PRAISE FOR *REPUTATION*

"Astonishingly timely and clever, utterly gripping."
—Lucy Foley, #1 *New York Times* bestselling author

"Sarah Vaughan has done it again. Superb."
—Shari Lapena, *New York Times* bestselling author

"An astonishingly timely, sharply written (of course), unsettlingly believable and impeccably just-one-more-page-paced thing of wonder."
—Ellery Lloyd, author of *The Club*

"Sarah Vaughan writes exactly the kind of women I want to read about—ambitious politician and mom Emma in *Reputation* is no exception. An incredibly gripping examination of the dangerous double standards women are held to, and the unjust pressures women face in the public eye. This novel races along through storylines so tense and sharp and well-crafted, there's not a minute to put it down."
—Ashley Audrain, *New York Times* bestselling author of *The Push*

"I simply couldn't put it down. It is current, compelling, and very clever."
—B.A. Paris, *New York Times* bestselling author of *The Therapist*

"Revenge, politics, and self-preservation collide as one woman desperately fights for her life. Masterful and nail-bitingly suspenseful, this story will stay with you long after you've turned the last page. Don't miss it."
—Liv Constantine, internationally bestselling author of *The Last Mrs. Parrish*

"Vaughan offers a cast of strong characters that are sharply realistic and consummately human. A complex, slow-burning examination of double standards, misogyny, and public image that shares strong appeal with Scott Turow's literary legal thrillers."

—*Booklist* (starred review)

"Vaughan considers the corrosive impact of social media on the lives of girls and women in this timely, twisty story . . . as thoughtful as it is surprising."

—*Publishers Weekly*

"Twisty."

—Vulture

PRAISE FOR *LITTLE DISASTERS*

"Taut, clever, compelling, and guaranteed to keep you on the edge of your seat."

—Paula Hawkins, #1 *New York Times* bestselling author of *The Girl on the Train* and *Into the Water*

"Each character is brilliantly drawn, and the book delivers surprise after surprise."

—Claire Fuller, author of *Bitter Orange*

"Vaughan is proving herself a master of suspense and an author willing to probe the darkest reaches of our psyches."

—*CrimeReads*

"This thrilling and emotional depiction of family drama, friendship, and trust will have you on the edge of your seat."

—CNN

"Powerful and compelling, the prose gets to the heart of parenting as well as self-doubt, anxiety, and heartbreak."

—*New York Journal of Books*

"Perfect for fans of Liane Moriarty and Celeste Ng, *Little Disasters* is an expertly crafted, uncanny thriller that offers mesmerizing characters, topical themes and unrelenting revelations."

—Shelf Awareness

"A great, twisting mystery until the end, and it's worth staying up late a night or two to explore this complicated drama."

—Associated Press

PRAISE FOR *ANATOMY OF A SCANDAL*

"A nuanced story line perfectly in tune with our #metoo times."

—*People*, Book of the Week

"A strong choice for book clubs. Former political correspondent Vaughan makes an impressive debut with this savvy, propulsive courtroom drama."

—*Kirkus Reviews* (starred review)

"Vaughan offers gripping insight into a political scandal's hidden machinations and the tension between justice and privilege . . . Absorbing, polished."

—*Booklist* (starred review)

"Skillfully interweaving the story of the unfolding scandal, Vaughan gradually reveals just how shockingly high the stakes are. . . . Sinewy . . . engrossing, twist-filled."

—*Publishers Weekly* (starred review)

"Vaughan weaves together a juicy courtroom drama set among the

British elite and told from the perspectives of three characters. . . . Exceptional."

—*Entertainment Weekly*

"A psychological thriller practically made for the #MeToo era . . . *Anatomy of a Scandal* is a win on every side: it has a gripping plot, but it's also an intelligent, kaleidoscopic look at the conversations surrounding sexual harassment going on today."

—Refinery 29

"*Anatomy of a Scandal* completely skewers the zeitgeist; cool, sharp, and beautifully written."

—Lisa Jewell, *New York Times* bestselling author of *The Night She Disappeared*

"Sarah Vaughan is sensational."

—Clare Mackintosh, internationally bestselling author of *I Let You Go*

"A nuanced, highly addictive read that resonates long after the final word."

—Kimberly Belle, *New York Times* bestselling author of *The Personal Assistant*

"A gripping dissection of deceit and desire . . . The definition of a page-turner."

—Elizabeth Day, award-winning author of *Magpie*

"This exhilarating novel . . . will have readers thinking about justice and truth and whether you can ever really, fully know someone."

—*Real Simple*

REPUTATION

A Novel

SARAH VAUGHAN

EMILY BESTLER BOOKS

ATRIA

NEW YORK   LONDON   TORONTO   SYDNEY   NEW DELHI

EMILY BESTLER BOOKS

ATRIA

An Imprint of Simon & Schuster, Inc.
1230 Avenue of the Americas
New York, NY 10020

Copyright © 2022 by Sarah Vaughan

First Emily Bestler Books/Atria Paperback edition July 2023

EMILY BESTLER BOOKS/ATRIA PAPERBACK and colophon are trademarks of Simon & Schuster, Inc.

For information about special discounts for bulk purchases, please contact Simon & Schuster Special Sales at 1-866-506-1949 or business@simonandschuster.com.

The Simon & Schuster Speakers Bureau can bring authors to your live event. For more information or to book an event, contact the Simon & Schuster Speakers Bureau at 1-866-248-3049 or visit our website at www.simonspeakers.com.

Interior design by Kyoko Watanabe

Manufactured in the United States of America

1 3 5 7 9 10 8 6 4 2

Library of Congress Cataloging-in-Publication has been applied for.

ISBN 978-1-6680-0006-9
ISBN 978-1-6680-0007-6 (pbk)
ISBN 978-1-6680-0008-3 (ebook)

To Ella and Anna

O, I have lost my reputation! I have lost the immortal
part of myself, and what remains is bestial.

WILLIAM SHAKESPEARE,
Othello, ACT 2, SCENE 3

I am Duchess of Malfi still.

JOHN WEBSTER,
The Duchess of Malfi, ACT 4, SCENE 2

8 DECEMBER 2021

The body lay at the bottom of the stairs. An untidy heap in this house that had been gentrified beyond all recognition. A jumble of clothes just waiting to be tidied away. His trouser leg had ridden up, and his ankle gleamed under my iPhone's flashlight. I couldn't bear to look at his face: turned away as if refusing to acknowledge that something like this could have happened to him.

There was no banister at the top of the stairs, just sleek white walls in keeping with the shiny oak steps, and the halogen spots that, once switched on, would reveal just how he had fallen. I touched the wall, pressing hard to gain traction; conscious of the need to stop myself from swaying. My heart was ricocheting, but my mind spiraled, too.

Why was he here? How did this happen?

More than anything: had he felt much pain?

For a sliver of time, so brief I later refused to acknowledge it, I allowed myself to imagine that he had.

PART ONE

One

11 SEPTEMBER 2021

EMMA

Looking back, it was the interview in the *Guardian Weekend* that started everything. Or rather, the fact I was on the cover. Exquisitely photographed, I looked more like an Oscar-nominated actress than a Labour politician.

It was hard not to be seduced by it all. The designer trouser suit elongated my legs, as did the suede heels: something I resisted at first because I always wore flats. But heels connoted power, according to the stylist, and it was a trope I chose to accept in that one reckless moment (the first of several reckless moments). In any case, I hoped the heels were balanced out by the message on my crisp white T-shirt: *Well-Behaved Women Seldom Make History*. It was something I vehemently believed. Only, when I saw myself on the front cover—with that defiant slash of red lipstick, my armor against a hostile world, and my thick bob blow-dried into a dark halo—I hardly recognized myself. I'd morphed into someone else entirely. Sex and power were the not-so-subtle subtexts of that photo.

Sex, power, and unequivocal ambition.

Even before the publication, I'd felt uneasy.

"Crikey!" I said when Dan, the photographer, showed me a couple of images through the preview screen on the back of his camera. They were tiny—three inches by two—and yet they were arresting. The back of my neck prickled. "I look pretty formidable."

"You look strong," Esther Enfield, the paper's newly appointed political editor, reassured me. "Strong and determined. It fits the interview.

Illustrates what you were saying perfectly. You didn't pussyfoot around with your message, and neither does this."

"I don't know. Can I see it again?" I leaned toward Dan, suddenly conscious of his physicality. He towered over me, long-limbed and energetic, like a teenager oozing testosterone, though he must have been in his early thirties. His breath smelled of artisan coffee.

"You look great." He was brisk, and I sensed his eagerness to get on with it.

"I just look a bit . . . hard?" I lingered on a shot of me in a butter-soft black leather jacket, the collar framing my unsmiling face. He'd captured a side to me I didn't like to acknowledge. Was I *really* as ruthless as he'd made me appear?

Esther shrugged, which made me feel foolish. In her mid-forties, like me, she knew what she was talking about and had sound instincts. Besides, this was the left-leaning *Guardian*, a paper more in tune with my politics, not the more right-wing *Daily Mail*.

"This will be good for your career, I promise." She seemed to read my mind, and then she gave me a proper, warm smile. And so, because this was my first national newspaper feature, because I didn't want to look weak, because I was flattered, I suppose, that the *Guardian* thought me sufficiently interesting to put me on their magazine's front cover, I let myself be swayed by her arguments. I let myself believe what I wanted to believe.

Besides, as Esther said, the photo would be balanced by what was inside: a sharp attack on the government's austerity measures, apparent in my Portsmouth South constituency, where the need for food banks had proliferated in the last couple of years; a critique of my party leader, Harry Godwin, as "ineffective and prone to self-indulgence"; and details of my private member's bill calling for anonymity for victims of revenge porn—the reason I'd agreed to this piece. It was a serious interview, worth doing, despite knowing it would irritate more established colleagues, and the photos would be seen through this lens.

"It's a fantastic shot," Dan, stubbled and artfully disheveled, said.

Later I wondered if this was the reason I caved in so easily: this simple flattery from a younger man who had coaxed me into being photographed like this. "Just a couple more. Head up, that's it. That's perfect. Sweet." Was I subliminally so desperate for male admiration? At forty-four, so conscious of becoming sexually invisible that, despite everything I stood for, I let myself be flattered by and play up to his uncompromisingly male gaze?

"Okay. Let's go for it," I told Esther. "As you say: no point pussyfooting around."

"Absolutely. Honestly, the pics *are* arresting, and it's precisely because of this that readers will spend time over this interview, and your colleagues will have to listen to what you say."

And so I quashed my critical inner voice: the one that used the waspish tones of my late grandmother, with a smattering of my ex-husband David's caution, and that always gathered in volume until I felt like shaking my head to be rid of it.

Pride goeth before a fall.

Of course, later I would regret this, bitterly, deeply, because that cover shot would be used repeatedly: the stock image that would accompany every Emma Webster story from that moment on. It would be the picture used when I was arrested, when I was charged, when the trial began. And this would rankle because, far from capturing the true me, it was a brittle, knowing version: red lips slightly parted in a way that couldn't fail to seem distinctly sexual; gaze defiant; a clear, almost brazen challenge in what the article would describe as my "limpid, dark eyes." A far cry from how I thought of myself, or who I'd ever been: a history teacher at the local high school; Flora's mum; or a junior politician who tried so very hard to serve her constituents while campaigning on feminist issues more generally.

A picture paints a thousand words. And yet this one reduced me to nothing more than a glamorous mug shot: my challenge to the camera not so different from the insolent expression captured in every custody photo snapped by the police.

Nolite te Bastardes Carborundorum. Don't let the bastards get you down. I had an old T-shirt with that message. Perhaps I should have suggested to the stylist that I wear it?

It would have been incendiary, of course. A clear middle finger to the trolls, the media, the critics in my own party—let alone my political opponents—who were poised, even then, to see me stumble.

Had I known what would happen, I might have put it straight on.

Two

11 SEPTEMBER 2021

EMMA

Twitter Thread

> **FiremanFred** @suckmycock: WTF! Look at the publicity whore @emmawebsterMP. A £450 leather jacket while hardworking folk r going to food banks.
>
> **Richard M** @BigBob699: Get back to work, love and remember who pays your wages.
>
> **FiremanFred** @suckmycock: Put it away, luv. No one's going to shag u.
>
> **Dick Penny** @EnglandRules: Shag her? Wouldn't touch that cunt if she was the last woman standing.
>
> **Richard M** @BigBob699: Agreed. Wouldn't even rape her. What a fucking disgrace.

The backlash to the interview was immediate. Seven a.m. on a Saturday morning, and my Twitter feed was already clogged with notifications. The need to check was stupid but compulsive. Vanity? Validation? A foolish, fleeting hope that my fears wouldn't be realized and I would find overwhelming support?

I tended to think of the trolls as sad little men whipping each other into an irate frenzy as they cowered in their basements. But then it was just one step away from imagining them masturbating furiously, and I had to remove them from their subterranean setting and see them as upstanding members of the community instead. The type of men who had spent their entire careers in positions of authority. Retired policemen or headmasters, perhaps. Men who would otherwise be tending to their gardens, or fundraising for local charities; who, perhaps, had wives and daughters (though I wondered how someone could hurl highly sexualized abuse at me and then behave civilly to their family. Perhaps the truth was, they didn't). I tried not to think of them as irredeemably bad.

It helped to remind myself that each could be responsible for hundreds of the notifications. That @borisshagger was a bot, for instance—I'd checked: he had no followers and a gray egg as an avatar; @BrexitBill123 and @TrumpRules4Eva were the same. So it wasn't that thousands of people thought I was un-rapeable, just that a few misogynists voiced it from numerous accounts. The interactions needled me, though, because while one person could have numerous accounts—multiple alter egos answering each other to create the effect of a pile-on—several people still thought this with a venomous intensity. Keyboard warriors, they called themselves. Such a pathetic term. Laughing at them, even if the laughter was hollow, helped a little, though it did nothing to unpick the knot in my stomach.

What worried me—besides the fact I might be missing cries for help from constituents—was that the volume meant I couldn't see the real threats. My fear was that there would be something that should be acted on—a rape or death threat—buried deep in the torrent of bile. Then there was the frustration that this overwhelming hatred could remain unchecked. Rape threats made on Twitter, or more usually in emails, could be referred to the police. But negative claims—*I wouldn't rape her if she was the last woman on earth*—didn't contravene any law. Neither Hampshire police nor the Met could act on a claim I was un-rapeable. Even if the open threat of rape was hiding in full sight.

I looked at the cover again as I stood in the kitchen of my Portsmouth home. This unfamiliar version of Emma Webster mocked me: her formidable expression, her way of holding herself, even her elegantly cut suit were all so at odds with me in my furry dressing gown, my eyes still sticky with sleep. I couldn't relate to her, and yet I felt a certain, shameful pride. I'd never thought I could look that *fierce*. And it wasn't just that. I looked hot, as Flora's best friend, Leah, might say. Should I want to look like this? Wasn't it anathema to everything I was trying to teach Flora:

the idea that you could make an impression, as a woman, without being sexualized? The appearance of strength was good, but the erotization of it? Surely not. Young feminists might celebrate their hotness, but I didn't think of myself like that. I hadn't had sex for four years. Most of the time I barely thought of myself as sexual. And yet here I was.

On autopilot, I flicked through more messages. For many, it was my attack on my party leader that was most incendiary. Maybe describing him as "lazy, and too reliant on a sycophantic coterie of hardliners" was reckless, though it was only what many of us in the parliamentary party believed. *The sooner Harry kicks her out of the party, the better*, said @Laboursympathizer, and there were several others in this vein—almost a relief after the tweets that criticized my appearance, then described quite how they'd like to punish me. I let the terms flow over me, the hard *c*'s and *t*'s, the *b*'s and *h*'s, the softer but insidious *p*'s and *y*'s, telling myself none of it meant anything. Sticks and stones and all that.

An early frost had coated my small garden, turning each blade of grass into a small, hard spear, and I tried to imagine being similarly protected. A line from the text popped out: *Close colleagues say she's focused and hardworking but somewhat humorless.* Who on earth thought that? Then I looked at the photos, again: particularly the one of me perched on the edge of a chair, back ramrod straight, my expression unsmiling, my expression not just formidable but aloof. I'd thought I looked serious, but now realized that I just looked as if I took myself seriously (a cardinal sin for a woman) or, worse, too seriously. I didn't look like the sort of woman you'd confide in; the sort of woman you'd gravitate toward at a party; the sort of woman with whom you'd want to share a glass of wine, a hug, or a joke.

I poured myself the remains of the coffee from the pot on the stove and sipped the thick dark liquid, my phone turned facedown on the counter. *Let it go*, the Disney refrain that Flora had once listened to incessantly filled my head. *Let it goooo*. The three hundred odd emails I received a day were bad enough, let alone the WhatsApp messages and texts from supportive—and, increasingly frequently, unsupportive—colleagues. I couldn't contend with any more electronic noise, let alone this barrage of Twitter abuse. More coffee, that's what I needed. I drained the dregs and turned my phone to silent, but not before reading a kind message from Claire, the younger of the two female politicians I shared a house with during the week, in London: *Ignore the bastards* 👊 👊 👊 👊 👊 👍 👍 👍 (Julia, our other housemate, more loyal to the party leadership, had been conspicuous in her silence.)

"You shouldn't keep looking at your phone. Isn't that what you tell me?"

Flora had sidled up behind me, quiet as a cat. Her yawn was feline, too: wide and luxurious.

"Hello, darling." The dull despair that had weighed me down since I'd woken wired, just after 5:30, eased as I saw my daughter. "Some breakfast?"

"I'll get it." She went to the fridge and pulled out some milk.

I wanted to slip an arm around her slight waist, to drop a kiss on her pimpled forehead, but my fourteen-year-old had grown as tall as me in the past few months, and with this new height had come a new reserve.

"Sleep well?"

She shrugged, too tired to answer, or maybe she thought it an unnecessary question. She'd been sleeping badly, finding it hard to drop off, and often waking with dark shadows beneath her eyes.

"Is that the interview?"

She was looking at the magazine cover and pulled it closer, her index finger hovering over my image.

"What do you think?" My breath was caught high in my chest.

"It doesn't look like you."

"It doesn't, does it?"

"Have they airbrushed you or something?"

"No." I half laughed with relief: thank God she didn't see this as the real me.

"You look good," she said, at last, as if she knew this was the answer she should give. I longed to pick it like an old scab, to dislodge it, to find the potentially painful truth. Obviously I resisted and moved the magazine to one side, signaling that it was something we didn't need to discuss further. I wiped the counter briskly, vaguely dissatisfied.

Flora poured a glass of milk and filled a bowl with Cheerios, which she ate dry. Better not tell her to eat properly: she was particularly prickly at the moment. Then she draped herself over a barstool, her long T-shirt swamping her slight frame. Despite her new height of five foot eight, there were still hints of a little girl. Her features had been softened by sleep, and her cheeks were flushed in contrast to her general paleness. "You're an English rose," I frequently told her. "I burn," she always replied—and yes, her freckled skin would turn an angry red if she missed a patch of suntan lotion: a burn that would feel like a rebuke because it was my job to protect my red-haired child from the sun, even if Flora hated me to fuss. She scooped her hair behind her ears and stared at the back of the cereal packet. Then she scowled, revealing a flash of necessary, ugly metal, and I felt helpless. Something was wrong, and I didn't know how to make it better.

I started asking her about her plans for the day. We agreed I'd pick up some forgotten PE gear from her father's, but then she slipped into silence.

"Did you hear what I said, Flo?"

She blinked through strawberry-blonde lashes.

"I've a constituency meeting this morning. I should be home by 1:30. Do you want to stay here, or shall I drop you in town?"

"Here's fine." She took her bowl and put it by the side of the sink, then finished her glass of milk.

"Good girl. I'll be back by lunchtime." As ever, I felt I had to make amends for working, though I did it every Saturday. "I'll get something nice for us to eat."

———

The Saturday town hall meeting, where members of the public came to complain about issues ranging from canceled benefits to garbage collections to the current state of politics, was held in a primary school in one of the more deprived parts of my constituency. Paint peeled from window frames that couldn't be opened, and the displays of children's self-portraits barely masked the chipped skirting and scuffed walls.

Business was brisk. I must have seen over twenty people by the time he walked in. It was a quarter to twelve, and I was ready for the end of the session. Patrick, my somewhat earnest twenty-three-year-old assistant, and Sue, the linchpin of my local office, who ushered in constituents, were also flagging. But a quick glance at the reception area showed we had at least another half dozen cases to get through.

"Baxter. Simon Baxter," he announced as he walked toward me and thrust out a hand to shake mine firmly. Mid-fifties, possibly ex-military, with a posture and trim physique that suggested he exercised, was assertive, and was used to being heard.

"How can I help, Mr. Baxter?" I smiled and indicated that he should take a seat. He did so, pulling the chair perhaps a little too close. He had fine bones and manicured fingernails, displayed as he placed one hand on each knee as if to indicate he meant business. A man, then, who took care of himself. Who was, no doubt, meticulous about keeping records or recording injustices—all helpful if there was a constituency issue I could help with, not so much if he had a grievance against me. He caught me assessing him—those squarely filed fingernails, the navy sweater, the polished brown oxford brogues—and the balance of power perceptibly tipped.

"Mr. Baxter?" I prompted.

"I'm here to complain, Mrs. Webster."

"Call me Emma, please." I'd always hated the "Mrs." tag, and now that I was divorced, it felt fraudulent to use it, though "Ms." sounded clunky.

"If you'd rather. Though I always find titles maintain a level of formality."

"If you'd prefer, that's absolutely fine. Now: how may I help?"

"I came in to discuss a matter close to my heart. As you might be able to tell"—a brief glance at his pristine shoes—"I'm a veteran. Twenty years in the marines before I retired and moved into private security. But I still have friends in the armed forces, still take an interest, and my son, Will, was in Helmand."

He paused. I gave the nod of approval he clearly sought.

"But I came to discuss the lack of provision for armed forces personnel leaving the military: the way we take our lads, send them on tours, and then spew them out as if they are disposable. The help to resettle—the so-called career-transition stuff—is wholly unsatisfactory: mental health provision, too. We treat them like dirt because they're working class." He stopped, as if he had briefly run out of steam. Whatever I'd expected from this man in his neatly pressed chinos and padded Barbour jacket, it wasn't that he would be concerned about veterans' mental health, nor that he would be some sort of class warrior. I opened my mouth to offer some platitude, but he was off again, a vein throbbing at his right temple, his face increasingly flushed.

"I hoped you'd help raise awareness of this issue," he continued as I smiled sympathetically. "But then I saw this—" And he tossed down a copy of the *Guardian Weekend* magazine. He paused, and the vein bulged like a pulsing worm. "I do not approve of, nor do I want, my MP, the person who represents me and my family in Parliament, to be preoccupied with such *self-publicity* when our lads are sleeping on the streets, ending up in prison, or falling down the cracks. You work for *us*. Isn't that right?" He paused, and I nodded, wondering how close to the edge he was; how liable to overstep the line that would see me reaching for the panic button in my bag. I glanced at Patrick, who was looking at his notes, apparently unconcerned. Perhaps I was overreacting, though my damp palms and increased heart rate suggested otherwise. I focused on breathing deeply, hoping I could still calm things down.

"I'm sorry you feel like this, Mr. Baxter," I managed eventually, in a way designed to appease. But he had reached the tipping point and ridden it, and I saw—from the way in which he now leaned forward, hands no longer on his knees but curled into fists—he had gone beyond the point of being talked down. His fury still came as a shock, and for half a second, I wanted to laugh: a defense mechanism, perhaps, or an embarrassed reaction to this very un-English display of aggression. "I'm sorry you feel like this," I repeated, more firmly this time. "But my giving an interview in a newspaper doesn't detract from my work for my constituents. If anything, by raising my profile, it only ensures that my voice is more likely to be heard."

The words tasted insincere. In what way would my interview achieve anything for Simon Baxter and his veterans? It wasn't that I was unsympathetic. I'd seen the impact of ex-military fathers coming home, the adjustment in families, the breakdown of marriages, through teaching at the local high school. But I'd learned I had more impact if I directed my energy at a few issues, and there were other causes I wanted to further first.

He saw straight through me.

"You're not interested in doing a thing for these lads." His tone was biting. "You don't give a damn about men who give up their best years for this country, only to be treated as if they're beneath contempt by the government. Nearly four years you've been our MP, and I've not seen a whisper of understanding on the issue from you. All you care about are women's rights. What about men's rights? What about the rights of these lads? Or maybe you're just concerned about yourself. *This*—" He gestured to the supplement as if he couldn't bear to touch it. "*This* tells me all I need to know about you.

"Because you're just in it for yourself, aren't you? You're as bad as the last one. In it to feather your nest, get yourself promoted, claw in the expenses—" He stood up abruptly, and I wanted to tell him to calm down but knew it would be inflammatory. My heart charged, but my mind was sluggish; clarity clouded by fear.

"Mr. Baxter. I really must ask you to be seated." Patrick was standing, his tone more strident than anything I'd heard previously. He looked young, and painfully thin, as if his six-foot-two-inch frame would snap if Simon Baxter so much as touched him. "There's really no need to be aggressive," he continued as the man took two steps closer. But then his reedy voice quavered, his innate good manners letting him down.

"I'm going to have to ask you to leave, Mr. Baxter," I said, standing up. The sight of him frightening Patrick emboldened me. "I can't have you intimidating my staff like this."

"Intimidating them!" The man snarled. "Christ! You think this is intimidation? You haven't seen the half of it."

"And I hope we won't need to," I said in my most teacher-like tone and watched his momentary surprise. That was better: I needed to speak to him as I would have to my most obstreperous student. "I have a panic button here, and I will call the police if you don't leave at once."

For what felt like several painful seconds, Mr. Baxter stood his ground. He was stuck, I realized: incapable of backing down without a severe loss of face yet still sufficiently bound by the ties of civil behavior not to go further, or to break the law.

"Mr. Baxter?" Patrick stepped in, galvanized by his indecision. "I need you to go now."

"For fuck's sake!" And there we had it. Civility, that gossamer-thin sheen he'd barely maintained, was cast off like an unwanted coat.

"Mr. Baxter," I repeated more forcefully.

"All right, all right, I'm going." He sidestepped Patrick, raised his arms to resist being manhandled. "I'll be watching how you spend your time, though," he spat at me. "I'll be watching *you*."

You do that, I wanted to say, though of course I stood rigid, a mirthless smile fixed on my face.

At the door, he stopped, turned, and glowered, just to make sure I'd got the message.

"You may think you're better than me, but you shit and piss just like the rest of us. I'll be tracking your every move. I'll be watching you."

———————

It took me a while to calm down after that. Of course I continued to be professional; to see the remaining constituents who had witnessed Simon Baxter storm out of reception, and whose queries about how to get into the most desirable schools, or pleas for me to intervene with bad land-lords, were comparatively easy to answer. Patrick kept a careful note of each new case.

"You're sure you don't want us to call the police?" Sue checked, once the last person had gone. "Just to log what's happened?"

I scrunched up my face. "I don't want to waste their time."

Like everyone, I was conscious of the murder, five years earlier, of a female MP, shot and stabbed by a constituent. That's why we took precautions. Why I informed the police whenever I held public meetings, and occasionally asked them to attend if I'd been particularly outspoken about violence against women and girls. But there was a balance. I didn't want to squander their stretched resources or cry wolf. Because what had really happened? A constituent had acted in a way that felt menacing and made a vague threat. I'd received far worse on social media. Had received worse in a letter. It was only that he had done it in such close proximity; that I could see the spittle on his lips, sense the power inherent in his biceps, see how his fists furled.

"If you think that's best," Sue said, and I realized that of course *she* would feel safer if I logged this with the police, and I was torn because I wanted to do anything to keep her. Sue was the competent heart of my office, but in her mid-fifties, she found town hall meetings draining; would need to have a nap once she got home. Her salary was modest, too, and she could earn as much in another office that never required her to contact the police or pick up the phone to be battered by abuse. The churn of MPs' staff was fast, but Sue had been with me from the start. Coffee, the odd sticky bun, effusive thank-yous, smiley faces on Post-its, extravagant toiletries for birthdays and Christmases: this—and ensuring I always worked harder than anyone else—was the currency with which I bought the loyalty of my staff.

"I'm sure he's got it out of his system by now," I tried to reassure her. "Wouldn't you agree, Patrick?"

The youngest member of my team bent his head as if to demur. He'd only been working for me for six weeks, so perhaps he didn't want to contradict me, or perhaps I had imagined the quiver and he hadn't been that shaken at all.

"He was *quite* aggressive." He paused and ran long fingers through his hair. "But, you know, that's public life, I guess. We can hardly keep you separate from those you represent."

"Exactly." I felt a sudden rush of tenderness. I needed to protect my staff, to minimize what had happened and convince them there was no reason for it to be repeated. Besides, there were measures we could and did implement: two 1.5-liter bottles of water placed on my desk in case of an acid attack; my car parked just outside the building in case I needed a quick getaway; waiting constituents scrutinized in case they seemed jittery; and bags searched after one lad—oblivious as to why it might be problematic—turned up with a knife.

"I've met plenty of Simon Baxters in my time," I said, "men who feel existentially challenged by every woman they meet," and I had: a school departmental head; a government minister; even—and I hated thinking of him—a former lover. "They're all noise and bluster." And then, with more certainty than I really felt: "He won't bother us again."

Later, once I'd left Sue and Patrick with further reassurances, I drove to David's to pick up Flora's gym clothes. He'd kept the family home after our divorce, since Flora would be spending the bulk of her time here and it felt less disruptive, but that decision still hurt.

Not as acutely as three and a half years ago, when I'd moved out with a few of my favorite pieces of furniture, my clothes and books. Then my shame and grief, my sense of failure at my fourteen-year-old marriage ending, had stung as sharply as lemon squirted on a cut. I'd had to fight against tears as I'd pulled the oak door closed for the last time, conscious I was turning my back on years of largely positive memories. "Don't worry, love. Perfectly natural," one of the removal lads reassured me as he started the ignition, and I said goodbye not just to a home but to a relationship I had assumed was pretty solid. "On to the new place now?"

The new place was a 1960s semidetached house on a small housing estate three miles away, chosen partly for its price and partly because it would be a short distance for Flora to cycle, but largely because, with its large windows and parquet floor and bright white walls unencumbered by cornicing or picture rails, it felt sufficiently different to the detached redbrick Edwardian villa in front of me now.

At least this no longer looked like mine. Under Caroline and David's ownership, Holmecroft had segued into a very different property. One that looked as if it had been styled for a home-improvement magazine: all tasteful shades of taupe and beige with various gadgets on display. There was a flat-screen television on the wall where I'd hung a watercolor bought on honeymoon in Wales, an expensive surround-sound music system, a noticeable lack of books or clutter. And, of course, Caroline's baby grand piano: a shiny black Yamaha that took up half the sitting room. Proof of Caroline's musicality and the reason why this cuckoo was able to chirrup her way into my nest—because Caroline, as well as once being a colleague who became a friend, had also been Flora's piano teacher.

I looked down at my hands and saw that I was clutching the steering wheel. Gripping it as if to center myself. My shoulders were hunched, and I drew my scapulae together to elongate my neck. It was mid-September and yet I felt chilled: the weather had changed as it always does at this time of year, and there was an autumnal nip, damp creeping under my jacket, insidious and dank. I wanted to feel the sun on my skin or the scorch of a log fire. I wanted, more than anything, to be held. David had been good to hug, and for a moment, I hankered for the days of campaigning when I would return home from a long day pounding the streets and he would hold me tight before I drifted off to sleep. We only had sex sporadically then—too much going on, we told each other—but there was still this tenderness. It was only when I became a politician that we rapidly fell apart.

For a moment that lasted only as long as it took to swallow my self-pity down with a swig of water, I craved that contact.

My God. Simon Baxter must have really got under my skin to make me feel this lachrymose.

———

"I think that's all the gym stuff. Caroline's washed it and folded it up. The sneakers are in this separate bag."

Flora's clothes were waiting on the bench in the hall.

"Everything okay?" As he handed over the bags, my ex-husband risked looking at me. His face had aged since I'd left, but in general, he looked better than when we were together. Caroline had introduced him to running—her antidote to hours spent on a piano stool—and he had the lean physique of a forty-seven-year-old man who ran three or four half-marathons a year in a bid to stave off middle-aged spread. There was also a new, neatly cropped, salt-and-pepper beard. Would I have found him more attractive if he'd looked like this when we were together? It was hard not to be conscious that his stomach was flat where it had been baggy, his arms and legs clearly defined. There was a new strength and energy to my once exercise-phobic husband, who had clearly been revitalized by his younger wife.

Which wasn't to say he looked at ease. He pulled at his nose as if tweaking it off, a tic he always did when he was nervous. "I saw you were in the *Guardian*. Front cover. Quite an accolade."

I glanced at him sharply. David shied away from attention; was all for caution and not provoking debate. He hadn't been happy about me standing as a politician, but I persuaded him it would take at least three attempts: that I might win by the time Flora was eighteen, having experienced the perfectly usual humiliation of losing a couple of elections before then. I wasn't *meant* to become a politician when she was ten. But that's the thing about politics, particularly politics these days. The old certainties can be shaken up.

I put on my best constituent-welcoming smile now.

"Thank you! Yep. I was thrilled to be interviewed—and so pleased I got the space to talk about issues that, as you know, mean so much to me."

"Look that's great, genuinely." He wasn't convincing, not least because he tweaked his nose again. "But what sort of impact will it have on Flora, your becoming more high-profile? Being on the local news is one thing, but this? Being some sort of cover girl? Aren't you making yourself too much of a target? Aren't you putting her at risk?"

I leaned against the doorframe and let my lovely old house prop me up. I was too tired for this. "Look. I've had the security audit done. We've had the panic button installed, the alarm, the extra locks on the door, the anti-explosive letter box." Just detailing the recent measures made me weary. "You know I'd never do anything to put Flora disproportionately at risk. But I'm doing this job to make a difference, and she understands that. She's okay with it."

"And what about the reaction she'll get at school?"

"She'll be okay." I plowed on, irritated by his ability to find the very thing that niggled at me. "This was a good interview, not a hatchet job, and as I'm sure you noticed, I made sure she wasn't mentioned by name." The piece referred to the fact I had a teenage daughter, but Esther had kept her word on this. "Besides, I doubt anyone in her class reads the *Guardian*, or if they read it online, they're not going to get to the magazine."

"I don't know." He seemed perturbed. "Let's hope so. Kids love to pick up on difference, don't they?" A pause, during which I was reminded how much it mattered to him what others thought. He stroked his beard—a new tic—as if wondering how to broach another subject. Then, almost as an aside: "Caroline wanted a word if you had a minute, by the way."

He gestured for me to come in through to the kitchen, then mumbled something about needing to get on and retreated to his study. Such a cowardly move. I had no real desire to talk to Caroline, who had encouraged me to stand as a politician, then moved with alacrity to fill my space once I got into office, but I couldn't be childish about this, however much I might resent her. We all owed it to Flora to try to be friends.

As always, the kitchen came as a surprise. It was a new addition: an extension that transformed the back of the house and rendered my old home clearly Caroline's. The new Mrs. Webster sat at a gleaming island, empty apart from a fruit bowl filled with Red Delicious apples that were so preternaturally large and shiny, they looked fake. Behind her, the garden with its striped lawn and impeccable herbaceous borders—a huge improvement on the jumbled tangle I'd never had time to get on top of—stretched beyond the new sandstone patio and bifold doors. Classical music was playing at an irritating volume: not loud enough to impose but enough to make its presence known. A piano concerto. Something, like Caroline, that was perky.

"Bit of Mozart?" I hazarded a guess.

"Number 23. A major." She smiled, as if I were a pupil who'd given the right answer. "Third movement can get a bit frenetic, though," she added, switching it off.

The room was instantly calmer, and simultaneously more exposing: as if, without the bright tinkling of the piano and the lush surge of the strings, our relationship, once close, now distinctly prickly, was stripped right back.

"David said you wanted to talk?"

"Just a quick chat." She came toward me and gave me a perfunctory peck on the cheek. Everything about her was dinky, from her petite physique to her straightened bob, to her clean Lululemons and the tiny pearl studs in her petallike lobes. "I just wanted to have a word about Flora. I'm sure she'll have told you, but just in case, I think she's had a bit of a falling-out with Leah. Nothing serious, but for obvious reasons, she's feeling more sensitive than usual this week."

"Oh." I felt wrong-footed. "She hasn't mentioned it, but she was exhausted yesterday evening and I've barely seen her this morning. I really should be getting back to her."

"Of course." Caroline made an irritatingly soothing sound that always reminded me of a wind chime.

"Am I missing something?" I hated having to ask. "You said 'for obvious reasons'?"

"Well . . . I mean . . . her starting her period." She paused. "Hasn't she mentioned it? Well, you know how private she is. It's okay. I had some pads in case. Gave her some Tylenol and a hot-water bottle. She was absolutely fine . . . well, a little emotional because it happened at school, I think, and she wasn't prepared, so she was embarrassed. But she let me give her a hug and then was her usual sensible self."

Somehow I managed to thank her and get to the car without betraying the shame welling inside me. My daughter had started her period, and it was another woman in whom she'd confided, and who had helped her out.

Of course I was grateful. Imagine if Flora hadn't had anyone to tell? If she'd soldiered on until I got home at the end of the week? But I was so saddened that she hadn't felt able to talk to me. And there was something else. What did Caroline mean about her being embarrassed at school? Had the other kids known and taunted her? Had she had to deal with all that?

I reached into my tote bag for a tissue, and my fingers ran over the silky front of that bloody magazine. Infuriated, I pulled it out. I'd thought I'd looked so strong with my red lips and my chin tipped up. That I'd exuded attitude. But the image, both familiar and so disarmingly other, now seemed pathetic.

With a satisfying rip, I tore off the cover and screwed it tight in my hand.

Three

12 SEPTEMBER 2021

FLORA

You'll be drinking acid next cunt.

Flora hadn't realized what the letter meant, at first. She'd been in her mum's office, helping Sue open the post at the start of the summer holidays. A bit of pocket money, though she'd have done it for nothing. It felt good just watching her mum in action. Having her around.

It was better than being at her dad's, where Caroline would only be nagging her about doing her oboe practice now that she'd given up the piano. "You'll lose that good embouchure. At least do your scales." Flora would practice the minor ones. Those with sharps, F-sharp minor, G-sharp minor, C-sharp minor—as if by doing so she could blast out her anger. "What about some majors?" But Caroline didn't get it. Didn't understand the need to be spiky and bad-tempered. "I know them *already*," she'd replied— before quacking out a chromatic scale.

The constituency office was hardly exciting, but it felt vaguely important, and somehow cozy. While Patrick and Sue manned the phones, she made cups of tea and doled out chocolate biscuits, shopped for food for a constituent whose Universal Credit had been delayed—bread, butter, milk, baked beans, pasta; the woman had cried when her mum dropped it round to her—and opened the post.

The envelope had been handwritten in a spidery scrawl, but the note itself had been printed on a computer. Copperplate Gothic. It looked so pretty that, at first, she had thought it was some sort of flyer.

"Oh!" She dropped the folded piece of paper.

"What is it, Flo?" Her mum looked up, concerned.

"Er . . . nothing. Not important." She shuffled the post, trying to hide it before her mum got to it. But her scalp was prickling, and she felt sick, like she did when Leah said something snide about her. Everyone was looking, and she knew she had gone bright red.

"Oh, Flora. Oh, my darling, I'm so sorry." Her mum's face had crumpled, briefly, as she'd read the words, and then she'd looked angry and very, very determined. "We need to tell the police and they will trace it. Look at me, Flora." She had grasped her by the shoulders and looked intently in her face just as she did when she was little. "I promise *no one* will be drinking acid around here."

But the police hadn't been able to track whoever sent the note. It was hand-delivered, and none of the prints on it matched any of those on their system. The sender remained even more untraceable than the Twitter trolls who threatened to rape and dismember her mum every day. The difference was that this man knew where her mum worked. He probably knew where they lived. He could be watching her mum come and go; could even be spying on her in her bedroom. He could be planning to throw acid in her mum's face, and there was nothing anyone could do about it . . .

She thought about that moment opening the letter, most days, though it happened nearly two months ago. Sometimes she managed to put it in perspective; at others, she felt overwhelmed. Often she couldn't sleep, her head so filled with the memory of it, with the fear her mum would be blown up, stabbed, or shot. Not that Emma knew she was this scared, though Flora couldn't hide her shock, straight after the letter was delivered, when the old cat door was sealed up and anti-explosive bags attached to their letter box in case a bomb was thrown in.

"Is it worth it?" she had asked, but in a too-small voice because she knew her mum wouldn't want to hear the question.

"Absolutely," her mum had said. "The very worst thing would be to be scared." She was typically brisk in her *don't worry about it, let's get on with it* kind of way. She hadn't understood what Flora was trying to tell her. To be fair, Flora barely knew herself, though now it seemed obvious.

Is what I want so unimportant to you? Is it worth my being this scared?

It was too late to try to explain any of this to her mother now. Too late to tell her mum *anything* that bugged her. Oh, her mum said she wanted to know. She would smile at her with that ever-so-concerned look on her face, but then her expression would glaze over as she remembered one of the hundred other things that she needed to do. Flora always wanted to talk at the wrong time, and her mum wasn't there late at night, when Flora's mind wouldn't stop whirring, or when Flora came home from school. She texted a lot: *How did the history test go? Did you do volleyball? I've ordered that music you wanted* . . . So it wasn't that she didn't *care*. But she was so fired up with her work that it sometimes felt there was no room left: that Flora's fears had to be squished around the margins, squeezed into the tiniest slivers of time. And if she couldn't even tell her mum she was scared of her being a politician, that sometimes she lay rigid until one in the morning, fixating on the threats she'd seen on her mum's Twitter feed, which her mum—*so* naive—seemed to think she was unaware of, then how could she explain things that might seem less important?

Particularly since she couldn't quite work out why the bad stuff was happening—let alone how she could make it stop.

Four

13 SEPTEMBER 2021

EMMA

"Fab piece."

Claire Scott—politician for Newcastle-upon-Tyne, captain of the parliamentary women's soccer team; my housemate, friend, and general right-hand woman—bounded into my office within minutes of my arriving there on Monday.

A pocket rocket. That was how some more seasoned politicians had viewed her when she arrived at Parliament. They knew not to underestimate her now.

Five foot two, and with her dark fringed hair pulled into a high ponytail, she looked younger than thirty-six and unthreatening: an unlikely attacking midfielder, though once you knew her, her chosen sport fitted. There was a grit to her, a practicality, a determination to play hard and fast, though with grace. Her voice conveyed this, too. A northern lilt that could be soft and lyrical but intensified when she became animated and suggested she knew far more about the harshness of life, the economic curve balls that could be thrown at you, than most of her colleagues in the easier south.

"Did you mean to wind up Harry quite so spectacularly?" She threw herself into the armchair opposite my desk, and grinned until her hazel eyes slitted.

I couldn't help but grimace. Our Great Leader had already let it be known he was displeased. Not that he conveyed that himself. (Subversive newcomers like me had no direct dealings with him.) But I'd received a terse message from Lou Greene, one of the parliamentary liaison officers: *It was crass of you to describe Harry as a misogynist. Don't do it again.*

I'd ignored Lou's text. I wasn't going to be told what I could or couldn't say, but I did wonder if I'd been reckless. I hadn't gone into the interview intending to criticize him quite so fiercely, but Esther had persuaded me to go on the record about a frustration that I'd previously expressed. Naive though it sounds, I'd felt a duty to be honest. Now that decision didn't feel so clever. My discomfort grew as Claire brought up the article on her phone and started reciting it.

" 'I'm not a fan of Harry, and it's no secret that he's not a fan of me. He shows scant regard for the need to change the law with regard to online hate crime, let alone revenge porn and cyber-flashing, crimes predominantly committed against women. It's such a blind spot, it's hard not to see it as entrenched misogyny.' " She let out an approving cackle. "You didn't exactly hold back. No wonder Harry's 'displeased'!"

"I went too far, didn't I?" Challenging the party leader this publicly now seemed needlessly provocative. I'd been flattered. Not just by Dan and the designer trouser suit—the shoot, with its euphoria and queasy trepidation, had come afterward—but by Esther's interest. She had played me rather effectively.

"Not sure about this bit: 'Emma Webster may be a good constituency MP, but her heart's less in local matters and more in issues of national significance.' I can't see your constituents liking that."

"I didn't *say* that—and I've already had one complaining." I told them about my Simon Baxter run-in.

"Ooh—he sounds nasty." Claire became serious. "You sure you're okay?"

I shrugged. "I'm refusing to let him worry me. *This* does, though. The comments about Harry, and that suggestion I'm not interested in local stuff. This is all going to backfire badly, isn't it?"

"Nah." Jazz, my twenty-six-year-old Westminster assistant, was matter-of-fact.

"You don't think it was too much?"

Jazz wrinkled her nose, her neon gel nails tapping away at her keyboard as she deleted messages, then reached for the mouse to check Twitter. "Not to me. It needed saying."

"Exactly," said Claire. "You didn't come here to be meek and sit quietly. Isn't that what you always say?"

And she was right. I'd entered politics, originally as a Labour councillor just six years ago, because I'd felt so angry about the poverty of some of
my students. Children who were having to attend food banks; were living
in substandard B&Bs instead of being provided with adequate housing;
were slipping through the cracks in a way they hadn't seemed to quite as
badly when Labour was in power. "Well, what are you going to do about
it?" my late dad, Graham, former docker, proud trade unionist, and then
a Labour councillor himself, had asked. It was the challenge he'd posed
throughout my teens, the refrain whenever I'd railed against capitalism
or the lack of a minimum wage; when I'd protested against road develop-
ments or discovered feminism; when I'd argued, with a sixteen-year-old's
passionate conviction, that I could change things if only I could persuade
others to agree. "What are you going to do about it?" was the rallying cry
that had inspired me to study politics and history, the first in my family
to go to university. I'd lost my conviction in my early twenties; had taken
the safest options—both with my husband and with my career. But as I
neared forty, his challenge resonated, and I finally found the confidence
to run for office.

"You wanted to use this interview to make an impact," Claire was
reminding me now. "To generate debate about revenge porn: shove it
further up the agenda. To stick it to Harry, really, for failing to support
you on this. And you've done that here."

She was right, of course. Though I was surprised Esther had included
quite so many photos and comments.

"Assume you kept off Twitter?"

"Yep." Jazz had kept an eye on it for me after the initial reaction on
Saturday morning, and I had concentrated instead on preparing for a
meeting with the home secretary's special adviser tomorrow, and on Flo.
Even that had left me dissatisfied, as if my meeting with Simon Baxter,
and the malevolence the feature had prompted, had bled into the entire
weekend. I couldn't get one thing right. Oh, I'd tried. Had roasted a
chicken and made a crumble that Flora had picked at before spending
hours applying makeup in front of YouTube—despite my suggesting we
watch a movie. "Can I see?" I'd asked at around 9 p.m. last night, trying
not to sound needy. And she'd opened the bathroom door and looked at

me, expressionless: her beautiful face greasy with makeup remover, the look she'd spent forty-odd minutes creating wiped clean away.

"I saw enough Twitter comments to know I *clearly* shouldn't wear red lipstick," I told Claire now.

"It's ridiculous," she replied. "You wear red lipstick when you're being fierce. You've worn it in the Chamber. These photos show that version of you."

"Tea." Jazz put a mug in front of me. It was a reassuringly strong brew. Jazz, lactose intolerant, didn't believe in adding much milk. From her desk came the click of a pop tab as she opened a Diet Coke. The mug, my favorite, was one of those made in a pottery café: decorated with baby Flora's handprint. I always washed it separately in case it chipped.

"What did Flora think?" Julia had slid into the room. Her expression was stern, but then Julia always looked serious. A bright resin necklace dangling over her navy dress was the only suggestion she could ever be less than somber, and even this seemed considered, as if a blast of primary colors would distract from her somewhat pinched face. She was thin, with cropped dark hair that might have looked gamine in her thirties but, coupled with her habitual look of disapproval, now seemed severe. She had taken me under her wing when I'd arrived, offering me a room to rent in the house she and Claire had taken on, and being kind when my marriage fell apart. Yet four years in, it sometimes felt like a friendship of convenience rather than something genuine. Like David, she had an unerring ability to home in on my insecurities.

"Oh, you remember what it's like to be a teenage girl. Faintly embarrassed, but deep down, I know, she's proud of me."

"She thinks the world of you," Claire said, with a glance at our housemate that suggested they'd already speculated about Flora's reaction. Julia remained unsmiling, and I itched to challenge her: to provoke her into saying I'd stepped out of line.

"Hope so," I said instead, and then, because I knew that sounded equivocal, I reached for my private mobile to remind myself of a message Flora had sent early this morning: a mother-and-daughter emoji with a pink heart between them followed by a yellow thumbs-up. Funny how Flora's phone allowed her to express things she'd never articulate in other ways. The sentimental emojis made me hope she would open up in a way she'd avoided the previous evening; reveal what Caroline had meant by her falling out with Leah, or even mention having started her period. (I'd put a box of tampons and a packet of pads on her bed, and they were moved, unacknowledged.) The iPhone she'd been so desperate for was our daily means of connection and, despite my concern about the amount of time she spent on it, a force for good in many ways.

"Look at this," I said, because the message was so sweet, and I wanted to prove my daughter felt close to me. And then I saw it: a message from an unknown number. My heart contracted, then flailed against my ribs: a quick one-two.

My phone had been on silent so that I could get some work done, and somehow this made it even worse. This threat had been there, hidden the whole time, in my handbag.

You think you're so fucking special. You'd better watch out bitch.

Five

6 OCTOBER 2021

EMMA

"The honorable member for Portsmouth South."

The Speaker sounded bored when he called my name during questions to the justice secretary. It was all smoke and mirrors. Ostensibly impartial, he was, I knew, sympathetic to my cause.

I rose to my feet. Two thirty p.m. on a Wednesday afternoon, and the baize green benches were less than a third full. The monthly question-and-answer session was hardly required listening for MPs who had just enjoyed the pantomime of Prime Minister's Questions. Many were still lunching and discussing the crucial question of which side won.

Wednesday afternoon was always a nonevent in the Chamber, but the meager audience hardly mattered. Jazz had emailed the people I needed to listen, the journalists who would turn my question into a story and give it a broader reach. I glanced up at the press gallery, saw the stenographers tapping away at their machines, a couple of anonymous bowed heads, and, crucially, the Press Association's parliamentary correspondent who within forty minutes would have sent my top lines out on the wire to every national and provincial newsroom. Everything had been perfectly set up. And yet I was apprehensive. This wasn't an easy subject and would make for uncomfortable listening, among those at home as much as those lounging on the benches opposite. My stomach did a quick flip, roiled and gurgled. This subject mattered—to me and, most of all, to my distraught constituent who'd raised the issue in such a powerful way.

A rustle of papers, a clearing of throats. I looked down at a card on which I had jotted my opening line and some bullet points. I needed to be succinct. I would be reined back pretty sharpish if this turned into a speech, but there were ways of demanding attention. "Military" was a good word to drop in, or "armed forces personnel." But "condolences" was the most effective.

It was hard to beat the death of a constituent to make people think.

"Could I ask the minister to offer his condolences to the family of my constituent Amy Jones," I began—and there it was. A hush came across the Chamber as the usual bickering and shuffling dissolved into a queasy silence. The minister, Richard Carlson, a lawyer and one of the more thoughtful members of the government, leaned back on the front bench and inclined his head.

"Amy tragically took her own life after being a victim of what is commonly referred to as 'revenge porn,'" I went on. A pause while some members calibrated that it was best not to titter, and those uncomfortable with the word thanked the Lord that none of their daughters were likely to get themselves into this state.

"Amy was only eighteen years old when her former boyfriend, Kyle Griffin, persuaded her that he should film her while they had sex. She was extremely reluctant, but he reassured her it was 'for his eyes only.' When Amy ended the relationship three months later, she asked him to delete the video clips. Instead he posted them on Facebook and sent the links to everyone he could think of in order to inflict the maximum humiliation. Amy's evangelical parents, who didn't know their youngest daughter was sexually active; her friends; her colleagues and her boss at a firm of lawyers where she had just been made an office junior. As if this wasn't enough, he put her mobile number and address—and a shot from the video—on a website advertising escort services. The first Amy knew of this was when her father opened the door to a potential customer who became verbally aggressive when Mr. Jones insisted his daughter wasn't a sex worker.

"Amy wasn't a particularly resilient young woman; not someone who, at some point, would manage to put this down as a hard lesson about some men's capacity for cruelty. She sank into herself. Refused to leave her room. Her sister, Freya, eventually persuaded her to go to the police, where she gave a statement. The police were sympathetic but warned her that, if a prosecution went ahead, she wouldn't be automatically granted anonymity. The Crown Prosecution Service would have to apply for an order requesting that. Nor could they prevent the video being further distributed. And while Kyle's behavior *could* lead to a prison sentence, there was no guarantee that for a first offense this would occur.

"Amy went home, and later that day, while her sister and parents were at work, she went into the family garage. There she hanged herself."

I paused and let the Chamber swell with the gentle murmur of condemnation; waited until the response burgeoned, then dipped, horror mingled with support.

"In a note left to her family, Amy said she could not bear the shame she had brought on them, and the fact she would always be known first and foremost as the girl in the video . . ."

Another considered pause.

"Kyle Griffin pleaded guilty at a hearing last month and was given a sentence of just one hundred fifty hours' community service. The maximum sentence, for the most egregious harm from a repeat offender, would be two years. Campaign groups have been calling for victims of revenge porn to be granted anonymity for the past eighteen months. This case highlights quite how urgent this need is. Would the minister be willing to meet with Amy's sister, Freya, and myself to discuss amendments to the forthcoming Online Harms Bill both with a view to extending sentences for those who perpetrate revenge porn and for granting automatic anonymity to their victims whose lives are blighted—or rendered seemingly unlivable—by such heinous acts?"

A chorus of hear-hears and general agreement. On the opposite benches, Tristram Sale raised an eyebrow in appreciation, while Barnaby Miles's lizard eyes flicked up and down, as if mentally undressing me. Then Richard Carlson got to his feet to offer sincere condolences to Amy Jones's sister, Freya, and her parents.

"Revenge porn is indeed something that the Law Commission has been assessing ahead of the forthcoming bill, and which my department has been looking at closely. It is yet another form of violence against women, which this government is committed to eradicating," he added, and I felt his words wash over me. Because what was he saying that hadn't been said before?

But then he surprised me: not offering the usual catalogue of supposed successes in the march against misogyny, or empty blandishments, but something concrete. "Amending the Online Harms Bill would be the swiftest means of protecting young women such as Amy. I will, of course, be delighted to meet with the honorable member for Portsmouth South, and with Freya Jones, to discuss ways in which we might do so—and I will be writing to her directly to arrange this."

And from my space on the backbenches, I beamed, warmed at the thought that my actions, my *speech*, had achieved something. That all the abuse—the anonymous rape-threat letters, the Twitter aggression, the interaction with the likes of Simon Baxter, the impact on my relationship with Flora—was worth it after all.

Briefly I thought of my father, the man who developed my social conscience. He died three years ago, twenty years after my nurse mum, Wendy, having seen their only child become an MP. "Now you can *do* something," he had said on election night, his pride emanating from his face, his body reverberating with excitement. "You've got some *real* influence."

I often feared I had far less than he believed, that I'd disappointed him in doing too little with the legacy he'd left me.

Well, I was doing something now.

6 OCTOBER 2021

EMMA

"Emma—could I have a word?"

Mike Stokes, the political editor of the *Chronicle*, was hanging around the edge of the Members' Lobby when I left the Chamber.

"Of course." I inclined my head to indicate he could approach me, an eccentricity of this place being that no member of the press could walk across the tiles unless invited to do so by an MP.

"Quite a speech," he said, as he slowed his jaunty pace. His casualness was studied. In his inside jacket pocket, there would be a pocket-size notepad he would draw out at some point in our conversation, perhaps raising an eyebrow to check I was happy to be quoted. I welcomed this professionalism. We'd worked together on a couple of stories, and as much as I trusted any journalist, I thought I could trust him.

"I'm glad you thought so," I said now. I felt elated: adrenaline from delivering my speech still coursing through me. Relief, too, that it had been so well received by my colleagues.

"Tragic case."

"Just horrible," I said, shaking my head. I thought of the video Freya had showed me, the visceral pain that built as I recognized the level of coercion. "That was just the bare bones of it. Wasn't sure anyone needed to hear the full details, but it was pretty horrific."

"I can imagine," he said.

He smiled at me again. With his sandy hair and trim physique, he could still be described as boyish, though he must have been in his early forties. He was unremarkable, except for his eyes, a dark brown that glinted with good humor as if he always expected something exciting to occur.

It was obvious what he was about to ask, but as we walked slowly toward Central Lobby, I let myself enjoy the dance of it: knowing that we probably would collaborate, yet waiting before I committed to doing so to see what he could do for my constituents in return.

"I wondered if you could tell me more about it, and if you thought the family might be willing to talk to us?"

"'Us?'"

"Well, if not me, the paper. Amy's story will resonate with our readers. It's every parent's nightmare, isn't it?" He had the decency to look embarrassed as he trotted out the cliché. "The enemy in the heart of your home. Or in your teenage daughter's bed.

"It could happen to any of our kids," he continued, warming to his theme. "And it taps into not just coercive control, and violence toward women, but that sense of the internet taking over our lives: of it being not just destructive—but inescapable. It's a human tragedy, first and foremost—a young girl shamed by her first boyfriend in the most heart-wrenching way imaginable—but it's so much more than that."

"Well, absolutely." I nodded in agreement. He got it. He really got it. Could see how we could take this individual story and show how it could affect every woman. I couldn't stop smiling at him, despite knowing I should be wary. Maybe I'd become too cynical. The *Chronicle* was left-leaning, after all.

"So, do you think Freya's parents—you didn't mention their names?"

"Frank and Lorna."

"Frank and Lorna. Do you think Frank and Lorna would talk to us? It could be with our star interviewer. It needn't be me . . ."

"Oh, I'm not sure, Mike. They're pretty distraught."

"Well, you know, that's *good*."

I gave him a look.

"I mean emotion is good. It conveys the impact this has had on them."

"They won't do it, Mike." I spelled it out. "They're very quiet people, very private. Evangelical Christians who hadn't considered that their daughter might be sleeping with her boyfriend. You can imagine their shock at receiving the video, and then their grief at what it drove her to do. This has *broken* them."

He scuffed a tile with his shoe. "What about the sister?"

"Freya? Yeah—actually she probably would. Particularly now that we've secured this meeting with the minister." I thought of Freya Jones's grim determination when she'd turned up at my town hall meeting and insisted on showing me the video. "I think that's a definite possibility."

"Great." He was beaming, and it transformed him. The rumpled hack, with his loosened tie and his hands in his pockets, seemed galvanized. Energetic. Irrepressible. As if he couldn't wait to get started on the story.

I suddenly wondered if he would be rather fun in bed.

"Let me talk to her, okay?" I said, blindsided by this idea of him in a totally different scenario, conscious that blood was rushing up my neck. "Run it past her first. Then I'll pass on your number."

"Or you could give hers to me?"

He clearly thought that I was stupid.

"I'll let *her* contact *you*," I said.

"Brilliant. Perfect. Thank you," he said, bouncing on the balls of his feet. "I don't suppose you could try her today, could you? I could see us really running with this story in a big way if she was willing to talk. And, as you know, that will force the issue up the agenda. In the meantime, we'll run a news story based on what you said in the Chamber and what the minister promised."

"Of course." I was flooded with relief.

"Fantastic. I could see us turning this into a campaign. Lobbying for an Amy's Law. That's got a great ring to it, hasn't it?"

By now, we had reached the lift to the lobby corridor where he would disappear while I walked through the cloisters of New Palace Yard to Portcullis House, and he stopped abruptly. I felt as if I should shake his hand to cement what we'd decided. Instead I fumbled in my handbag for my phone.

"Just checking I've got the right number."

He leaned a little closer to check I had his mobile in my contacts.

"Ah—got it," I said, moving away. "I'll call her straightaway. And let's chat later? In case you need any more quotes?"

I looked too keen. Too eager to get Amy's story across, but a tabloid campaign was exactly what I needed to keep ramping up the pressure on the minister.

"Perfect." There was that smile again.

I turned to go toward Portcullis House, conscious that he was watching as I walked away.

Seven

6 OCTOBER 2021

EMMA

I should have felt giddy with the relief by the time I unlocked my bike and set off for Cleaver Square, at around 8:30 that evening. It took less than ten minutes, slipping over the Thames, braving the traffic hurtling across Vauxhall Bridge, then rattling down Kennington Lane. I varied my route, and I usually felt safer than when I took the Tube and walked back from the station. Cabs were reimbursed past 8 p.m., but how could I take a taxi when my constituents relied on food banks?

Perhaps it was my apprehension about how my speech would play out on social media. (The usual trolls were already vicious.) Or maybe I was still feeling the effects of the adrenaline that had fired my speech in the Chamber and a couple of broadcast interviews, and that still coursed through me like radioactive dye. Either way, by the time I left the Commons, I felt vulnerable. A stiff breeze brushed the nape of my neck as I wheeled my bike to the gates, and as I glanced behind me, I felt horribly exposed.

It was a dirty night, rain lashing, spray rearing up my legs and soaking my trousers. The Thames was dark and glassy, but I barely glanced downriver as I pedaled away. Instead I kept my head down, concentrating on the traffic that throbbed at my back: malevolent, predatory, insistent. Rain seeped between my cycling helmet and my GORE-TEX, a cold trickle that wriggled under the collar of my blouse.

At the lights, a pimped-up Golf GTI revved its engine and almost cut into me as it turned left to race toward the City. "Fuck's sake!" I yelled in shock at him ignoring my flickering lights and fluorescent tabard. I screeched on my brakes, then turned right onto the Embankment, the glitz of the Houses of Parliament slipping away.

And as I turned onto Black Prince Road, the houses on either side seemed suddenly unfriendly. The few trees waved witches' fingers as a stiff breeze sloughed off any remaining leaves. Then a couple of boys on bikes raced across the road: no lights, hoods up, skinny legs pedaling furiously before they glided, elegant as skaters, looping backward and forward toward me.

The rain was pelting down still, their wheels slicking on the wet tarmac, and as the elder boy came close, I caught a glimpse of his mocking expression and pale, pinched face. The teacher in me wanted to shout at them to use their lights; that without them, they were undetectable until a car hit them; that their lives were not as cheaply expendable as they might think. I already felt cowed, riding in the dark, flustered by the turbocharged Golf, by the aggression seeping from this restless city and coming at me now. *Slick, slick, slick.* The older boy—thirteen or fourteen, with a shadow of hair on his upper lip—bore down on me. Calves burning, I surged on, eyes trained on the curve of the neoclassical terrace ahead. Was he toying with me? A cat giving his prey a chance before closing right in?

Kennington Lane startled me with its light and noise: all cars, fast-food outlets, and real estate agents. I followed in a bus's slipstream and stuck close to its taillights, reassured by the thrum of its engine and its familiar red bulk.

But as I peeled off down a side road to my own flat-fronted Georgian terrace, I risked checking that the road behind me was empty. And there he was: lackadaisical, his arms crossed against his chest. A wide, cocksure grin on his face, he looped from one side of the road to the other, just avoiding the cars parked bumper to bumper, judging the distance expertly with the slightest twitch of his hips. He raised one hand in a salute, but as I turned back, cycling feverishly, feet slipping from the pedals, rhythm lost in a flurry of panic, I sensed him gaining on me.

I swerved onto Cleaver Square; came to a halt outside our house, flinging my bike against the iron railings, fumbling with numb fingers to attach it with the U-lock. *Come on, come on.* My heart juddered, then seemed to miss a beat entirely as the boy cycled past, giving me a dead-eyed stare. He was circling the square. Fuck. He had followed me home, and I had to get inside. Had to get inside before he completed all four sides—a brutal tease? a dare?—and caught up with me. I had to get inside *right now*. My key twisted in the bike lock, and then I was running up the five steps to the front door, horribly exposed as I fumbled with my keys.

There was no one home, but the security light clicked on as I stood at the top of the steps, fiddling for the correct key, fired by a panicky desperation. The lock turned, and I was in. As the alarm blared, I keyed in the code, then leaned against the door, fearful he was on the other side. Waiting to post something through the letter box, perhaps, or just listening out for my breathing, for a cry, for some evidence I was frightened. The floor tilted upward, and my heart thudded so loudly it seemed impossible he wouldn't hear.

I tried to breathe deeply. To calm myself. To tell myself I was being ridiculous. He was a kid. It could be a complete coincidence he had come this way. Even if he had followed me, he'd have cycled off now, clearly bored by my response. But my heart was stuttering, and I felt both hyper-alert and befuddled by the blood whooshing through my head.

A buzz from my backpack, and I drew out my phone. Another unknown mobile. Not Mike's. Simon Baxter's? Or this kid's? Ridiculous. I was being ridiculous: it was my personal number. How would a random boy who'd spooked me in the street have access to it?

But it seemed someone did.

And as I glanced at it, I started shaking so fiercely I dropped the phone, a fine crack running diagonally across it.

Because the message read:

I'm watching you bitch.

Eight

7 OCTOBER 2021

FLORA

Her mum was on the news again.

Which was great. Really it was. Or at least it was good for her mum, for the causes she was passionate about and for her profile. But it wasn't so great for Flora. And she knew she was being selfish, but she couldn't help feeling that way.

It wasn't exactly *easy* being the daughter of an MP. Apart from the constant stress—making mental pacts to try to keep her mum safe as she visualized acid, gun, and knife attacks—it was also that people assumed she was rich. Posh. Stuck-up. To be fair, they'd thought it even at primary school. That's what happened if you were called Flora—who called their child *Flora*?—lived in a nice house, and had parents with good jobs: one a local councillor and teacher before she was elected, the other working in IT.

But her mum becoming an MP meant things rocketed to another level. She was proud of her. That went without saying. So proud, the first time she saw her on TV fired up by something she cared about, she literally thought she would burst. But Flora was also "conflicted," as Miss Harwood, her English teacher, would say. Because it wasn't enough for her mum just to be a politician who kept her head down, voting as she was told, getting on with the job, and sometimes being quoted by the local paper. It was as if she went out of her way to get publicity. Or perhaps that wasn't fair. But she didn't do anything to avoid it: seemed to think that any risk was justifiable if it helped her cause. Of course, Flora got that she wanted to champion feminist ideals. She didn't know anyone who was *anti*-feminist, apart from the boys in her year who said it to get

43

a rise. But she wished her mum would tone it down a bit. Realize that, while she might like being high-profile—and Flora could see she got a kick out of being on the TV—not everyone wanted to stand out. Not everyone wanted to be different. And at fourteen, Flora didn't want to be different at all.

To be fair, her mum's increasingly high profile probably wasn't the only reason Flora's life was so awful at the moment. But had she still been a teacher, still been with her dad, still been a normal mum—there to pick her and Leah up from volleyball matches, or take her round to her friends' houses, or just be *around*—she reckoned none of this would be happening.

Not that Flora wanted to admit to what "this" was, to be honest. Because it felt like—and she still couldn't get her head around it . . . well, it felt like she was being *bullied*.

"Celery," they called her. Or "The Stick." And she laughed along with them because what was the alternative? To stand there, her eyes filling with tears? To say in a tight, choked voice, *Please don't call me that?* No one liked someone who couldn't take a joke. And so she told herself that a nickname was a kind of endearment. Easier to believe when Leah stuck to Celery, a soft, silly sort of nickname; harder with the more brittle The Stick, which suggested she wasn't even human.

It was the Snapchat "opinions on" Leah had posted that had really got to her. All those comments about her that her friend had encouraged, had *invited*. It was just a joke, Leah later said. Flora wasn't even meant to see it. She'd been blocked from the chat; had only discovered Leah's post because Kat had shown her since she'd "thought she ought to know." By this stage, there were several comments: a pile-on from that question until more than thirty of her class were chipping in, and the responses—most of them anonymous—had shifted from tepid interest to full-on attack.

What's with her face? 😰 😰 😰
Too round by half, man, and so fucking pale.
What's with the invisible lashes?
Albino girl or what?
I wd srsly kill myself if I looked like her.
But wd she do it properly?

She's clever.

Yeah. But she don't understand the world, man. Look at how she was with Leah in Superdrug.

Yeah.

Talk about resting bitchface.

Just like her mum. Bitch thinks she can boss us about.

"You're not upset, are you?" Kat asked after she'd borrowed Flora's phone to take a snap of the comments on her phone. (They both knew Kat couldn't take a screenshot on her phone without Snapchat alerting Leah that she'd done so.)

"'S okay."

"I mean *I'd* want to know if people were saying this about me . . ." Kat peered at her with big, concerned eyes.

"'S *okay*, I said. Don't tell her." She wiped her nose with the end of her sleeve, ducking her head so Kat couldn't see that her eyes were smarting. *Don't let her see me cry. Don't let her see me cry.* She wished Kat would just leave her alone.

It was nothing. Pathetic behavior, her mum would say if Flora told her about it (though, *obviously*, she wouldn't). Her mum had no idea what it was like to be a teenager these days. A throwaway comment, a joke that had an edge, was like a single strike of a match—and before you knew it your whole life was in flames.

Later, much later, she would realize that it was partly her reaction when Leah nicked that Benefit highlighter from Superdrug that triggered everything. She'd distanced herself a bit after that: made it pretty clear that she disapproved. What was it that Dumbledore said to Neville in *Harry Potter and the Sorcerer's Stone*? Something about it taking a great deal of bravery to stand up to your enemies, and just as much to your friends? Of course, she hadn't quoted Harry Potter. Leah—who'd seen the films, not read the books—would have laughed in her face. But Leah had picked up on her unease. "You looked right down your nose at her," Kat said, while Abi added: "Just because your mum's a politician, it doesn't mean you're better than everyone else."

"It's not my fault my mum got that job," she tried to tell them, and "I can't help my face." She'd never been very good at hiding her emotions.

With hindsight, it was Charley Morris's fault. If Leah hadn't been obsessed with becoming like her, perhaps none of this would have happened. Because, to move up the school hierarchy, Leah had to rid herself of any embarrassing friendships: the girls who weighed her down.

Flora was deadweight. They'd been close in middle school—part of a group with Abi, Evie, and Kat—but Leah was socially ambitious. Having joined the varsity soccer team at Victory Academy, she was on glancing terms with Charley Morris, *the* most popular girl in the year. Charley was a bae-girl. Confident, mean, hard—both in attitude and looks. There was nothing soft about Charley, from her straightened hair dyed a defiant black to her sculpted eyebrows, skin the color of caramel, heavily mascaraed lashes, and acrylic nails.

From the moment she joined the team, Leah changed. It happened so swiftly that, only three weeks into the school year, she was drawing on thick eyebrows and applying fake tan. Flora was thrown. There was something sad about Charley, who looked twenty on her Insta account. And yet she couldn't tell Leah that. Last year, they might have mimicked her—sucking in their cheeks, batting their eyelids, pouting their lips—giggling over how *obvious* she looked in her tiny bikini accessorized by a strategically placed vodka bottle. Now Leah seemed to have lost her sense of humor.

And then, last week—the day before the Snapchat pile-on—Leah just ghosted her, and Abi, always closer to her than to Flora, copied Leah.

U okay? Flora WhatsApped her best friend. But though she knew the message had been read, there was no reply. She waited, hoping for a cross-eyed emoji. But there was still nothing, and when she glanced across in geography, expecting an eye roll when the teacher lost it with Hayden Symonds, Leah casually turned her body away.

At lunch, Leah and Abi pushed ahead of her, and when she joined them at their table, Leah refused to look at her and just said: "Sorry, that's taken."

"But there's no one here."

Everyone in the lunchroom seemed to be looking their way.

"It's saved." A blank look, as if Leah saw right through her. The burble of chat resumed, but Flora stood riveted. Then Samuel Briggs jostled her with his backpack, and Marc Williams shoved past, and she took her chicken wrap, which she wouldn't be able to eat, out onto the playing fields. And it felt as if everyone watched that walk of shame.

The next day, Leah, with a changeability that was becoming predictable, started talking to her again. There was no *soz* or emoji suggesting she regretted ghosting her; no acknowledgment that Flora had seen the pile-on, let alone an explanation for why Leah had started it. Just a *K?* when Leah asked if she'd done the math homework, and could she have a look? (It was never a straight *Can I copy it?*)

"Actually. No, I haven't," she said, which was a lie because Flora always did her homework, and Flora knew that Leah knew this. When she handed her book in, she felt Leah's eyes tracking her back to her seat.

Leah didn't speak to her for two days after that, but she did by the Friday, and for a while, Flora was allowed to tag along. To rejoin the group in a temporary way. She chatted more to Evie and Kat, who were willing to survive on the crumbs of Leah's friendship, and she accepted that her position was precarious: that she was about be dropped.

And she hated herself for putting up with this type of friendship, but what other option did she have? To hang around the playground on her own like the sort of freak she suspected she might be?

"All okay with Leah?" her mum had asked last weekend. Perhaps Caroline had mentioned something? And then she felt guilty because she'd confided in her stepmum a bit when Caroline guessed she'd been crying. Sometimes it was easier to talk to her because she was less busy and because she was there.

She couldn't tell her mum anything, really. Emma had made it pretty clear that what Flora wanted—for her no longer to be an MP, for life to somehow revert to how it was when she was a little kid—was no longer possible. And she believed Flora's friendship circle was as tight as it had always been.

And so she always smiled when her mum asked her about her friends. When Emma mentioned that she'd always liked Leah—"a strong character but lots of fun, yes?"—or that Kat was "dependable" . . .

Flora told her what she wanted to hear.

Nine

7 OCTOBER 2021

EMMA

Twitter Thread

> **BrizzleBert** @BB1457433: See feminist freak @emmawebsterMP wants to protect slags who give it out.
> **Andy Madeley** @madmancunian: Takes one to know one.
> **BrizzleBert** @BB1457433: LMFAO. My thoughts exactly, m8.
> **Dick Penny** @EnglandRules: Yeah. Rkn there's a reason she's promoting this slags charter.
> **Andy Madeley** @madmancunian: Bet she's absolutely *filthy*.

Kennington, 6:50 a.m., and I stood in my basement kitchen, downing my first tea of the morning, and peering past the rain-slicked pavement at the slowly brightening sky.

Once upon a time, this would have been the domain of the maid and the cook: the downstairs to the light, high-ceilinged rooms where a Georgian merchant would debate the issues of the day. These days, the basement was the hub of the house, with sleek floor-to-ceiling cupboards, the obligatory island, and a seven-foot distressed oak table, at which we were more likely to work than eat. Beyond the table were French doors that opened onto a courtyard garden with plants no one remembered to water and a view of two hulking high-rises. There was a rickety garden table, but even on sunny evenings we rarely sat there. It was impossible not to feel watched from above.

The three floors above were divided up so that we each had our own space. Julia had the top floor, with her bathroom, bedroom, and the best views; Claire, the middle; and me, the raised ground floor with its additional tiny bedroom or dressing room, for the very few occasions when Flora came to stay. The kitchen was the only communal space. The place where we regrouped and caught up over mugs of peppermint tea if we were trying to be virtuous or glasses of wine as the week dragged on. Where we—or, more usually, Claire and I—gossiped and plotted and tried to put the world to rights; where we reminded each other of why we'd chosen this job; and where I counseled Claire as she became more despondent about whether Matt, her thirty-two-year-old policy wonk boyfriend, would ever commit to her and the idea of children, or whether she should shed him or her career.

And I liked the irony of this: the fact that, although we could pop into each other's rooms, we converged in this space that was practical and intimate. The ghosts of the women who'd worked here, and they were always women, could be felt all around. And if that sounded fanciful, then the atmosphere was benign. The Kennington house wasn't my home. I'd kept my bedroom deliberately austere—an iron bed, clothes hidden away, just the one black-and-white photo of a ten-year-old Flora—and it felt right that this was as uncluttered as a nun's cell: a space in which to work, not play. But we had to kick back somewhere, and the kitchen—even this kitchen with bars on the window and extra locks on the back door, thanks to this house being assessed following the acid-threat letter—seemed to be the place.

I didn't feel as if I could relax this morning, though. Even here, in the place I should feel safe, I felt nervous. I'd slept particularly badly, *I'm watching you bitch* spooling incessantly through my mind. I only had to glance at my phone's cracked screen to be reminded of the message I'd received as I'd slammed the front door. Who knew my private number and would send that to me? Who would use a burner phone, too? (Because I knew the police would be unable to trace it.) Late last night, I changed my settings to block all unknown numbers, but I couldn't do that with my work mobile since I needed to be accessible. If someone was sufficiently determined, they would keep on sending these messages to me.

I took a slurp of Assam tea: my first drink before I moved on to thick black coffee. Dawn was properly breaking now, the sky a watery blue tinged with flamingo pink. I tried to remind myself that I loved this part of the day. With my housemates up at seven, the hour before was the only time I could be guaranteed some peace and quiet, and I used it to read through the previous day's ministerial statements. All too often, worries about Flora distracted me, but today I was obsessing about the message, and the shameful fear that had gripped me as I'd cycled back, pursued by that malevolently smiling man-boy.

It had to be some sort of coincidence: him *and* the text. I shouldn't think any more about it, nor the excessive abuse I'd unleashed by talking about Amy in the Chamber—a deluge of tweets detailing *exactly* what should be done to me that muddied my mind. Perhaps the news would make me focus. I switched on the radio, and there was a clunk as the device tripped: a frustratingly frequent occurrence, our landlord's renovation not extending to a complete rewiring. I unplugged various things, then trudged upstairs to the fuse box under the next set of stairs.

With power restored, I returned to the radio and BBC Radio 4's *Today* program. A familiar voice sent an immediate chill through me: a shiver that ran straight from my coccyx to my bowels. I started to shake. That man. That *bloody* man. Marcus Jamieson, professor of politics at University College London, but better known as a controversial commentator and columnist for the most right-wing newspapers. The sort of media whore guaranteed to get a rise.

"The issue is that the woke lobby," he sneered, "now dominates the agenda to such an extent that your average middle-class, middle-aged white man has been silenced." "But surely—" the presenter began before Marcus cut in: smooth, urbane, the fake working-class accent he'd adopted years ago when he was my politics tutor at Brighton dropped now that there was no need for any pretense that he was anything but a privileged man. "It's not up for discussion. The snowflakes have become so dominant it's impossible to compliment a woman without being seen as predatory, or to question someone's gender without being transphobic." Oh, for God's sake. He wasn't even original. I swiped the volume dial so that he was silenced, then clicked it abruptly to completely cut him off.

That man always brought out the worst in me. Inevitably I remembered our last conversation four years ago. His voice with its hint of sly laughter, its clear condescension, the balance of power tipped firmly in his favor, just as it was when he was my lecturer and I his student struggling to keep up. Well, fuck him. I needed to block out him, the boy, the Twitter trolls from what was important. What I needed to do, I realized as I spooned coffee into a pot and placed it on the burner, was to concentrate on how best to help Freya.

And I was back there, at our first meeting two weeks ago, a week after Kyle's derisory sentence. Freya sitting hunched in that primary school classroom, fizzing with anger, then subdued by grief. At first, I'd struggled to understand, the twenty-year-old almost whispering, as if her emotions were too overwhelming to be expressed. But then she became clearer, articulating her fury not just with Kyle, the sort of toxic male whose good looks had curdled into a hardness, but also with a system that meant her sister died after realizing that, if a prosecution was brought against him, she would be shamed all over again.

"She couldn't carry on. Her *boss* saw it; our *dad* saw it. Look—I'll show you."

"It's all right. There's no need."

But Freya was jabbing at a video on her phone. "I want you to understand what he *did* to her. Why she felt so ashamed."

The screen flickered, then jolted into action to reveal the top of a girl's head, her mouth on a man's penis. Filmed from above, the girl paused and laughed self-consciously, embarrassed at being recorded, perhaps at having to do this at all. At one point, she had looked up at her lover, and it was this that had splintered my heart. *Am I doing this right?* the look said, and *I can trust you, can't I? You're not* laughing *at me?* I shivered at the memory of a similar glance myself. Of a distant time when that sharply felt, oh-so-poignant need to please had been of the utmost importance to me.

"Okay. I think I've seen enough." I cleared my throat, began to shuffle some notes.

"You need to see this bit: to listen to what he says here." Freya was insistent.

"I really don't." I was firm. "I don't need to see any more of it at all."

She'd been confused. "But you have to *see*. See the look on his face and hear what he tells her."

"Another time," I said. "I've seen more than enough for today. Look, it's horrific." I tried to placate her. "I can only imagine how humiliated she must have felt. How much this must have felt like the ultimate betrayal."

"The bastard. The absolute *bastard*. He ruined her life. He *took* her life and he's not even going to prison." She was shaking. Fear ambushed me like that, but for Freya, it was anger: a fury so excessive her skinny body quivered with rage.

"There's nothing any of us can do," she went on as she looked at me to contradict her. And it was then I realized I faced a choice. I could offer my sympathy but say there was little I could do to change the law. Or I could promise that this would be an issue I took on. Something that would define me as an MP but, more importantly, would alter society in some small way so that the Kyle Griffins of this world faced a proper deterrent: a far stiffer prison sentence that would make them think before posting a private video online.

Ten past seven. I would ring Freya at nine, just to check she was genuinely happy about being interviewed by Mike's colleague. Had she agreed to it too readily? The suspicion niggled like a piece of grit in my eye.

"And you're willing to talk to the *Chronicle*?" I'd asked last night after telling her about meeting the minister. "Mike Stokes is a good man: I wouldn't suggest this otherwise." I hadn't mentioned my reservations about Jenni Collins, the star feature writer who was known for being ruthless.

"As long as Mum and Dad are kept out of it, then that's fine." She had paused and then sounded firmer than I'd heard before, her voice swelling with conviction. "I have to do this for Amy, don't you see?"

Ten

8 OCTOBER 2021

MIKE

Sister's Heartbreak for Revenge Porn Victim
by Jenni Collins

The last thing Amy Jones told her sister, Freya, was that she loved her.

Freya was surprised. "We're not a lovey-dovey family," says the student, sitting in the neat semidetached home she shares with their parents. "We're not the sort of sisters who say such things."

An hour later she realized why the 18-year-old had uttered those words.

Because when she tried to push open the family's garage door, she couldn't.

Her little sister had hanged herself.

"I'll never forgive myself," Freya, now twenty, says, with tears in her eyes. "I knew she was desperate, but I hadn't realized she couldn't see any other way."

She doesn't only blame herself.

Her greatest anger is reserved for Kyle Griffin, Amy's ex-boyfriend, who Freya says drove Amy to suicide by sending a video of her performing a sex act to Amy's parents, her boss, and colleagues, and posting it on social media. Last month, Kyle was sentenced to just 150 hours community service after pleading guilty at a court hearing.

"It was more than Amy could bear."

Mike threw his copy of the *Chronicle* back on the desk in his office, tucked away down the lobby corridor in the House of Commons. There was a double-page spread, complete with a picture of Freya conveying just the right combination of sorrow and fury. He had to hand it to her. Whether through luck or judgment, Freya had got it just right.

The desk had been thrilled. After months of grumbling about a lack of exclusives, his news editor had barked a gruff "Good work" when Mike rang in. "More of the same, please," he hadn't been able to resist adding—which was all very well for him, but Mike was the one who would have to do it. With print journalism dying, every hack—even one with the experience and acumen of a political editor—was only as good as his last story. And with young blood snapping at his heels like a pack of Jack Russells, he needed to nab more exclusives.

He rubbed a hand over his face as if to smarten up his features. He hadn't done anything noteworthy to get hold of this tale. It wasn't just that it had been handed to him on a press release; it had been spouted in the Chamber and then relayed on the wires. Still, without his contacts, this would have been at best a news-in-brief. It was the human element—Freya's grief, Amy demure as a fourteen-year-old bridesmaid in a photograph far removed from the video clip that Kyle distributed—that gave this story legs. And if it weren't for his powers of persuasion, Emma wouldn't have given him access to this: would have gone to Esther Enfield at the *Guardian*, which, with a broadsheet's disdain for human interest, would have thrown away the story. Buried at the bottom of page six, at best.

He texted Emma his thanks and suggested they meet for a coffee to discuss how to throw the story forward. She'd reply quickly. Was passionate about Amy's case. And while she might enjoy the publicity—he'd noted the *Guardian* cover, the tilt of her jaw, an intriguing confidence he hadn't seen to this extent before in the Chamber—she still had the best of motives. A conviction politician, that's what she was, and all the more refreshing for it. There were too few of them around these days.

"Great show, big boy."

Guy Black, the most junior member of the *Chronicle*'s political team, burst into the cramped office, slung a man-bag on his chair and his jacket on a peg in an elegantly choreographed movement while simultaneously placing two takeaway cups of coffee on the desk.

"Thanks, mate." Mike nodded at the flat white that had miraculously appeared. He thought the Portcullis House coffee overrated, preferred strong PG Tips, but Guy, ex–private school, ex-Oxbridge, and one of the paper's graduate trainees, had never been seen to dunk a tea bag in a mug of hot water, and seemed to have money to burn.

Mike sat up straight. He didn't think "big boy" referred to his physique, and he hoped it wasn't a reference to his sexual prowess. There'd been no one since his wife, Niamh, died twenty months earlier: it had been far easier not to consider a new relationship, but to focus on a career that, if he wasn't careful, was also in danger of slipping away. No, the nickname was intended as a reference to Mike's position in the office's hierarchy, though he had little doubt this twenty-four-year-old—as enthusiastic and well-bred as a working Labrador pup—would at some point effortlessly supplant him. Guy, insufferably smart, was adapting fast: the odd glottal stop littering his speech; references to soccer, not the rugby he'd played at school, peppering his chats with the special advisers. And they loved him back at the office. The *Chronicle*, while proud of its working-class heritage and paying lip service to diversity, secretly loved a bit of posh.

"So—Freya Jones," Guy began winningly.

"That'll be *my* story, Guy." Give the boy an inch and he'd be all over this.

"Fair enough, skipper." The trainee folded his long limbs beneath his tiny desk, clear apart from his iPhone 11 and his coffee. In contrast, Mike's was a jumble of papers, of reporter's notepads, of pens without their lids, and a mug with the dregs of yesterday's tea festering in the bottom, a scum of curdled milk skimming the top.

Mike lifted the fresh coffee to his lips. Felt a twinge at having been sharp. He was meant to be mentoring Guy, though the idea that this cocky so-and-so needed help was risible. Still, this office was too small for bad humor to fester. He glanced across at Guy, skimming the *Guardian*'s rolling politics blog in case he'd missed anything while on the Tube, flicking over to Twitter. He was keen, or good at appearing keen, he'd give him that.

"Just for argument's sake: if you were the desk, what would you want now from the Amy Jones story?" he asked.

"Well . . ." Guy leaned back in his chair, put his hands behind his head. A trouser leg rode up; he had posh socks and posh ankles. "In the absence of some fresh dirt on Kyle . . ."

Mike dismissed the idea with a wave of a hand. "Someone in the office will be working on that. We'll get a call. Ideally us and not the *Record*. Another girlfriend? I bet there is one. Another life blighted by this shite."

"Yeah." Guy looked a little taken aback by his vehemence. "Well, in the absence of that, I suppose I'd want something concrete to move the Amy's Law campaign on. An interview with the minister?"

"Not going to happen . . ." Richard Carlson would far rather a full-on Saturday interview with the *Times*.

"Her parents' anguish?"

"Good. But they're keeping *schtum* at the moment. Can't really blame them. What father wants to talk about watching his daughter giving someone a blow job? Doubt even Jenni could bulldoze her way into that."

"Then working on your top contact." Guy gave him a sly look. "Your MPILF."

"Easy, tiger."

"Bloody appalling, more like." Rachel Martin, his deputy, thirty-two, sharp, and hardworking, marched into the office. She'd joined politics from the showbiz team and had the killer combination of good looks and a refusal to be cowed.

"Sorry, Rach." Guy ducked, anticipating a cuff to the head.

"Unfortunately, you're right," she said, barely sparing him a glance as she slid into her seat at the terminal next to his. A flurry of activity as she logged on, shoved a pile of papers to one side, pressed the remote so that the monitor flickered into life: a square of poison green with the words *House not sitting*. The room suddenly felt busy, and Mike realized he was slouching.

"Emma Webster is Mike's secret weapon," Rachel continued, looking at her boss sideways and tucking a hank of hair behind her ear. "And he, believe it or not, is hers, because our banging on about an Amy's Law is only going to make her stock rise higher. She'll be bending over backward to help us. Am I right?"

A clatter of her keyboard as they all demurred. "So, where do you reckon you should take her?" asked Rachel.

"I was thinking the cheeky Italian off Millbank?"

She pulled a face. "Too old-fashioned. Too ordinary. I'd go a bit more upmarket. She's not a cheap date."

"She's not a date at all." Post–#metoo, you couldn't be too careful.

"She's not a date. But she *is* a top contact," Rachel corrected herself. "And top contacts deserve a bit of nurturing, a bit of pampering. Somewhere special. A Soho dining room, sufficiently far from here to feel ultra-discreet. You want somewhere where she'll open right up . . ."

" 'Easy, tiger' yourself," Guy said, with his infectious gurgle of a laugh.

"In your dreams." Rachel lifted her cup and implanted a kiss of red grease on the plastic lip, preoccupied as she dismissed him. "Isn't there a Home Affairs select committee you should be going to? Committee room seventeen?"

Guy pulled a face, and Mike hid a smirk in his cup. The new boy didn't like Rach, who'd been working for a decade, pulling rank, and she didn't have much time for him.

From somewhere, Mike's phone began to buzz: a rhythmic vibrating like a trapped bee.

"It's under your pile," Rachel said without looking up from her screen.

She was right, of course, though it still took a while to locate it from the mound of papers, discarded press releases, and business cards to the side of him.

Emma, he mouthed to Guy as he moved a copy of the *Standard* to retrieve the battered handset.

"Hope your ears are burning," he said into it, and he was conscious that his voice had lowered, his tone curiously intimate, as he turned away from his colleagues and his words curled into the phone.

One or both of them snorted, and in one neat move, he sprang up from his desk and moved into the corridor, leaving the sound of his colleagues' gently mocking laughter behind.

Eleven

8 OCTOBER 2021

FLORA

Hi. Saw u around.

Flora ignored the Snapchat message at first; went to delete it as she did with any message from a boy she didn't know. But first she checked the avatar.

Jake Cummins.

Not Jake Cummins in year eleven? He'd played the sax in band but dropped out because it wasn't cool.

She clicked on his stories, where a photo confirmed he was as lovely as she remembered: tall, good lashes, unusually clear skin. He was pulling a typical boy pose: hand on his chin, concentrating on something in the middle distance, making fun of the whole Insta thing. There was something about the tilt of his head, the exaggeration of the pose that implied this. (Her teacher had been talking to them about implications in English.) The moody filter helped.

Sorry ur friends r giving you a hrd time.

She dropped the phone onto her bed as if it burned her. How did he know? Had he seen what had happened in the school lunchroom? Or had he seen @FreeeeeeakyasF on Insta? Because that had been Leah's latest "joke." An Instagram account of unflattering pictures of Flora she wasn't able to edit: with a double chin; slouched over; goofing for the camera, because she hated having her photo taken and so always fooled around. The filters made her look even worse, and no one held back in the comments. *Freak. Fucking freak. Freak girl.*

Was he trying to trick her, now? Except he had no reason to be cruel.

S'Okay, she typed—and waited, watching the telltale dots, willing him to reply.

His response was immediate.

Don't let them get u down.

So how u doin?

K

They still getting to u?

Yeah

U can tell me u no

Flora paused for a moment.

It's NBD, she messaged back, then added a 🙂.

Leah hadn't spoken to her for three days, and so Kat, Evie, and Abi were ignoring her, too. That evening, she'd thought about cutting herself. Had taken a vegetable knife from the kitchen and sat in the bathroom, pressing the blade against her inner thigh, poking the point into her soft flesh and wondering if a slash would bring some sweet release. But then Caroline had knocked to check if she was okay, and she'd hidden the knife in a towel; put it back in the kitchen later. She was such a flake.

A quizzical emoji pinged back, and a question mark.

Maybe she should tell him more? Risk being honest?

It was late, 10:15 p.m., and in her bedroom, she felt safe. Her bedside lamp cast a warm glow, and Jake seemed genuinely interested. Bit sad he didn't acknowledge her at school, but then guys didn't unless they were *linking*.

So what do u think of her rly?

U won't say? she checked.

A 😶. Then: *U just seem 2 clever, u no, 2B hr* 👭.

Flora wasn't sure how to respond.

NGL, I don't get it. Ur pretty

I hate myself.

? 😟

They hate me. Call me The Stick. U must hv seen?

Yeah. 😟😟 *But u can tell me.*

And even though she knew that trusting him made her vulnerable, still the relief of opening up to someone was something she craved. And so she started to talk about how she felt in lengthy Snapchat messages. And he listened. And encouraged.

Do you tk she hates u?

It was what she feared, but still she hesitated before typing: *Yeah*.

She still your BFF?

No hesitation now. 🌀 Then: *No. No way*.

A pause while she wondered if she dared admit to what she really felt. Why not? It wasn't as if he'd tell Leah.

I think I hate her, she said.

———————

The messaging became more frequent after that. It didn't feel sexual, and she wondered—almost with relief because she couldn't handle her intense feelings for him—if he was secretly gay.

It wasn't as if there was anyone else she could tell. Her friends hadn't spoken to her for a week, and their coldness had infected the entire year. The Stick was how everyone now referred to her. Dried out. Unfeeling. *Insentient* (that's how her teacher would describe it). Something to be thrown to a dog. Something to be burned.

Sometimes she thought Kat and Evie seemed confused. Before the blankness clouded their eyes—*Did you hear someone? Did someone say something?*—they looked embarrassed, as if they knew that what they were doing was cruel. She didn't blame them. It was a clear case of survival of the fittest. If Leah Smythe decided Flora Webster wasn't worth speaking to, then *obviously* everyone agreed. She kept thinking about how she'd reacted when Leah nicked the makeup: "*Don't*, Leah. Don't be *stu*pid." Why couldn't she have hidden her disapproval? Why couldn't she have a less expressive face?

But she'd dealt with it badly—and this was the result. At least she had Jake to talk to. At least his messages made her life okay.

Tk u, she Snapchatted after a particularly bruising day in which Leah had rolled her eyes when she answered a question in English, then muttered something that sounded very much like, "You are *so* asking to be raped."

"What did you say?" her teacher had asked.

"Nothing," Leah had replied sulkily. But she *had* said it, Flora was sure of it.

4 what? Jake messaged back now. She took a deep breath, but messaging helped her say things she would never have the courage to say in real life.

Her mum would say that was the danger of social media.

4 helping me cope with that fucking bitch.

––––––––––

And then it all came crashing down.

"So, you think I'm a bitch."

It was the next day. Leah stood in the doorway of the girls' bathroom, flanked by Charley Morris.

"What?" Flora crinkled her forehead, but she didn't need to act incredulous: she felt it. "I never said . . ."

"You think I'm a 'fucking bitch'. Does your mum know you use language like that? Not very nice, is it? The daughter of our MP speaking to her constituents like that. But you've always thought you were better than the rest of us."

"What are you going on about?" She was physically trapped. Leah and Charley had stepped into the communal area by the basins and barred the path the door. Charley tossed her head in her direction as if she were barely worth acknowledging. "I'm sorry," Flora said. "I don't understand."

"Oh, I think you do." Leah sounded grim, as if it brought her no joy to impart this. She waited a beat, and Flora felt her insides dissolve.

" 'Thanks for helping me cope with that fucking bitch.' He was kind, wasn't he, spending all this time listening to you moan on and on . . ."

"I don't know what you're talking about," Flora repeated, because *surely* he wouldn't have told Leah?

"Oh, come on." Charley Morris gave a mirthless laugh. "You didn't really think that Jake *Cummins* would be interested in you?"

She could hear the rhythmic dripping of a leaking tap, and the slow *clack-clack* of Charley's gum; heard, too, her heart thud as if she were doing cross-country: a fierce rhythmic *whoosh* pounding through her head.

"I—I thought . . ."

"That he liked you?" Leah asked, as if she were a child. "Ha!" Her laugh echoed around the bathroom. "He doesn't give a shit."

"But he . . ."

"He chatted to you on Snapchat? Aww, bless. Don't you know you should never take anyone online at face value?"

She didn't know how to answer, felt her face burn a vibrant red.

"You particularly shouldn't take people at face value," added Charley, "if they've a face like Jake Cummins."

"A body, too," Leah chipped in.

"That as well," Charley drawled, in a way that made it clear she was speaking from experience. She looked away then, feigning coyness; inspected the state of her nails.

Leah threw Flora a look of triumph. "I wouldn't worry about it. There'll be other boys. Just not ones in Jake's league." She gave a brash laugh, too loud and excessive, that made Flora want to punch her, to pound her head against the chipped ceramic basins.

"But next time: careful what you tell them, 'kay?"

Twelve

17 NOVEMBER 2021

EMMA

Unapologetically UnPC WhatsApp Group

@BarnabyMilesMP: God, she's so sanctimonious

@TristramSaleMP: Hot though? Particularly when she gets
self-righteous.

@PJacksonMP: Fair play to her. She deserves to celebrate tonight.

@TristramSaleMP: Something you're not telling us?

@PJacksonMP: I wish. But a source tells me she's going out—and with
insalubrious company.

@BarnabyMilesMP: The dirty bitch. Well, perhaps they'll show her a
good time.

"Do you come here often?"

Later, when I tried to track back to where things steered so badly off
course between us, I wondered if I set the wrong tone. If this throwaway
line, made just after we took our seats at the dimly lit table, had created
a false idea from the start.

Mike had flushed, a pinkish tinge forming high on each cheek. He
looked suddenly younger. Really quite good-looking. As if the day-to-day
cares of being a political editor had been lifted from him; a weary layer of
his identity peeled away.

"Sorry," I said, feeling confused. "I just meant it's a bit far from Westminster for an average lunch." Though of course this was a dinner. "I've
never been here before."

It was, I realized in the taxi, little more than a mile from the House of Commons. But this candlelit dining room, down a tiny street in the heart of Soho, belonged to a different world from the restaurants fringing Westminster, with their men in suits and white linen tablecloths, or the bright clatter of Portcullis, a goldfish-bowl-like environment where you only took a contact if you wanted to be seen.

This eighteenth-century townhouse, furnished with dark wooden tables and mismatched chairs, was a venue in which to be secretive: to cut deals, woo clients, begin affairs. There were oysters on the menu, I couldn't help noticing. And truffles, which I'd last eaten fifteen years ago, in Italy: the holiday when I conceived Flora. I crossed my legs automatically. I wouldn't be having truffles tonight.

"It can all get a bit claustrophobic over there," Mike was saying. "It's good to get out of Whitehall, remember what London has to offer. Besides, the food's good—and I owe you."

"Oh, hardly." He didn't owe me anything; I thought I should make that clear.

"I reckon so. This is a celebration, isn't it?"

A young waitress was hovering discreetly, but she came forward at this point.

"Shall we have some champagne to start?"

"You're not going to call me a champagne socialist?" I regretted the words as soon as they flew from my mouth.

"We're a bit beyond that, aren't we?" His face was sheened with surprise before he gave a rueful smile. "Come on, Emma. I owe you big-time. Thanks to you, I've outrun the hounds."

"Really?"

"Well, not literally." He shrugged. "But the desk's off my back for a bit. They can be pretty relentless. Now, what about just a glass? I'm having one. I think we've earned it." He gave me a beguiling look. "Come on. What do you say?"

"Oh, all right, then." I needed to loosen up a bit, and he was right: we *had* earned it. Besides, I'd had a killer of a day. A particularly nasty email from Simon Baxter that made me wonder if I'd been naive in not contacting the police, though there was nothing specific to fear; it just throbbed with menace. Then an anonymous text via my work mobile—*Don't get too carried away celebrating*—that could have been from an MP irritated by my rising profile, but which I couldn't help but read as a threat. Perhaps as a result, I'd failed to look as I'd waited to cross Great George Street and head toward Whitehall for a meeting, a fellow pedestrian pulling me out of the path of a cyclist running the lights. As the rider raced past, I'd had to fight off the sensation that he'd deliberately aimed at me.

So I'd been tempted to cancel tonight, except that Mike had been suggesting a meal ever since we started working together and I would have felt obliged to rearrange it. And we *did* have something to celebrate. We were going to change the law! Thanks to the Amy's Law campaign, the Online Harms Bill had been amended so that victims of revenge porn would be granted automatic anonymity in line with victims of other sexual offenses. Sentencing would also be altered to reflect its new definition as a sexual offense rather than a breach of technology law. Kyle Griffin might have got away with a lenient sentence—though the police were looking into an earlier case with another ex-girlfriend, who'd come forward thanks to the coverage—but the Kyles of the future would be looking at up to seven years in prison.

The champagne, which arrived swiftly, was, as I'd hoped, crisp and dry, cold and buttery. I hadn't eaten for eight hours, and perhaps because of this, it seemed to go straight to my head.

Across the table, Mike was smiling. We'd been in contact a lot these past few weeks. It wasn't just the quick coffees or snatched phone calls but also the conspiratorial texts and debriefs after each news story and meeting, the checking in, the 9 p.m. email when I'd thought of another way in which to up the pressure, the sense of having some sort of colleague with whom to force the minister's hand. I'd enjoyed working with him; had liked the validation he and his paper offered me, the praise that went with the sense of a job well done. And our mutual trust and goodwill was heartening: an antidote not just to the grim nature of Amy's case but the daily misogyny, the casual spilling of hatred I increasingly faced. (The Twitter rape threats had burgeoned since the day I mentioned Amy: and yes, like the most craven addict, I sometimes crept online.) Mike reminded me that, despite the constant hum of abuse, despite my jumpiness whenever

I cycled home or received a text—the abusive ones now exclusively on my work mobile—some men might be okay.

He stopped talking and smiled at me suddenly, his look curiously intimate. We were two-thirds of the way through a bottle of Merlot. I felt warm—and this was an almost-forgotten sensation—almost pampered.

"Here's to Amy," he said, raising his glass.

"To Amy," I said, immediately a little more sober.

"And to Freya."

"To Freya."

"And to you. You've been brilliant."

"Thank you." I felt uncomfortable, but I should take the compliment. Shouldn't do that peculiarly British and largely female thing of putting myself down. "We've done a good job," I conceded, because deep down, I knew he was telling the truth. "We've done something really worthwhile. If only it was as easy to get all areas of life right."

Later I wondered quite why I said that. Why I crossed the line from political contact to something more intimate, and whether it was deliberate—or an accident, as I told myself at the time. Because this was one of those moments I would look back at later, after everything altered: when I began to talk to him not as a contact, or at a push as some sort of colleague, but as a proper friend.

"God, tell me about it." Before I could dial it back, he said something about all the mistakes he'd made. He rubbed his face with his hands: a variation on David's nose tweaking, but with him, it was endearing. "Sorry," he added. "You don't need to hear me talking about this."

"Try me," I said because it was easier listening to someone else's screw-ups than my own. Except that it transpired he hadn't screwed up; he'd been widowed. He'd previously mentioned a Niamh, but I'd assumed he was divorced: his marriage, like mine, a casualty of his career. But she'd died nearly two years earlier from late-detected bowel cancer, he now told me. They'd been together twelve years.

His face softened as he talked of her, as he recalled how they met: she'd been a sub on the paper; had tightened his copy; had taught him how to write better. How she'd tolerated his workaholism and occasional bad temper—this said with a wry, self-aware smile that deflected any faint warning bells that should have rung. She'd been planning a sabbatical and a possible career change when she became properly sick.

"She was so creative. Made jewelry; was getting good at it, look—" And here he stretched out his right hand to show me an intricate Celtic band. Without thinking, I took his hand in mine and turned it palm upward, following the fine gold she had woven around his ring finger, admiring the delicate craftwork. His skin was dry, his fingers warm. I dropped his hand, vaguely embarrassed, but not before I caught his expression: a mix of grief, pride, love—the love of a decent man—and a flicker of something else. Perhaps a recognition that it was time to move on.

"Any children?" I dared to ask.

"Not with her," he said, and he gave a sort of grimace. "I've a sixteen-year-old son, Josh. He lives in Middlesbrough with his mum and stepdad. Cath, my first wife, left me when he was a toddler. Of course I love him—but I wouldn't say he and I were particularly close. Haven't done that well, have I? What would Wilde say: looks like carelessness? Losing not one wife but two, and effectively losing a son . . ."

And he began to talk about how he missed his boy. How he'd seen more of him when he was little but had only ever been a once-a-fortnight dad: taking him to soccer and knowing that Cath's partner, Matt, would take him on alternate Saturdays; would be there for the parents' evenings, the soccer training, and all the matches in between. How this semi-connected parenting wasn't what he'd planned when he became a dad, and yet he only had himself to blame. His job was all consuming, and he'd got the balance wrong; he could see that now that Josh, with younger siblings, a girlfriend, and a social life two hundred miles away, didn't need him in any way. He could hear it in his son's voice: the relief when their weekly phone call came to an end; the sense of obligation to a man who had given him half his DNA but too little commitment, too little time. Mike drank deeply, emptying the red wine in his goblet. "I'm just hoping that at some point in the future he might want to spend time with me."

"Of course he will. I'm sure he appreciates your texts and calls, however reserved he might seem. They want to know you're there for them, even if they can't convey that," I said, speaking more from my experience as a teacher than as a mum. And then the niggling anxieties about Flora began to spill out. "This is completely off the record," I checked early on, and he was suitably dismissive.

"I think you can take that as given. Shall we get another bottle?"

And another bottle of Merlot swiftly appeared.

"I guess I'm not used to her becoming so detached," I went on. "Has my absence caused that? The fact I don't see her from Monday morning to Thursday night?" Or more often Friday, because David's house was closer to school and Flora preferred to remain there during the week. "Or is it just because she's a teenager? She's fourteen: there's no reason for me to know what she's up to all the time, and that's fine. It's just it's a contrast to how we used to be, even a year ago, and I worry that there's something that's making her anxious. She spends a lot of time in her room online. I've always assumed she's working, but perhaps it's not that."

"You're not worried she might be being groomed?"

"No, no. She's very sensible. Her dad and I have drummed that into her. I suppose there might be a boy. But she's studious and now she's in her senior year, so there's a real ratcheting up of homework."

"She's not being bullied?"

"No. She's got a very secure group of friends. I just fret that there's something preoccupying her that she can't tell me about, and that bothers me . . ."

The main course arrived. Sea bass for me, duck for him. I ate, hardly registering the taste. I hadn't confided any of this to my housemates. Neither of them had children, though Claire craved them, and it seemed insensitive to obsess. Mike was easy to talk to. Inevitable for a journalist, I suppose. If he posed a question, I couldn't help but answer it.

"Sorry—this is gloomy," I said at one point when I felt close to welling up, and he poured more wine. Getting drunk suddenly seemed like sensible behavior. We were no longer toasting our professional success but sharing our parental failings.

"Change of subject?" he said.

"Absolutely."

"So—why did you become an MP?"

"Oh God. Good question!" But I told him about a girl I'd taught who was found to be suffering from malnutrition; about the boys who didn't have winter coats; about my dad and his high expectations of me, his insistence, even more than my mum, that I challenge everything; that I always strive to do what was right. About my sense, too, as I neared forty, of the passage of time; the fear that if I didn't act as my dad suggested, if I didn't at least *try* to help rectify the societal injustices that troubled me, it would soon be too late.

"Sorry—bit heavy," I said after a while; then, with a self-conscious smile. "Change of subject?"

"Chocolate torte or tiramisu?"

"There's a choice. Maybe just a brandy?"

"That sounds decadent."

"Or we could share the torte with coffee?"

"And two brandies?"

"Well, why not," I said.

Was this how we moved from a heartfelt discussion to weaving amiably through Soho, the taste of coffee, chocolate torte, and brandy in my mouth? I hadn't felt this reckless in years—and I smiled, nostalgic for the young woman I'd once been, for a youth I'd taken for granted and that only now I realized I should have mined more deeply for experiences. Perhaps would have, if I hadn't become involved with an older man—a while before David—who tore my confidence to shreds.

At some point, I slipped an arm through Mike's, and we walked through the quieter streets of Soho, the atmosphere shifting to one of delicious uncertainty as his upper arm nudged against my left breast. There had been a young couple at the table next to us in the restaurant on an early date: their conversation freighted with expectation as she'd played with her hair and fleetingly brushed something from his cheek. I wanted to feel like them, I realized when he turned toward me in a slim alleyway off Oxford Street. To be poised, anticipating something delicious, reveling in the possibility. I wanted to shock my neglected middle-aged body into existence. I could do that, couldn't I? Because at that crucial moment—one I'd regret soon afterward, and that I'd rue throughout the court case—I trusted him.

"Fancy going on somewhere else?" I said.

Thirteen

18 NOVEMBER 2021

EMMA

I wasn't sure where I was at first. The room was too dark: the curtains hanging heavily, a shaft of light filtering where they weren't quite closed. The mattress was too soft, and the pillows so excessive that I had difficulty hauling myself up. My head had been cleaved in two, and my temples throbbed as if a blade had been left inside: it hurt to turn even an inch. A migraine? But my mouth tasted as if I had eaten a rat, and then I knew—and the realization was mortifying because it was so entirely avoidable—that this was a vicious hangover.

It must have been over twenty years since I'd felt like this, and yet somehow I'd retained the capacity. The memory of a buy-one-get-one-free student night rose from the depths of my subconscious: the sound of house music; the taste of tequila and, soon after, the acid tang of vomit; the determination to never, *ever* drink like that again.

And yet here I was. I needed water, Tylenol, perhaps carbs: my gut craved food and grumbled at the thought of it. I needed a shower to wash away the sweat and shame, the heat and stench that seemed to be coming from my body, or not just from me, because there was a musky smell in the room: earthy, sexual, male.

There was a man in the bed next to me. I registered the fact, taking in the shape of the body lying on its front, while memories of the night lay around me like pieces of a jigsaw puzzle. Then I retched and stumbled to the bathroom, propelled not just by alcohol but by disbelief.

I closed the lid of the toilet, drank deeply from the tap, splashed my face with water. I still smelled, but I couldn't cope with a shower just yet. The towel was worn and thin, but I wrapped it around my body, shielding my breasts and stomach and the very tops of my thighs. My skirt and blouse were splayed on the grubby dark carpet, where one of us must have tossed them. If I crept back in, perhaps I could retrieve them before locking myself away.

Moving back from the bathroom, I saw that he was still fast asleep. His back was hairless, and his face, turned toward me on the pillow, crumpled with sleep. The sex—because I could remember quite a bit of it now—had been surprisingly good. My instincts had been right. Or perhaps I only thought this because it had been so long since I'd been touched. What had seemed an inevitable consequence of getting divorced—my celibate life—had soon become a deliberate decision: I didn't have room in my life for a relationship, and one-night stands had never appealed. Maybe I had felt so intoxicated, my sensations heightened, my behavior *hungry*, because of those long barren years?

But no, I wasn't so out of practice that I'd forgotten the difference between good and bad sex. A series of images flickered in quick succession: his mouth, his eyes, his thighs, his hands. My lips felt bruised, and just for a moment, I let myself remember his energy, his strength, his grip.

I shivered, a chill running up my spine as I scrabbled for my clothes from the floor and searched for my underwear. My tights and bra were nowhere to be seen. I would shower first, hope I could pinpoint them once I was half dressed. It wasn't the least bit funny, but for a moment I felt hysterical. I had fucked a tabloid journalist and was considering leaving my underwear like a calling card. Like evidence. It was almost as if I had a self-destructive streak.

Never mind that the sex had been good, that it had been consensual, that I had initiated the whole thing—or at least had suggested booking into the misnamed Luxury Inn off Oxford Street (practical, anonymous, affordable; *deeply* unromantic) when we found ourselves ducking into doorways and pressing against each other like desperate teenagers, when we grappled with one another in alleyways I usually would never venture down in the dark. I needed more of him: more than the taste of his mouth, the feeling of being encased, the knowledge that we were doing something illicit, decadent, and entirely removed from reality. I wanted to know this man: to trace his skin; to watch him drink me in; to see if the connection we'd felt over dinner could be improved on, could be magnified, once we were stripped right down.

Taking him back to Cleaver Square and risking the judgment of Julia—Claire might have approved—was never an option. But neither was going back to his apartment, not just because I feared a cabbie might recognize me, but because I would come to my senses before we got there. If we were going to do this, then the need was immediate and intense. His mouth on my neck, my lips, my breasts. A glance that was unequivocal: desire distilled efficiently. He was inside me within a minute of my slamming closed the cheap hardwood door.

I stopped dressing for a second, remembering my elation at knowing I could feel so swiftly aroused, that I could arouse him so completely. *Pride goeth before a fall.* But I was just so relieved that that part of me that had felt dormant had woken up—like the dried stick of an orchid in my bathroom that, given a perfunctory water, had suddenly decided to burst into flower.

There would always be this between us now: this awareness not just of how we looked naked—he had seen the fine stretch marks streaking my inner thighs; I knew his penis bent to the left—but of how we looked at the moment at which we were our most exposed. He wouldn't rat me out over this—he wasn't a shit, even if he was professionally ruthless—but he would *know*, and I would never be able to catch his eye across a crowded lobby without fearing a smirk. He had seen me come. He had *made* me come, had heard me whimper and judder and cry. For a millisecond, my mind filled with a certain heavy-lidded look of his before I slammed the memory shut. Could we do this again? Oh God, it was so good—and I liked him. I genuinely liked him. But how could he fit into my life when the last thing I had time for was any sort of relationship, let alone with a tabloid hack? The sensible thing to do would be to shelve this as a good experience, make clear we should revert to being purely professional, and regretfully move on.

Perhaps it would be best if I slipped away before he noticed. The clock radio read 5:37 a.m. I could be out of here and back to Kennington before he or either of my housemates woke up. Closing the bathroom door, I showered quickly, scrubbing the cheap shampoo through my tangled hair, then soaping beneath my arms, my breasts, in between my legs. My skin tingled under the tepid water, and as I dried myself, I was conscious both of the ache in my groin and an inner voice that insisted my behavior wasn't just unprofessional but sluttish. *Stupid slut*, as the Twitter trolls would clamor. *Sexually emancipated*, a small voice replied.

I pulled on my clothes, my skin still wet and clammy. My tights and skirt were the sort an MP might wear; my silk blouse, worn without a bra, perhaps not. I felt, briefly, deliciously indecent: my dark nipples nudging through the fabric that clung to my damp breasts, my hair wild, my lips bee-stung from his stubble. My skin was flushed from the shower, from alcohol, from lack of sleep. I looked, as Jazz might put it, as if I'd been up all night screwing. But my expression, enhanced by my smudged mascara, was out-of-kilter. I looked completely wired.

I had never slipped away from a lover before (I had only had four previous ones), so this didn't come easily. But after snaking a hand under the covers to retrieve my bra, I knelt down on the floor to fumble with the clasp. Out of sight, I reached into my bag, my fingers brushing against my phone. I had put it on Do Not Disturb in the restaurant; had forgotten to alter the settings and now saw there were three missed calls, and four texts from Flora and David. With the chill certainty that something had gone horribly wrong, I scrolled back through.

David: *Please call. It's to do with Flora.*

Then: *Please ring asap. It's important.*

Finally: *Emma, I'm sorry it's so late but please do call.*

And from Flora: *Mummy, I'm so so sorry. I've done something awful but it's not what Dad thinks.*

There were a couple of voicemails from David, too. I played back the most recent, the phone clamped to my ear so that his words wouldn't seep into the room. "Emma. Re earlier messages, please call, *however* late you get this." My ex-husband's voice was brisk, but the way it rose at the end of the sentence suggested panic. Something had scared him: I had rarely heard him sound like that.

I stayed very still, crouched on the worn carpet, as if by doing so I could think precisely. The last text came at 1 a.m., the phone calls petered out at 12:50 a.m.: less than five hours before. They'd have been thrown by my silence. Had I been in Kennington, of course I'd have answered: the phone would have been charging by the side of my bed. Here it was in the bottom of a suede bag, and I had been distracted. It was just my luck that this was the one night in the four years since becoming an MP and living apart from Flora that I'd failed to check it before going to sleep.

"Christ, I feel rough." Mike startled me as he propped himself on one elbow, his hand clutching his forehead. Slowly he focused. Realization dawned as he took in the fact I was fully dressed and scrabbling around on the carpet. "What are you doing? Come back to bed . . ."

"I need to go," I said, stumbling as I tried to stand up straight.

"You're going?" He looked befuddled; his face, softened by sleep, sharpening as the reality dawned on him. "You were going to sneak away?"

"I'm really sorry. Something's happened. Last night was fun—" I stopped, realizing I sounded dismissive, that this in no way captured the connection—physical and emotional—I was sure we'd both experienced. "No, it wasn't just that. It was really good . . ." And it was, I realized; in a different life, it was something that I'd very much like to repeat. I sat down on the bed next to him, conflicted: I wanted to touch him. "But I think this was probably a mistake."

His expression dropped, his disappointment and incredulity clear.

"I trust you'll be discreet?"

He gave a whinny of disbelief. "This wasn't some *setup* . . ."

"No. I know that."

"Look—it's early." He shifted to sit up, then rubbed his forehead. "I feel rank; you, too?"

"I'm fine." It came out wrong. Far too clipped.

"I didn't mean—"

"Sorry, I have to go. I've got to get in touch with Flora—"

"She okay?"

"Something's happened to her." I stood, irritated with myself having a conversation I didn't have time for. My voice spiraled in panic. "She's been texting. I've *got* to go . . ."

"Of course. I'll call you."

"No, I'll call you." I needed to be in control of this. "And please—"

My voice was too harsh: authoritative and just a bit manic. "*Please* can you just forget everything I've told you about her?"

Even in the gloom of the room, I could see that I'd hurt him. His expression had hardened to such an extent he seemed unrecognizable, though it was one that I would see again. I put my hand on his bare shoulder, my instinct always to try to fix things, but he shrugged it off like a child in a sulk. Well, fuck that. His ego wasn't my priority.

"Just forget about me. I have to go. I have to find out what's happened to her."

Fourteen

17 NOVEMBER 2021

FLORA

Double PE. First period. Flora always hated it. Not the exercise so much, though that was sufficiently embarrassing (she was clumsy, flat-footed), but the getting changed in front of everyone else.

It was bad enough before the bullying. She would pick a corner, her body turned toward the pegs so that only her curved back was seen and, in a complicated maneuver, swap her school shirt for a PE top. She moved quickly so that no one would glimpse her tiny breasts. Even then, Leah couldn't resist a dig ("Do you even know what puberty is, Cel?" "I don't know why you bother with a bra," "Must be *weird* not having your period . . .")—always said with a bark of a laugh to signal this was just a joke, to take the sting out of it, to dismiss any possible response as an overreaction. Completely over-the-top.

Once the bullying began, the whole process became increasingly torturous. With wearying predictability, items of her clothing would disappear so that she had to stand in the middle of the changing room and ask, "Has anyone seen my shirt? It's not in your PE bag, is it? Would you mind looking?" Slowly, reluctantly, legs would be moved aside, and girls would glance at her with contempt before the crucial item was discovered, stuffed under a bench, coated in dust, and stamped with a muddy footprint, and she would have to go down on her hands and knees to scoop it up.

Since the revelation that she'd been catfished, the discovery of the lost items became even more delayed—so that the entire class had changed before her hidden top *and* shorts just happened to "turn up." The day that changed everything, she spent five minutes searching for them, her chest tightening as she imagined the after-school detention she'd receive for not having her gym clothes.

Finally Leah put her out of her misery.

"Oh! Were you missing these?" She held the shorts up in one hand and the top in the other, her face twisted into a moue of disdain.

"Where did you find them?"

It was a stupid question because Leah had found them exactly where she had hidden them. Leah knew that Flora knew this, but what could Flora possibly do? Far from looking embarrassed, Leah gave a wide smirk. They'd read *Lord of the Flies* in year nine, and without wanting to sound melodramatic, Flora thought there was something Jack-like about Leah's behavior. Did that make Flora Piggy? She bit the inside of her mouth, concentrating on the pain to prevent herself from giving into self-pity and risking the tears that seemed so close to the surface these days.

No one else seemed interested, of course. Somehow she got through the trampolining. Afterward, she slumped on a bench in the middle of the communal changing room, half shielded by a forest of discarded tracksuit bottoms and coats. She wanted to shrink away, tried to do so while ignoring the stink of sportswear that hadn't been washed all term and the stench of a blocked toilet. Trampolining had been dire: the girls in her class not even bothering to hide their harsh laughter as she tried to bounce, then teetered on the edge. She closed her eyes, trying to shut out the memory of her humiliation, but Leah's too-loud voice kept intruding, infused with its casual cruelty masquerading as good humor.

"Oh, Evie. That's a bit *too* much!"

So, Evie would be Leah's next victim. Flora, hidden by the coats, peered through a gap between two PE bags to spy on what was going on. How had she not recognized Leah's true nature long ago? Her smug self-regard that made her raise one eyebrow sardonically at poor Evie, who'd gone a deep red; her confidence while standing in the middle of the changing room in her underwear—black lace panties and sports bra—while everyone else changed quickly and discreetly, and that meant Leah loved herself in a way very few others could.

Flora *hated* her for this. She hated her for being so comfortable with her body. Despite her rounded tummy and the fat bulging over her bra, she liked herself enough to parade around the changing room, her double-Ds shoved up, her head tilted to one side. Then she took off her bra, while standing in front of Evie, flaunting what she had, even doing a little shimmy like a mock striptease as she stuck her boobs out, because Evie was self-conscious about being a 34A. It was this, when Flora tried to rationalize it later, that made her do it. That made her take out her iPhone, push it through the coats, and lightly touch the photo button so that she snapped a picture of Leah preening, her large breasts thrust up, her black push-up bra twirled from one hand. The phone was on silent, so no one noticed her capture the live shot—taken from slightly below, not above, which would have minimized her tummy. A moving shot that captured Leah's vain sashaying and the moment her smile twisted into a leer. Flora thrust the phone deep in her bag, not daring to check if it was in focus, just feeling as if she had got one up on Leah. As if she had somehow wrested back a tiny bit of power.

Because Leah wasn't all *that*. She thought she was, but Flora had permanent evidence now that she wasn't. It was the sort of photo Leah would hate others to see.

"Where's The Stick? Is she hiding somewhere?" Leah's voice rang across the room, and it was this that made her suddenly retaliate; that made her do something so reckless that her heart jolted, excitement and boldness combining for one brief, sensational moment.

Touching the forward symbol, she selected a contact—someone who wouldn't dream she had his number—and quickly pressed send.

Fifteen

18 NOVEMBER 2021

EMMA

The police were there when I arrived.

"They're in there with her," Caroline half whispered as she opened the door to me. It was just before nine. I'd run for the first train out of Waterloo, but in my panic had boarded a slow one that stopped at every station on the way down.

The journey had been a nightmare. David had conveyed the bare outline of what had happened in a single text, but when I called, the line kept breaking up and then my battery ran flat. No charger in my bag. No clean clothes. A toothbrush and paste snatched on the concourse with some Tylenol, water, and a large black coffee. I felt grubby and unmoored without my usual means of connection. I'd managed one text to Mike—*Last night was lovely. Sorry to rush*—aware that I'd left on a sour note; perhaps conscious, even then, that I needed to do some damage limitation; that he had the potential to turn.

"She's okay. She's been desperately upset, but she's stopped crying," Caroline added as she ushered me into the hall. The door to the living room was closed, but I could hear the murmur of deep voices. "Do you want to go straight in or freshen up?"

I gave an odd laugh, and the murmur of voices paused. Freshen up? A prim euphemism—or a dig at how I looked?

"Yeah . . . actually, okay." I was suddenly conscious of my pint of coffee and scurried to the downstairs bathroom.

Like everything else in the house, it had been recently made over: a hefty bequest from David's childless great-aunt no doubt funding the limestone tiles, exorbitant room spray, and sleek basin. I scrutinized myself: straightened my blouse, recombed my hair, and reapplied a slash of red lipstick to draw attention from my bloodshot eyes. I was battle ready. If not the imperious woman of the *Guardian* photos, then someone who could hold their own. I might have felt exposed, dismantled even, when I'd stood in the hallway, but now my carapace was back on.

Flora looked so slight when I entered the room.

"Mum." Her voice was tiny, and I spied her ghostly predecessor: Flora, aged ten, who'd sat quietly as David and I explained that we were separating; who'd been determined, even then, to be a good girl.

"Oh, my love." I went to her to give her a hug, but her pale face was closed and she shifted away. "We'll sort this all out," I contented myself with promising as I gave her shoulder a squeeze.

"Emma Webster." I turned to the police officers, who introduced themselves as Detectives Matt Blackwell and Karen Swinburne. "I'm sorry I took so long." I rolled my eyes, trying to endear myself with a common grumble. "South West Trains as punctual as usual . . ."

Detective Blackwell, in his early thirties, gave a thin-lipped grimace. His colleague, in her mid-twenties, didn't respond.

"Why don't we all sit down and discuss this." David gestured for me to join him and Flora on his new L-shaped sofa. I felt a rush of gratitude as I sank into the too-soft cushions. Beside me, Flora managed a watery smile.

"Detective Blackwell was just explaining what happened and why they're here," David summarized. "It might be helpful if you could start again," he told the officer, "since we've had some communication difficulties—not in general, you understand, just today . . ." His voice petered out as his joke fell flat. "Emma: does that make sense?"

"Yes. Thanks. Fine." To be honest, it was a relief he was leading this conversation like a business meeting: perhaps we could deal with it quickly. "David told me that a photo had been taken of Leah," I addressed the detectives. "I must confess I can't see why anyone needed to involve the police?"

"We were contacted yesterday," Detective Blackwell said, "by the parents of Seb Frinton."

"Seb Frinton?" The name meant nothing to me.

"He's this boy Leah likes," said Flora, so softly I had to strain to hear.

"Mr. and Mrs. Frinton contacted us because Seb had been sent a photograph of Leah Smythe from your daughter's phone."

"Okay. Well, that doesn't mean she was involved. Perhaps someone borrowed her phone without her permission?"

The detective smiled patiently. "Flora has confirmed that *she* sent the photo."

"Is that right, Flo?"

A slight, barely perceptible nod.

"And what was the photo of exactly?" I kept my voice light.

David cleared his throat and looked pointedly at our daughter, whose face crumpled as it did when she was tiny and knew she was going to be told off.

"Flora?" I asked gently, because even though I knew the explanation would be bad, I clung to the idea there was some sort of misunderstanding. But she pulled at the cuticles of her left thumb, tearing the tender skin away.

"The photograph was taken as Leah was changing after PE," Detective Blackwell said when it was clear my daughter wouldn't speak.

"Was she *naked*?" I willed him to deny this.

"She wasn't naked. She was wearing her panties, but she was topless." He let the words sink in.

"Was she *posing* for the photo?" There was a cockiness to Leah, an overweening self-confidence, and I could imagine her forcing Flora to take her picture on her phone and then sending it on to a boy. Yes, that could be it! I felt myself lighten, risked glancing at David, as if he might back me up on this. But he had had twelve hours to work out what had happened, and he remained ominously silent, his face drawn with the trauma of it.

"It seems that Leah didn't know that Flora had taken this photo—nor that she had forwarded it," Detective Swinburne spoke, for the first time, in a surprisingly gentle Edinburgh accent. She was tiny and somehow fox-like: with a fierce shock of short auburn hair, a heart-shaped face, and bright, dark eyes.

"Is that right, Flo? That Leah didn't know you'd done this?"

Another almost imperceptible nod.

"Oh, sweetheart—and Seb? Is he a boy in your year?"

"In year eleven, not our year."

"A fifteen-year-old boy . . ."

"Seb Frinton is sixteen," Detective Blackwell said.

Next to me, Flora began to weep, and the bemusement I'd started to feel—the frustration that she could have been this stupid; the embarrassment that she could have done this to another girl—was obliterated by her guttural sobs. I put my arm around her shoulders, feeling the rigid tension of her upper body slowly ease as she finally let herself lean into me. "Shh, shh, it's okay," I said, kissing her hair.

Detective Blackwell cleared his throat, and the moment—the exquisite moment that reminded me she was still my kindhearted girl—was instantly over as Flora wriggled away from me and sat up in one fell swoop. David passed her a tissue, and Flora dabbed at her blotched face and blew her nose noisily before reaching to take my hand.

"Why did you send the photo?" I asked her at last.

She shrugged; then: "She trolled me. She catfished me."

So much misery in those six small words.

I looked to David for more clarification, but it was Detective Swinburne who spoke.

"Flora has told us there was a sustained campaign of online bullying against her and that this was her way of retaliating. I'm sure she'll fill you in on the details. The issue, as I'm sure you'll be aware, is that this was an indecent image, and because it was *live*, was effectively an indecent video of a child sent on to a third party. She distributed an indecent moving image of a child."

"It was a retaliation for bullying!" I heard my voice rise, sensed my desperation at the idea that my fourteen-year-old could be perceived as having distributed child pornography. "Of course, sending it wasn't acceptable, and Flora's clearly well aware of that. But surely"—and here I was careful to make my tone placatory, to smile at the detectives, to be my most charming—"we can deal with this proportionately, as parents. Surely this is nothing more serious than that?"

The detective gave me a slight smile, but her eyes remained cold. She couldn't be more than twenty-five, and it felt completely ridiculous that she could have such an impact on my daughter's life.

"We've spoken about this to Flora, and to Mr. Webster, before you arrived," her colleague said. "She is aware of the magnitude of her behavior—of the fact that it could constitute a criminal offense, that we will be discussing this with the Crown Prosecution Service, and that we will need to consider how to proceed."

He stood up, signaling that this was the end of his visit; pulled his suit jacket down with a neat tweak.

"I'll see you out." David bustled them out of the room while I remained with Flora, who was weeping quietly.

"Flo . . ." I gave her hand a squeeze, momentarily at a loss as to what to say.

"Oh, Mum." She looked at me, her eyes welling, and in her expression, I read incomprehension, shame, and fear.

"This is going to be all right. You will get through this. You will be okay," I said, knowing I was reassuring myself as much as her. It was the mantra I'd told myself when David said our marriage was over, the one I'd used when the police said they couldn't trace whoever sent the acid-threat letter: *You will get through this. You will be okay.*

"We will get through this," I repeated because I refused to believe my daughter's life need be defined by this. "This is a mistake which you'll learn from and then we'll move on," I continued as I held her tight, because neither of us could guess the ramifications of her behavior.

And besides, what choice did I have?

Sixteen

20 NOVEMBER 2021

EMMA

Emma Webster MP Facebook
12,867 followers

Proud that the Online Harms Bill, with the government-backed amendment strengthening prison sentences for revenge porn, has passed through the House of Commons. Proud to be tackling violence against women and girls, and proud on behalf of my late constituent Amy Jones.

Dave Hislop: Dearie me, Emma. Talk about hubris. Haven't you heard that pride goeth before a fall?

Mary Tanner: What about violence against men and boys?

Bax S: Not as headline grabbing and our Emma loves the limelight. But we'll be watching to see how she deals with it. And we'll be there when it dazzles her.

What on earth did he mean by that?

I usually resisted looking at my official Facebook page, but I was procrastinating. Putting off a difficult phone call. And this page tended to be softer than other forms of social media: a more accurate indication of my constituents' concerns.

We'll be watching. . . And we'll be there when it dazzles her. That had to be from Simon Baxter, but was it a sly dig or a coded threat? A development of his threat at the town hall meeting or of those menacing texts? (Which weren't necessarily from him—since the police couldn't trace the numbers, they had no proof—though, if not, it seemed rather coincidental.) *We'll be watching* was more muted than *I'm watching you bitch*, so perhaps I was worrying unnecessarily? It wouldn't be unlike me to read too much into it.

I pressed my knuckles into my eyes. A sleepless night, and the emotional turmoil of the past few hours, was wreaking havoc with my judgment. Checking Facebook was completely detrimental, I knew that, but I was paranoid that news of Flora's behavior had somehow spilled out. And so I scrolled feverishly through my feeds, discounting the common insults as I scoured the comments for anything about my daughter. There seemed to be nothing. Just this comment, reminding me I was forever being scrutinized, that had snuck under my skin.

I closed the page. Clicked on my contacts. I needed to focus on rectifying the situation. Urge the chief constable not to make an example of my daughter, if that wasn't too heavy-handed? And make this necessary and highly uncomfortable call.

"Stef?"

"Yeah?"

The voice on the other end of the line was wary—then, once she recognized my voice, skeptical and defensive. I understood that. We'd barely spoken in the past couple of years, for no particular reason except our daughters no longer needed us to organize their social lives, and now that I was calling, I was very clearly in the wrong.

Stef Smythe was Leah's mother, and she was someone to whom I owed an apology. Because, while I might reassure my daughter that all would be well—that I supported her; that she shouldn't have behaved as she did, but that this didn't mean she was a terrible person; that even though she had been suspended from school for two weeks, this was surmountable—I still felt a heavy shame that she could have done this to another girl.

Which wasn't to say that Leah was blameless. She'd behaved like a little bitch. (Not that I'd articulated it like this to Flora.) Pretending to be a boy so that she could coerce my daughter into criticizing her; manipulating her; humiliating her—both by suggesting no one would ever find her attractive ("Boys do like breasts, Flo" was one of the kinder put-downs my daughter recounted) and by initiating the Snapchat pile-on and mocking Instagram account. When Flora shared the extent of the campaign against her, I felt both acute sorrow and a primal rage. Though it cut against all my feminist principles, I could absolutely understand my daughter's need for retaliation. (In fact, my immediate, swiftly dismissed reaction was to imagine pummeling Leah's face . . .)

My next response, though—and thank God it was nearly instantaneous—was to rein in my anger and make sure I didn't convey it to Flora. And my third response, *obviously*, was to acknowledge that there was something deeply problematic about my daughter forwarding a picture of a topless young girl.

I was aware of the irony, of course: that Flora's behavior, with its intention to humiliate, was somewhere along a continuum that led, at its most extreme, to Kyle Griffin and everything I was spending my professional life opposing. But apart from this, and my guilt that I had got my parenting so wrong, I felt huge sympathy for Leah, whose topless photo had now been seen not just by Seb Frinton and his parents but also by various members of Hampshire police and the Crown Prosecution Service, who would decide if a charge should be brought against Flora. And I kept imagining how I would feel if I were Leah's mum.

So here I was. On the back foot. Ringing a woman with whom I'd failed to keep in contact, despite our seeing quite a lot of each other in those long-ago days of primary school; desperate to put things right.

"It's Emma Webster," I said, injecting a dose of good cheer and warmth into my voice. And then, stupidly: "Flora's mum."

"Oh, yes?" Her tone remained brittle. She wasn't going to make this easy for me, and I couldn't blame her.

"I'm ringing to say how sorry I am for Flora's behavior. Obviously the police are involved now, and she's been suspended from school, but I just wanted to stress how mortified she is that she did this to Leah and to say that I hope, eventually, the girls can move on . . ."

A pause at the end of the line. Then a scoff of disbelief. "You have to be joking, don't you?"

"No. No, I'm completely serious. We are both *so* sorry."

"Sorry that she was found out, do you mean?"

"No—I didn't mean that." I sounded too well-spoken: as posh as Stef no doubt believed me to be.

"Then what?"

"That I'm—we're—just so sorry she did this. It must have been incredibly upsetting for Leah—and for you and Chrissie." I remembered her older daughter. "Flora's very conscious of that." I paused, and to try to convey the magnitude of my daughter's emotions, the fact she wasn't a sociopath who could act like this without considering the impact on others, I added, "She's been pretty distraught, too."

"Oh my God—the cheek of you."

I remained silent, aware that she needed to have her say.

"You think I *care* that your precious daughter's '*distraught*'? Perhaps Leah was pretty bloody distraught about her picture being forwarded and seen by the police and that boy's parents. Perhaps *my* daughter was '*distraught*' about you and Flora treating her with such contempt . . ."

"I can assure you that's not the case." There was some misunderstanding. Our wires were clearly crossed.

"I don't mean just about the photo. I mean when you dropped her. Leah loved coming round to your house, and then suddenly there was no time for her. It was as if you thought she was beneath your daughter. Flora treated her exactly the same."

"I didn't 'drop' her." I was genuinely bemused. "That was just . . . life, Stef. I became an MP, I got divorced, I left my home . . . I barely spend enough time with my own child: you know what it's like as a working parent." Stef worked three twelve-hour shifts a week, or did, when Leah and Chrissie were small. Too late, I remembered that until I became an MP, Leah came to ours at least once a week; that I'd feed her each Thursday after volleyball, cooking meals I knew Leah liked and taking an interest in her so that her friendship with my daughter might grow. Or was I subconsciously aware that I needed to protect Flora even then? To shore up some shared experiences, and lavish her friend with kindness, because it was clear Leah was the dominant one, the cooler girl who might be less loyal, less consistent, who could turn on a dime? I had thought Leah emotionally robust: resilient, self-confident. I hadn't realized how much this contact might have mattered to her.

"Yes, well." Stef sounded chastened now, as if she knew I had a point. "I know why you're ringing now anyway . . ."

"I wanted to apologize."

"To get me to tell the police not to press charges . . ." She sounded triumphant. "But it's nothing to do with us. Not our choice, the detective told us. It's up to the Crown Prosecution Service to decide . . ."

"I wouldn't dream of trying to influence you," I said, conscious I was giving a politician's answer. I might not *dream* of influencing her, but I very much *wanted* to do so. "Look. This all feels rather heated—"

A snort of incredulity at the end of the line.

"—and I don't expect you to accept what I'm saying," I went on, "but I'm grateful that you've listened."

"For God's sake."

Her open antagonism felt like a slap across my face. For a moment, I was stymied: incapable of knowing how to continue.

"Well, goodbye then—and I'm sorry."

The line went dead as she hung up.

And I was left feeling distinctly unsettled. As if, far from managing to smooth things over, I had somehow made things much, much worse.

Seventeen

26 NOVEMBER 2021

SIMON

What the hell was that skinny bitch of an MP up to now?

Simon Baxter hung back a little as Emma Webster walked up the steps of the police station.

He'd been following her for the past two Fridays, ever since her office had refused to engage with his emails. A clipped *Thank you for your interest. Ms. Webster is very busy and cannot reply personally.* That was the standard response.

It riled him more than if she'd ignored him completely. Which was why he'd decided to keep tabs on her. He didn't do it obsessively. Self-control was important, so for the moment he was restricting it to when she was local. Just enough to feel he was on top of things. Because, while there'd been a certain satisfaction in imagining her reaction to his emails and barbs on social media, he couldn't be certain they'd been seen.

But following her, well, that stepped things up—and he was going to do it quite a bit. Because the memory of her condescension, the way she'd spoken to him as if he were some common thug—*I'm going to have to ask you to leave, Mr. Baxter. I can't have you intimidating my staff like this*—had gotten under his skin. As if he'd done nothing for his country. As if the tours of Afghanistan and Iraq, not to mention Northern Ireland, accounted for nothing at all! And what about Will? He hadn't wanted to mention his son—unlike Emma, in her campaign literature, he didn't exploit his family—but had she been sympathetic, he might have told her about his boy. How he was a different lad since Helmand: not sleeping, drinking too much, having flashbacks. The GP mentioned PTSD; mentioned, too, that the waiting list to see a psychiatrist was over six months.

Recent cuts had hit the provision of mental health services, the doc explained, and that was all well and good, but it was hard to take when his lad was trembling and nauseous. In a state no man of twenty-eight should be. Not that this mattered to Emma Webster, treating men like shit while prioritizing *women's* issues. Well, she was going to have to listen—given that he paid her fucking salary!

So here he was. It had been easy to tail her from her home, where he'd been waiting since 6 a.m.; to park at the other side of the parking lot; to follow at a distance. He had a good vantage point, in an office doorway, opposite the police station, and she hadn't clocked him once.

That was partly due to her focusing on that teenage girl. Must be her daughter, given that she'd just put her arm around her; was protective of her just as he was of his boy. Odd that she'd want to take her kid to a cop shop, though.

Perhaps there was something she wanted to report. Online abuse? He'd been careful on Facebook: he wasn't stupid. Didn't use bad language. He could understand why she might want to complain—but good luck with that! If you dished it out, you had to take it back, and it was clear she couldn't. Not on Twitter, where, pathetically, she tried to win critics round; not when she appeared on telly, where she got emotional; and not in person. But the woman was a hypocrite. No doubt thought she was entitled to special protection. Which was presumably why she was marching into a police station now.

Though why would she take the girl? Unless—and sweet Jesus could this be it?—unless the *daughter*, for some reason, was in trouble with the police?

He'd clock the girl's expression when they came out. He was good at judging people. You learned to do that in the forces: read reactions, assess when someone was frightened. And from her thin, stiff body as she approached the building, he'd say she was pumped with fear.

Good job Mark was on the front desk, a former colleague who'd nabbed an admin job with the police when he was decommissioned. It still bugged him that Mark, never the sharpest tool in the box, had had the foresight to do this. Still, he had his uses. Was deliciously indiscreet. A couple of pints should do the trick. There would be a record of what this was all about, and if Mark didn't know the answer straightaway, he could access the files easily. No one would think to question it.

Simon shifted in his doorway. The thought of exposing Emma fucking Webster—of ensuring he got the better of her—was oddly arousing.

He had her in his sights now.

Eighteen

29 NOVEMBER 2021

EMMA

The text message from Mike froze my insides.

Been contacted about a story involving Flora. Be good to hear your side of it. Victoria Tower Gardens in ten?

I bolted down to the patch of grass beside the House of Commons, trying to assess what he might know, praying that he hadn't had a tip-off. It had been eleven days since our visit from the police. It had been three since we'd gone to the police station, where she was cautioned. Managing her anxiety, dealing with her two-week suspension from school, and trying to minimize the fallout had been pretty all-consuming.

I hadn't seen Mike since leaving the Luxury Inn; hadn't communicated apart from the text message I'd sent on the train, and a phone call hours later, in which I'd minimized my concerns about Flora—*Just teenage angst*—and stressed I wasn't interested in a repetition of what had occurred.

Now I hoped our conversation would remain professional. His text had certainly suggested as much, even if our most recent phone call, made in the aftermath of the police visit, when I'd realized it was madness to even contemplate a relationship with a tabloid reporter, had quivered with rejection and hurt.

"Emma."

His tone as he ambled toward me was distinctly cool.

"Mike." I was more effusive. Instinctively, I wanted to touch his arm. But the lack of any recognition that we'd been allies, let alone anything else, made me keep my distance. "Are you okay?" I said at last.

A curt nod. "Shall we walk? I want to run something past you."

"Okay." I smiled and tried to catch his eye. "You're making me nervous. You said it was about Flora . . ." I heard myself babbling.

He remained silent as we walked toward the river, and my apprehension grew with every second.

"Could you just spit it out?" I said as we paused to look out over the leaden river. "You said you wanted to talk about my daughter?"

He turned and looked at me directly, his expression holding a flicker of something close to compassion. *He knows. He fucking knows*, I thought while trying for a poker face.

"There's no easy way to say this," he began. "We know Flora's been quizzed by the police for distributing child porn. That she's only just avoided prosecution. Now: we can go hard on this, or, with your help, we can dress it up softly. What do you say?"

Think on your feet. My experience as a teacher and an MP had completely deserted me.

"I don't know what the hell you're talking about," I finally said.

"So, you don't deny it?"

"I don't . . . I'm not saying anything. No comment. Absolutely no comment. I'm not discussing this." I started to walk away.

"I think it would be in your interests to talk, Emma. Seriously . . ." And there was something in his tone, some reminder of the decency he'd shown that night, that stopped me from racing away.

"We know she forwarded a moving image of a topless fourteen-year-old girl and has been investigated by the police. We have all the details," he went on. He knew she had a criminal record. That she'd been given a Youth Conditional Caution. That she'd had to write a letter of apology to Leah and was attending sessions with the youth offending team. That though this wouldn't be automatically disclosed in any criminal record check, it would in an enhanced one if she wanted a career exempt from the Rehabilitation of Offenders Act, such as a doctor, lawyer, or teacher, or if she applied to certain universities. He even knew that she'd been suspended from school, that she'd been distraught as the caution was read to her, and that, as we left the station, she'd been in floods of tears.

"Okay. Enough." I couldn't bear to hear any more.

"So, you'll cooperate. Tell us your side of the story?"

I looked at him, appalled. He really didn't get it. "Absolutely no fucking way."

"Oh, Emma." His tone was one of marked disappointment.

"No bloody way. I am not discussing it. And there is absolutely no way you could print *anything* about her. She's a child. Under eighteen. You'd be breaking the law if you touched this story. Besides—would the *Chronicle* really do this to a kid?"

He gave an unapologetic shrug. Clearly breaking the law, not to mention industry guidelines, was a risk his rag was willing to take.

"Calm down," he said, a response guaranteed to inflame. "Just think about it. This is a very relatable story. We will find a way to run it—but it would be far better for everyone if you were up front about it and came on board . . ."

"What the hell do you mean by that?"

"Hey, we'd do it gently." He seemed impervious to my anger, held both hands up as if to placate me. "You know . . . it's every parent's nightmare, isn't it? That their child will do something stupid with their phone, or on social media, and before they know it, they've got themselves involved with the police."

I wanted to hit him. He had the *audacity* to parrot back the line he'd used on me when discussing Amy, to think not just that I wouldn't remember but that I'd *fall* for it: this touchy-feely, ever-so-softly approach. It was just an insidious way of screwing me over! I took a deep breath, tried counting to ten—but it was no good. My rage, which had simmered like molten jam, came to a boil.

"I am *not* exposing her to this and, my God, I will come after you if you *dare* to name her in print." I jabbed at him with my finger. "We are not even having this conversation. This is *strictly* off the record." Because for all I knew, he would not only be taking this as confirmation of the story but choose to quote me.

I turned and started to walk toward the pewter Thames, swollen after a heavy rainfall, the surface all currents and eddies whipped by a stiff breeze. Bloody *hell*. I was hopeless at playing this game. I needed a moment to calm myself and so concentrated on a cruise boat sailing downriver: a few chilled tourists shivering in rain capes, pinched faces gazing at the House and Big Ben. They were probably anticipating a place of sophisticated argument, not grubby compromise; of intellectual discussion, not ruthless backstabbing. *Focus and think.* That was better, though my breathing was still too rapid, my body betraying me once again.

"Look, Emma . . ." Mike had caught up, and though his tone sounded reasonable, his words were cold and far more cynical than I'd have thought possible from our night together. "We can run the story without your help. Get a Tory MP to ask a question linked to the Online Harms Bill, in the Commons; then it'll be covered by privilege and can be reported. Or perhaps it could be leaked to a website—and once that happens, it's a free-for-all. But it would be far better to talk to us: that way you'll have control over the narrative. You'll be able to shape exactly how it plays."

"I can't believe you would even think of doing this to me, let alone a child. My God, I *trusted* you. We *slept* together."

"This has nothing to do with you and me," he said, looking at me calmly. "It's a great story. A watercooler issue."

"For fuck's sake." My voice was too loud. "Where's your *humanity?*"

"Come on, Emma. You don't mean that." His tone was dismissive now, and I wanted to claw and spit at him like a cat protecting her young. How dare he do this to my girl? Instead I stepped back and started walking away from him and the Commons, following the river west. The wind was picking up, and my shoes slid over the sludge of the fallen leaves. Behind me, I could sense his footsteps: he wasn't going to let me leave with this unresolved, and I needed a way to shut it down fast since my arguments seemed to have glided straight off him. *Think, Emma, think*—but my thoughts had turned to porridge.

For one wild moment, I wondered about trading his silence for a different story: Harry's affair—widely rumored—with a married Labour peer. But really, who cared? Besides, that wasn't my style. I had to cling to my principles because if I didn't have my integrity, what did I have?

I would have to brazen it out. Remain firm. Keep insisting I wouldn't cooperate. Seek legal advice. A stern lawyer's letter sent to the *Chronicle?* Could I do that? Would that somehow do the trick?

I turned to look at him, his face—the face of a decent man, I'd thought, over that candlelit table in Soho, a good man, even—now revealed to be that of a weak one. A man without scruples, or with scruples that could be abandoned with little compunction at all.

Had he been rooting around for this ever since our night together? *I've got to get in touch with Flora. Something's happened to her.* Was that what had whet his interest, or was it my brusqueness—*I think this was proba-bly a mistake*—that had provoked him? Was he pursuing this because of dented pride? I'd sensed he could turn; glimpsed his changeability in his sulkiness, the shaking off of my hand. But I'd underestimated him, not wanting to consider the extent of his ruthlessness. And later? Well, then his ability to turn on me became painfully, fatally clear.

At that moment, though, by the Thames, I thought I could—just— handle him. I was persuasive, and I was in the right, wasn't I? Surely I could curb this? Could stop him, even if I couldn't win him round?

I thought of the *Guardian* cover: the slash of lipstick, the well-cut suit, the fierce tilt of my head. I remembered the resolution and strength that image conveyed, and I concentrated on channeling it as the wind struck me, fresh off the water.

"You're getting nothing from me."

Nineteen

1 DECEMBER 2021

EMMA

FiremanFred @suckmycock: I'd take a razor to @emmawebsterMP's smug face, only it would blunt it.

Richard M @BigBob699: Worth it to strip it to ribbons, though.

Dick Penny @EnglandRules: Strip HER more like.

FiremanFred @suckmycock: Nah—not worth the energy.

Despite the bravado I'd shown Mike, our encounter in Victoria Tower Gardens marked the moment my fear became all-consuming.

It didn't help that the anonymous texts had resumed. *Like mother, like daughter* was the latest, sent to my work phone. Did this, with its restrained venom, the lack of a *bitch*, which still made itself felt, come from Mike? Was he capable of that? Or was it sent by someone else?

Checking Twitter last thing at night, and first thing in the morning, also intensified my anxiety. I told myself I needed to see if anyone else had a sniff of the story, and I soon fell down a virtual rabbit hole into the minds of those who hated me the most.

Filled with self-loathing, I found a link to some deepfake porn: my face superimposed on a naked body, unspeakable things done to this counterfeit me. I finally contacted PLaIT, the specialist Met police team dedicated to looking after the security of those in Parliament, and they promised to investigate. But I wasn't that reassured. Even if they tracked down its creator, there would be others out there who wanted to hurt me.

I was walking toward College Green, two days after being confronted by Mike, when I first sensed I was being followed. It was Wednesday lunchtime, and Parliament Square was cluttered with the usual hodge-podge of protestors: an anti-vaxxer, a man wrapped in an EU flag, and a masked man impersonating a priapic prime minister, as he'd done each day since the Tory leader came to power.

The pavement was heaving. Until recently, I'd been comfortable in crowds, or more comfortable than walking down a side street or using a subway whose long tunnels hid menace. I'd thought there was safety in numbers. But as Mike had shown me, danger could hide in plain sight.

It was the synchronized tapping of footsteps that perturbed me. The way they mirrored mine precisely. I glanced over my shoulder, but the sea of faces only shifted, blank eyes staring back.

Perhaps I was imagining it? The gunmetal skies didn't help. The threat of a downpour made everyone move more quickly, and even the Japanese tourists, who typically blocked the path to find the perfect photo of the Commons, rushed to find cover before the heavens burst. The atmosphere felt oppressive: the black barricades forbidding, the armed police excessively heavy-handed as they stood by St. Stephen's Entrance and New Palace Yard. Most of the time, I was inured to their humorless expressions, their flak jackets and semiautomatic rifles. But against the backdrop of rolling thunder and the first fat raindrops, their presence now seemed particularly menacing.

A second roll. The crowd upped its pace, and I strained to hear the footsteps that snagged at my attention. Perhaps I was just jangled by Mike's threat? I'd been awake since half four, had downed three strong coffees that had made me jumpy. So perhaps I was primed to feel on edge.

But there it was again: a particular footstep beneath all the others, like the steady beat of a metronome, rhythmic, insistent, keeping neatly in time. I walked a little faster, and it caught up with me; slowed down, and it mirrored me. I crossed the road, onto the side of Westminster Abbey, telling myself that I'd shake it off; that of course it wouldn't follow me because it was a coincidence, a trick of my imagination—and yet there it was.

I didn't dare look round because if I did, he might just catch me. At least my destination was in sight. By the time I reached College Green for my interview with the BBC, I was walking more than briskly, had stumbled into a fast trot until I was almost running. Thank God I was wearing smart biker boots and could still run, though I was relatively unfit. As my feet hit the grass and I spied the gazebo where the camera crew was sheltering, I abandoned any pretense I felt calm.

"You okay?" asked the BBC's chief political correspondent as I was fitted with a mike before going on camera.

"Yeah, fine," I said—because I didn't want to look flaky; didn't want to create the impression I was anything but the articulate, assured MP he knew.

But I was preoccupied, still assessing if this had been a stalker. If there was someone whose footsteps receded as I ran away.

The feeling of being watched continued that evening. I hadn't cycled—my bike had a puncture—and both Claire and Julia had evening engagements, so I took a cab and tried to relax in its relative privacy, resisting the cabbie's eyes in the rear mirror.

He knew who I was, of course. He'd picked me up from the rank in New Palace Yard, but I hadn't had the energy to engage; to listen to why I was wrong about the prime minister or my own party leader, why revenge porn wasn't an issue worth getting excited over, or why the recession was a mere blip. I reached for my phone and sent Flora a good-night text, then fumbled for my house keys and splayed them surreptitiously in my right hand, slotting them between my fingers, because that's what women do when they are out alone at night. The driver caught my eye and I looked away, embarrassed that he'd caught me, resentful that I'd felt the need to do so. I clutched my bag tight, poised to spring from the cab as soon as it stopped, eager for the moment I could shut the door on him and everyone else who probed and questioned and made judgments and comments about me.

The street was dark once the taxi pulled off, my having thrust a tenner at the cabbie and not waited for a receipt. The streetlight near our house had blown, and the square felt unusually eerie. A twig snapped, and I glanced round sharply as if expecting that the sound had been made by somebody else.

There might have been no one in the street, and yet there was a flicker, quickly extinguished, from inside a car parked a few meters from me: a dark blue station wagon with its lights off and, I couldn't help noticing, someone slumped down inside. I took a step closer. That was unusual: for someone to wait without the engine running and the heater switched on, given the near-freezing temperature of a December night. Another step. There *was* someone in the driver's seat: the light was sufficient to detect something shifting and to catch the paleness of a hand, not on a steering wheel but lifting something. Something bulkier than a mobile phone . . .

Heart thudding in my ears, I turned and ran up the steps, despite knowing I was in full view, that I was making myself a target, because I needed to get away from whoever it was who was stalking me, who was directing something at me right now.

My key was primed in my hand, and it slotted into the lock straightaway so that I almost fell as I thrust the door open and slammed it quickly behind me before fumbling for the alarm. And then I started crying. A whimper, hastily suppressed, in case whoever he was had followed me up the steps, was on the other side of the oak. *You'll be drinking acid next cunt.* The words from the threat letter blasted through my head. And the texts, and some Twitter comments. *I'm watching you bitch. Not worth raping. I'd take a razor to @emmawebstermp's smug face.* All this venom directed at me—and what if someone wanted a physical outlet? If they were no longer satisfied by empty threats?

Well, what are you going to do about it? I would just have to deal with it, wouldn't I? Like I always did because no one else would so do! I checked the bolt. Just the one, in addition to the key. Our landlord had been reluctant to ruin the house's Grade II listed features with additional fittings, despite the recommendations of the security audit that we fit three extra locks to the door. Now that stance felt obscene.

I would have to move out. This was the second time someone had stalked me here, and I didn't feel safe: in this house with just the one lock; with its steps to the door where I was a standing target; with its large sash windows designed to show off the house's inhabitants, the very last thing I needed, particularly with my bedroom at the front on the raised ground floor.

And then a self-pitying sob bubbled up because I'd liked living in this elegant house with two women I was close to, though my relationship with Julia had soured recently, and I wondered if I'd feel safe anywhere at all.

My throat tightened and I gave in to the relief of tears, the release of all my pent-up anxiety. I hated feeling reduced to this. Being this scared: constantly on edge, needing to be vigilant, feeling as if I was always being watched and followed.

When I checked from the top window, ten minutes later, the car had gone.

Twenty

4 DECEMBER 2021

EMMA

Amy's Law MP feeling the strain

Revenge porn MP Emma Webster shows the strain of battling for justice for revenge porn victims this week as she was snapped outside her Portsmouth home.

Friends say family worries are also taking their toll on the 44-year-old divorcée, who has a 14-year-old daughter. "She's a working single mum with a teenager: that's tough," said one. "She's lost so much weight recently she's looking gaunt and anxious."

Our pic comes just weeks after this one printed in another newspaper—and shows her dramatic weight loss and lack of va-va-voom. A friend said: "It's not just her curves that have gone, but her confidence."

Here's hoping the Amy's Law champion resolves her family issues soon.

The photographs showed me putting out the trash cans. Hair mussed up, dressing gown tied tight around me, Flora's sneakers shoved on hurriedly when I'd woken to the garbage truck's distinctive whine and rattle as it drove down the street.

Next to it was that bloody *Guardian* picture: the red lip, the fitted trouser suit, the heels—and yes, of course I looked more confident, more ballsy: there'd been a stylist and a makeup artist. But it wasn't just that. That photo had been taken before the anonymous texts began; before I started being followed; and, crucially, before Flora became involved with the police.

It was the fact they'd taken this new picture outside my house that distressed me far more than the photo itself—though I looked like an old bag lady with my bedhead hair and startled, pillow-crumpled face. I'd only overslept because I'd finally taken a sleeping tablet after my week of restless nights. I still hadn't spoken to David about Mike's threat. Crazy, given everything that would come, but I think I was in denial, or rather, I feared I was overreacting, that my judgment was clouded by lack of sleep. And then there was that mantra-like challenge: the expectation I always imposed on myself. *Well, what are you going to do about it?* Irrationally, I hoped I could deal with it myself; that Mike's bravado would fizzle like a damp wick and there would be no need for me to lob this particular grenade into my Portsmouth life. That I could avoid my ex-husband's anger and, more importantly, protect Flora from ever knowing that anyone else knew what she did to Leah.

Still, I couldn't continue like this. Would need to be frank, at least with David. My ex-husband didn't buy the paper, so I suppose I could have kept it from him, but I would have been incandescent if the tables were turned. If I discovered *he* had been staked out and photographed while our daughter was at his house, and he'd failed to mention it, I'd have hit the roof. And I needed to share the burden of what Mike knew.

Because there was something particularly creepy about the fact that the *Chronicle* had sent a photographer here, to the home I shared with Flora, and that they had had me under surveillance. The photographer might have been waiting outside all night, while we slept. For what must have been the twentieth time, I peered out at the front of the house despite telling myself that, since the paper had what it wanted, there was nobody there. Then I triple-checked that the front door was bolted and the kitchen door doubled-locked. My skin goose-pimpled, a draft from the window in the utility room suddenly sinister: it had no extra lock because it was too small for anyone to clamber through it, but what if it had been forced and a camera planted? If I was being observed outside my house, then who was to say I wasn't being watched inside it as well?

My stomach churned, the black coffee I'd downed making its way back up until I tasted it again, bitter and bilious. In theory I should be safer here than in Cleaver Square, with its inadequate locks. And yet my 1960s home now felt flimsy: the large windows that had first attracted me too wide, its postwar bricks and paneled glass naively trusting—as if inviting an intruder to step right in. The fact that a photographer had obviously been parked straight across the street from my home for quite some time and nobody in the neighborhood had thought to question him, was perturbing. This breach of my privacy, coming on top of the acid-attack letter, the abusive texts, the fear I was being stalked—and I could see now that the car in Cleaver Square might have been a photographer or a junior reporter put on the case by Mike—scared me. This all felt so horribly close to home.

And it was hard not to read the copy as a threat. I knew exactly what Mike was doing. "*Family* worries are also taking their toll on the . . . *divorcée*, who has a 14-year-old *daughter* . . . 'She's a *working single mum* with a *teenager*' . . . Here's hoping . . . the Amy's Law champion a rocket scientist to glean that the source of my anxiety was my teenage girl. That this fourteen-year-old was making my single parenting "tough" and had done something specific to make me look so "gaunt."

I dialed my old home number and, of course, Caroline answered.

"Are you okay?" She was always good at sensing when something was wrong, I'd give her that. Emotionally intelligent. Empathetic. It was how she'd grown close to David; why, I suppose, I'd gravitated toward her in the staff room when we first met. She'd sensed a colleague was making me uncomfortable—always sitting too close, dominating my attention, ignoring my frequent references to my husband—and was direct in seeing him off. "Stop sniffing around, Ian. You're embarrassing yourself." Did she say something worse? Either way, it served as lighter fuel to our relationship.

I cleared my throat, the words sticking because I didn't like admitting to my vulnerability.

"Not really. Are you both around?"

"I could kill him."

David's fists were clenched, his knuckles beading in his large, tensed hands. His color was heightened, and when he closed his eyes, his lashes quivered like the wings of a butterfly hovering in front of a flower.

I'd never seen him this angry. The David I'd married had been relatively mild: his emotional blandness one of the things that had attracted me after my previous toxic relationship. He would get irritated by minor things—my clutter, the cat shitting in the flower beds, next door's occasional house parties—his exasperation expressed in passive-aggressive tics. But sheer unbridled fury? A threat—however hyperbolic—to murder someone? That just wasn't like him.

But then this newly lean David was a fresh take on the man I'd married. Perhaps this aggression came with the three-and-a-half-hour marathons, the gym sessions, the protein shakes, and the vitamin supplements that Flora told me he religiously took? Or maybe it was just that his teenage daughter was under threat? From upstairs came the plaintive sound of Flora playing a Bach concerto on her oboe. Since the "Leah thing," she'd started practicing again. For two or three hours a day, she would obsessively perfect each phrase. Now the melody spiraled upward in a sequence; a phrase and reply that meandered into a minor key in an elegant contrast to her father's visceral growl.

"The question is: what are we going to do about it?" Caroline asked, and I felt a rush of gratitude for this acknowledgment that this was a problem we faced together. "Emma: do you have any contacts on the paper you could talk to?"

"I do—but I don't think he would help."

"Really?" She looked bemused, and I wondered if she could read anything into my reluctance to approach my source. I'd hoped to get through this without admitting to knowing Mike, and I still had no intention of telling them we'd slept together: it was none of their business. But telling them we'd already rowed about him running some sort of story—and that I'd failed to dissuade him—now seemed inevitable.

"The political editor sees it purely in terms of a good story. He approached me and offered to tell it from our side." I filled them in quickly on my conversation with Mike. "I thought I'd warned him off by reminding him Flora's a minor, but the paper is ruthless. This"—I jabbed at my picture in the *Chronicle*—"is its way of showing me they intend to find some way of getting the story out."

"Can't you appeal to his basic decency? Does he have kids himself?" David's face was no longer a heightened red, and I felt a flash of exasperation at his good nature. Mike and the *Chronicle* operated under a different moral code.

"The thing is," I said, offering a version of the truth, "he made a pass and I made it clear I wasn't interested in him, so I wonder if this is personal. He has a reason to get at me if his pride is hurt."

"Oh, come on—" David began.

"*David.*"

"It's fine. I'm not offended."

"It's not that." David looked irritated at his wife assuming he'd thought it impossible anyone would find me attractive. "I meant: he's an adult, isn't he? Would he really behave like this because of that?"

"Oh, sweetheart," said Caroline, in a tone designed to flatter. "You're far more generous-spirited than most men . . . But this does mean that there's no point in Emma approaching him again. Perhaps you or I should try to have a chat?"

David clicked his finger joints as if limbering up for a fight. "I don't think I'd trust myself to speak civilly to the bastard."

"Yes, you've told us you want to kill him," Caroline said dryly, and she caught my eye in a rare, shared moment of exasperation. "So, it will have to be me."

"You?" David was surprised. That was interesting: he underestimated her, whereas I no longer did and hadn't since doing so had proved fatal to my marriage.

"Why not? I love Flora. And she's so fragile at the moment. Can you imagine how she'll react if she sees this story? If what she did to Leah is exposed in any way?"

"Christ." David shook his head.

"Exactly," said Caroline. "I don't want to think about what she might do if they went further. Besides, I can be quite persuasive."

And she smiled, her perkiness not quite masking a glint of steel.

I didn't trust her. In that moment, I knew I couldn't risk the woman who had cuckooed her way into my home negotiating with Mike, a man who had made it clear he was happy to trounce my daughter's reputation and disregard her well-being. Besides, it was *my* job to dissuade him. I would just have to think of another way.

"Mike's made it pretty clear he's not susceptible to persuasion," I said, in a voice that held a tiny quiver of anger. "Tabloid journalists don't tend to respond to appeals to their better nature." I gave a hollow laugh that made me sound a little manic. "Believe me, I've tried. And I *have* contacted a lawyer. They could write a letter to the paper's legal department warning they'd be in contempt of court if they ran the story. The only thing is the letter would cost five grand; ten if we instructed someone really good, which isn't insignificant." I swallowed, waiting for them to offer to help. They didn't, and so I was forced to be completely frank with them. "I think we should do this, but I just don't have the money."

"We could split it," said David, as Caroline gave a little mew of disbelief, then looked at him intently, no doubt semaphoring her desire for another renovation project.

"David, we don't have that sort of spare money," she squeaked.

"We'll find it." He looked grim.

"Thank you," I said, and I was grateful. "I'll call the lawyer first thing on Monday morning."

I left, feeling resentful toward Caroline, and ashamed for having foisted this on them. Because were it not for my job, Flora's behavior would have been part of a steep learning curve: a highly regrettable teenage misdemeanor; a stupid, adolescent mistake.

It was because of my reputation that hers risked becoming a tabloid story.

And so I had only myself to blame.

Twenty-One

6 DECEMBER 2021

CAROLINE

There had never been the slightest doubt in Caroline's mind that she should try to persuade Mike Stokes to drop the story. She kept reminding herself of this as she stood outside a takeaway coffee shop, opposite the House of Commons, waiting for him to turn up.

Emma, more involved than she cared to admit, was clearly out of the question. As for David, he was falling apart, and no number of lengthy runs—he'd done a sixteen-miler after Emma came round—or sessions with his punching bag in the garage would calm him down sufficiently to make him persuasive, or even coherent.

So, it had to be Caroline. Just as she was the one in whom Flora had confided that awful Thursday when Seb had replied to her texted photo with a curt *Who the fuck IS this?* And just as she had been the one who'd held her as they'd told David, Flo so incomprehensible that at first, he had no idea what she was talking about. It had been Caroline who'd taken the phone call from the police, and who'd tried to charm the two young officers with an offer of a cup of tea, as if this was a social call and not an investigation; Caroline who'd been up in the night when she heard Flo retching in fear.

And where had Emma been during all of this? Uncontactable.

Not that Caroline resented any of this. She loved Flora almost as much as if she'd been her own daughter, she was convinced of it. She was, after all, the Webster she had grown to love first. Her stepdaughter had been her piano pupil, the conduit through whom Caroline, at first just a colleague, had become Emma's friend and later, though she had no intention of this happening, had fallen in love with David. As a means of becoming enmeshed in the Webster family, Flora—if it didn't sound icky—had been her gateway drug.

"Can I help you?"

"A skinny decaf latte, please," she told the young male barista. "One shot." She'd been waiting for Mike Stokes for ten minutes. Not so long as to know he was playing some sort of power game, but long enough to feel conspicuous. Besides, the December wind was bitter, and she needed warming up.

The shop was playing some banal pop—G major, when really this was a B-flat minor kind of day—but the milky liquid soothed her as she remembered those early months of knowing Flora: a time when she'd been particularly glorious—engaging, bright, and possessing a musicality far beyond her years. Watching her scamper through scales, learn Mozart sonatas, or enjoy the swing and rhythm of twelve-bar blues, Caroline had realized she craved a daughter like her. She was thirty-four by then and painfully conscious that as a peripatetic piano teacher it was near impossible to meet eligible men. (None of her teacher colleagues were that attractive, and most of those she met through the choral society she rehearsed with were either married and elderly, or gay.) She'd looked into sperm donation, but it felt too clinical. What she wanted—and what she came to appreciate David wanted—was a partner *and* a baby.

And the idea of him fathering her child grew to feel inevitable. She knew—way before him, though not, she suspected, before Emma—that his marriage wouldn't last the Parliament. The first glimmer was clear the night Emma was elected, the second the result was called. For a fleeting moment, just before she adjusted her features into an appropriate expression, Emma had seemed stunned. Was she calibrating what it would mean for her marriage? Her unintentionally breaking the agreement she and David had hammered out late at night—that she would stand this time but not win—without understanding that outside forces might affect their bargain? That, in the mercurial world of politics, she was powerless to control her future after all?

"She didn't want this. She didn't really want this," David would insist, clinging to his theory for the first few months she was away until it became clear that his wife loved her new career; that she was more than thriving—she was *flourishing*, was *intoxicated*, during this honeymoon period, by her new political life. As a performer, not good enough to be a soloist but sufficiently proficient to play semiprofessionally and to have experienced applause from an audience, Caroline recognized this only too well. Emma had found her *voice*. Not one challenged by precocious teenagers but one that people listened to; one that gave her a taste, however illusory, of power.

It was the day when Emma appeared on the BBC's *Six O'Clock News*, talking about domestic violence, that David finally realized he had lost her. Caroline was teaching Flora that Monday, 5:30 to 6 p.m. as usual, and David had asked if they could stop on time so that Flora could watch it. (She was so rewarding that Caroline frequently overran.) Emma had texted, *Think I'm on the Six!!! Can you record?*—followed by a fist pump emoji and a party popper. No mention of David or Flora. Caroline ended the lesson, and it seemed only natural to join them on the sofa to watch.

And Emma was breathtaking. Glossy and confident. Articulate. A little earnest as she spoke directly to the reporter, not the camera, but impassioned and genuine. It was fair to say that David was transfixed.

Afterward Flora tried to call. Then David. "We watched. You were wonderful. Do call back?" His voice had rounded with pride as he left the message, and then his expression had slipped to one of unsurmountable sadness, as if he knew it would be hours before she rang.

"Have we time for Flora to go through her new piece?" Caroline had asked, desperate to buoy them both up, and he had nodded, grateful.

Flora was learning the *Pink Panther* theme tune and mastering the walking bass. She soon lost herself in the puzzle of getting it right, and when she became frustrated, Caroline rattled off "The Entertainer" to distract her pupil from fretting about some muddled fingering, and the bigger issue of why Emma was failing to call.

Caroline had stayed to eat, as she sometimes did, and as she left, she touched David's arm. A light touch. Nothing sensual. But he was startled. "Sorry," she muttered on the doorstep, not because she'd touched him, though she'd never done that before, but because she sympathized with how he was feeling. Then: "I hope she gets back to Flora. Take care."

She later learned that Emma had been in a series of votes and hadn't texted until past 11 p.m.—by which time, of course, Flora had cried herself to sleep.

The next day, David rang asking her to lunch, and they began from there.

————

There still wasn't a baby, of course. They were moving on to IVF now. Thirty-eight. She still had time—though the odds were less than 50 percent, and they only had the money for two cycles. Or rather—and here she took too large a swig of coffee so that it burned her throat—they *had* the money, kept back from his great-aunt's bequest and set aside from the renovations (which she sometimes cursed, though she had been desperate to rid the house of Emma's presence), except that David had just offered to pay for that lawyer's letter. And *of course* they had to do whatever they could to protect Flora. She knew that absolutely, felt embarrassed now by her selfish reaction. But still, if Mike could be persuaded without this money being spent, that would be *fantastic*. And she might have a chance of a baby after all.

The lack of one, while it made her feel inadequate, did at least make her appreciate Flora more intensely. This might be it, this not-quite-proper version of motherhood; this *cheat's* version, as she sometimes thought of it. Her only chance—which she had to get right. Well, she'd failed at that. She'd let Flo down: she felt this acutely, not because she'd been the catalyst that had blown the Websters' marriage apart—she'd only speeded up the inevitable—but because, with David so poor at communicating with his teenage daughter and Emma away, she should have picked up on Leah's bullying earlier.

After all, she'd known that Flora was unsettled, if not actively unhappy; that she wasn't mentioning her friends and was closing conversations down whenever Caroline suggested seeing them. It had been a tricky balance: wanting to be involved and yet not wanting to intrude. And she had clearly tiptoed around her stepdaughter too much: being too hands-off, failing to appreciate that what she'd thought was a usual case of teenage girls falling out could escalate to such a toxic situation. So this attempt to persuade Mike Stokes was driven not just by love, or, less nobly, by a desire to save money, but also by guilt.

He was fifteen minutes late now, though, which was bordering on rude, and somewhat surprising. He'd seemed refreshingly keen to meet her—which possibly had something to do with the fact that she hadn't been a hundred percent truthful about her motives when she'd rung.

"I'm the wife of Emma Webster's ex-husband," she'd said when she was put through via the paper's news desk. She'd concentrated on making her voice sound deep—a true contralto—and as seductive as possible. "I wonder if we could meet. I think I have something you might like to hear."

Now, though, she was nervous as she saw a figure similar to his Twitter picture sprinting across the road toward her. Sandy-haired, not unattractive, and fizzing with an animal dynamism that made her chest tighten with apprehension about how he'd react when he discovered she hadn't told the truth.

"Mrs. Webster?" He smiled affably.

"Caroline." She smiled back.

"You okay for a coffee?"

She gestured to the cup in her hand. "I'm fine—but you get one."

"Nah. Drink too much of the stuff, anyway." That might account for why he was bouncing on the balls of his feet as if he had too much energy inside him. "Are you happy to walk somewhere quieter?"

Somehow she found herself being guided across Westminster Bridge, making inane conversation until they stopped at the midpoint and turned to look back at the House of Commons. She felt a little vulnerable, conscious of the previous terror attack that had happened near this point, aware they were hardly being discreet. Perhaps that was part of his plan though there were only a couple of Italian tourists anywhere near, and neither seemed interested in the two of them. Beneath her the Thames surged, gray and molten, while the ashen clouds spat the odd needle of rain. It didn't seem the most auspicious place to talk.

"So—you said you had something you could tell me about Emma Webster," Mike began.

"Can I just check this is completely off the record?" She was suddenly intensely nervous. "I don't want to be quoted in any way."

"Of course." He was looking at her as if she was a truly fascinating person. It was unnerving: made her realize she couldn't sustain a conversation in which she appeared to offer one thing but wanted another, that she needed to be honest from the start.

"I'm not here about Emma. I'm here about Flora."

"Go on." He seemed more interested. Of course she would know about the Youth Caution. Perhaps he thought her a wicked stepmother, prepared to betray her?

"I'm here to ask you to drop all this now."

"All what?" A nerve twitched at the side of his mouth.

"You know what I'm talking about. I'm sure we can find a way to prevent you writing this legally, but in the meantime, you've exerted massive pressure with that photo of Emma. What will you do next? A picture of Flora with her face blurred to obscure her identity? Or another story with hints any of her classmates would understand? I'm appealing to your good nature. To your humanity. I don't—frankly—really care what you do to Emma." At this, Mike smiled. "She's put herself in the public eye, she has to cope with the repercussions. The payback. But I'm asking you to think about what you're doing to a young girl."

"Is that what you came all the way up here to ask me?" He shook his head slowly, and at that moment she felt a surge of rage at him daring to be sardonic. "Your stepdaughter's hardly some blameless innocent. She sent revenge porn. A moving image of a fourteen-year-old girl. Exactly the thing her mother's been campaigning against. I suggested to Emma we do this in a sensitive way. Start a public conversation about the pressures our teenagers are under. Discuss online bullying and the impact on teens' mental health. Show the full picture. But if she won't cooperate, it's in the public interest to expose hypocrisy of all sorts."

Christ. She wanted to hit him. Could understand now why David, normally so placid, felt murderous. Mike inhabited a totally different moral universe from them all.

"But she's a *child*."

"A teenager who'll be fifteen in three months. A teenager with an iPhone who took a topless video of a girl her age and sent it to an older teenage boy in an extreme act of retaliation. I'd say that was revenge porn."

He paused as if the conversation was over.

"Please." She felt frantic. "I'm worried about her self-harming, perhaps even worse."

And there it was. A flicker of sympathy—or, if not that, then the tiniest glimmer of doubt. Something had resonated. Whatever he might profess, he wasn't entirely comfortable with this either.

"Do you have a child?" she pressed. "How would you feel if this was them?"

The sound of a mobile cut her off. An angry buzz from his inside pocket. Mike took it, and the expression on his face switched from disquiet to excitement. "Look—I have to take this. Thanks for agreeing to meet—"

"But I—"

"Gotta go! Sorry!" He held up his hand, effectively dismissing her.

And with that, he walked briskly back over the bridge, mobile rammed to his ear, deep in conversation, leaving Caroline peering deep into the Thames's abyss.

Twenty-Two

6 DECEMBER 2021

MIKE

Well, *this* was a fucking turn for the books.

Mike barely glanced at the traffic speeding over Westminster Bridge as he jaywalked across it and back to the House of Commons.

A white delivery van gave a long blast of its horn, but he merely held a hand up in apology, he was so preoccupied with what his caller was saying, so intent on reaching somewhere they could speak alone.

His thoughts freewheeled as he hurtled through the ramifications of what he'd just heard. Jesus fucking *Christ*, but this was incendiary. An exposé that, with its fallout, could last *days*, would bring him long-lasting credibility with the desk, and would *decimate* a reputation, making a mockery of everything that had stood before.

Because this was something that would blow the Flora Webster story *way* out of the water. *That* tale would be a peripheral ripple compared to the tsunami unleashed by what he was being told. And to be honest, he'd been having his doubts about how they could run the story of Flora's teen porn retaliation and her mother's hypocrisy. Without Emma's collaboration, it risked looking exploitative. The deputy editor had raised the issue of adolescent mental health—his nineteen-year-old daughter was rumored to have depression—and the lawyers were getting a bit twitchy. But with *this*, there were no concerns about anyone being underage. The story might be historic, but everyone involved was an adult at the time. Most importantly, it sounded as if would stand up. There were pictures. If what he was being told was correct, most would be too X-rated for a decent family newspaper, but there would be some shots that could be edited and pixelated and, critically, it would be incontrovertible.

It was the reason he'd been late to meet the new Mrs. Webster. There'd been an initial, tantalizing message left on his voicemail first thing this morning, and the source was potentially so destructive Mike had waited, hoping they'd respond to his text and call him back. They hadn't, and Mike had spent the conversation with Caroline distracted by the thought that they could be making contact. Irritated, too, that she'd proved such a waste of time.

Although nothing was *really* that in this job, he had to keep reminding himself. Every tidbit overheard or overseen, every cup of coffee with a contact, had the potential to add an extra strand of color. He now knew that the new Mrs. Webster, though younger and a perfectly attractive woman, lacked the charisma of her predecessor: that element that made Emma political box office material; that had made him fall for her so totally that surreal, almost cinematic Soho night.

Caroline hadn't given him what he'd wanted, nor what he'd expected. She had only provided a little insight into the taste of Emma's ex-husband, but in the grand scheme of things, he didn't mind.

He basketed his fingers together and stretched as if limbering up for the work ahead. He had a new story to focus on now.

Twenty-Three

8 DECEMBER 2021

EMMA

The day that it happened began particularly badly. Standing in the kitch-enette down the hall from my office, I smashed the mug with Flora's baby handprint, knocking it hard against the tap.

I'd been rushing. It was four days after my unsatisfactory conversation with David and Caroline, and my reactions were quick and snappish, my answers to the most anodyne questions defensive. As I stood wondering if I could glue together the broken pieces, I started crying. "You okay?" Jazz asked, clocking my red face when I returned to the office. "'S nothing," I brushed her off. But it *was*. A reaction less about breaking a cherished possession, and more about the constant strain of living in this state of heightened apprehension and fear.

It had been a tense few days. On Monday, I'd instructed a media lawyer to send a lawyer's letter to the *Chronicle* reminding them they'd be breaking the law if they printed anything about Flora, but I still couldn't believe this would be enough.

That night, I'd bickered with Claire over where we should hang the mistletoe (that and a poinsettia our only concessions to Christmas). It was uncharacteristic: the strain of the last few weeks making me snap. We'd concluded with her telling me I *clearly* needed my own space. I didn't, but I needed somewhere more secure, ideally in a block with an entry phone or in some sort of gated complex. We could move together, I told them, last night, after mulling the argument over for twenty-four hours, but it might be easier if I looked alone.

Claire was understanding. But Julia accused me of overreacting, and clearly resented the prospect of being burdened with a new housemate.

"We all experience abuse," she'd said, as if it was a competition. "It's inevitable if you speak on a feminist agenda. But it doesn't mean you should feel *hounded*. There's no need to panic. Just be logical and you'll ride this out."

"I don't feel safe." My cry came out too loud, my tone ragged, as if I'd lost all sense of perspective. "You *saw* the pictures the *Chronicle* posted of me."

"But that was at your *constituency* house," she reasoned. "And they got what they wanted. I don't mean to minimize this, but the stalker in the car must have been a photographer, and he's gone now. And the other incident—the boy on the bike—was just a kid."

"Have you rung PLaIT?" asked Claire, referring to the specialist Met police team, who hadn't come back to me about the porn creator.

"No. I was trying not to make a fuss." Immediately I felt stupid for this decision.

A long, hard stare from Julia. "Well, then. There you are."

I'd felt bruised by last night's argument and found it hard to sleep afterward. Unusually, I didn't set my alarm for six and delayed breakfast to avoid seeing either of them. They were out by eight: it was easy, for once, to be the last to leave. But I'd found it hard to focus, all day.

"Go home," said Jazz, at around four, as darkness shrouded the windows and it was clear I was achieving little. "You still got that headache?"

I nodded. A viselike snare banded my temples, tightening as the light dimmed.

"No point being a martyr," she went on, and there was an edge to her voice: if I'd caught something, she didn't want to get it. Then her tone softened: "No offense, but you look a bit shit."

I cycled home, legs pedaling furiously as shadows licked the asphalt, then bit at my ankles. A quarter past four, and the roads were relatively quiet before the rush-hour swell. I was skittish, unnerved; thought a car, hanging back, was tailing me until it peeled off to the left at the lights. At the next junction, I sensed someone behind me: another cyclist with his front wheel too close to my back one, trailing me too closely. Had he been doing it a while? The wind had picked up, a mizzle of rain blustered against me, but it wasn't just that, was it? His breath seemed to goose-pimple the back of my neck.

I sprinted after that: head down, thighs burning; the road slipping beneath me as the rain grew far heavier; needles pricking at my cheeks, soaking my legs. My sense of danger was all-consuming, and I managed the journey in record time. Twelve minutes, three seconds, my Apple Watch told me as I chained my bike to the railings, engulfed by a wave of dizziness that suggested I'd pushed myself too hard. Crouching down, I tugged off my gloves and helmet, then held on to the railings, using the cold of the iron to steady me before I considered taking the steps up to the door. I closed my eyes, listening to the dried branches of the plane trees clattering against one another, the distant drone of traffic, the wail of a siren. The rain was dying off, but the cold galvanized me into action and, still a little woozy, I stood up.

I knew, as soon as I opened the door, that the house wasn't empty.

The silence had a peculiar quality to it: as if it had recently been disturbed. The motes of dust had been disordered, the air passed through another's lungs. Beyond the front door, the London traffic thrummed, but inside, the silence was freighted with expectation. Someone else had been here. Someone was here still.

The alarm should have been set. A nasal blaring that usually blasted as soon as you pushed open the heavy oak door, and which stopped mid-note when you tapped the code into the keypad.

It didn't blare now.

The others weren't back—I'd passed both their offices on the way out—but perhaps it hadn't been turned on? Setting it was instinctive: as automatic as brushing my teeth or taking a multivitamin while the kettle boiled first thing in the morning. Part of the natural rhythm of the day. I had set it as I left the house, I was sure of it, but Agnes, the cleaner, was in today. She came fortnightly, and there'd been a previous occasion when she'd forgotten to do it correctly. Though I knew it was unlikely, it was possible the ominous silence was down to human error. Someone else had screwed up.

It was dark, though. The lamp in the hall should have been on a timer, but it wasn't, and the house was blanketed in darkness: the light that automatically clicked on when someone stood on the doorstep shone palely, but the back of the hall remained in the gloom.

I flicked the switch. Nothing. Perhaps the circuit had fused? That must be why the alarm hadn't worked. I needed to find the fuse box in the cupboard under the stairs, get the lights back on, restore order. I leapt on this explanation, though my heart still beat a rapid *da-dum, da-dum, da-dum* as I fumbled for the flashlight on my iPhone and tiptoed down the hall.

Why did I do that?

It was a question I would come to dread. Why on earth, when it was possible that someone had entered my house, didn't I, a woman who had been hounded by the press, who was receiving abusive text messages, who had been threatened online and in person, simply run out of the house and call the police? Given the level of vitriol I'd received—the acid threat, the anonymous texts, the Twitter trolls—I must have known that was the wise thing to do, rather than step directly into probable danger?

And yet I made that choice: to try to cope without asking for help. *Well, what are you going to do about it?* My father's challenge meant that I thought I ought to deal with this alone.

"Hello," I called, trying to make myself sound bold, though my voice held a distinct wobble. "Hello? Is anyone there?"

I wondered if I could hear footsteps . . .

The tread of a hard sole, the creak of a leather shoe.

I took a step closer.

And that's when it happened. That's when everything went wrong.

PART TWO

Twenty-Four

13 JUNE 2022

EMMA

I have had bigger audiences before. But none so critical.

Sitting in the dock of Court Seven of the Old Bailey this first morning, I have never felt so exposed.

There must be forty sets of eyes on me: the judge, her clerk, her usher, and two rows of press—far more than would usually attend a trial, even in this setting. But then my case has already attracted massive publicity. The prosecution's opening speech, I know without hearing it, will make the front pages. It might even lead the six o'clock news.

The public are craning to get a look at me, too: those who can angle themselves to peer into the dock from the public gallery. And, of course, there is the jury. Five ordinary men and seven ordinary women on whose skills of analysis, and sheer gut instinct, my entire future hangs.

I judge them as they are judging me, trying to calculate what the ethnic makeup or the gender balance might possibly mean. It's a London jury: more diverse than it would be in my constituency. Three of the jurors are from Black or Asian backgrounds; two have sworn on the Koran. Is that reassuring? Women are less willing to convict, and I'm tempted to smile at these: to try to win them over. Because never has an audience's judgment mattered so very much.

The judge is talking now. Her Ladyship Fiona Costa. Petite, Cambridge-educated, and in her late fifties, her true self barely visible: just a thumbprint of a face beneath horn-rimmed spectacles, and squashed between her wig and gown.

And I'm envious of this. Because in this environment, in which mobiles are banned, there can be no Twitter memes. No trolling. No ridicule.

And certainly no deepfake manipulation, of the sort I've experienced, in which her head is imposed on a pornographic image and shown having sex with—and here my eyes flit to the royal crest suspended on the wall behind her—a unicorn or lion. Protected by contempt laws, Her Ladyship can act, safe in the knowledge she won't be publicly vilified. Anonymous. Androgynous. Revered—or, if not that, then at least respected. Her word is, literally, law.

She is laying out instructions to the jury now. High on her throne, above the banks of the lawyers, the lawyers, the police, she is stipulating how they must behave.

"You mustn't put anything on social media or respond to anything on the internet in any way about this trial. You mustn't go looking up people involved in this trial on Facebook. And don't go on the internet looking for information. Please ignore any media reports you might have come across inadvertently." A pause here, and I want to laugh because how can they disregard the news? "It is imperative you are not influenced and that you make your decision, for which you have taken an oath, entirely on the evidence you hear in this court."

The jurors are attentive; only the shambolic student in the back row, a mountain of a man with a greasy fringe he keeps flicking from his eyes, seems unimpressed by her directions. A woman in the front row in a too-tight jacket stares with open suspicion, and I stare back, just a little defiant. *She doesn't look as good as she does in the photos*, I imagine her thinking, and I hate caring that this is the case. I've lost over twelve pounds in the past six months; my hair is falling out in clumps; I've noticeably aged. Inevitably, I imagine her wondering: *Is it guilt that's made her look like this?*

In front of me, the lawyers wait: the prosecution to my left, the defense to my right. Judge Costa is still talking, her clipped voice quiet and authoritative as she finishes the housekeeping and discusses the hours the court will keep. Ten thirty to one, she tells them; then two to four fifteen. My lawyer has already warned me that the days will stretch interminably, the pressure of concentrating exhausting. The judge, schoolmarmish and stern, repeats this warning. "You will find them quite long enough because you will be required to pay close attention," she says.

"Now, Miss Jackson." She inclines her head toward the prosecuting counsel, Sonja Jackson, the back of whose wig I stare at intently.

A stately woman, she takes her time in rising, and though it may only be a couple of seconds, while she arranges her notes and takes a preliminary sip from her glass of water, those seconds stretch. It's all part of an act. Let your audience wait. Tease them with anticipation so that they'll be poised to listen to your every word.

A slight coughing fit from one of the jurors. Miss Jackson waits until he has stopped. Until the courtroom is free from rustles and tics and murmurs. As close to silence as it will ever be.

"This is a charge of murder," she says, and her voice is low and commanding, a voice imbued with the gravity of the situation. "This is a case that concerns the death of a man called Michael, or Mike, Stokes."

Twenty-Five

8 DECEMBER 2021

CAROLINE

Caroline is getting ready for bed when Emma calls, 10:35 p.m. She wouldn't usually pick up at this time, but a phone call, instead of a text, means that something is urgent.

Still. David's already in bed, and she's sitting on the edge of it, moisturizing her calves. It's important to keep some boundaries.

"It's a bit late," she begins.

It's clear at once that something is up. Emma is making a strange gulping noise, as if she is trying to keep things together: percussive, guttural, more animal than human. When she finally speaks, her words flow too fast.

"Are you okay?" Caroline asks, though that's a stupid question because clearly she's not, and her distress feels contagious. "Slow down: I can't understand."

The torrent begins again. A jumble of words rattled off at a high pitch. *Flora. Sorry. Contact. Injury. Police.*

"Police?"

"The police are here. I've been trying Flora since eight. Her phone's off. I need to explain." Four staccato facts are machine-gunned out.

"Flora's in bed. Everything's fine," says Caroline, though everything is very much not fine: Flora was as distressed this evening as she's ever seen her. She presses her palm against her forehead as if to smooth out her thoughts. She needs to help fix whatever has happened, but it's impossible with Emma speaking like this. "Slow down. Start from the beginning. Please."

More slowly now, but in the same high-pitched voice that threatens to career off at any moment, Emma manages to relay the bare, horrifying facts.

"I came home and found Mike Stokes in the house. He'd got in somehow—and he, he'd fallen down the stairs."

"Are you okay? You're not hurt?" Caroline concentrates on keeping her voice calm and low. But even now she is busy calculating what this will mean for Flora, already sufficiently distraught about her police caution and frantic about news of it leaking. If the police have been called about Mike breaking into Emma's London house, will they be able to keep that from emerging, too?

"I'm fine," Emma is saying now. "Well, of course I'm not fine. It . . . it was fucking awful." And here her voice cracks and she is crying now, properly crying. Caroline's heart clutches: Emma doesn't cry and rarely swears.

The bed creaks as David turns toward her inquiringly. She shakes her head: she needs to focus on what Emma's saying.

"I'm so sorry. What do you mean he'd fallen down the stairs?"

"He's okay. Well, he's not okay. He's in the hospital and he's unconscious, but I hope he'll be okay." A great gulp of breath as if she is steeling herself. "But . . . but when I entered the house, I found him in the kitchen—at the bottom of the stairs. He'd been drinking. The hallway was wet. There's been torrential rain. The police think he got in somehow. They think he wanted to look through my things—and then he must have slipped.

"I need to speak to Flora," Emma carries on, the words still pouring from her as if she needs to rush out all this information at once. "But her phone seems to be off, and I can't leave a message like this."

"Of course not," Caroline says. She's surprised Emma hadn't called David or her first. This isn't the sort of news Flora should receive unfiltered. And though, of course, she's concerned for Emma, her priority is her stepdaughter, who has had quite enough to deal with thanks to her mother being in the public eye and, frankly, knowing this man.

"Her phone's in the kitchen," she says, dealing with Emma's immediate demand, though she is preoccupied, trying to make sense of everything, though it feels like something is missing, a key detail just outside her peripheral vision. "We agreed she wouldn't have it in her bedroom. Why don't you FaceTime her on my iPad first thing in the morning?"

"I don't want her to hear it from anyone else."

"She won't. She's having such trouble getting to sleep, we have to wake her at seven at the moment." Of course, Emma, not being here on week-days, won't know that. "She won't have heard anything by then. Anyway, are you sure it will be picked up that soon?"

"I don't know." Emma's answer comes out as a sigh. "Yes. I expect so." She seems resigned to it, or perhaps exhausted. She might behave as if she is invincible, her pride preventing her from ever asking anyone for help, but she sounds properly scared. It's no wonder. The *Chronicle*'s snatched photographs were bad enough, and the knowledge that Mike knew all about Flora. But discovering Mike was stalking her to the ex-tent he'd broken into her house? Caroline shudders. She can't imagine anything worse.

"Is it safe for you to stay there?" She is suddenly struck by the practi-calities of what's happened. "Where are you staying?"

"We're being allowed back in after the police finish up." Emma gives an odd, dissonant laugh. "It's not as if he's going to get in again. There's a police officer outside his hospital door."

"Oh, Emma." The enormity of it builds like a sustained crescendo. "Do they know how he got in?"

"No. There's no sign of a forced entry, so they think the cleaner might have let him in."

"And all three of you are staying there together?"

"Yes. Claire's been really supportive. Julia . . ." A deep sigh at the end of the phone. "Well, she's been a bit more difficult."

"Difficult?"

"She got back soon after me, so she's understandably a bit more shaken. But yes, we'll all be staying here."

They talk a little longer, Caroline repeating her reassurance that she'll make sure Flora doesn't look at any news websites before seven; Emma confirming that, yes, she has contacted PLaIT.

"I hope you manage to get some sleep," Caroline says, and she realizes it's perhaps the most genuine conversation they've had for four years.

"I doubt it—but thank you," says Emma, her voice just held by a thread of despair.

———————

David remains silent as Caroline switches off the phone. To be fair, he's quiet at the best of times, but there's an intensity to his silence that means he is working up to saying something. He lies back on the pillows, his hands behind his head.

"This is going to be dire, isn't it?" he says eventually. She remains silent. He's clearly heard Emma's end of the conversation, and his question doesn't require an answer. She is just wondering how they can try to soften the impact on their fourteen-year-old girl.

"Does it strike you as a bit odd?" He looks at her. "Him being in the house?"

She has started smoothing shea butter into her hands: caressing her long pianist's fingers, working the cream into the cuticles. "Oh, I don't think so," she says. "It's the sort of thing journalists on his paper do, isn't it? Think of the lengths they've stooped to already. We already knew he was pretty ruthless. That he wasn't bothered about breaking the law."

"You didn't like him, did you?"

"There was nothing to like." She pauses, weighing her words, trying to be fair. After all, the man *is* in the hospital. "Perhaps that's unkind, but I thought him rude. Dismissive. I could absolutely see him muscling his way in."

David rolls toward her, his face still troubled.

"Christ. What a hideous thing to happen."

"I know." She climbs into bed, lies back against the pillows.

"Emma's going to hate this being in the papers."

"I imagine—I *hope*—there'll be a huge amount of sympathy for them. Three female MPs experiencing a male journalist breaking into their home? It must have been absolutely terrifying." She gives a little shiver: not for the first time relieved she has a strong man in her bed—someone she would send into the house first if they were ever broken into.

He is silent again, and she senses he's wrestling with whether to articulate something.

"What are you thinking?" She helps him out.

"I don't know." He pauses. "I mean: Emma's hugely honest, isn't she? I can't remember her ever lying, but I just keep wondering how I would behave if I found him in my house. I don't think I could possibly be civil. I'd feel quite violently toward him—and I'm never violent. I'm not a violent man."

"What are you saying?" She looks at him, wide-eyed. Wasn't he listening? "She found him at the *bottom* of the stairs. He'd already fallen down there. He was unconscious. They didn't have any conversation at all."

He looks at her directly, his gaze sharp, his eyes—his best feature, the thing that had most attracted her to him—a clear, hard blue. "Do you believe her?"

"Yes, I do. Absolutely!" She is emphatic as the shock of him suggesting this runs through her. "She's scrupulously honest. Painfully so." She thinks of Emma's outrage when David told her about their relationship. It was their deception for those few short weeks between him embarking on their affair and telling Emma their marriage was over that had shocked her the most, and that had taken her the longest to get over. It was as if she didn't believe they could have lied.

And Emma couldn't have lied now—could she?

"David." She props herself up on her left elbow so that she has the slight physical upper hand. "I think Emma's fundamentally incapable of lying." He looks at her, somewhat doubtful, and she holds his gaze.

"But irrespective of that, for her sake and, most importantly, for *Flora's*, we don't have an option. We *have* to believe what she says."

Twenty-Six

9 DECEMBER 2021

EMMA

"Emma?" The letter box clatters shut, then scrapes open. "Emma? Claire? How are you both feeling this morning?"

The camera crews and a straggle of snappers have been outside my house since first light. I resisted leaving at my usual time, preoccupied after speaking to Flora and needing to ready myself for the reaction in Westminster. Now, at 8:30, it's clear that was a massive mistake.

It's obvious that this will be immense. When Julia left around seven, tight-lipped and refusing to acknowledge the media's presence, the story was being mentioned on the early bulletins, but there were few details. Now the press has gleaned that it was *I* who discovered an intruder in our house.

Somehow the news has leaked out. Through the police? Perhaps through Kate Buckby, a friend of Julia's and a Labour backbencher who trumpeted the story on Twitter last night? *Intruder breaks into home of 3 women MPs: "When will our security be taken seriously?"* Someone wants it to be known that it was *I* who came across Mike, though their identity remains unknown. And as if by osmosis, the knowledge is spreading. Because why else would these questions be being directed specifically at me?

"Emma? Can you tell us how you feel?" The voice coils through the letter box: sinuous, winsome. "We just want to chat to you."

Deep and male, it's another form of intrusion: stretching toward me, demanding that I react.

I race up the stairs, knowing his eyes, framed by the letter box, will be watching my departing heels, calves, and thighs; will be noting the fact I

131

fled from future comment. I sidle upstairs to Claire's bedroom, move to the window, and watch them watching us.

"They're talking about it now." Claire points to her laptop, where the ITV reporter I can see below gestures earnestly at the house as he delivers his piece to the camera: his expression animated, his cheeks pink from the biting cold.

"We understand that, after the scene was examined for several hours last night, the three MPs were able to return," he is telling the anchor in the studio, as if he's imparting some insider knowledge rather than information he must have gained from a Metropolitan Police briefing. "But though we believe two of the women, Emma Webster and Claire Scott, are still inside, no one has offered a comment so far."

"Anything new online?" I ask Claire, my eyes fixed on her laptop screen. "Why is he bothering to comment on our saying nothing?"

"Has to fill airtime?"

"I know—but it makes us sound unhelpful." I move away from the window to peer over her shoulder. "Why should we have to talk to the press about something this traumatic at all?

She flicks to the *Guardian* rolling news blog, then to the BBC website. "They're still running with 'a forty-two-year-old man.'"

My stomach contracts, the nest of snakes that have coiled there since I opened the door last night and found the alarm hadn't been set knotting even tighter. That line's not going to hold once Mike fails to arrive at work. I need to get to the Commons to discuss this with Harry and other colleagues before Mike's name is leaked. And yet, to do that, I have to brave the swelling media clustered around the bottom of our steps.

Claire's phone vibrates, and she glances at a text, gives a small nod of approval.

"Cab's a minute away. All set?"

She has her coat on already, grabs her bag, is primed to confront the pack of seven or eight reporters now circling outside our door. I turn back to the window as a sedan sweeps into the square and waits, its engine running. The pack—all men bar one young woman who's not quite part of their gang—turns to the house, their faces alight with anticipation, craning to see when we will emerge.

It is a taste of what's to come, and once we're outside, the surge of bodies—phones thrust into our faces, mikes invading our space, broad male shoulders jostling around us—makes me flinch despite my telling myself I mustn't. Claire grabs my right hand and tugs me along.

"Emma—how are you feeling this morning?"

"Can you tell us what happened?"

"Emma, Sky here: it must have been terrifying for you?" The man is so close I can smell the cigarettes on his breath.

"ITV News, Emma. A horrific ordeal. Good you're all okay. A quick word for the camera?"

I turn to the last speaker, a political correspondent I recognize, and give him a look that says: *Please—leave me alone.* Later the image will be played on what feels like a never-ending loop, and my expression is pure rabbit-in-the-headlights. Like a cornered animal, I can't help but semaphore my fear.

"Okay?" Claire asks as I collapse in the back of the Uber and the driver pulls away at some speed. Her soft features seem to have sharpened this morning: there are dark smudges under her eyes because she, too, has failed to sleep properly. She sat up with me until one; found me shortly after six, rooted at the bottom of the stairs; staring at the spot where he'd lain.

"I handled that badly." I chew at the inside of my mouth. "I should have said something—but I felt under attack. My God. What are they going to think?"

She shrugs. "Don't worry about them. Everyone who matters is concerned. Look—" And she flicks between the parliamentary Labour WhatsApp group and the Labour women's group, reading out a steady stream of support.

I can't help fearing this is just the beginning, that she's being naive in thinking we can dismiss them. She must sense I'm unconvinced because she takes my hand in her tiny palm and grips it until it almost hurts.

"There's nothing you need to explain," she says, her expression fierce, her conviction intense, and I feel the most immense gratitude that she doesn't doubt me. "There's nothing you need to account for at all."

The atmosphere's calmer when we arrive at the Commons. The taxi drops us in New Palace Yard, where we are safe from the possibility of being chased by camera crews. Still, we're stopped by three or four MPs on our way to our office, and it's clear it's not a morning in which we will achieve much work.

"Oh my God. Are you okay?" Jazz guides me to my desk as if I'm an elderly constituent who's had a bad fall. "The phone's been ringing off the hook. So many people are worried—and there've been loads of requests for interviews. Will you be putting out a statement?"

"I don't know." I shake my head, as if by doing so I'll think more clearly. "What's everyone saying?" I've avoided Twitter during our journey, but now I log on to my computer, fearful that Mike's identity—which will lead the press to muse on his connection to me—has leaked out.

"They're overwhelmingly sympathetic. Nobody's being snippy—oh, and Harry's office just called. He wants to see you straightaway, and then the Speaker wants to talk to you."

"The Speaker?"

"Maybe he's going to announce a new review of security?"

I nod. This really doesn't look great for the parliamentary authorities.

"The BBC have called. ITN. Sky." She ticks the news channels off on her manicured fingers. "I told them you weren't talking to anyone at the moment, just as you said."

"Thanks." I sit down at my desk, already overwhelmed at the thought of how I'll deal with this. The memory of Mike—railing at the bottom of the stairs after he recovered consciousness, then being stretchered off to the hospital—rears against me, and I tamp it straight back down. I've so much to do, I can't allow myself to think about how he is yet, though I'm desperate to call the police to check on his condition. At the same time, I feel furious that he put us in this position, having broken into our house. The different Mikes I've known coalesce: collaborator, colleague, friend, lover, *stalker*, threat. Warm eyes smiling at me over a Soho table, cold ones in Victoria Tower Gardens. Which Mike will emerge if—no, *when*, because I have to try to be positive—he recovers from this?

Jazz is still chattering on. I'd called her as soon as we'd seen Kate Buckby's tweet last night and filled her in on what had happened; decided that, since Mike had been arrested, a strict no-interview approach was the one we should take. Now I wonder how long this will stick. On the BBC News website, our break-in is still a small story, but there's an ominous "more to follow," while on the *Mirror*'s rolling blog, and the *Guardian*'s, momentum builds. Has Julia been spinning to distance herself from me? The one consistent detail being accurately reported is that *I* came across the intruder, and *Julia* alerted the emergency services. "BREAKING NEWS," shouts the *Mirror*: "Intruder discovered by revenge porn MP. Housemate called the police."

On the news wires, there's plenty of coverage of my work in opposing revenge porn, with opinion pieces I'd written for the *Chronicle* quoted at length. And the hacks have picked up on the fact we've all campaigned against sexual violence—and that I've been particularly outspoken. *Did intruder target MP campaigning against revenge porn? Did intruder target all three female MPs?*

But the story's very confused. For the next thirty hours, it will run in diverse directions as reporters fly with different theories. *Intruder was dressed in balaclava. Possible link to high-profile robberies. Police probe terror motive. Was intruder planning acid attack?* My eye snags on this one—and I am back in the hallway: the fear that someone would spring out at me and fling acid in my face absolutely all-consuming. Has some detective from South Hants leaked details of my acid-threat letter?

I scroll faster now, searching for the hashtag #EmmaWebster, then the key words "MP" and "Intruder"; barely listening to Jazz's list of friends and colleagues who have called again and again. It is only a matter of time before Mike's name gets out—and the story catches even more fiercely, the flames that are licking around us bursting into a fierce blaze.

And here it is. The thing I have feared—in case it leads to the revelation I slept with the man and, from that, to the fact he was investigating Flora—announced in less than 140 characters by ITV:

"Breaking news: MPs intruder was tabloid journalist."

Twenty-Seven

9 DECEMBER 2021

EMMA

"So you know him? He's the reporter you've been collaborating with?"

"Yes, but that makes it even more frightening. He's a reporter whose paper's trolled me by running an unflattering photo of me—and now he's broken into my home."

"Of course." Harry Godwin clears his throat and glances at Duncan White, his aide, as if unsure of how to handle this. The Labour leader is wary of women, and given my criticism of him in that *Guardian* interview, our relationship is somewhat strained.

Still, he's obviously concerned. Three of his female MPs have had their home broken into by a male tabloid reporter, the police are involved, and the intruder remains unconscious. The shock of it keeps coming at me in ripples: or, more, like rogue waves that catch me out when I least expect it. I think I'm behaving rationally, but then I'll snap, just as I did with Harry. Here, in the Leader of the Opposition's office, I'm ambushed by the enormity of what's occurred.

"You'll be aware that I collaborated with Michael Stokes on a story sparked by the death of my constituent," I manage at last, and it's a relief that my voice sounds calm, though my heart is flurrying so fast I wonder if I'm experiencing some kind of heart condition. "We succeeded in getting the Online Harms Bill altered, which was quite a coup. But I have no idea why he was in our home. I would *never* invite a contact there." I gesture to Julia, joining us because she contacted the police. "My—our—experience has been terrifying."

"Well, quite," he says.

"I think it's impossible to understate quite how horrific this experience has been," Julia adds. "I came home to discover this *journalist*"—she says the word with palpable contempt—"at the bottom of the stairs with Emma crouched over him. The police think he'd charmed our cleaner to inveigle his way in. He'd been drinking heavily at a Christmas lunch, and he'd been in Emma's bedroom . . ." I shudder as she says this, imagining his hands spilling through my lingerie, pulling out my drawers. "The police think that, given that the hallway was wet with rainwater, he must have slipped and fallen down the stairs."

She goes on to detail her horror and her quick-wittedness in calling 999. There's no mention that she dismissed my concerns about security the night before; instead she stresses that all three of us had been worried about it for quite some time.

"I think this should serve as a wake-up call for the whole political establishment," she says. "The risks MPs—and particularly, it saddens me to admit, *female* MPs—run on a daily basis are now unacceptable given the level of security we're afforded. I'd ask you, Harry, to press the Speaker for another review of security, and to call for tighter controls on the press. Of course, we need a cultural change—a whole shift in how people behave toward MPs on social media, even without addressing the issue of sexual harassment and specifically stalking—but in the meantime we need better protection for MPs like Emma who are subjected to extreme misogyny. This *man*"—she spits the word—"this *journalist* might have *seemed* innocuous, but he was clearly absolutely fixated with her."

"Oh, I'm not sure we know that," I begin, because the last thing I want is for Julia to intimate our relationship was anything other than professional.

"Emma: he broke into our home," she spells it out. "Now either he was doing that because he was investigating you for a story—and his paper had already hounded you, they clearly thought they were onto something"—she gives me a hard stare—"or, having collaborated with you on the Amy's Law campaign, he was obsessed with you and, when drunk—because I could smell the alcohol coming off him, Harry—he broke in to tell you this. Either way, what he did was illegal, and intensely frightening. This was *our* home. *Our* sanctuary. It should have been a place we could feel safe."

I nod, unable to speak, consumed by self-pity. It *was* my sanctuary. The one place, in a world where I so often felt hounded, that I could drop my guard. I'm so grateful to Julia for articulating this: for behaving like the ally I need, and that I haven't felt she's recently been. There is something about someone else spelling this out that validates my reaction when I entered the house, that reassures me I *wasn't* being irrational in experiencing such intense fear. My throat tightens and my eyes burn. I am back in the hallway, wondering if I am imagining the creak of the floorboards or if my worst nightmare is about to be realized; back to seeing his body. I meet Harry's eye and can only nod.

The Leader of the Opposition clears his throat, and his manner seems softer now, more unconditionally supportive. He values Julia, a member of his close-knit frontbench team, who has always been loyal, and he is sympathetic to her and, by extension, me. As we leave, he reaches to shake my hand, then clasps it firmly in both of his. Harry at his most intense, his most empathetic, is not something I've previously experienced, but I feel almost tearfully relieved.

"I want you to know," he says, his tone studiedly sincere, "that this was totally unacceptable, and I support you wholeheartedly."

The morning is filled with phone calls and meetings. Julia goes back to Cleaver Square to discuss improved security arrangements with officers from PLaIT, and I talk to the London mayor and the Speaker. At around eleven, I manage to squeeze in a phone call to my ex-husband, since Flora is constantly on my mind.

She was almost hysterical when I FaceTimed her at seven; then, after her initial reaction, she seemed to shut down: her answers nearly all monosyllabic, her expression pinched. I doubt she's made it into school, or rather to the isolation unit she's supposed to have been attending since Monday, after her school suspended her for two weeks.

"She's at home with me." David's voice is guarded; she is clearly in the room. I hear him move around the house to talk more openly. "Well . . ." A long, heartfelt sigh. "She's done her usual thing of clamming up, but, you know, she's not holed up in her room; she wants to be around me, even asked for a hug—so that's a good thing." There's a lengthy pause, but the atmosphere's not hostile, and as my heart yearns for Flo, I'm grateful for his familiarity down the line. His tone softens. "How are you? Is it as bad as it looks with the press?"

"Oh, you know . . ." And a memory comes at me again, another image that blindsides me: of Mike's body, crumpled; of a wound that glistened under my flashlight's beam. My chest tightens, and my heart repeats that scurried beating that frightens me, being so out of sync. How am I? Pretty bloody furious that Mike broke into our home—and the impact that's had not just on me but on my daughter, too. Anxious about his condition, and what happens next. Dumbfounded—because I still can't process why he thought he could do this. Another flurry of heartbeats, and I press my hand against my ribs, as if by doing so, I can still my heart. I can't articulate any of this.

"The home secretary's office is on the line," Jazz whispers, and it's a relief not to have to explain this but to finish the call instead.

But Greg Collins, the home secretary, wants to hear what happened from me, too. And so, despite him being briefed by the Met Police, I repeat the account I gave to the officers yesterday, laying out each fact like cards from a deck.

I tell him how I opened my front door, concerned that the alarm hadn't been set and the light was off; how, because of this, I feared someone was inside; how I then discovered what I thought initially was a jumble of clothes, but realized, with a keening horror, was a body at the bottom of the stairs.

And despite my attempts to keep this clinical, I am back there: heart banging so fiercely against my ribs I was sure it was audible as I crept down the hallway, listening out for creaking boards and knowing, from the texture of the silence, that I wasn't alone. "Hello," I called out. "Is anybody there?"

"As I understand it," Greg Collins says, "Michael Stokes remains under arrest?"

"Yes." I try not to think of Mike in a hospital bed: still unconscious, according to the news feeds I keep constantly refreshing. Nor of his boy, Josh, who might become fatherless because of this.

"And you're okay?"

And the simplicity of the inquiry, posed by someone so senior, strikes me abruptly like a football flung at my chest. No, I am very far from okay. But I can hardly admit this to a man who holds one of the four great offices of state. The home secretary knows me as someone capable of changing the law. An effective campaigner, an assiduous politician, willing to defy the Twitter trolls and my political opponents in the Chamber to discuss something as deeply uncomfortable as revenge porn. A grown-up in a world where there are surprisingly few of them. What will he think if I reveal my vulnerability?

Besides, it's not in the culture. When the 2017 Westminster terrorist attack occurred, MPs were offered counseling. I heard that few took up the offer. You had to organize it yourself, and frankly no one had the time. It also smacked of self-indulgence. For someone with constituents barely subsisting, or living with the daily horror of domestic violence, trotting off for therapy would have seemed like self-absorption. I was elected the following year, but had I been an MP, I'd have brushed the idea aside.

"Emma?" Greg Collins has realized I'm distracted. He's a nice man: the father of two daughters, both a similar age to Flora, who I doubt he sees enough of. A people's politician in a party led by a narcissist. Too center-right to be home secretary for very long. But does he really want an honest answer?

"I'm okay," I say, in part because that's the answer he's expecting, in part because I need to convince myself. "Or at least, I'll be okay."

———————

The news that our intruder was a journalist has given the story fresh legs—particularly since the *Standard* is sufficiently confident it's correct to plaster it across its front page. The *Chronicle* barely mentions the story, and the BBC remains circumspect about the unexplained presence of a journalist in the home of three female MPs.

But the story of extreme tabloid intrusion is too intriguing for the broadsheets and other broadcasters to ignore. The headlines spool across the bottom of the TV monitor in my office—*Tabloid man found unconscious in MPs' home*; *Reporter in the hospital after invading women MPs' home*; *Tabloid journalist breaks into home of three female MPs*—briefly interspersed with other headlines but returning with increasing regularity. Could something positive come of this? Might it be a tipping point? The moment we finally acknowledge the press and public have gone too far in hounding public figures—politicians, celebrities, *royalty*, because it's impossible not to think of Harry and Meghan—in person and on social media?

Over on College Green, TV crews have pitched gazebos and are questioning my most media-savvy colleagues. *I can't discuss this while a police investigation is ongoing* remains my response to requests for interviews because the last thing I want is to jeopardize proceedings if Mike stands trial for breaking in. I keep wondering how he is. My hands, hovering over my keyboard, tremble: another wave of shock and exhaustion lapping at me. I turn up the TV's volume. Turns out that there's no need for me to be relaying each detail because, while Jazz and I hide in my office, my colleagues are happily providing a commentary some five hundred yards away.

Against the honeyed backdrop of the House of Commons, David Lloyd-Brown, the influential chair of the Digital, Culture, Media and Sport select committee, is holding forth about the "toothless" regulatory powers against the press, nine years after the phone-hacking scandal. The *Guardian* has already published a comment piece about a "broiling media crisis," and Sky's media correspondent is asking any politician he can get his hands on if "the tabloid press has gone too far?"

There's no shortage of MPs willing to share their own experiences of trolling, stalking, or social media intrusion. Cora James, a relatively new Tory backbencher, reveals she had to take out a restraining order against an overattentive constituent and details her fear so vividly that I make a note to email her my support. Male MPs voice their strong concerns. But when Dennis Armitage, a former Labour home office minister, describes me as an "unlikely have-a-go heroine," showing "pluck and determination" when confronted by this man, the BBC anchor, Olivia Edwards, picks him up.

"But there's no indication Emma Webster confronted him in any way? As I understand it, she arrived to find him injured, having fallen down some stairs?" She turns to the camera. "We must stress that the police have made no suggestion that there was an altercation, and that the intruder, whom BBC News is not naming for legal reasons, remains in the hospital under police guard."

"Any idea why he's saying that?" I ask Jazz.

"Nope. Everyone knows he's not with it these days. Remember that meme of him falling asleep in the Chamber. Why?" She looks up from her screen, and I worry that she's watching me quizzically.

"I just don't like people making things up."

The phone rings. "Duncan White for you." She transfers the call.

"Emma." Harry's adviser's tone is curt. "We're sending a press officer round. You need to make a statement on this. We'll keep it all legal, but given the interest, it's untenable to keep silent and refuse to engage at all."

"I can't face being on camera." I think of this morning's scrum: the camera flashes, the reporter's breath, the feverish pack. *Well, what are you going to do about it?* I'm going to hide away because I don't like where the story's heading.

"Just make a short statement, and we'll make it clear you're not taking questions. Agreed?"

———

With the help of a press officer, I draft a brief statement confirming I experienced a break-in but going into few details. As suggested, I stand outside St. Stephen's Entrance, scene of many a leadership challenge and telegenic resignation, to face the throngs of reporters primed for the latest twist in the tale.

"Over here, Emma."

"Can you look this way, love?"

Quietly, I do as I'm asked. I want to get this over with quickly, in part because the temperature's near freezing, the air crisp and sharp as daylight leaches away. I'm wearing a wool maxi coat, and I can't stop shivering, the cold seeping through the thin soles of my shoes and biting at my fingers as I clutch my piece of paper, dusk blanketing me as the photographers' flashes flare. Opposite, the windows of Westminster Abbey glitter gold; to my left, the river is strung with lights. It should feel festive—a Richard

Curtis version of a London Christmas—and yet, even here, in the heart of the capital, a bleak midwinter has us firmly in her grip. The paving stones shimmer with a crystalline frost; my breath forms ephemeral puffs; the raw cold obliterates the smell of exhaust and purifies the air. But I don't find it bracing; instead it all feels too heightened. As if my senses have been overstimulated and all my usual reactions have stepped up a gear.

And in the footage broadcast later that night, I look pinched; swamped by my coat, bought in October in the hope it would look smart for any outdoor broadcasts about the forthcoming Online Harms Bill; embarrassed that I appear a frightened woman when what I want to convey is my rage. In a too-small voice, I confirm I came home to discover an intruder; that I have been shaken by the experience, will be making no further statements, and would appreciate some space.

There's a flash of cameras, a wave of cries.

"Emma—how well did you know the man?"

I turn away, my heart pounding—*What do they know? Why do they ask that?*—but refusing to react as desired.

The press officer puts up his hand as if stopping traffic, and I rush inside where the chief whip, Anne Wright—tall, blonde, austere—gives me a curt nod. I did well not to be drawn; now I need to remain quiet about it. "Let's hope the police resolve this quickly," she says, and her tone is grim.

But I should have known that a three-line statement would never be enough. That what the media wanted to see and hear was a display of intense anxiety. That, while the press is being ripped to shreds on live TV, it seeks validation and must acquire this through the sort of fast-changing, emotive story that will excite its readers and viewers and have them panting for more. That a woman in the public eye must cooperate with those who've promoted her in the past—and that because I've forgotten this crucial part of the contract, the press will turn against me. That, by refusing to pander to them, I have only made them more determined to find out what went on.

By early evening, everyone, even the cautious BBC, is naming Mike and running with the story that my intruder was a reporter with whom

I had collaborated on stories. I didn't feed the media beast, and so it has become more ravenous, and now it has turned.

Just before 7 p.m., Julia comes into my office. Jazz has popped out to make some tea and, left alone for the first time that day, I am close to crying. I press my knuckles to my eyes as the words swim on the screen.

"Thank you for speaking to Harry," I say, feeling a swell of warmth. "He listens to you, and I was explaining myself badly. I really appreciate your flagging the security issue."

"Not a problem."

My words rush from me. "And I'm really grateful you recognize it was a big deal, that you acknowledged I'd been properly scared."

"Well, I was clearly wrong not to do so earlier, wasn't I?" she says, a hint of acid in her tone. "Rather unfortunate this had to happen to prove you right."

"We should *all* have moved out earlier." My voice is too high: I sound strident and hysterical, caught out by the emotion of the day. I concentrate on becoming calmer and more conciliatory. She was with me, waiting for the ambulance to arrive, and she *saw* how terrified I was. There's no reason for her to be harsh: she was shaken herself. "None of us should have experienced this."

"Well, I think we all agree on that," she says dryly. Her lips have narrowed into a thin line, the telltale sign of her disapproval, and it takes all my self-control not to retaliate because Julia isn't being just passive-aggressive, but also rather unfair.

She *was* unsympathetic, and my fears *were* valid—so why is she behaving so coldly?

And as she leaves, I can't help feeling deeply unsettled: as if I've made a fundamental error in further alienating a one-time friend.

Twenty-Eight

10 DECEMBER 2021

FLORA

She's been crying again.

Flora watches her mum when she returns from the bathroom in her constituency office, noting her red-rimmed eyes, the fact she's been in there too long. Now she's using her perky voice as she chats to Patrick and Sue. The one that exclaims over the messages of support that have been flooding in, the emails and cards added to the tally of thank-you notes pinned above her desk. The one that tells Flora that everything is going to be absolutely okay.

Nothing is okay. Nothing has been okay since Flora sent Seb Frinton the Leah photo and Seb messaged: *Who the fuck IS this?* For one long month, anxiety has been pressing down on her chest. At moments, she's felt completely crushed, the weight perhaps at its most intense when she received the caution from the police (and the shame of that memory still makes her want to vomit). But then the *Chronicle* printed that picture of her mum, and her mum failed to win round Mike Stokes. (Her parents think she doesn't know, but of course she eavesdropped on their conversation when her mum went round to discuss it.) But nothing, absolutely nothing, has stressed her out as much as learning that her mum found Mike Stokes at the bottom of the stairs.

She reacted badly to the news. "Hysterical" was how Emma put it when she FaceTimed yesterday morning to tell Flora about it, and about the police's involvement. *Please don't be hysterical, sweetheart.* But what did she expect? The reporter who had been stalking her mum, who was pressuring her to talk about what she, Flora, had done to Leah, was in the hospital after falling down the stairs at her mum's London home. ("Still unconscious," her dad told Caroline last night, and he'd looked particularly grim.) It's been on the news, and now that policeman, PC Berwick, has called—and her mum's been crying again. Perhaps Mike's still unconscious? Would that really be so bad? Is it wrong to hope he stays that way?

She doesn't think her mum has *any idea* what it's been like: knowing there are people willing—no, *eager*—to hurt her mum; knowing, too, that Mike's paper has been actively stalking her. Flora may no longer be allowed a smartphone, but her laptop gives her access to social media and all the twisted things men say they want to do to her mum—rape her, cut her, lynch her—deep into the night.

Obviously she hasn't been to school. Now that her two-week suspension has ended, she's supposed to be going to the isolation block—for kids with behavioral or mental health issues because that's a *really* good mix; it was a choice between this or expulsion and homeschooling—but she can hardly go when everyone will be discussing what's happened to her mum. Which means she's had more time to scroll through the news stories and the comments below the line. Reading what everyone's thinking about Emma, the doubts and suspicions—*What was he doing in her house in the first place? Bet the whore invited him in. She just "discovered" him, did she? Slut. Fucking cunt*—until doing so has felt like some sort of sick addiction.

At least she's ahead of the curve. Her mum's given up trying to shield her from the news. How can she when there were camera crews outside their home this morning, and Flora came down to discover her listening to BBC *Breakfast* news *and* Radio 4's *Today*? The way Flora sees it, she's gaining the maximum information to try to protect her. Because isn't knowledge power?

At least she's got her home now. It doesn't look as if she'll be going back to London anytime soon. Not while the security at Cleaver Square is so bad (and the place has always given her the creeps—all those trees in the square where someone could hide and spring out at you). Not while the press is still hanging around the house. Flora had tried to convey her relief at her staying here, but her mum got defensive. "It's not as if I'm hiding from them. I mean look!" She'd gestured at a local reporter approaching the constituency office. "I've even got them here!"

Flora goes to her now, while she sits at her desk, and rests her head on top of her head, puts her arm around her shoulders. She wants to cling to her, just like when she was little and had to be in the after-school program: when she would count down the minutes before being picked up at the end of the day. When Emma arrived, Flora would cling to her like a limpet: arms tight around her waist; face buried in her stomach, hiding from the other kids, who happily continued playing and thought her behavior weird. She didn't care; or rather, the need to show her mum quite how much she hated this separation overruled this. Embarrassment mattered less than being left.

"You okay, darling?" her mum asks now.

She shrugs, because of course she isn't. They both know that.

Her mum wrinkles her nose at her in a *sorry this is horrible* sort of way, then pretends to go back to working through her emails before flicking straight back over to the *Guardian*'s rolling news blog. Better to be honest, really. To accept that all everyone in this room is thinking about—even Patrick, trying to find emergency accommodation for a victim of domestic violence—is how Mike Stokes is.

And then her mum's phone rings again, and Flora watches her expression as she glances at the name of the caller and answers immediately.

"Yes," she says in that serious tone she uses when a senior politician calls—they've already had the shadow home secretary on the phone—or the police. Then the color drains from her face completely like a Popsicle with the juice sucked from it. "Thank you for telling me," she says, and then, in a quieter tone, "Yes, of course. I see."

She switches the phone off very deliberately and pauses for a moment before she meets their eyes: Patrick, off the phone now, and staring at her behind the finger-smeared lenses of his glasses; Sue, in the process of making another round of coffees, a teaspoon of granules held midair; and Flora, who knows with pin-sharp certainty that this is another of those moments—like the moment when she sent the photo to Seb—when life changes completely, when the universe laughs at you like Charley Morris in the girls' bathroom. Because no matter how much she might want to prevent her mum from saying what she's about to say—and she wants this so desperately she imagines lunging at her to clamp her mouth shut—there is absolutely nothing she can do to stop it.

Twenty-Nine

10 DECEMBER 2021

EMMA

They're all looking at me, and I'm not sure how I can get the words out. Because right up until I answered the call from PC Berwick, I was praying for a different outcome. Right up until he said, "Ms. Webster," in that too-somber tone, I thought things might be okay.

"PC Berwick here again," he said, in a way that didn't fit the round-faced twentysomething who'd had the misfortune to be the first on the scene when Julia called emergency services.

It was his second call to me in an hour, and I knew, viscerally, that what he was about to tell me was going to change everything.

"I'm sorry to inform you that Michael Stokes hasn't recovered consciousness." A pause, and then he spelled the brutal fact out for me. "He died at St. Thomas' Hospital at 1:17 p.m."

I pressed the mobile to my ear so that the words couldn't seep out; kept my face turned away from the others, as if by doing so I could protect them, or as if, until I told them, this wouldn't become real.

"Ms. Webster?" he checked. "Did you hear me?"

But my body had let me down: my throat tightening so that I couldn't provide an adequate, let alone appropriate, response.

"Yes," I finally managed, and my tone was too abrupt, as if I was irritated by him calling. Then: "Thank you for telling me."

I give myself a second after finishing the call before turning to face the others.

"That was PC Berwick. He has some bad news, I'm afraid." I clear my throat because it's a struggle to get out the words none of them want to hear me say. "He said that Mike Stokes hasn't regained consciousness. I'm afraid that Mike Stokes is dead."

The three of them stare at me, but it's Flora I focus on. Even paler than usual, she vibrates with tension, her eyes wild with incomprehension.

I need to talk to her alone.

"Oh, Emma," says Sue. "I'm so sorry. What a terrible shock. Will you be wanting to say something?"

"Yes." My mind's gone blank. "Yes. I imagine I will."

"Well, there's no rush, is there?" She pauses, waves of sympathy emanating from her as she fiddles with her handbag, not knowing what advice to offer. "I think I'll take my lunch break now. Are you coming, Patrick?"

And after she gives him an uncharacteristically pointed look, they leave.

On the other side of the room, Flo has turned away, back hunched, shoulder blades poking like sharp wings through her sweater. It's the same spiky energy that signaled a meltdown when she was two or three.

The door has barely closed when she turns to me.

"Mum . . ." Her face is pink, her eyes too bright, and for a split second, she seems poised between tears and terrible, inappropriate laughter. "I know this sounds awful, but he can't get to you anymore, can he? Mummy"—and her voice is too high, sounds somehow manic—"maybe this means things will be okay?"

My chest is straitjacket tight. I can't quite take this in. In her childish optimism, she seems to think his death is beneficial. How have I managed to produce a child who could think this? I need to explain that no death can ever be good and, more immediately, to prepare her for the fact that things are going to get far worse. Because an intruder who breaks into the home of three MPs is one thing; an intruder who dies after doing so is quite another. There'll be a postmortem. Christ, there'll be a postmortem and the news story is going to run and run.

I can't allow myself to think of Mike's sixteen-year-old son, Josh, or his friends and colleagues, who will mourn him. I can't—I just *can't*—allow myself to think of Mike. It seems incredible that someone so energetic— in conversation; in bed; and, yes, even when he regained consciousness and was swearing at the paramedics—no longer exists. Forever etched in my memory, not as a man who, briefly, made me feel desired; not as a colleague with whom I shared jokey texts, numerous coffees, and a sense of common purpose; not as someone who then became frightening—but as a body, alien, lifeless, at the bottom of the stairs.

For a moment, I am back there: approaching him with trepidation, not knowing if he was alive or dead, only to feel a sense of reprieve when he gave a groan that signaled he was conscious. A sob burns my chest and bubbles up into my throat, but I swallow it down hard because I need to be the adult here.

"Flo, darling." I put a chair next to her and put my arms around her, feel her resistance ease as I pull her into a hug. "It's not a good thing that Mike has died—though it might feel like it, at the moment. But your relief, though it's perfectly natural, is not something you can ever admit to *anyone* else, okay?"

She nods, wide-eyed. I've spoken to her as if she were a far younger child, but she's responded to this, seems to welcome this guidance. She wriggles: my fingers are pressing too hard on her shoulders, and I release my grip.

"You've seen the press reaction in what happened so far, and they will become far more interested. For a bit, it will feel relentless, but I promise you we will be okay. These things have a limited shelf life. It will be really tough for the next forty-eight hours, perhaps a little more, and then everyone will get bored. They'll move on, I promise." I swallow. I don't believe this for a minute, but I need to take this gently, and I have to be positive for her sake.

She looks unconvinced, so I try a different tack.

"Do you remember when we tried surfing in the summer?"

She nods, like a small child craving reassurance.

"Remember how frightened we were initially, when the waves crashed over us and we had to be carried along? But then it was over, and it wasn't as bad as we'd thought? That huge wave broke, and the surf fizzled in the shallows, and we survived. We'd swallowed too much water, but we were basically okay—and it will be the same with this."

She gives me a watery smile as I pray that she doesn't remember that a heavy wave can also cause a wipeout. "Mum, you're shaking." She points to my knees, which have developed an involuntary tremor. My left hand quivers, and I shove it between my thighs.

"Well, it's been a bit of a shock," I say, sounding too bright and no-nonsense. "Do you want to grab a sandwich?" It's 2 p.m. now. I'd forgotten to suggest she get lunch.

"We could go for one together?"

"Oh, I'm sorry, sweetheart." I need to take in what Mike's death means for us and to work out how to respond. "I have to make some calls."

Her face falls. She's only just holding it together, and guilt courses through me as she reluctantly leaves with the promise that she'll be back in twenty minutes.

And I am online before she closes the door, turning to the news blogs, to BBC News, to Twitter; scouring them for references to the story, and to the reaction that spills out faster than I can read. *MPs' intruder dies. Journalist dies after break-in. Reporter who preyed on female MPs is dead.* The stories are still sympathetic, but the headlines are morphing into an uneasy mix of sympathy and something rather more circumspect: *Chronicle man was fine reporter.*

And here they are. The questions that drip doubt and judgment; that somehow imply that there is a kind of female MP who might ask to be stalked and harassed, to have her home broken into. As if the woman might be to blame. *Was dead reporter fixated on one of three female MPs? Was journalist still working with MP? Did female MP invite reporter to her home?* The office landline starts to ring, and my WhatsApp pings wildly. I silence my mobile, ignore the phone. The tide is turning, I can sense it; the swell is building, and soon there's the risk that I could drown.

Because what I fear—what I've feared ever since Julia called the police—is that the world will discover I slept with Mike Stokes. And that matters, not because it casts doubt on my judgment—*a feminist who sleeps with a tabloid journalist!*—and not because I should be ashamed of casual sex—I tell myself I shouldn't—but because who knows where this fact will lead? Anyone knowing we'd had sex could look at the *Chronicle*'s decision to publish those snatched photos and wonder why they'd mentioned my teenage daughter. And fellow reporters would truffle out the real story here.

My breath is high and light as my mind catastrophizes about the leaking of Flora's secret. It was a childish mistake; it cannot be printed; she *cannot* be shamed. The shame is all mine: as her mother, and as a woman who allowed desire and the need to be desired to override her usual sensible, sound judgment. Because the sex wasn't worth it. Christ. It really wasn't worth it—I know it, even as a flash of Mike moving against me, and his tenderness afterward, stubbornly shunts its way into my brain.

And here it is: the tweet I have been anticipating, in some form or another—and it strikes me in my solar plexus hard. The insinuation is Technicolor-bright, acid sharp, and for a moment, I'm stymied:

Breaking news: Intruder was MP's lover.

The reaction comes thick and fast, fresh details adding speculation and nuance. *MP's intruder was spurned lover. MP was being stalked by ex-lover. Trysts and turmoil for the MP and the hack.*

Where has this all come from? I scour the tweets, but there's no attribution. It's all *it is believed* and *sources say.* Does this mean that Mike had bragged about our tryst to colleagues, or that one of my housemates guessed?

And if this is out there, who knows what else is?

Thirty

11 DECEMBER 2021

Twitter Thread

Dick Penny @EnglandRules: I hear a certain female MP was spotted going into Charing Cross Police Station this morning.

Richard M @BigBob699: Naughty, naughty.

Dick Penny @EnglandRules: Crying out for a bit of discipline, that one.

FiremanFred @suckmycock: Still wouldn't touch her, though that journo certainly did.

Dick Penny @EnglandRules: #GooseyGooseyGander

Richard M @BigBob699: ???

Dick Penny @EnglandRules: It's a nursery rhyme. Just a hunch. Look it up, FFS.

The Record (online edition)
Sleeping with the Enemy
Marcus Jamieson, the Prof Who Speaks for the People

Is the relationship between the press and politicians too cozy?

The answer is a massive YES.

You only have to look at the tragic death of political editor Michael Stokes to see why journos should maintain a healthy detachment from MPs.

Because politician Emma Webster is currently being questioned about his death—which follows a fall in her £3M London home—after it was revealed the couple had been good contacts in more ways than one.

I taught Emma Webster, in my Brighton Uni days. I'd like to say she was a top student, but as she was to prove during finals, hers is a second-class mind.

Perhaps if she was as brilliant as she's led us to believe, she'd have remembered that no good ever comes from sleeping with the enemy.

Portsmouth Post (online edition)
Letters to the Editor
Local politician and journalist's death.

To the Editor

Re Emma Webster, I have always found her to be kind, caring, and the most hardworking politician. She has been absolutely brilliant, following my sister's death, in working to get the law changed, and me and my parents are proud to know her.

Yours truly,

Freya, Frank, and Lorna Jones

To the Editor

I am reading much support for Mrs. Webster, but I have found her far too preoccupied with her own publicity—and her pursuit of women's issues—than in her constituents' concerns.

On the very afternoon that Mr. Stokes was fatally injured, my son, Corporal Will Baxter, who served in Helmand with the 1st Battalion Welsh regiment, took his own life on the train tracks outside Winchester after succumbing to depression and PTSD.

I had repeatedly asked Mrs. Webster to look into the provision of mental health services for veterans but, despite my numerous emails, received only a lukewarm response.

If she had only listened and concentrated on issues like this, it might have proved better, for him—and her.

Simon Baxter

(Letter removed from website at 6:16 p.m. for legal reasons.)

Thirty-One

11 DECEMBER 2021

EMMA

They said they just wanted to ask me to answer a few questions. To clear up some details. Twelve noon. Charing Cross Police Station. I could bring a lawyer, but there was really no need.

"Thanks for coming in, Ms. Webster—or are you happy for us to call you Emma?" says Detective Chris Parkin as he ushers me into a conference room just beyond the outside desk. I'm given some tea in a foam cup: the drink and the use of the first name no doubt both attempts to suggest this is perfectly cordial. But his quick smile is more of a grimace. It doesn't reach his eyes.

We sit opposite each other at a bare table. Beside him is his colleague, Detective Kelly Blake: in her late twenties with a clear complexion and heavy bangs that create the impression of a girl next door. I haven't got a lawyer, though Claire is trying to find one who comes well recommended. Now, as the detective starts recording our conversation, I wonder if my decision not to bring one was woefully naive.

"We know you gave an initial account of what happened when you entered your house on 8 December to PC Berwick, but we wondered if you could run through it again?" he asks before leaning back, arms crossed across his chest. His biceps bulge through the crisp whiteness of his shirt, and despite the seriousness of the situation, there is something almost comic about his obvious pride in his gym-buffed torso. I half expect his muscles to twitch.

"It was as I said," I say, my tone calm and matter-of-fact, because there's some security in repetition, and as I recite this, I see it all happening. "I came in. The alarm was off. The hall was dark. I thought the lights had blown, so I found the flashlight on my phone and started to move toward the fuse box, underneath the stairs. Then I heard a sound from the kitchen: I shone the flashlight down the stairwell and saw what I thought was a pile of clothes at the bottom. I went down and found a man. Michael Stokes. He was just lying there."

"You see the thing is, we have a witness who heard arguing through your adjourning wall, at around 4:23 p.m.?" says Detective Parkin, as he watches closely for my reaction.

I shrug and pull a *search me* face. "I don't know why that would be. The houses are terraced. Perhaps he heard an argument from his other neighbors or in the street?"

Detective Blake tilts her head to one side. She is not, I sense, a woman's woman. Is more the type to screw over a female colleague if it means endearing herself to a man.

"You didn't have an argument with him?" she asks, her tone light.

"I didn't have an argument with Mike Stokes," I say, with careful precision, "because when I found him, he was already at the bottom of the stairs."

Detective Parkin sits forward and watches me through slitted eyes. For three long seconds, none of us say anything; then he gives another of his empty smiles.

"Let's talk about your relationship with Michael Stokes, shall we?"

"My relationship with Michael Stokes, as I told Officer Berwick, was professional. He was a contact with whom I worked on the Amy's Law campaign."

"We've looked at his phone, and there seem to be rather a lot of text messages between the two of you. Nearly two hundred and fifty of them?"

"As I said, he was a good contact. We worked together closely." I hold his gaze. He'll have read the news stories. *Intruder was MP's lover.* Is he going to challenge me on this?

"What about the message you sent on the day he died?"

"What?" I feel winded because I have *no* idea what he's talking about now.

"'Meet me at mine. 4pm. Have something you'll want to hear.'"

"I really don't know what you mean." Things have taken on an *Alice in Wonderland* quality, and my voice sounds bright and high.

The detective smiles. He's surprised me, and he likes that.

"The message was sent to Michael Stokes at 10:46 a.m. last Wednesday, 8 December, from a Messenger account that appears to be connected to your Facebook."

"I don't really use Messenger. If I wanted to speak to Mike, I would text him—as you've seen." My mind feels cloudy. Are they trying to trick me? I *didn't* do this—so either someone else did, or they've made some sort of mistake.

"So you didn't suggest meeting him at 4 p.m. at your Cleaver Square house?"

"No."

"And yet you turned up there shortly after that time, where you found him injured, and lying at the bottom of the stairs?"

"Yes, but that must be a coincidence because I didn't send him the message you describe. I returned home earlier than usual because I had a bad tension headache. You can ask my parliamentary assistant, Jazz MacKinley."

"We'll make sure we do that," he says. "We also have CCTV footage from a camera on Kennington Lane which suggests you would have arrived at your house shortly after 4:21 p.m. That was a full eight minutes before your housemate Julia Cooke came home and called an ambulance. Can you tell us what you were doing in that time?"

"Was it really that long?" I am genuinely confused. "It felt like far, far less. I don't know. I was very upset. I'd come in and found this man in my house. I think I just felt paralyzed by fear."

"You didn't think to call an ambulance when you discovered that a man had apparently fallen down the stairs in your house?"

"No, I didn't—not before Julia did, no." I redden at my apparent lack of humanity, can feel myself getting defensive. "I think I just panicked. I was in intense shock. It wasn't a normal situation in any way."

"I see," he says, his tone methodical and calm, if a little bemused—like a principal trying to get to the bottom of a behavioral issue. "Can you look at it from our viewpoint? There are a few things—the message, the argument, the delay—that just don't fit . . ."

"Well, when someone breaks into your home, you don't necessarily behave as rationally as you would like," I say, growing warm because the atmosphere is suddenly oppressive. I breathe deeply, trying to hold the stale air in my lungs, to calm myself as I might before a speech.

There's a knock at the door, and it feels like a reprieve.

"Yes?" Detective Parkin is curt.

A young woman almost curtsies to him. "The results you wanted have come in."

The detective and his partner exchange a glance I can't decipher, and he leaves us.

"Would you mind waiting here?" says Detective Blake, as if I'm in a dentist's clinic.

"I'd like to call a lawyer."

"Of course." She gives me a look as if to say, *At last you've come to your senses.*

And she follows her colleague.

———

They are gone for almost an hour. By the time they come back, their absence feels excessive, manipulative, and, of course, sinister.

Thankfully, the lawyer, John Pearson, has arrived. A slim, ascetic man, he has already advised me that, from now on, I should make no comment. I know he's only trying to help, but surely it's best to cooperate? To get this over and done with? It's that old desire to be a good girl, to always answer questions. It's a decision I will regret.

Detective Parkin looks particularly pleased with himself as he enters the room, and I know, unequivocally, that I don't trust him. I don't trust the smirk lingering at the corner of his mouth as he starts to speak.

"Emma Webster, I am arresting you on suspicion of murder. You do not have to say anything, but it may harm your defense if you do not mention when questioned something you rely on in court."

And though it feels bizarre that he is reciting something I've only heard on television, still this is simultaneously, terrifyingly real. Arrested for *murder*? My scalp prickles, and ice creeps up my spine. The air feels knocked from my chest, and then my heart flurries like a drummer's military tattoo, getting faster and faster. *Ta-ca-ta-ca-Ta-ca-ta-ca-Ta-ca-ta-ca-TA-CA-TA-CA.*

––––––––––

I am booked in; am read my rights; have my DNA taken. A swab swiped inside my mouth and my fingernails scraped. Cleaver Square has become a crime scene once again: is being analyzed far more thoroughly for any remaining forensic evidence than when this was judged a break-in. I've had to hand over my phone so can only imagine Julia's anger: the narrow pursing of her lips, the tell of tension—a sharp twitch just below her eye.

The interview room in the custody suite is bleak and unforgiving. A table screwed into the floor, bare walls soundproofed with some sort of felt material, one high window. In its Cold War starkness, it's intimidating in the extreme.

Detective Parkin leans forward.

"I expect you were wondering what that interruption was about?"

I shrug, refusing to pander to his wielding of power as he drip-feeds information.

"We'd just had some very interesting results from the postmortem." He pauses, as if expecting me to ask him about it. I refuse to oblige.

"You see, the postmortem indicates that Michael Stokes sustained a couple of injuries before the fall that couldn't have been self-inflicted."

For a moment, I am speechless.

"I don't know anything about any injuries," I eventually manage to say.

"He had a fresh cut on his left cheek and another just above to his left temple," Detective Parkin continues. "These cuts don't fit with him falling down the stairs." Another long pause while he assesses me. My throat tightens and I swallow: even if I wanted to, I'm not sure I could speak.

"What's more, the cut to his temple caused a blood spatter at the bottom of the stairs," the detective says, his tone conversational. "Now the nature of these things means that spattering only happens when there's a second blow—the blow to the head as he hit the bottom of the stairs—do you understand?"

I nod.

"For the tape, please."

"Yes," I say.

Next to me, John Pearson, a stranger until an hour ago, wonders if he might have a word with his client?

"Is that what you'd like, Emma?"

I nod, desperate for the chance to reorder my thoughts, for the officers to leave me alone. Detective Parkin stops the recording device.

Once we are alone, John is earnest. "Are you sure you want to persist like this?" he asks. "My strong recommendation is that you answer no further questions. Make no comment, and once we receive full disclosure of their evidence, at a later date, we can review our position. Saying anything further risks making things worse."

I put my head in my hands, trying to disappear. I was so desperate to shut down their questions, I didn't see they were curating evidence ahead of receiving the postmortem findings. Wouldn't it be easiest now for me to give them an explanation that makes sense?

"There are some details I left out," I say, so quietly that John strains to hear.

"Some details?" A flick of irritation passes over his face.

I start weeping, then swipe at my eyes with the back of my hand. Competent, fearless Emma Webster, MP, seems to have disappeared.

I have spent my life trying to be honest—and now that I haven't been, it's backfired badly.

"I'd like to tell the truth," I say.

PART THREE

Thirty-Two

13 JUNE 2022

EMMA

Tom Tillett, the lawyer instructed to argue my case in court, had warned me that the prosecution's opening speech would feel particularly damning. After all, Sonja Jackson's job is to persuade the jury that I am guilty of murder. That I didn't kill Mike Stokes by accident but intended to do so. That I was vicious and acted in a grossly disproportionate way.

Still, it comes as a shock to hear myself spoken about like this. It's the disconnect between the story she weaves and the measured way in which she lays out her case. There's no need for hyperbole or bombast: the story's sufficiently dramatic, and the jury can accept it easily.

And they're intrigued, sitting upright, curious and attentive; eyes flitting from this stately lawyer, with her regal posture and authoritative yet accessible way of speaking, to me, a politician whose fall from grace has already been trumpeted this morning on the TV. It's the women who worry me the most because women judge other women more harshly, don't they? I watch the two eldest women jurors: a grandmotherly figure in her mid- to late seventies with a tight gray perm and a woman in her late sixties with a sleek ash bob. I remember their names from when they took their oaths: Rita and Margaret. Permed Rita. Ash Bob Margaret. Both Tories? I think this instinctively as Ash Bob Margaret glances at me with open curiosity and Permed Rita's eyes narrow just a little. Just as they judge me, I judge them.

"On Wednesday, 8 December, at around 4:29 p.m.," Miss Jackson begins, in her measured way, as if she's telling them a bedtime story, "a woman called Julia Cooke arrived home and discovered the body of a man lying in her basement kitchen. He was unconscious, and he appeared to have fallen down a steep flight of stairs.

"The man, who had a fatal head injury, was a journalist, Michael, or Mike, Stokes, and sitting next to him was her housemate Emma Webster. The question of how he came to be there—of whether he was deliberately pushed down the stairs with the intention of killing him, of whether he was *murdered*—is the question at the heart of this trial.

"At around 4 p.m. that day, Michael Stokes went to the Cleaver Square home. He knew Ms. Webster. They had worked together on news stories and, in fact, as you will hear, they had a sexual relationship." At this, Permed Rita and a young juror in a hijab look surprised: perhaps they haven't read the papers. "Ms. Webster had ended it some three weeks earlier, but he believed she had invited him over. In fact, he'd received a message that appeared to suggest this: 'Meet me at mine. 4pm. Have something you'll want to hear.'

"He arrived and was let in by the cleaner, Agnes Molnár, who had to go to another job and left him there. It is agreed that at some point soon after this, the lights in the house fused due to a filament bulb in the hall lamp, which was set to a timer, being blown. Shortly afterward, at 4:21, Emma Webster arrived home. Around eight minutes later, Ms. Cooke came back and discovered them. She called an ambulance because Emma Webster had failed to do so. Mike Stokes briefly recovered consciousness but then slipped out of consciousness on the way to the hospital. He died there, less than two days later."

Sonja Jackson pauses; looks down at her notes as if inviting us all to consider the fact of his death. It's all part of the drama, but just because this rhetorical device is familiar, even hackneyed, it doesn't mean it doesn't work.

I look across the courtroom, at the soft pine benches with their poison-green upholstery, the swaths of dark-suited police officers and press, the gowned and wigged lawyers, then up to the public gallery, where Claire is watching and Patrick's taking notes. The silence builds, and with it my sense of guilt. In the well of the court, there's a teenage boy sitting with his neatly dressed mother. He's in shirt and tie and looks in danger of being overwhelmed. But as Sonja notes his father's death, Josh looks directly at me—and Cath squeezes his hand.

"Members of the jury, at first this incident looked very straightfor-ward," Sonja goes on, her voice deepening and becoming even more somber. "Mr. Stokes had been drinking at a reporters' Christmas lunch. Ms. Webster told the police that she had returned home to discover him at the bottom of her stairwell, and it appeared that he must have drunk-enly fallen down the stairs.

"But this was a blatant lie. It was one which Ms. Webster persisted with not just in her initial account to the police, on the night of the mur-der, but in her police interview when she was arrested three days later. The truth is that, when she entered her home in Cleaver Square that late afternoon, she was surprised by Mike Stokes standing in her hallway in the dark. They began to argue, and that argument became physical. Emma Webster accepts all of this. At some point, the Crown says, their fight escalated until she pushed him down a thirteen-step flight of stairs.

"You will hear from a neighbor," Sonja Jackson goes on, "who tells of hearing raised voices and thudding, which, the Crown says, was the sound of Michael Stokes's and Emma Webster's feet as they fought in the hall. You will also hear from the forensic pathologist who conducted the postmor-tem on Michael Stokes. His findings indicate that Mr. Stokes was kneed in the testicles"—a pause: several of the male jurors look queasy—"and that he sustained a cut to his left cheek and another to his left temple.

"You will also hear from a blood-spatter expert that there was blood in the stairwell that indicated he had been hit before he fell—and that Emma Webster used hot water and bleach to try to remove this."

Another pause, during which a juror in her late twenties, blonde hair scraped into a high ponytail, raises a dark sculpted eyebrow at me, and her neighbor pulls his chin reprovingly into his chest.

"In any police inquiry, DNA tests are carried out," Sonja continues. "Once it became clear that a fight had taken place, detectives found a trace of Mr. Stokes's blood on the prong of Ms. Webster's house key, suggesting Ms. Webster had used the keys she was clutching in her right hand to assault Mike Stokes, forcing them into his face. She then grabbed a ceramic bowl from a console table in the hall and smashed it against his left temple. At this point, the Crown says, she kneed him in the groin.

"By this stage, the fight was taking place toward the back of the hallway and opposite the descending flight of stairs to the basement kitchen. If you look at tab one of your jury bundle, you can see a layout of the hall and the spot there." There's a flurry of activity as the jury open the fat blue files in front of them, containing photos, CGI body maps, and the layout of the house. "At some point, Ms. Webster managed to push him away from her, the Crown says with the deliberate intention of him falling down the stairs onto the basement kitchen's hard slate floor." A beat, and Sonja allows the silence to stretch as she looks from one juror to another. "It was the act of doing this that led directly to his death.

"The defense will argue that this was a clear case of a woman acting in self-defense when confronted by an intruder. The issue remains, given the circumstances, whether this would have been a reasonable or *proportionate* response."

Her tone is so mocking I want to stand up and rail against her. Instead I push the nails of my left hand into my right palm until I wince.

"It will be the Crown's case that this was not *reasonable* self-defense. Besides, having not merely pushed him away but *pushed him down a steep flight of stairs*, what did she do? You or I, acting in self-defense, but then faced with this terrible event, might be expected to ring an ambulance, and run from the house for help. But Ms. Webster failed to do either of these things—and the ambulance was only called eight minutes after she returned home and at the instigation of Ms. Cooke.

"The fight would have taken a matter of seconds, the Crown suggests. No more than a minute, considering the evidence of the sound of the argument and the extent of the injuries. In the time before Ms. Cooke arrived, Ms. Webster swept up the broken pieces of the ceramic bowl and deposited them in the recycling bin. She also moved a bunch of mistletoe, the Crown says, which was hanging from the first light fitting in the hall when her housemates left for work, and strung it from the second, directly opposite the flight of stairs. Why did she do this? We say to give credence to her claim that she pushed him in retaliation for a sexual assault—after he lunged to kiss her there.

"When the police arrived, Ms. Webster offered her version of events— her *lie*—that she had found him at the bottom of the stairwell leading to her kitchen. We say her having the wherewithal to lie so quickly, and her behavior in running around tidying up, hardly indicates the behavior of someone acting in self-defense."

There's another pause, pregnant with judgment, and I feel it seeping into every corner of the courtroom. She can't just present her theories as fact! But my lawyer has explained she can. That I must listen while she presents her case and calls witnesses to prove it. And so she continues.

"The Crown does not have to provide a motive for why Emma Webster did this: it is enough for us to prove that her behavior, despite the very real anxiety she may have felt, was disproportionate. But we say that Michael Stokes was investigating an unfavorable story about her and a family member. His newspaper, the *Chronicle*, had already printed unflattering photographs of her strongly indicating their intent.

"Ms. Webster knew that he was doing this. You will hear from a witness who saw them arguing nine days before their fight. Who heard her warn him she would 'come after' him if he dared to name the family member in print. And you will hear a voicemail Ms. Webster left on his phone on 4 December, the day the photographs were printed, in which she tells him to 'leave me fucking alone.'

"Ms. Webster is a public figure. Someone who, before these events took place, was becoming high-flying and high-profile. Who had a reputation for being a relentless, telegenic campaigner: who was far more than just a good local politician.

"Ms. Webster knew Michael Stokes well. They had collaborated on several stories, had drinks and dinner together. You will hear that there were hundreds of texts bandied between them; and that, three weeks before this—on 17 November—they went for dinner together, after which they booked into a hotel and had sex. But now she was angry with him for pursuing this story. She was anxious about her reputation. We say she pushed him because she was concerned with maintaining her good name."

I risk looking at the jurors then, and wonder if they buy this version of me as a callous, ruthless woman? I've already had six months of being viewed as this. Six months of working on my own: the Labour party rejecting me as soon as I was charged and making it clear I shouldn't be seen in Parliament. Six months of being judged by the police; in prison, where I spent two nights before being granted bail; by the judiciary, my colleagues, my friends. I thought I was prepared for this. That I could cope, knowing how forcefully I'd argue against it. But my eyes burn. I can't allow myself to give in to tears.

I focus instead on the back of my lawyer's head, trying to distract myself from my fear and anger. Tom Tillett, sitting in front of John Pearson and brought in by him to advocate persuasively, is a bruiser of a man: shaven-headed, six foot plus, broad shouldered, with a slightly protruding stomach, he is someone you would want on your side in a fight. Despite his bulk, he has physical grace, moves lightly, is chivalrous. The sort of man to open doors for women, something I find strangely comforting.

I like his junior, too. Alice Bradby: early thirties, uber-efficient, sharp, tenacious, and pregnant. Her billowing gown masks it, but the slight mound curving below her dark waistcoat is unmistakable, as is the green tinge to her face. No one acknowledges it, either out of embarrassment or because it's not deemed relevant. Just once, as we wash our hands together in the court bathroom, I catch her exhausted gaze in the mirror and murmur a soft "You okay?" She nods briskly and turns away to the dryer, keen to deter further inquiry.

Sonja has been talking for an hour and a half now, and I have let my mind float, as if incapable of taking in the details, though I know the case against me, have thought of little else for the past few months. I look down at my hands and notice that my fingernails have left a row of sharp little bites. My right eye twitches, and when I move my jaw, suppressing a yawn because the courtroom is stuffy, it clunks. I've been grinding my teeth in my sleep for the past six months. I shift, feeling my navy trousers—part of the suit I'd worn for that bloody article, a suit I'd subsequently bought because it made me feel good and I'd hoped to channel that feeling in this courtroom—hang from my waist, slip against my thighs. I trace the fabric's weft, then stop abruptly. For Christ's sake, I must concentrate.

Because Miss Jackson, as the judge refers to her, is now reaching her conclusion. The definition of murder, and the questions the jury will have to address.

"The law says a person is guilty of murder it they unlawfully kill another person with an intention to kill or cause really serious harm," she says, looking along the jurors, ensuring each clearly understands. "This means that the prosecution must prove two things: one, that the defendant killed the deceased, and two, that at the time of the killing she intended to kill him or at the very least cause him really serious harm.

"It is the Crown's case that Michael Stokes, a man Emma Webster trusted sufficiently to spend the night with, was unarmed, posed no real threat to her—and knew something that would ruin her reputation. We say that this is a clear case of murder."

Thirty-Three

13 JUNE 2022

EMMA

The general housekeeping of the court and the prosecution opening have taken longer than I expected, and it isn't until after lunch that the first prosecution witness is called.

It is Julia, of course. We have had very little contact over the past six months. None, bar some texts when I was first arrested, Julia being particularly irate at being evicted from Cleaver Square for three days. Then, once it became clear she would be a prosecution witness, not speaking to her became a condition of my bail. Still, she could have found a way to convey her support, through Claire, had she wanted.

Yes, it's fair to say that Julia hasn't proved an ally. There's no reason why she should, really, the strands of friendship more strained, more tenuous, over the past four years. I guess it was inevitable: petty irritations, such as my mistakenly putting chicken on her shelf in the fridge despite her being vegetarian, allowed to fester; larger ideological differences never adequately addressed. In the months before Mike's death, the once-weekly shared meals that had proved so crucial to smoothing out concerns had stopped, none of us having the time to cook or the inclination to fix a date. Did she resent my higher profile? As shadow transport secretary, working hard in an unglamorous field that rarely made the news, I'm sure it rankled, as did my reaction to my trolling: after all, *she'd* put up with plenty of misogyny during her twenty-year career. And then, of course, she was the one who found me bent over Mike. From that moment, any irritation with me seemed to immediately harden, and it feels as though she judged me as guilty from the start.

I think I sensed it from the moment she stood at the top of the stairs leading down to the kitchen.

"Hello? Is anybody there?"

Her voice filtered down: higher pitched than usual, with a note of trepidation. For a moment, I couldn't respond: my throat felt flayed. Finally I managed to squeak: "I'm down here. The fuse box must have blown."

I could hear her fumbling in the understairs cupboard, then flicking the switch so that the hall was flooded with light, though the stairwell remained gloomy, the basement floor where I squatted the other side of Mike shrouded in darkness still. Up in the hall, the light blazed, and Julia stood illuminated like some avenging angel. A querulous note crept into her voice as she peered down the stairs, her head tilted. "What on *earth* are you doing down there?"

Now, as she stands in the witness box, dressed in a somber shift dress with her trademark resin necklace—black, white, and pink, like an assortment of candies—and her angular, heavy-framed glasses, she refuses to look at me. Perhaps it's easier to knife someone if you fail to acknowledge they're there.

Sonja Jackson is asking her about when she first walked in and stared down at me from the hallway.

"I asked her what had happened."

"And what did she say?"

"That there had been an accident. I asked if she was hurt—and she said no, but that someone had got in. I started down the stairs, and realized that what I had assumed was her coat and bag on the floor beside her was, in fact, the body of a man."

"And what did you do then?"

"I stopped on the stairs—I couldn't get all the way down because the bottom was blocked by his body—Emma must have stepped over and was crouched the other side of him—and I asked if he was alive."

"And what did she say?"

"That she didn't know. That she hadn't checked." Julia's upper lip is a narrow line that she folds over when expressing disapproval; now it seems to entirely disappear.

I remember how frantic she seemed as she shouted at me to check his pulse. My fingers ran over his hair, thick and coarse with a sheen of grease to it, and his skin, disarmingly warm. Somehow I picked up a thready *da-dum*. Bile rose in my throat. "I can feel his pulse," I said, and just for a moment, it felt as if everything could be made better because of course I didn't want him dead; I wanted him to survive this. "He's alive. Oh my God. He's alive!"

"She found his pulse," Julia says now. "I managed to get close enough to the bottom on the stairs to lean and switch on the light—the switch is at the bottom of the stairwell. Then I ran back upstairs, shouting that I was calling 999."

"You were the one to suggest calling 999?" Miss Jackson clarifies.

"Yes."

"Emma Webster didn't suggest that?"

"No."

"And she didn't say she had called it?"

"No." Julia pats her necklace to her chest. "I went back upstairs because the phone reception's better in the hallway, but I told her to move him into the recovery position."

"And did she follow your suggestion?"

"No. When I finished the call, he was in the same position as before."

I interlock my fingers, stunned by this callous version of myself she's describing. I was scared of shifting him; couldn't remember how to do it; was confused, too, as I heard her speak to the operator in between barking orders back down.

"If we can pause for a bit, I think we can play back the recording of your phone call to the emergency services," Sonja Jackson is saying. And for the next three or four minutes, we are catapulted back to that moment, Julia's tone more vulnerable than usual: a quiver as she tells the operator, "I think he's alive." In contrast, I am silent on the tape: I was at least four yards away, bending over him; telling him everything was going to be okay, though he was unconscious, and I think I knew, even then, that that was a lie. "Is someone with him now?" asks the operator. "Yes—my housemate," says Julia, and I look at the jurors, who seem rapt, and I'm so grateful for this reminder that I was there.

The recording ends, and Sonja Jackson tells the jury that it took the ambulance seven minutes from the point at which Julia gave our address to its arrival. She turns to Julia and asks her what she did after ending the call.

"I went to help," she says, her chin upright, her tone self-righteous. "I told Emma the ambulance was coming, and I went back down to the bottom of the stairs to see how I could help."

Was it really like that? As she clattered back down, Mike had given a groan and opened his eyes, his expression glazed and uncomprehending.

"Mike? Mike?" I was frantic. "He's conscious, Julia. He's conscious!" I'd placed my hand on his chest.

She crouched down and touched his leg, the part of him closest to her, and kept machine-gunning orders. "Talk to him. Keep him with you. Tell him his name."

I started speaking gibberish: just repeating his name over and over while his eyes remained on me, his mouth worked wordlessly. His torso was warm, compact, reassuringly that of a living, conscious man. I pressed against it, so he would know I was here, with him; so that he would know I wasn't going anywhere.

"Can you describe Emma Webster's behavior while you were waiting for the ambulance?" Sonja Jackson asks.

"She seemed agitated."

"Agitated?"

"Yes. And quite hysterical. She kept repeating: 'He was just lying there.' Said it over and over."

"And what happened then?"

"The paramedics arrived and I showed them down. Mike became unnerved when he saw them."

And I am back there as Mike reared up and flailed against the paramedic: "Get off. I'm all right. I'm all right, I said." His voice shimmered with bad temper and a manic, unpredictable quality. "Need to get out of here. Get fucking out of here. Get fucking off me!"

"And how was Emma Webster while this was happening?"

"She looked frightened, just as I was, then she started asking whether this was a good sign."

My voice spiraled in panic, my questions incessant. "It's a good sign, isn't it? Is it a good sign? That he's conscious, that he's talking?" I could hear myself sounding ridiculous, but the need for reassurance was far more acute. The paramedics were focused on their job in hand, though, strapping him to a stretcher, wheeling him down the hall toward the ambulance. I followed them up the stairs, then disappeared into the downstairs bathroom, desperately trying not to throw up.

"And if we could just address the issue of the mistletoe?"

I'm roused from my memories and sit, alert, watching Julia. On the Monday night—less than forty-eight hours before this happened—I'd had that disagreement with Claire over where we should position the mistletoe. She had thought it looked too unsubtle, strung at the front of the house. I'd thought it looked more festive and had won the argument.

But on Wednesday morning—after everyone had left—I moved the mistletoe to the second light fitting at the back of the hall, as Claire had suggested: still smarting from their reaction when I said I'd wanted to leave and keen to make amends. The prosecution can't accept this—and argue that I shifted it after pushing Mike down the stairs, so that I could accuse him of sexually assaulting me beneath it. And so Sonja is now questioning Julia about it.

"When I left in the morning it was hanging at the front of the house, as Emma had thought it should, and when I returned, it was hanging from the second light fitting," Julia explains. "I noticed it as soon as I put on the light because she'd made such an issue of not putting it there at first."

"Did you mention it to anyone at the time?"

"I told PC Barker, the policewoman who arrived, because I thought it was odd."

"And did you notice anything else?"

"Yes. There was usually a ceramic bowl on the console table in the hall. I was rather fond of it: I'd bought it on holiday in Dorset. After the paramedics left, I realized it wasn't there."

"Thank you, Ms. Cooke," says Sonja Jackson as she gives her a nod of apparent satisfaction. Some of the jurors look bored by the detailed questioning about the mistletoe. But Sonja has what she wanted.

"No further questions," she says.

"I won't keep you too long, Ms. Cooke," Tom begins, before taking her back to the mistletoe argument.

"I think it's right that during this row, Claire Scott was upset and said Ms. Webster 'needed her own space'?"

"Yes, that's right."

"And Ms. Webster looked distressed by this?"

"Yes."

"Would you say that Emma Webster is a 'reasonable' person?" Tom asks, his tone all warmth and reasonableness himself.

"Yes, generally," she says.

"She never made a fuss about having the ground-floor room, for instance, despite you all agreeing it was the most exposed?"

"No."

"So, isn't it perfectly possible that, having reflected on the argument with Claire Scott on Monday night, she decided to move the mistletoe before she left for work on Wednesday morning?"

"Well, I *suppose* so," she concedes.

Tom gives her a slight nod as if to say, *There, now, that wasn't too bad, was it?* She rewards him with an acid smile.

He continues in this same reasonable tone as he introduces the suggestion that she holds some animus against me.

"Were you close to the defendant when you lived together?"

"We'd been housemates for four years."

"That doesn't quite answer the question."

"I suppose there were certain tensions, as is inevitable with any house share."

"I believe Emma Webster had told you, the previous night, that she was going to move out because she was concerned by the house's substandard security?"

"Yes, that's right. It's a Grade II listed building and our landlord was reluctant to introduce further measures, such as an entry phone, further locks or bars on the windows. Emma told us she felt unsafe living there and wanted to leave."

"And as I understand it, you felt exasperated by this?"

"Exasperated is too strong, but I was a little irritated, yes. We all live busy lives and finding a suitable new housemate takes time, as does finding alternative accommodation if that isn't possible. Whatever the tensions, we were used to living together. I thought that counted for something. With hindsight, I underestimated how frightened she was."

"You knew, I think, that Emma Webster had received a death threat. A letter threatening an acid attack?"

"Yes."

"And that she regularly received rape threats, on social media?"

"Yes."

"Even that she was receiving anonymous abusive text messages?"

Julia has the grace to look embarrassed. "I—I didn't know the details."

"But you knew of them? Indeed, I believe you were in her office when she received one of them, and she showed you?"

"Quite probably."

"'Quite probably?'"

"I mean, yes."

"I think you *were* in her office, on 13 September, weren't you? You were discussing a feature she appeared in in the *Guardian* when she received a text message saying: 'You think you're so fucking special. You'd better watch out bitch.'"

"Yes." Julia is typically pale, almost washed out. Now the center of each cheek blooms with a patch of red.

"And you knew that she'd been put under surveillance by the *Chronicle*: you'd seen the photos they'd printed of her, and she'd told you she felt anxious because of it?"

"Yes, that's right." Her tone remains bright, almost defiant, but some of her usual self-regard has gone.

Tom stands a little straighter. He does not need to belabor the point he is building up to; we can all see where he is heading. "She was 'agitated,' you said, when you found her at the bottom of the stairs. 'Agitated' and 'hysterical'?"

"Yes. She was quite beside herself." Julia's lips thin again.

"She had just discovered an intruder in her house, hadn't she?"

"Yes."

"And this intruder was the man who was pursuing her for a story?"

"Yes."

"And her home was the one place she wanted to feel safe?"

"I suppose so, yes."

"It was dark in the hall, without the lights on, wasn't it?"

"Yes."

"Well, I would have thought being 'agitated' and 'hysterical' would be a perfectly natural reaction?"

A pat at the necklace again. "Yes, perhaps," Julia says.

Tom looks down at his papers, takes his time. His tone is gentle, curious.

"Do you recall the paramedic saying she appeared to be in shock?"

"Yes." Julia seems diminished.

"No further questions."

And with a flourish and speed that belies his size, Tom sits back down.

Thirty-Four

13 JUNE 2022

EMMA

I am exhausted after the court finishes sitting for the day, and simultaneously adrenaline-jangled. Claire sweeps me into a black cab, grim-faced as the photographers push and jostle around.

She is renting a two-bedroom apartment on the nearby Golden Lane Estate. Once Cleaver Square became a crime scene, the house share fell apart and Claire moved in with her boyfriend, Matt. Four months on, he left her, and she is living in an apartment she can't afford in an unfamiliar area of the city. She'll need to give it up soon but has offered me her spare room throughout the trial.

The apartment, built in the 1950s, ex-council and a modernist classic, is white-walled, stark, large-windowed. My eighth-floor room looks out at other blocks, each with a balcony in a primary color. Mine is acid yellow; those opposite, like pieces of LEGO, are turquoise and terra-cotta red. There are tennis courts and a community garden, but all I can think about is whether anyone living in the apartments opposite might be watching. *I'd take a razor to her smug face, only it would blunt it. You think you're so fucking special. You'd better watch out bitch.*

I shiver and draw the curtains. Claire brings me a mug of tea, and this simple act of kindness makes me cry.

"It's okay," she says as I step out of my unfamiliar heels and rub my stockinged feet on her parquet floor. I put the tea down, incapable of drinking, incapable of doing anything but giving in to the tension that has gripped my body. My shoulders are meshed as tight as chicken wire; my back's so rigid, I fear it will snap. "Come here," she says as she gives me a hug.

"I sounded so awful," I whisper into her hair. "The stuff about me sweeping up the ceramic bowl . . ."

"Shh, shh," she says, though we both know that's the most problematic part of the case. She pulls away and makes me look at her. "This was the prosecution's turn. You haven't told your side of the story yet."

We deconstruct the day a little more. Discuss the jurors. Is Permed Rita particularly disapproving, or the girl in the hijab? The hard-faced blonde with the expressive eyebrows? What about the men: the skinny thirtysomething with the air of disappointment, the bearded fortysomething who looks thoughtful, florid-faced Blazer Man?

"I wonder if Mike's family will be there all the time?" She looks at me inquiringly. I have no idea. I think of Cath, his ex-wife, petite, perfectly made up, who I imagine is there for her son. The way Josh looked at me—hatred and hurt conveyed with his father's eyes—is my abiding memory of the day.

I change, then sit on the double bed in the small second bedroom, and FaceTime Flora. Now fifteen, she is old enough to watch my trial, but of course I won't let her, and have turned down David's hesitant but genuine offer to attend. I strive to keep my tone upbeat: "Yes, I'm glad it's started. There might be footage of me tonight. Best not to watch it: it's the prosecution's job to make me look bad, but you know that's not what really happened. Now, how are you feeling? Did you go into school? Oh . . . Okay. Well—did you do any schoolwork online?"

My daughter is near monosyllabic, her voice tight with anxiety. Who am I fooling? She's acutely aware of the seriousness of what I'm experiencing, far from being convinced that everything is okay.

David is at work, so she hands me over to Caroline.

"Is it awful?" Her face is pinched with concern.

I nod, raw-throated, ragged.

"I expect it might be on the *Six O'Clock News*," I say at last. "I can't bear to watch . . . Can you reassure Flo that it's the prosecution's job to make me look this bad? That it doesn't mean I did it? That none of this includes my defense?"

"Of course." Her voice is soothing. "She knows all this, of course she does; we've repeatedly told her, but I'll remind her, anyway."

Later I try to eat: Greek yogurt, which cloys; pea soup—warmed and then discarded. Claire has to go into the Commons to vote but leaves me with a bottle of white wine. I glug down a glass, then pour myself a second; desperate for something that will make me relax.

But I'm too unsettled. Resisting the news, I scan Matt's books, still lining the shelves in the second bedroom: Rawls's *Theory of Justice*; Locke's *An Essay Concerning Human Understanding*; Bagehot's *The English Constitution*; set texts by Descartes, Berkeley, and Hume that I doubt he's opened since university. Nothing that would distract or immerse me, that would constitute a good read. There are a few thrillers (though I'm hardly in need of suspense) and the program notes to a recent production, at the nearby Barbican, of *The Duchess of Malfi*.

There's a copy of Webster's revenge tragedy, too, and I start reading, reminding myself of this political figure derided for her sexual autonomy. *A lusty widow. A strumpet.* And yet, at the point of death, she is still asserting her refusal to be cowed by her brothers, her identity, her strength.

She is judged, her reputation tarnished, and yet her sense of self persists. "I am Duchess of Malfi still," she proclaims.

Thirty-Five

14 JUNE 2022

CAROLINE

"MP Emma Webster will be back in court today after being accused of pushing her former lover to his death. The Labour backbencher smashed a ceramic bowl and a bunch of keys in his face, then lied repeatedly to police, the Old Bailey was told yesterday. The case, which has provoked massive publicity, is expected to last at least two weeks . . ."

Caroline reaches for the dial on the radio and silences the Radio 2 headlines. It's been pretty relentless. The BBC is leading on it, the *Mail* is splashing on it, and friends are taking to Facebook, airing gossip as concern.

Upstairs, Flora is obsessively playing Ferling's oboe studies. In other circumstances, Caroline would be thrilled by this excessive practice, this desire to get it exactly right. But there is something too dogged about her metronomic timing and meticulous repetition. There needs to be some rubato, some flexibility, some sense of leaning into the phrasing, some *musicality*. Some evidence, perhaps, of her sorrow and pain. But Flora has shut down, refusing to discuss her mother's trial for murder—though she reads about it voraciously online. And just as her face is blank, when you raise the subject, so, too is her playing is expressionless. This is music devoid of any emotion at all.

Like a cat wailing, according to David. "It's a duck," she corrected him automatically when he made this criticism yesterday. "In Prokofiev's *Peter and the Wolf*, the oboe's the duck; the clarinet's the cat." He had looked at her, his face an incredulous mask. Fair enough. This was hardly the time to be pedantic. The fact of Emma's trial has hit him hard. To know someone for twenty years, and for something of this magnitude to happen? Well, they're all having to recalibrate things.

He can't let himself think she could have done it. He's emphatic she didn't do it. Caroline has been more circumspect (despite what she might have told him). After all, the prosecution believe she murdered him, rather than acting in self-defense. And Emma is not to be underestimated. Look at how she became an MP in a marginal seat within two years of becoming a councillor. She has always had the ability to surprise.

In some ways, and this obviously isn't something she could admit to anyone, Caroline could do with Emma being out of the picture. Life would be easier without her implicit judgment. (She knows Emma's sniffy about how she's done up the house, and some of the clothes she's bought Flo.) But Caroline's not a bitch, whatever Emma might think. And the horrible truth is that whether Emma's guilty or innocent isn't, to an extent, the issue. (And that is taking some getting her head around.) The issue is what will happen to Flora, already sufficiently stressed, if Emma is convicted. It's something Caroline doesn't want to contemplate. And so all that matters is that Emma gets off.

She sits at her piano, fingers resting on the keys, and starts working through a series of arpeggios to calm herself. She begins with the majors, then shifts to the minors. C, then working through the keyboard: C-sharp, D, E-flat, hands flying up and down the octaves as if the noise and blur of activity will drown out her less admirable thoughts.

There's a tiny, mean bit of her, a bit she can't tell David, that is relieved Emma has experienced this fall from grace. Although Caroline has ostensibly "won" any conceivable competition between them—gaining her man, her house, and even, part of the time, her daughter—she's never felt like a winner. From the moment Emma and Caroline met in the staff room, and Caroline noted the way younger male teachers sought out Emma's approval and advice, she has been constantly outshone.

Because Emma is something of a golden girl, professionally and politically: she has known what it is like to stand in the limelight and bask in the applause, the attention, of an audience, in a way that Caroline can only manage when accompanying her choral society (and even then, her role is diminished: she might conduct from the piano in rehearsals but is pretty peripheral once they perform).

Emma has always had the moral upper hand. Blameless in the disintegration of her marriage. Or at least, if her working in London during the week was undoubtedly a factor, then it was unintentional, not calculating like David's decision to embark on, and Caroline's instigation of, an affair.

But now Emma is learning what it is like to have her reputation trounced. It is something Caroline knows rather a lot about. It's impossible to be the Other Woman, to be someone instrumental in the breakup a relationship, without having your character, your integrity, smeared. Not that her true friends would think this, but teacher colleagues kept their distance once she became involved with David. *Perfectly pleasant as a workmate*, she could see them thinking, *but not someone you'd choose if you wanted to keep your husband. Not exactly* trustworthy.

David hasn't experienced any of this, of course. She moves to a chromatic scale starting on a low C, the ominous double-handed rumble conveying her bad temper. It helps that he doesn't come across as slick and self-confident: looks bumbling and self-effacing, as far removed from the stereotype of an adulterous husband, the perennially unfaithful philanderer, as it is possible to get. But it's also that old sexual double standard. Since Eve, it's always the woman who's been the temptress, and though Caroline dresses demurely (work wardrobe from M&S, weekend sportswear from Next) and though her friends in the Bach chorale would think her quiet, even a little uptight in her near teetotalism, her refusal to touch sugar or red meat, her perfectionism ("All well and good, but it's not as if she's giving recitals at the Wigmore Hall; that ship has passed, lovey," as one of the more waspish tenors once observed). Despite all this, she was the one people looked at with raised eyebrows. *Good old David: trading his wife in for a younger model. Caroline? Mmm. Did you know she was the daughter's piano teacher? Funny how it's often the quiet ones . . .*

Except weren't they both just trying to make the best of life? To catch at happiness, often slippery in the best of circumstances. Okay, so she'd had a moral choice. She needn't have been the one to instigate their first kiss; needn't have given him an ultimatum shortly after they'd first slept together, hustling things along, conscious of the tick-tock of her biological clock. But they were adults. She didn't have time to prevaricate. Wanted to be decisive. In musical terms, she favors the mathematical precision of the Baroque period over the lush indulgence of the Romantic. Is more Bach than Brahms. Can't bear the drama of Sturm und Drang.

But her role as the Other Woman means that now she lacks decent female friendships. Ironically, the woman she always wanted to be closest to was Emma, and sleeping with her husband, and then becoming the second Mrs. Webster, has rather put paid to that.

Emma sounds as if she could do with more support. Perhaps doing so, and ostensibly accepting her innocence, whatever she privately thinks, might help not just Flora, Emma, and David—but herself. Because, much as she knows the Other Woman tag is ludicrous, it has stuck to her like Velcro, and she doesn't like it. She, as much as Emma, is preoccupied with her good name.

Thirty-Six

14 JUNE 2022

EMMA

Day two of my trial, and I wake, soon after 5 a.m., feeling deeply apprehensive. I reach for my laptop. The opening of the case has been covered extensively by the papers, and the headlines are ruthless. *MP pushed lover to his death. MP failed to call 999. MP lied over lover's death.*

"See—none of them lead with the ceramic bowl," Claire tries to reassure me as we sit, shortly after six, analyzing them together. But it's the second point mentioned in the BBC headlines; is mentioned high up in the *Times, Guardian,* and *Mail.*

We walk to court, her trying to quell my nerves with local constituency gossip. There's an edge to her criticism of her local chairman, who is hounding her for accompanying me for a second day and has even muttered about her being deselected for her marginal seat.

"I thought he'd value loyalty. Would understand the concept of innocent until proven guilty." She strides up Ludgate Hill, clearly rattled. Her workload's so heavy, she was never going to attend the whole trial, and I realize I can't ask her to do so beyond today.

I'm embarrassed to have put her in this position, and my shame only intensifies once I'm back in the dock, watching Darren Berwick walk into the court to give evidence. He was one of the two officers who arrived on the scene along with the paramedics: young, seemingly inexperienced, keen.

He was kind and solicitous, too, as was his colleague, Heidi Barker. It might have helped that I was physically shaking, knees trembling involuntarily so that I had to press them down.

"If we could just ask you a few questions," he said once the paramedics had stretchered Mike out and Julia had been escorted to a separate room by Officer Barker. He gave me a smile, warm and reassuring, as he guided me to sit on a kitchen chair.

He took me through my arrival, my reaction when I realized the alarm hadn't been set, my fear that someone had entered.

"I walked down the hall, using the flashlight on my phone, and then I saw him." The lie I'd started to formulate as I spoke to Julia solidified as I repeated it. "He was lying at the bottom of the stairs."

"Did you know him?" Officer Berwick said after he'd clarified that this was the first time I'd seen him in the house.

"Yes. He's a political journalist; I'm an MP. We'd worked together on a story." The details came tumbling out. It didn't occur to me to lie about this connection. They would find out anyway.

"So—is he a friend of yours?"

"No. Not at all." I shuddered. Far from it, but I could hardly elaborate.

"Did you have a bad relationship with him?" He had noticed my reaction. Beneath the table, my knees knocked against the wood.

"I'm sorry. Could I get a glass of water?"

"Of course."

"I just—seeing him like that. It was such a shock."

I got up abruptly and filled a glass, the water slopping over my hand as I wrenched the tap on quickly. With my back turned, I gulped it down. I was conscious the officer would be watching me. *Just a preliminary chat. Nothing to worry about.* And yet how could I not worry?

"I was asking what your relationship was like with Mr. Stokes?" Officer Berwick said as I sat back down.

"We didn't have a relationship." I lied without thinking about it.

"So, you hadn't invited him to your home?"

"No. He's a tabloid journalist. A work contact," I explained, as I would three days later to Detective Parkin. "He was someone with whom I've worked on a couple of stories. But I've never invited him to either of my homes. That's the very last thing I'd do."

"So, you came in, the alarm was off, and then what?"

"I found him at the bottom of the stairs."

"Just that?"

"Yes."

"And what did you do?"

"I went down to him."

"And did you call the ambulance?"

"No. Julia called it. I think I got in a couple of minutes before her. I didn't phone because mobiles don't work in the stairwell—you can't get great reception there; you have to go near the back doors toward the garden or back upstairs, and I didn't want to leave him. And I just froze. I'm sorry." I realized I was babbling. "It's just a shock . . . I didn't know what to do."

The officer made a detailed note, his writing spidery and painstaking. He seemed to accept my explanation, and his colleague appeared similarly satisfied when she returned after interviewing Julia. There seemed nothing untoward in anything we said. We were two politicians; Mike was a tabloid journalist. Neither are deemed particularly trustworthy, but two sober female MPs had to be more credible than one drunk male intruder. There was no reason for us not to be believed.

They would be in touch, Officer Berwick said, if they needed to interview us again. "And we'll update you on Mr. Stokes's condition."

"Thank you." I should have thought to ask about him before the officer mentioned it.

Officer Barker's phone started ringing, and she went into our courtyard garden to take the call, her back turned toward the kitchen. When she came back, her gaze flitted to me before she spoke to her colleague— and I knew then that everything was about to go horribly wrong.

It was her look of apprehension that did it: a certain wariness as if she sensed that things were to become far trickier.

"That was the hospital. Mike Stokes is unconscious again."

———

Remembering that moment, from my spot in the dock, a chill of fear runs up my spine. The feeling intensifies as Sonja Jackson starts to play back footage from Officer Berwick's body cam. The video is splayed across two screens: the first directly opposite the jury on the other side of the courtroom; the second to their right, on the left of the judge, and visible to the assembled lawyers and me.

The woman captured by the camera that December night looks wired. She talks too fast, guilt almost tripping her as she spills her story. She is eager to offer an explanation and shut down questions, far too willing to please. The woman on the screen doesn't seem to be aware she is perjuring herself because her mind isn't spooling that far ahead. Her hair is flattened from her cycling helmet, but it's better cut than it is now, and she's smartly dressed in the blouse and cashmere cardigan, the tailored Jigsaw trousers she'd worn that day. But the sleek trappings—the clothes and minimalist kitchen—can't hide her feverishness, the slightly hyper energy she emits, and there's a palpable disconnect, as if the sound and images of the video are slightly out of sync, though the IT's all working correctly, and you can hear me enunciate clearly.

"If we can just pause the tape there," Miss Jackson says, and she taps at her laptop to stop the recording. "Emma Webster is telling Officer Berwick what happened when she entered the house. You have the transcript of the interview in your bundles, tab two, section one, but if I can just read the pertinent section, she says: 'It was too quiet, but I thought someone was there. I walked down the hall, using the flashlight on my phone, and then I saw him. He was lying at the bottom of the stairs.' Isn't that right, Officer Berwick?"

"Yes," he says.

"And I think you double-checked that with her. You asked her"—and Miss Jackson skips through his evidence, her voice less monotone than Officer Berwick's, but the exchange still matter-of-fact—"'So when was the first time you saw him?' And Ms. Webster replied: 'When I saw his body. His body at the bottom of the stairs.'"

"Yes."

"No further questions." Sonja Jackson sits back down, having firmly established my initial account in the jurors' minds so that she can later depict me as a liar.

It is a tactic she will use again and again.

———

Before we hear from the paramedic, Miss Jackson calls the next-door neighbor who claims to have heard the fight. Alex Marber is an eighteen-year-old student, who was studying at home on the afternoon in question. I hardly knew the Marbers beyond chatting to Ian, the disarmingly good-looking father, on the rare occasions we found ourselves locking our bikes to our respective railings after arriving home at the same time. Nikki, his fellow doctor wife, was always trying to rope me into the residents' association, and I felt so embarrassed for refusing that I kept my distance. The parents both worked at St. Thomas' Hospital; had two children at university and a third, Alex, who was still at home.

I barely recognize him as he ambles into the box. He has his father's charmed good looks and an additional height: he must be six foot three or four, has grown six inches since last summer. And like a sunflower that's rocketed, he sways slightly, as if unsure of his sudden growth.

But if this suggests he's uncomfortable, he's not. His expression, as he glances at judge and jurors, is a beguiling mix of shyness and provocation. He is studying English, music, and drama, he tells the court, and he has a certain presence, born of being an extremely good-looking, privileged young man. The jury sense it, the potential foreman sitting a little straighter, the young blonde woman with the expressive eyebrows taking note. You can imagine him onstage: he holds your attention even though he's doing nothing more significant than stating his name and filling in this background, and I worry they'll find his evidence convincing merely because of his charisma and looks.

Sonja Jackson takes him briskly through his statement. On Wednesday, 8 December, Alex was home from college and had been studying, with his noise-canceling headphones on in his attic bedroom.

"What were you playing?" asks Sonja Jackson.

"Nirvana. 'Aneurysm,' I think."

There is a pause while the tragic irony of him listening to this shortly before Mike sustained a fatal head injury reverberates around the court. He must sense it because he rushes to elaborate. "And 'Heart-Shaped Box.' All the classics."

"Nirvana is a rock band, isn't it?" She gives the jury a little smile that suggests she remembers these hits. "Yes," he says, a little sardonically.

"And how loud were you playing it?"

"Pretty loud. That's kind of the point."

At about a quarter past four, he went from his second-floor bedroom down to the kitchen, in the basement.

"Why was that?"

"I felt a bit hungry. Thought I'd raid the fridge."

A murmur of recognition ripples among the jurors. Both the ample woman in the front row with the Chelsea bun face and the woman around my age who sits behind her smile indulgently. Mothers of boys, I'd guess.

"Were you listening to the music as you went downstairs?"

"Yes."

"And as you came back up?"

"No. I stopped listening in the kitchen. It was 'Smells Like Teen Spirit.' I'd listened to it too much, so I just put my headphones round my neck."

There are more details about him making a cheese sandwich and fetching a pint of milk, and the possible time it took for him to do this. (No more than five minutes.) Then Alex was keen to get back to work. He started climbing the stairs, still without his headphones on, and as he reached the top of the stairs and entered the hall, he heard muffled voices.

"It sounded like there was a row going on. I could hear footsteps clattering around and a man and a woman. They were having an argument."

"What makes you say that?"

"Well, it sounded quite heated."

"Were the voices raised?"

"Not the man's. His was quieter, as if he was trying to calm the woman down, but hers was louder. Higher pitched. Going on and on. Nagging. Then she shouted at him."

"So his voice was quieter 'as if he was trying to calm her down,' but she shouted at him," Sonja Jackson repeats, as if this is quite astonishing. "Could you make out what she said?"

"Not at first—I was just getting into the hall, only listened for a few seconds—but she must have spoken particularly fiercely because I heard: 'Get out. Get *out*!'"

"And how did she sound, as she said this?"

"Really shrill and fierce. Like he was being told off. Like a teacher might be, or my mum when she loses it." He gives a slight smile, and I wonder how Nikki Marber will feel, knowing her son has told the Old Bailey of the outbursts I'd occasionally hear.

"And what did you do then?"

"Well, I went back upstairs to do my work."

Sonja Jackson waits, head cocked to one side.

"I felt a bit as if I was intruding. Eavesdropping," Alex continues. "I didn't want to hear their argument: it was none of my business. And I needed to get on. I had an essay to get in the next day."

He looks at me then, this young man, and I wonder if I can read guilt in his expression. How strange that the run-up to the most fraught experience of my life was overheard by someone who thought he shouldn't intrude. How events would have changed had he hammered on the wall; had he come around; had he been more curious, less polite; had he not been a typically self-absorbed teenager, preoccupied with finishing a lengthy assignment on time.

I can't blame Alex for trudging upstairs when he heard our argument. And yet I'm overwhelmed with sadness that he didn't come and help. Resent, too, that he dismissed me as shrill. If he had any idea of the terror I felt! That while anger was coursing through me, so, too, was a chill fear that made my movements erratic and aggressive and my voice loud and piercing. "Really shrill and fierce"? I was fucking terrified.

I glance at the press benches, where all this is being scribbled down as Sonja wraps up her examination.

"He was trying to 'calm her down,' you said?"

"Yes."

Sonja Jackson smiles. She has what she wanted, and she will leave it at that. "No further questions," she says.

———

Tom Tillett is reassuringly effective. Urbane, modestly spoken, he stares into the middle distance, as if contemplating how to approach this, but I am beginning to understand it is all a trick. A good lawyer, he has told me, should never ask a question without knowing the answer, so I'm reassured that he knows exactly what he's doing, and that this contemplation is staged.

Tom comes at Alex from a tangent, asking about school, reiterating that he is studying English.

"Yes."

"In fact, I believe you're just about to embark on your university entrance exams now, and that you hope to study English and drama at university?"

"Yes."

"At Bristol?"

"Yes."

Alex looks rather pleased with himself, and Tom gives a slight nod. A top university. Jolly well done.

"One of the texts I believe you are studying—that you were writing an essay on that night—is Shakespeare's *The Taming of the Shrew*, is it not?"

"Yes, that's right."

"'Froward, peevish, sullen, sour . . . And thus I'll curb her mad and headstrong humor.' A problematic text, isn't it? Would it be fair to say that the shrill and shrewish behavior of women was something that was on your mind?"

"I guess it's possible . . ." He is slightly less confident now.

"'Higher pitched.' That's how you described Emma Webster's voice, wasn't it?"

"Yes."

"Isn't it possible that what you heard wasn't a shrill woman telling someone off, like your mum, as you put it, but a woman who was terrified?"

"Well, I suppose so, yes."

Tom looks pointedly at the jury and waits three beats, not needing to lay it on thick. My lawyer has no desire for Alex to explain away an argument. A fight took place: the postmortem injuries bear it out, and I haven't disputed it. Indeed, it is part of my defense that I was sufficiently terrified for our argument to become physical, to my intense regret and shame. But Alex's inference that Mike was trying to "calm me down," that I was shrill and overreacted, is an impression we can't allow the jury to mull over.

As he leaves the witness box, Alex Marber's beautiful face is tinged with pink, and he looks slightly less sure of himself.

Thirty-Seven

14 JUNE 2022

EMMA

Unapologetically UnPC WhatsApp Group

@BarnabyMilesMP: Christ, have you seen the stuff coming out of
  court?

@TristramSaleMP: "Get the fuck out"? She's hot when feisty.

@BarnabyMilesMP: Would love to tell her to calm down, dear. 😄 😄 😄

@PJacksonMP: Being serious, her lawyer's good.

@BarnabyMilesMP: Not as good as Jackson. For a woman, she's legal
  dynamite.

I feel cold when Jago Harris, the lead paramedic, enters the box. Just
the sight of him takes me back to that moment at the bottom of the
stairs when Mike started railing against him, my adrenaline spiking as I
wondered what he might say. The jurors are getting used to witnesses now
and show only the mildest interest. But as he stands there, calmly, in his
uniform, I suspect they will trust his evidence.

He was nearing the end of his shift when he got the call to go to
Cleaver Square on 8 December, he tells the court. He and his colleague
had been told a male was unconscious having fallen to the bottom of
some stairs.

"And where was Mr. Stokes when you found him?" Sonja asks.

"Right at the bottom of the stairwell. On his back—as if he'd fallen
straight down from the top and bumped down the stairs."

"And could you explain his condition?"

"He was conscious but very disoriented. There was some blood on his left cheek from what looked like a superficial wound and another cut above that on his temple. It was bleeding a bit, so I put some cotton wool and surgical tape on it, but I was more concerned about the fact he'd banged his head. There was a visible bump at the back, so I ran through some questions—where he was, the date, his name. It was clear he had suffered a concussion. He seemed stunned, complained of feeling dizzy. Then he became argumentative."

And suddenly I find my breathing is short and shallow as if I am hemmed in. My vision blurs and I lower my head, then put it between my knees. Out of the corner of my eye, I can see the security guard looking at me. "I'm okay," I manage to whisper, because the last thing I want is to draw attention to myself. Instead I concentrate on the floor between my feet and on regulating my breathing. Slowly the room tips upright; the air begins to feel less oppressive; I bring my head up and try to listen to what the paramedic says.

But the memories are stronger than his evidence.

"Get off. I'm all right. I'm all right, I said." Mike's eyes looked wild, his expression belligerent. "Need to get out of here. Get fucking out of here. Get fucking off me!" His voice shimmered with bad temper and panic, with confusion and fear.

I noticed a spatter of blood on the wall near his head; hoped the paramedic hadn't, too. He didn't seem to; was more preoccupied by the lump on Mike's temple, the wound on his cheek.

"Let me clean that for you," Jago Harris was saying. "There you go. Now we need to get you to hospital."

"I'm not going. I'm not fucking going." And it was then that Mike became properly agitated, batting the paramedic's hands away.

"He became upset," Jago Harris says now. "Aggressive. He had obviously been drinking, and he kept insisting there was nothing wrong with him."

He describes wheeling Mike out on the stretcher, and I see myself asking incessant questions. "It's a good sign, isn't it? That he's conscious, that he's arguing?" I had followed the stretcher down the hall, watched as it was carried down the steps and into the ambulance. He was still conscious, and I couldn't square this: the fact I'd thought him dead and now he was talking again.

I seemed "panicky," the paramedic now tells the court.

"'Panicky?'" The way Sonja says it makes it sound bizarre.

"Well, no more than you would expect from someone who had come in to discover a man in their home."

My throat tightens at him acknowledging my shock. At last, a witness understands that, confronted by an intruder, I *was* completely terrified.

Only when he leaves the witness box and casts a glance in my direction, I can't help reading disappointment in his expression.

His role that night was to try to save a life. Does he, and everyone else, believe that mine was to take one?

———

There's a brief break, due to a delay in getting hold of Agnes Molnár, our cleaner and the next witness. There's not enough time to meet Claire, so I pop to the canteen to buy a coffee; then sit, trying to look inconspicuous, where it's relatively quiet.

Someone's left behind an early edition of the *Record*. It's the one paper I haven't read, and like a woman bent on self-destruction, I riffle through its thumb-smudged pages, desperate to discover what they're saying about my trial.

And while the news story offers nothing new, they've gone to town with a sketch of the opening day by Marcus Jamieson, the "Prof Who Speaks for the People," and my old tutor. I trace his out-of-date photograph: his silky hair in its foppish center parting, his sharp cheekbones, those cruelly clever eyes. He's ten years older than when he taught me. More hawkish; a little heavier; his early beauty toughened so that, objectively, he's a strikingly handsome man. Yet all I can see is the curl of his sensuous top lip. His very palpable sneer.

And his scorn drips from his pen: perfectly calibrated to wound while stopping just short of being legally prejudicial. It's a scorn I know, that I *remember* all too well. Once it was so effective, I'd physically recoil, or jump to do his bidding. Even now it kindles shame, apprehension, and deep unease.

It's the hottest ticket in town, *writes Marcus Jamieson, the Prof Who Speaks for the People*. And I had a front-row seat.

Not since Jeffrey Archer was in the dock for perjuring himself has a public gallery at the Old Bailey fizzed with such anticipation.

Because, in the opening speech alone, we were promised this would be a tale of sex and lies (though no videotape).

We were there to watch Emma Webster, MP—once a rising Labour star, now a woman whose party has disowned her—stand trial for murder.

The murder of her ex-lover, no less.

She's the first MP—let alone the first *female* MP—to be charged with such an offense. Quite a first! And no doubt she was aware of the distinction. Head bowed, she struck me as frail—with none of the feistiness you might expect from someone who, we heard, in the course of a frenzied fight, kneed her ex in an area no man *ever* wants to be kneed.

And I'm shaking, though I know it's *pitiful*, this drivel. He's *still* doing it. Trying to trash my reputation—as he's been doing for the past twenty-five years. Back then, it was a case of downgrading my essays, of marking my exams as mere passes, of diminishing my confidence so much I dropped my beloved politics. Now it's by depicting my downfall with undisguised glee.

All because this manipulative older man was my first lover. And though it took a while to extricate myself from his clutches, he has never forgiven me for rejecting him.

———

I can't think about him once I'm back in court. The next witness is our cleaner, Agnes Molnár. Listening to her take the oath, I realize I didn't even know her surname before this all occurred.

She used to come to us every other week. Leaving a strong smell of bleach and making our lives immeasurably easier—yet I saw her so little, I referred to her as "the cleaner."

I certainly wouldn't have recognized her as she is now. On the handful of occasions when we've met, she would have been wearing jeans and a sweatshirt, her manner efficient and perhaps a little harried, head buried in the cupboard under the sink. Now her dark hair is tied back, revealing a pale face, sharp cheekbones, and pointed features, offset by a severe black jacket and a tight, short skirt. Her English is good, but she doesn't seem completely sure of it, and so her voice often sounds interrogative, her "yes" rising at the end of the sentence in a clipped and somehow breathless "yah." This, and the fact she tilts her chin up as she answers a question, makes her appear defensive.

Sonja walks Agnes through her evidence gently, requiring nothing more than a "yes" as she asks her leading questions. She ascertains that she cleaned our house every other Wednesday, from two until four o'clock, and that on Wednesday, 8 December, it was raining heavily.

"In fact, in your statement you say it was 'filthy wet' and you were 'worried about getting soaked as you went to the Tube'?"

"Yes."

As she was trying to put her umbrella up just inside the hall, a man came up the steps toward her, she tells us.

"Did you know him?"

"No—but he showed me a card from his paper. It said he was political editor, and his name was Michael Stokes."

"Did he say anything else?"

"Yes." The answer comes quickly as if she is keen to get it out. "He said he had come to meet Emma Webster, and could he come in."

"And what did you say to that?"

"I said I didn't think it was a great idea." She shakes her head. "I didn't think I should let a man into the house. I didn't think Julia would like that at all. But it was raining a lot. The rain was blowing into the hall. He didn't have an umbrella. He had the collar of his coat up and was . . . How do you say? Bunched up . . . trying not to get wet. He waved his phone at me. He had a message from Emma, he was saying, and he kept trying to show it to me."

"And what happened then?"

"His phone was wet. It was an iPhone 7, I think, and he couldn't make it work in the rain, so I let him shelter under my umbrella. Then it seemed . . . I don't know, silly . . . getting wet like that. So I let him stand in the hall, on the mat, just inside the door." She gives an apologetic shrug. "He had a nice smile," she adds. "I had good feeling. That he was a good man. That he was telling the truth."

The jurors are watching her intently. The skinny, ratlike man in his thirties with the receding hairline nods along to her evidence; his bearded neighbor's expression is sympathetic, and I suspect that "he was a good man" is something that will resonate, that they'll discuss in the jury room. I'm not sure it's as simple as that. He was as flawed as any of us, and that late afternoon, he was far from "good." But I can see how he would have seemed charming and unthreatening, even with a few drinks inside him. After all, Mike Stokes had been successfully persuading reluctant interviewees to allow him over the doorstep ever since he was eighteen.

"Did he enter the house itself?" Sonja says.

"Yes. Not far in. Just on the doormat, and I stood next to him as he looked for the message on his phone."

"And what did the message say?"

" 'Meet me at mine. 4pm. Have something you'll want to hear.' "

"And did you believe him when you saw this message?" Sonja asks.

"Yes. The message said it was from her. I knew Emma had worked with him. She had articles from the paper about Amy's Law pinned on her bulletin board." Agnes looks at me then, and I make myself return her gaze.

"So, you let him stay in the house?"

"No." Her voice swells and cracks, her defensiveness increasing as she details her thinking. "I let him stay on the doorstep. It was just after four. We thought she would be a couple of minutes, and the rain was getting so bad it was coming in. I was late for my next job in Clapham. My agency is quite . . . strict: I need to get next house done before my clients get home at half six. And so I told him to wait there, under the ledge. I wanted to say he should pull the door closed, so he wasn't in the house, but I didn't . . . I didn't want to look rude by being suspicious. And I didn't set the alarm. I was so late for my next job, and I thought, if he was there on the doorstep, I didn't need to do it."

Sonja Jackson takes her time in appraising Agnes. She leans her elbows on the lectern as if recognizing we all need time to contemplate Agnes's foolish, and ultimately devastating, act of kindness, and when she speaks, it is more in sorrow than in condemnation.

"So—you left him in the house, standing on the doorstep, alone?"

"Yes."

"Were the lights on when you left?"

"The lamp in the hall, on the little table, is set to a timer, and that had clicked on. The others were off."

"And when you left Mike Stokes on the doorstep, with the door open and the hall light on, how long did you think Emma Webster would be?"

"I thought she would be back any second."

Another lengthy pause.

"And if we can just turn to the mistletoe, do you remember where it was hanging when you left?"

She chews her lip, apparently unable to answer. Apprehension sharpens my senses, and I sit more upright. If Agnes claims it was hanging from the first fitting, the prosecution case against me is stronger. I cannot help willing her to give the right answer as the court sits transfixed.

"I—I don't know," she says at last. "I clean so many houses. It was a long time ago. I look at the floors, the surfaces, the skirting boards. The areas people notice. Julia said not to bother dusting the picture rails, the lampshades. I just focus on what's important—so I look down all the time."

My breath eases out. I had wondered if she would fail to give a definitive answer for fear of making a mistake. But the explanation is more prosaic.

A quick nod. "No further questions."

———————

After lunch, we hear from Mel Reed, the IT and telecoms expert witness.

Cool, slim, in her mid-thirties, she doesn't seem to help the prosecution's case. She tells the court that the message was sent from a Messenger account, linked to Facebook, but from a deleted user, and that, though it used my name and profile picture and so gave the impression I'd sent it, there is absolutely no evidence it came from me. She could not say which device this message was sent from, but it wasn't from any the police knew

of: neither my personal or work mobiles, my laptop, or my work computer, all of which were seized.

Sonja looks disgruntled as she sits. No doubt she's resigned to Tom
pressing the witness on the crucial point of who might have sent the
message. And my lawyer doesn't disappoint.

I have been adamant all along that I did not send this and that Mike
or a colleague of his must have done so to justify his presence and provide
him with an excuse to enter my house. He would have to have known that
Agnes was cleaning at that time, but since his paper had been keeping me
under surveillance, this wouldn't have been impossible to find out. He'd
also have had to gamble on her letting him in, but we all know doing this
was part of his trade.

Tom's aim is to clarify that I couldn't possibly have sent the message
and then to suggest Mike as an alternative.

"We have heard that there is no evidence Ms. Webster sent this message from any of her known devices," he says. "And we have heard that,
when this message was sent, a fresh Messenger chain—indicating it came
from a different account—was set up?"

"That's right," Mel Reed agrees.

"Can you think of a reason why Ms. Webster would have created a
second account, accessed from an unknown device, from which to send
a message when she already had a perfectly good account connected to
her Messenger?"

"No," Mel Reed says.

"And to be clear, it is possible that Mike Stokes sent it to himself, on
an as-yet-undetected device?"

"Yes, that's possible."

From the back of Tom's head, I think I can detect a nod of satisfaction.

"No further questions," he says.

———

I am drained after the day's evidence. Tom had warned me that parts
of the trial would lag. What I hadn't realized was that concentrating so
intently would feel like the most colossal strain.

When the court disbands, shortly after four, I have a brief discussion with my legal team, then take a cab with Claire back to her apartment. The streets are heaving, and there's a pulsing energy: a peal of delighted laughter, brisk footsteps heading for the Tube or to bars. I should be making the most of every drop of freedom. Instead we discuss whether Agnes's "he was a good man" will resonate, and if the jury think I sent that message. Then I text Flora: *All good. Give me a call when free?* An hour later, I still haven't heard, so I ring David, fretting about how she'll be feeling, needing to be reassured.

"Do you want the honest answer?" He's a kind man, but his voice is tethered with resentment about the effect this is having on our daughter.

"Of course I do." My voice creaks with dismay.

"She's finding it tough. What's so hard is that there's no one to interpret what's happening, to filter it and help her understand. It helps that you ring and text, of course it does, but it doesn't stop her worrying there's so much you're keeping from her, so much you can't say."

"I've tried to do that. Tried to reassure her."

"I know. But it would be only natural for you to put a positive gloss on it. Meanwhile, she's scrolling online, reading everything she can get her hands on—and you know how news reports distort things: only conveying the most dramatic lines. She's getting no sense of balance, or proportion, from this." A pause. Then: "I understand you don't want me up, but Caroline's offered to come up tomorrow, if that would help. So that she can give Flo a more balanced view. Report back. Tell her how you're doing. You never know: you might find it helpful to have someone there?"

"Oh, I couldn't ask that of her." I've no desire to be judged by the woman I've judged for the past four years.

"She'd like to come—for Flora."

A long pause, and he has me there. Because how can I say no to this? How can I actively reject an offer that might ease my daughter's anxiety?

I clear my throat. If I can't sound enthusiastic, then at least I can try not to sound begrudging.

"Yeah. Yeah, okay. Well, if she really doesn't mind, then thank you. I'll see her there."

Thirty-Eight

15 JUNE 2022

CAROLINE

Caroline has never sat in the public gallery of a court before. Despite the seriousness of her being here, her need to report back to David and Flora, and her sympathy for Emma, who's painfully thin—really far too thin—and understandably nervy, there's something almost *exciting* about the drama of it all.

She feels as if she's among the gods up here, perched on the front bench, where, if she cranes to the right, she can just see Emma. This, after all, is a form of performance. More a play than a recital, of course.

Emma had warned her it might feel dull. But the first witness, the cabdriver who took Mike Stokes from Westminster to Cleaver Square in the sleeting rain, is almost comical: he seems like a bit of light relief.

Yes, the gentleman seemed in a good mood, Bill Redman says. He'd been to a Christmas lunch, you see. Curry house in Westminster, and here Bill starts to offer his opinion on the merits of this particular restaurant compared to its competitor before Sonja reins him in with a question: did he seem a little worse for wear?

"I'd go as far as to say he was jolly. Keyed up. Full of Christmas spirit, if you know what I mean. But he wasn't someone you had to be wary of: I wouldn't be charging him £100 for the pleasure of scrubbing down the back of my cab." And here Bill gives a quick smirk, playing to the gallery, where the woman sitting next to Caroline chuckles. "No risk of vomit," he clarifies, as if this isn't abundantly clear.

"Did he tell you where he was going?" the lawyer asks.

"He was popping round to a friend's, he said. I got the impression it was a lady friend."

"What made you think that?"

" 'I've been summoned to a friend's,' he said, and he gave a sort of wink. I said I hoped she was pleased to see him. 'Hope so, too!' he said. It was just a bit of banter, really—then we talked about politics a bit, of course. Just because of where I picked him up. Or rather, I talked, come to think of it." He pauses, and Caroline notes that the judge is suppressing a smile.

"Did he seem aggressively drunk in any way?"

"No." Bill Redman is clear. "I've had enough nasty drunks in the back of my cab in my time to be wary when someone's been on the lash, but he was a complete gent. Hadn't drunk enough to be lairy. Delightfully tipsy, you might say."

"Did you notice any marks on his face?"

"No." He pauses as if thinking. "None that I can think of," he says.

Caroline glances at her former friend. She has difficulty imagining her lashing out at Mike with her keys: Emma, who was irritatingly condescending, not snappish, when cross with David; prone to using a "teacher voice"; unflappable, serene. The blood on the key is proof she shoved them in his face, but she must have been utterly terrified to do so. Caroline can imagine doing so quite easily. Who knows how anyone would react in a moment of intense stress?

Sonja Jackson looks pleased as she sits down, and Emma's lawyer makes minimal headway. Ascertains that Bill Redman has no medical training but doesn't press the point. Caroline thinks he should. "Delightfully tipsy" was how the cabbie viewed Mike. And didn't the cleaner describe him as "a good man"? The picture being built up about Mike Stokes is of someone anodyne, good-humored, with none of the arrogance or casual dismissal Caroline remembers when she met him two days before all this happened. A man to deal with Emma's hysterical behavior. To calm her down.

And how Emma would hate the thought of any man doing that! Why shouldn't she feel hysterical? Caroline is suddenly filled with white-hot anger: a sisterly desire to defend this woman, who she still isn't truly sure is innocent (though she's keeping that to herself). She peers down and sees that Emma looks stricken and frail: breathing, she reckons, not from her diaphragm but from her chest. The security guard is glancing at her, and Caroline looks at the judge. Surely she can see that Emma's not well? Can't she halt proceedings?

But the paradox is that, though this whole performance is concerned with the fate of Emma Webster, the structure of the trial means that, for the moment, she is waiting in the wings.

———

The door to the public gallery opens, and a man sneaks in: in his mid-fifties, smartly dressed, apologetic. Caroline tuts at the intrusion, as does the woman next to her. Doesn't he realize they need to concentrate on the next witness, Guy Black?

Emma has warned her that the point of calling him is to suggest that she had some sort of sustained relationship with Mike.

"But you didn't, did you?" Caroline had checked with her.

"No. I slept with him once. The time everyone knows about." Emma had given a tight sigh. The irony of her discussing a clandestine sexual relationship with the woman who'd slept with her then husband wasn't lost on either of them. "But if the prosecution suggests we had some sort of ongoing friendship, at least, then they could argue he wasn't an intruder—or at least that he wasn't as threatening."

"Oh." Caroline could see how that might work.

Now, as she peers down at Guy Black, she begins to understand how the jury might find him persuasive.

"How would I characterize Mike's relationship with Emma Webster?" he repeats Sonja Jackson's opening question. "Well, at first, she was just a contact, though a good one." He glances in Emma's direction before delivering the sting. "Emma Webster is a media-savvy MP. Always willing to chat to the press, which could make her unpopular among her colleagues, but which made us love her. She'd quoted for various stories and, through the Amy's Law campaign, she and Mike became . . . close."

Caroline sees the jurors take this in, imagines them appraising Emma in the light of such telling phrases. If being "media-savvy" is suspect, then so is being "close" to a journalist. It's such an intimate word. And Guy seems to relish peppering his evidence with innuendo. Hands resting on the front of the box, he takes his time, letting his eyes sweep over each juror, playing them like a consummate performer before providing them with another tantalizing morsel.

"Of course, though we teased him about it, we didn't realize they were getting quite *so* close."

"You teased him, you say?"

"Ribbed him. Quite a bit. Just banter in our office, and the odd text."

"I think we can go through some of the texts here. If you look at tab four in your bundles, you can see some examples," Sonja Jackson explains, and the jurors riffle through their bundles. "On 26 October, at 2:13 p.m., for instance, you text: 'Emma Webster rang keen to chat.' And then, later that afternoon, at 5:17 p.m., three hours later: 'EW rang AGAIN'—and the 'again' is in capital letters, suggesting some urgency?"

"Yes."

"There's another here, on 2 November, at 11:17 a.m., 'EW verry keen to talk' and you can see that the 'very' is elongated—again for emphasis?"

"Yes. She was just very, very keen."

Sonja pauses and looks down at her papers. "But then the texts in this vein stop. From Thursday, 18 November. Why was that?"

"Because Mike made quite clear that they should. Not initially—but a couple of days after. The morning after they'd gone for their meal, he looked really rough, and was a bit noncommittal. He'd bought himself a double espresso, itself unusual, and a Diet Coke, so I made a lame joke. Said something like, 'Not get any sleep last night?' and he said, 'Something like that,' and changed the subject."

"And I think you surmised from this that something might have happened between him and Emma Webster, but you weren't to press him on it?"

"Yes. I mean it was just speculation—I didn't know they'd had sex; I thought he might have made a drunken pass at her—but you'd have to be pretty stupid not to guess something had gone on. So the next day, the Friday, I tried again. Made some crappy joke about their hot date and he kind of snarled at me to 'leave it out.' Look, I'm not pretending this was some great love affair, but it was clear she'd rejected him, and he was pretty crushed."

Emma looks drawn at this. She's a kind person: must hate hearing how

Mike felt wounded. And it can't help her case, Guy normalizing him like this. A few of the jurors are looking pensive: a woman in her thirties with short cornrows and an intelligent face, a middle-aged woman with tired blonde hair and an anxious expression. Are they thinking about their own rejections? Are they empathizing with Mike Stokes?

Guy mentions that he would like to read out a eulogy he's written, and Sonja Jackson looks panicked as she stands abruptly and says that that really won't be necessary.

Judge Costa looks irate. "Mr. Black," she says, and she offers him a very tight smile. "The role of this court is to address the circumstances of Mr. Stokes's death. To determine if he was murdered. While we are apprised of your loss, I cannot for one moment believe you think this an appropriate forum." She glares at him. "It is not," she adds, to quash any doubt about the matter. Then: "Miss Jackson?"

"No further questions." Sonja looks nettled.

"Mr. Tillett?" The judge could be offering chocolates at a dinner party.

"Just a few, Your Ladyship," he says smoothly, and there is something about the casual way in which he implies he will be brief that alerts Caroline to the possibility he will be anything but.

"Mr. Black," he begins, as if embarking on a courtly dance, a quadrille perhaps. "We have heard that you sent messages to Mr. Stokes concerning Ms. Webster?"

Guy Black nods, and Caroline wonders if he is looking just the tiniest bit less sure of himself.

"If we look at one, in tab six of your folders." He waits for the jurors to find it. "Sent on 24 October, in the middle of the Amy's Law campaign, it reads: 'Your MPILF called again.'" Another pause. "Could you explain what you meant by the abbreviation?"

Guy has the grace to pretend to look abashed. "'MPILF' is a play on 'MILF.'"

There is a snicker from one of the jurors, and from behind Caroline a sort of guffaw of contempt from the man who snuck in late. She glowers at him. Pervert. This reflects badly on Guy, not Emma.

"Which is?" Tom Tillett isn't letting him off the hook.

"Look, it's not very PC, not something I ever imagined being read out

in court, but Emma Webster was terribly attractive. She regularly topped
the lists of sexiest female MPs. 'MPILF' is a play on the well-known compliment 'MILF.'" Emma's lawyer is still not helping him out. "'MPILF'
stands for, well, it stands for 'MP I'd like to fuck.'"

There is another pause as the court assimilates this information. There
are telling phrases, Caroline realizes, critical moments that will stick in
the jurors' imaginations, and this assessment by Guy seems to be one of
those. She watches the faces of the two eldest women jurors. Both look
repulsed. Guy, meanwhile, has gone an interesting pink. He might use
language like that with his mates, but he'll be aware of context. A well-
educated young man whose words are being reported by his peers, and
heard by women old enough to be his grandmother, knows he shouldn't
talk like that about any woman, let alone one older than him and in a
more authoritative position.

"There are, I think, eight texts in total that refer to Emma as 'the
MPILF,'" Tom Tillett goes on, his tone placing quotation marks around
the phrase and conveying his contempt for it. "They run up to 18 November: that's the day *after* we know Mike Stokes and Emma Webster spent
the night together." He directs the jury to yet another printout of the relevant texts and takes them through them all. And as he recites this casual
litany of misogyny, Caroline watches Emma's face crease. The whole time
she thought she was being taken seriously, this entitled man, just young
enough to be her son, was texting about her dismissively, referring to her
offensively. She had thought she was among colleagues, but they—or at
least Guy—had objectified her just as efficiently as the trolls who hound
her on Twitter: the men unable to refer to her without resorting to words
like "cunt" or "slut." And Caroline finds that any schadenfreude she suspected she might feel—because the woman who had judged her so harshly
is now being judged, and in such a public way—doesn't exist, and she feels
a swell of solidarity, of sympathy, that Emma was ever viewed in this way.

"'Your MPILF rang AGAIN, big boy!' 'Your MPILF rang. Must be desperate!'" Tom Tillett's deadpan tone makes each text incongruous and gro-
tesque. And then the possessive pronoun is dropped and an anonymizing
definite one introduced, the night Mike and Emma met in the restaurant:
"'Good luck with the MPILF!' followed by an eggplant and a taco emoji.

"And I believe an eggplant emoji represents a penis and a taco a vagina?" Tom Tillett asks pleasantly.

Guy, who by now looks as if he'd rather be anywhere but in the witness box, mutters something.

"I'm sorry. I didn't quite catch that," says Judge Costa, peering at him over her heavy, dark-framed spectacles.

"That's correct, Your Honor," he says.

The judge continues to scrutinize him because he's addressed her incorrectly. After a painful couple of seconds, he realizes his mistake and flushes deeper. "I mean, Your Ladyship."

Her tone is glacial. "I see."

"And I believe the use of this abbreviation was part of the joshing about his relationship with Emma Webster in the office, is that right?" Emma's lawyer continues, relentless.

"Yes. It was just a bit of banter. Nothing was meant by it—except that it was clear Mike liked her. That he valued her as a contact, but also that he found her attractive."

"From the texts, I think we can see that Mike didn't use this abbreviation himself?"

"No—but he didn't discourage me from using it," says Guy, somewhat defensively.

"So, far from viewing Emma Webster as a professional equal, she was viewed—by you and your boss—as someone to be spoken of in sexual terms, someone whose sexual attractiveness was of paramount interest, is that right?"

"Well, I wouldn't say that was of *paramount* interest . . ."

"And yet that's how she's consistently referred to—and this wasn't discouraged. We have eight texts in which this is mentioned," Tom says evenly.

There is a pause, during which Guy gives a shrug as if to say, *Okay, you've got me there.*

Behind Caroline, the man mutters something that sounds suspiciously like, "Bet she loved it."

In the dock, Emma looks straight ahead, her expression pained.

"No further questions," Tom Tillett says.

Thirty-Nine

15 JUNE 2022

EMMA

"Well, I think now we have Miss Martin as our next witness, do we?" the judge asks Sonja, who agrees that we do.

"In which case, would counsel agree this is an appropriate juncture at which to remind the press of the earlier matter?"

A flicker of confusion among the jurors, perhaps at the erudite language, perhaps at the thought of what the "matter" might be.

"Members of the press," she says, leaning slightly forward, and my heart tightens because she's repeating the warning about Flora, made before Sonja's opening speech. "Just to remind you, the following discussion is subject to a reporting restriction—section 45 of the Youth Justice and Criminal Evidence Act. That means that nothing can be printed which risks leading to an identification of Ms. Webster's daughter, Flora Webster, as a person concerned in the proceedings. Neither her name nor the subject matter can be reported. Is that understood?"

The journalists lay down their pens, obedient as small children listening to a respected teacher.

"Very well." She gives them a hard stare. Then: "Miss Jackson?"

Sonja Jackson rises and ruffles her gown around her like a crow rearranging its feathers. "Members of the jury," she says, "you will hear that Michael Stokes had been working on a story which involved Emma Webster's fourteen-year-old daughter, Flora. Michael Stokes had discovered that Flora Webster had been investigated by the police for taking a live photo of another teenage girl when she was topless—and sending the moving image to a sixteen-year-old boy."

The lawyer pauses. A couple of the journalists smirk, and one of the young women journalists glances at me, narrow-eyed. Rita, with her cotton candy perm, pulls her chin in like a chicken primed to peck. Margaret, with her ash-blonde bob, gives a shake of her head.

"Now, we are not here to judge Flora Webster," Sonja Jackson goes on in the self-satisfied tones of someone whose child would never do this. "The fact she was interviewed by the police and given a Youth Conditional Caution is only relevant because it was something that Michael Stokes discovered, and that Emma Webster was anxious he shouldn't report. We will submit that this tension explains the animus between Ms. Webster and Mr. Stokes." She directs the jury to the text message I received from him on 29 November, suggesting we meet in Victoria Tower Gardens, and explains how I went to discuss what he'd discovered. A pause. "If we could call Miss Martin?"

Rachel Martin was once, if not my key contact on the *Chronicle*, then a woman whose calls I would take and who would smile at me when we passed in the Commons. Now she looks at me with palpable disdain.

Everything about her smacks of anger: from the way she pulls sharply at the bottom of her crisp white shirt, then tugs at the lapels of her jacket, to the jut of her chin and slight toss of her head. Guy might have championed Mike, but it was Rachel, he once told me over a coffee, who was his closest colleague. Rachel who sat alongside him for four years, sculpting stories, trading nuggets of information, sharing late-night drinks and commiserations about the demands of the desk and the relentless nature of their jobs. And as I think of her animosity toward me, I wonder if she ever viewed him romantically. His widower status, his aura of being wounded, his apparent dishevelment could make him disarmingly attractive. And if I fell for it, another single woman might well, too.

I view her differently, through this prism, judging her as she judges me. But I also note how her voice becomes less strident as she covers some of the ground already discussed by Guy. Yes, there *was* a distinct shift in Mike's behavior in the aftermath of our Soho meal. Yes, she knew that something had happened, and after a few days she managed to prize the information out of him. "You could call it female intuition," she tells the jury, because, like Guy, she's a born storyteller. "Or perhaps it's journalistic instinct, but really it was just obvious."

"How so?" Sonja asks.

"In the run-up to their meal, he was . . . well, upbeat, I guess. It wasn't that he was lovestruck. He was forty-two, had been around the block a few times, but it was as if his cynicism was wearing off. He started talking about the changes to the revenge porn law that they'd brought about through the Amy's Law campaign with the zeal and enthusiasm you'd expect of a journalist trainee. He just seemed visibly younger. Far less jaded about politics, and about the chances of anything ever being changed. And you know when someone has 'mention-itis'? It became a running joke between Guy and me: how frequently he could shoehorn references to Emma Webster.

"And then, after the meal, he became cold, or at least detached, when she was mentioned. Quite curt. We'd thought, Guy and I, that we'd get some great mileage out of it. That we'd rile him a bit—but that clearly wasn't an option, at all." She gives a hollow laugh. "I realize we don't come out of this very well . . . I took Mike for a drink on the Friday night because he had clearly been hurt and it was affecting the atmosphere in the office. Frankly, I'd thought I could laugh him out of it; get him a bit drunk; remind him that *we* valued him, because we did, we really did." Her voice thins, the past tense hitting her. "I hope he realized that at the end."

Sonja gives her a moment, lets her grief land. Then she presses on. "And did he say anything about Emma Webster during that drink?"

"Yes. He didn't go into details, but it was clear she'd rejected him."

"And I think you found his attitude to her had hardened?"

"Yes. It's a defense mechanism, isn't it? It was clear he didn't want anything to do with her. He stopped mentioning her, so it wasn't as if he was criticizing her or being cruel. I remember a colleague from another paper made a reference to her in passing as 'Mike's top contact,' and he sort of gave a shrug and said, 'She's all Rachel's now.'"

"And were you happy about that?"

Rachel dismisses me with the most perfunctory of glances. "Emma Webster was perfectly entitled to reject Mike. It doesn't mean I have to like the way in which she handled it. But I'm a professional. She's a good source of stories, and she had a good relationship with the *Chronicle*. The editor would have been keen we maintained that. I wasn't going to let that go."

The female juror my age looks at me now, and I wonder if I can spy pity in her glance, because there's real acid in this dismissal from a younger woman. But I don't have time to dwell on it because Sonja is turning to 29 November, when Rachel spotted us while walking to the Commons from the BBC's Millbank Studios.

"I'd just been on the *Daily Politics* show," she says, a touch of pride in her voice. "It must have been just after midday. I thought I'd done okay, but I was a bit hyped and wanted a moment to myself, perhaps to walk along the river."

"Did you walk along the river?"

"I didn't, no."

"And why was that?"

"Because as I made my way down, I saw Mike and Emma Webster, and they were clearly having an animated discussion. She looked furious. Her posture was rigid, and she was jabbing her finger at him, standing too close and speaking quickly as if she was really having a go. I got a bit nearer, still staying out of sight, and I heard her say: 'I will come after you if you *dare* to name her.' Then she turned abruptly and stormed off, striding along the path bordering the river, and he sort of sauntered after her. His body language was interesting. He looked confident. As if he knew he had her rattled. As if he was the one in control."

Rachel goes on to detail how she went back to the office but didn't raise the incident with Mike.

"Why not?"

"Because it felt too personal. I assumed it had to do with their one-night stand, or whatever it was."

"But I believe that, on the day Mike Stokes died, 10 December, you rang the police and told them what you'd seen that day?"

"Yes."

"Why was that?"

"Because it was clear Emma felt real animosity toward him. Look—I didn't know about the Flora story then. Even though we worked together, Mike was operating on a strict need-to-know basis: only the editor, the news editor, and a couple of photographers were in on it. But Emma's reaction and the fact she was willing to behave like this in a public place seemed extreme. We all lose our temper at times, but she'd gone beyond that: was on the edge, out of control."

Sonja waits. Lets the significance of her words settle in the minds of the jurors. It's a favorite tell of hers. This pause to allow the audience to dwell on what they've heard. It's a technique I used as a teacher, and if I ever make it back to the Commons, and if I ever have the strength to stand up in the Chamber—both of which seem inconceivable at the moment—it's one I must remember. To underline the significance, there are no further questions from the Crown.

Tom takes some time establishing that I had some justification for "losing my temper" with Mike, that lunchtime. Rachel confirms that the *Chronicle* had me under surveillance from 29 November, when they received the tip-off that Flora had been to the police station and I refused to cooperate. That this involved photographers staking out both homes and culminated in a newspaper article on 4 December, describing me as a single parent who was "gaunt and anxious" because of a "family issue." If the jurors looked at tab nine in their bundle, they would find the article there.

And as they turn to the relevant photocopy, it strikes me how obscene it is that I experienced this, and that I somehow accepted it as inevitable: the payback, the flipside to being an MP. Just like the water placed on my desk in case of an acid attack and the bag checks for knives before I met with constituents; just like the panic alarm carried within touching distance and the extra locks suggested for the door. Just as I'd normalized the fear that coursed through me as I cycled home, always terrified I was being followed, or the fact that constituents might cause my heart to race, like Simon Baxter shoving his face so close to mine I could almost taste his spit.

But there was nothing normal about any of this.

"Miss Martin," Tom concludes, after the journalist confirms these details in a frank, businesslike way. "Have you ever been placed under surveillance?"

"No."

"Or had an unflattering news story alluding to your fracturing mental state published?"

"No."

A long, thoughtful silence.

"In your experience as a seasoned journalist, do the subjects your newspaper targets welcome being treated like this?"

"No." A note of incredulity creeps into her voice.

"And you're an emotionally intelligent woman. Would a female MP who believed she was stalked, and who was already trolled at length, feel some frustration at this happening?"

"Yes—but she was a public figure."

Another silence, and his tone is quieter, exquisitely thoughtful.

"What difference does that make?"

It's a fair question, but in its simplicity, it's breathtaking. Ash Bob nods as if to say he has a point while the greasy-haired student looks pensive. *Let's hear her wriggle out of this*, his expression seems to say.

"If you're a public figure, then you're fair game, to an extent." Rachel's voice rises as she grows defensive. "And if you're a politician, paid to represent us, to pass laws governing the rest of us, then you're open to greater scrutiny. They understand—or they should understand—that that's the deal."

"And that includes having photographers keeping you under surveillance twenty-four hours a day? Having snatched photographs published of you in your nightclothes; knowing that your teenage daughter risks being exposed for criminal behavior, yes, but the sort of mistake an impetuous fourteen-year-old might make, if a way can be found of doing this that doesn't break the law? That's the deal, is it?"

"Yes," she says dryly.

"That's in the public interest? Or is it that, as far as your paper is concerned, it is publicly interesting?"

"I'd argue it was both." Her eyes flash. He has touched a nerve.

Tom looks down at his notes. I can't see him raising a skeptical eyebrow, but I've observed him enough in our consultations to imagine him doing this. He takes his time before moving on.

"'I will come after you.' That's what you claim Emma Webster told Mike Stokes?"

"Yes."

"How far away from them were you when you heard this?"

"I suppose around five yards."

"But neither of them saw you, so is it possible it was more?"

"They didn't see me because I was standing behind a bush. And I very much doubt it was more than five yards."

"You must have very good hearing?"

She shrugs. "She said something to threaten him, and it sounded very much like that."

"'We all lose our temper,'" he continues. "But then you noted that Emma Webster 'turned abruptly and stormed off, striding along the path bordering the river'?"

"Yes."

"So, having apparently threatened him and lost her temper, she chose to remove herself from the situation. To defuse it by walking away?"

"I guess so, yes."

"In fact, *he* pursued *her*. 'He sort of sauntered after her,' you said. 'He looked confident,' you added. 'As if he knew he had her rattled. As if he was the one in control.' This doesn't appear to be a situation in which he felt threatened, in which he was *frightened* by her behavior?"

"No," she agrees.

"No further questions," he says.

The court adjourns after Rachel's evidence. I have never been more desperate to get away. It is one thing to know that trolls are thinking the worst of you; another to hear that people you've worked with, who you thought liked you, at least professionally, hold you in contempt. It's not so much the MPILF comments, which I knew about, the Crown Prosecution Service having had to disclose those texts in the run-up to the trial. It's more that Rachel, who I always thought liked me, clearly didn't.

If you're a public figure, then you're fair game.

Caroline is waiting for me in the Old Bailey's grand hall once I've said goodbye to my legal team. She looks slight against the grandeur of the neobaroque surroundings: the gleaming marble floor and columns; the ornate murals; the axioms—"Right lives by law," "Law subsists by power"—decorating this vast room.

"It's quite something, isn't it?" she says, gesturing at the ornate dome flanked by four marble goddesses—Justice, Mercy, Temperance, and Charity. She is standing near a statue of the prison-reform campaigner Elizabeth Fry, and I give an involuntary shiver: prison and a life sentence being the outcome I fear above everything else.

"Shall we go?" I ask, suddenly desperate to be away from this heavy Edwardian symbolism—the pity conveyed by Mercy, Fry's benign expression.

But as we start to walk toward the stairs, I spy the back of a dark head a few yards in front of us. Broad shoulders, a Barbour jacket. Simon Baxter? There's no reason for him to be here unless he's making good his threats. *I'll be watching you. I'll be tracking your every move.* The thought that he could have been watching from the aerie of the public gallery makes my heart stutter. Am I being paranoid—or *could* it be him?

"Do you see that man?" I ask Caroline, gesturing ahead, but he's been obscured by a large family group jostling as they pour out of a courtroom.

"Where?" She cranes her neck but can't see. "There was a bit of an oddball, muttering in the public gallery. I'd quite like to avoid him."

"What was he like?" I ask as we set off down the wide, Sicilian marble stairs.

"Middle-aged, respectable, quite dapper."

Simon Baxter? Or any number of men.

I keep my head down, though, as we traipse to the bottom, apprehensive not just about seeing him but about running the gauntlet of the photographers. On the previous days, I've made sure I've been flanked by John and Alice as I've left the building, ensuring there are no usable shots of me alone.

This time, I've left a little earlier, and the vast staircase is busier so that, as we prepare to leave the exit, we're in a throng of people. And I realize I've timed this all wrong because we've caught up with someone I would really rather not encounter: a sixteen-year-old boy, gangly and still in the throes of acne, but with the incontrovertible eyes and dimple of his dad.

"Wait a sec," Caroline whispers, putting her hand on my arm to hold me back.

But Josh, who's been distracted by his mum, looks up and catches my eye. His pupils dilate, the anger he'd directed at me in the courtroom swapped for shock at seeing me out of that setting. For a moment, he's no longer a young man, but just a small boy who has lost his father.

Guilt isn't finite, I've discovered in the six months since Mike's death. It ambushes me at the most unlikely moments, but sitting in the dock, I thought I'd experienced enough. That I'd applied a tourniquet to that emotion by dwelling on the terror Mike inflicted by inveigling his way in, by having me under surveillance, by threatening to expose my child.

I've tried not to remember the Mike bubbling with excitement as we met in Central Lobby, the Mike who made me laugh over that restaurant table. The man who made me feel desired and fell asleep with one hand cupped around my left breast. The Mike who seemed to crave intimacy, who let himself show he was vulnerable, who was clearly hurt by rejection. "You were going to sneak away?" he asked, bemusement on his face. And while I was frustrated at the time—I needed to get to Flora; I couldn't pander to his ego—I also realize I judged him harshly, because he'd been eager for warmth, for kindness.

Josh's reaction—before he turns in disgust and barges away from me, determined to put as much space between us as possible—reminds me of that.

Forty

16 JUNE 2022

The Record (online edition)

Marcus Jamieson, the Prof Who Speaks for the People

The Emma Webster trial is proving to be quite an eye-opener. Hacks who make crude jokes about the sexual attractiveness of politicians; one-night stands in three-star hotels; and now, the Old Bailey heard yesterday, the MP in question issuing threats.

"I will come after you" may not be the sort of thing we expect our politicians to say—but perhaps we should welcome this show of vim and spice.

This Emma Webster reminds me of the feisty student I once taught. She didn't have a first-class mind, but she had gumption!

Like so many of us, I'd far rather a politician with character.

Emma Webster MP Facebook

13,234 followers

> **Freya Jones**: Anyone wishing to send cards of support to Emma, please could you drop them at her office so I can pass them on when I attend court next week.
>
> **Bax S**: "I will come after you?" But she doesn't like being held to account herself. Talk about hypocrisy.

Forty-One

16–17 JUNE 2022

EMMA

The next morning, the jury attend the Cleaver Square house, now, of course, no longer rented by Claire and Julia. Their files contain detailed floor plans of the place I used to live, and they have watched footage taken by Officer Berwick's body cam showing the hall and staircase leading to the kitchen and the spot where Mike fell. They've also been video-walked through the house, with R2S, or "Return to Scene," software. But Tom thinks it's crucial they understand the relatively cramped nature of the hallway, and the dangerous proximity of the stairs. For them to grasp this, they need to go there.

It takes up an entire morning: the jury meeting at the court, then being taken off in a minibus with the clerk as if they are on some macabre school trip. When they get back, they seem more upbeat, less restrained. As if they've all being playing truant; or as if, outside the confines of the jury room and the designated seats they file into dutifully, their fledgling friendships have burgeoned. The woman my age smiles at Ash Bob as they realign their files; the mountainous student mutters to his lean neighbor; the hard blonde grins at the bearded fortysomething as he shifts some paper away. The cloying atmosphere of the courtroom has perceptibly lightened, and it takes a couple of minutes of Sonja Jackson standing silently, looking down at the papers on her lectern as if they are indescribably scintillating, for the jurors to quiet down.

They do so pretty swiftly once she introduces the next witness. Rebecca Smith is a forensic scientist who's been called to discuss blood spatter: the smear of blood found on the bottom step and a fine halo on the wall at the bottom of the stairs.

"When you examined the area where Michael Stokes fell, what did you find?" Sonja begins.

"Initially the walls appeared very clean," Dr. Smith says, with a smile, as if she knows she is about to impart something of huge significance, and my chest tightens because I know what is coming. "Someone had recently scrubbed them with hot water and bleach—you could smell the cleaning product—so that no blood was visible to the naked eye."

And I am back there. Two in the morning, my hands thrust into a bucket of scalding water, scrubbing away at the wall. Was I trying to get rid of any evidence—as Sonja suggested in her opening? It was less rational than that: a visceral need to rid the house of any hint Mike had been there.

Sonja presses Dr. Smith on how she discovered the spatter.

"We use luminol, a chemical which creates a bright blue luminescent glow when it reacts with iron in the blood's hemoglobin and reveals blood, despite any amount of antiseptic or bleach." A perky smile with a hint of gritty determination. "If there's blood, then the luminol *will* detect it."

There's a lengthy discussion about the pattern the blood formed, the direction in which it spattered and the nature of the stain. These were telltale "exclamation marks"—a long spine of blood, then a distinct dot—which indicate the blood had spattered at a low, obtuse angle once Mike's head hit the floor.

"The crucial thing about blood spatter is that it occurs the second time someone is hit," explains Dr. Smith as the jurors listen intently. "So, the wound has already been inflicted and the spatter occurs when that wound's either struck again, or shaken on impact with a hard surface, such as the concrete at the bottom of the stairwell. The low angle at which the blood spattered and the closeness of the spatter to the head are specific to the head striking the floor."

Miss Jackson nods to the expert and indicates she has no further questions.

"I have just the one," says Tom, and I can hear the smile in his voice. "We have heard, from the paramedic who attended Mr. Stokes at the scene, that he was agitated. He reared up against him, *flailed* against him, pushing him away. Is it possible that in the process of doing this, he banged his head himself—creating this spatter?"

"Well—I suppose it's possible," Dr. Smith says.

"Thank you." Tom sits back down. His question is designed to muddy the waters: to suggest that Mike could have caused this injury himself, and so diminish the idea he was struck forcefully before falling and striking the floor. Some of the jurors are making notes; the bearded fortysomething and his older neighbor look thoughtful. But none of the doubt that Tom is sowing, meticulously and gradually, in his cross-examination of witnesses seems sufficiently forceful. It's as if he's chipping away at the marble of the prosecution case, removing delicate slivers, when what I need is for it to topple with one colossal blow.

I am alone during the day's evidence. Caroline couldn't get out of her teaching commitments, and Claire can't miss a committee. I pretend I don't mind.

From time to time, I glance up at the public gallery, fruitlessly hoping Jazz or Patrick will have arrived. But there are no reassuring faces, and it's impossible to detect anyone beyond the front row. At one point, I sense a dark-haired man standing at the back, but he disappears. Simon Baxter? My skin goose-pimples at the unsettling awareness he could be hiding in plain sight.

I take a cab back, sufficiently rattled to imagine I could be followed. My thoughts are of blood spatter; of the pictures I'd tried so hard to neutralize, the wound glistening on Mike's forehead, that fine spray of blood I'd so desperately hoped that no one would detect.

Flora FaceTimes later and is more upbeat than on previous evenings. Having Caroline reporting back has obviously helped, but her blind optimism worries me. "You'll be okay, Mum, I promise," she says. But what if I won't? I can dismiss some of Sonja's grandstanding, but the factual evidence from a forensic expert is far harder to shrug away. It's proof that Mike was struck sufficiently hard before he fell for there to be a wound that bled. And the fact the blood was cleaned up, confirmed by Dr. Smith as she explained about the luminol, makes me sound so calculating.

I am sitting, agonizing over this, when Claire returns around 7 p.m.

"You okay?" Her round face creases with concern as she takes in mine.

"Not really. The evidence today about the blood felt pretty damning. The jurors perked up when they heard I'd cleaned it with bleach." I try to make a joke of it. "You should have seen some of the looks."

She throws a shop-bought fish pie in the oven, pulls a bag of peas from the small freezer. "Got to make sure you eat properly."

Because I won't in prison, I want to reply.

I feel infantilized being looked after. It can't have been easy for Claire: deciding to believe someone charged with murder; offering to put me up during the trial—a bail condition—let alone walking into court with me those first two days. She's not only antagonized her local party but ensured she'll never rise through the ranks, those close to Harry making it known that her loyalty to me is seen as "unwise." So why is she doing this?

"Because you've been there for me," she says as she places broccoli in a steamer, and I pour her a glass of wine. "Four years of listening to me bellyache about this job and eighteen months of me banging on about Matt have to count for something, right?"

And I think of our shared history: my sitting up with her at one in the morning as she fretted over an error she'd made in the Chamber, for which she'd been publicly reprimanded by the Speaker; or discussing whether she should give up a career she still believed in, but which meant she was unlikely to ever have a family of her own; or, for the most part, listening as she obsessed over Matt—who, immediately after ending the relationship, came out as gay.

"I feel as if everyone's laughing at me," she says, and her expression's bleak: she looks drained of her usual dynamism, her good humor. "I feel so judged. I'm supposed to be intelligent, astute, good at reading people—and I didn't see this. I didn't know, though he was my partner—and others did. I feel so naive. So ashamed."

"No one's judging you," I say, thinking back to the end of my marriage. "And even if the odd one does, it doesn't matter, does it?"

But I know this is of little consolation. Because the fear of judgment, coupled with the sense of betrayal, means that she is immersed in shame.

My sleep is disrupted. Fractious. I dream of spatter: blood expelled, pro-
jected, or cast off by a weapon spraying the crisp white walls. I dream of
gushes, splashes, arterial spurts; drops and stickiness; pools and wounds
that flow unstinting. Of smears that reemerge: brighter, bolder, more
incriminating, more crimson, every time I manage to wipe them down.

I wake, the white sheets so badly soaked that for a moment I think
I've wet myself, my heart quick-stepping so that when I stumble to the
bathroom, I bang into walls as I sway. Four seventeen a.m. The streetlamp
casts shadows, and Mike rears up, agitated, furious. *Get off. Get off me.*
A flick of the light switch and I send him packing. Then I pull on some
jeans, an old jumper of my dad's, a baseball cap brought in case I needed
to feel anonymous. It's still night, but twilight is creeping in and dawn will
break before five. I suddenly have the most intense urge to get out of here.
To walk the quiet streets, knowing that no one will expect me to; that, for
once, I needn't fear being followed. I leave a note for Claire and slip away.

And so I set out, tracing liminal parts of London: squeezed between
the City and Fleet Street; to the east of Covent Garden, the west of the
Square Mile. I wriggle up tiny lanes that whisper of Dickensian characters;
trudge past elaborate Victorian buildings, triangled between office blocks
of glass and steel. I get lost around Holborn Viaduct, before finding
Hatton Garden, Leather Lane, streets that sound familiar; trudge back
down the grimy thoroughfare of Farringdon Street to Ludgate Hill, where
I hang a left and see St. Paul's emerge in all its domed and colonnaded
splendor like the most elaborate wedding cake. The city's waking up: a
delivery truck stops to stock a supermarket; cleaners slip into offices.
Dawn breaks—salmon pink, crepuscular, hopeful. My night has been
filled with dreams of blood, but the world spins on, oblivious. Conscious
that my days of freedom might be limited, I need to taste more of this
fresh morning air.

I walk back up Farringdon Street, hang a right, and find I have come
across a vast, redbrick building. Smithfield Market. The street is busier,
and the air smells different: there's a ferric tang that grows bloodier, more
intense. The atmosphere is male and good-humored as vans off-load their

contents: vast carcasses of meat—sheep, pigs, quarters of beef—that hang, white-marbled and vermillion red. *Make not your heart so dead a piece of flesh. Flay off his skin.* Fragments of *The Duchess of Malfi* surface, and I shake my head. *Who would have thought there would be so much blood in him?* Wrong play, and there wasn't that much, was there? I tried, with the bleach and scalding water. I really tried to wipe it away.

A porter, white-coated, red-cheeked, sees me staring at his trolley and peers a little closer.

"Cheer up, love! It might never happen!"

Once upon a time, I'd have turned away, automatically irritated by the "love" and the suggestion I should feign cheeriness on his behalf. Now his good-humored statement nearly breaks me. Because I think "it" already has.

———

There's a different atmosphere in the court when I arrive three hours later. Perhaps because it's a Friday and the promise of a weekend free of having to concentrate from 10:30 to 4:15 stretches before the jurors. Or maybe because they are due to hear from the Home Office forensic pathologist, who will give them insight into something they wouldn't experience elsewhere.

Just before he appears, Sonja's junior, Dan Jacobs, reads from a toxicology report that confirms that Mike had 160 milligrams of alcohol per 100 milliliters of blood. There is also a report from Andrew Mattison, the consultant neurosurgeon who looked after him at St. Thomas' Hospital, which details his treatment and the fact he was declared dead at 1:17 p.m. on Friday, 10 December. The court is quiet as the dry fact is read out, as if taking a moment to mark this. Josh and his mother haven't been present since I surprised him as we queued to leave the building on Wednesday, and I'm grateful. If I were Cath, I wouldn't want my son to hear.

Nor would I want him to hear from Dr. Ash Chatterjee, whose entire appearance hints at his precision: from his sculpted goatee to his neat torso buttoned into a single-breasted suit. His speech is precise, too, as he confirms he conducted the postmortem on Michael James Stokes once the initial examination revealed evidence that couldn't be explained by his fall. This anomaly was the discovery of the cut to his left cheekbone and the separate cut to his left temple: lacerations caused by separate objects, he will tell the court, and whose infliction before Mike fell was corroborated by the evidence of the blood spatter, about which we've already heard.

Sonja takes a while to walk him through his credentials—his position as a lecturer at Imperial College London; his fourteen years' experience as a pathologist, after qualifying as a doctor at Guy's and St. Thomas's Hospital—before moving on to Mike Stokes's height and weight. Five foot eleven and a half, and 170 pounds "in old money," as she puts it.

She raises the toxicology results. "I believe this equates to double the drunk-driving limit?"

"Yes."

"So, would he be visibly drunk?"

"It would depend on his capacity, his tolerance for alcohol. The analysis of his liver suggested a moderately heavy drinker: twenty to thirty units a week. With this level of consumption, for a man of his size and weight, he might be unsteady on his feet—particularly if he was pushed off balance," Dr. Chatterjee says.

"If we can go through the injuries detailed in tab nine of your files," Sonja continues as the jury open their binders and reorganize their pages in an audible flurry, "I think image one shows a laceration, to the left cheek, measuring 0.6 centimeters by 0.2 centimeters, and 0.2 centimeters at its deepest point?"

"Yes."

"Image two shows a cut above, to his left temple, measuring 2.1 centimeters by 0.1 centimeters, and 0.3 centimeters at its deepest point, with some bruising around it? The cut the Crown says was caused by a ceramic bowl?"

"Yes."

"Image three: the palm of the deceased's right hand shows a bluish-purple bruise, around 4 centimeters in length and 3.5 centimeters wide, and image four shows a similar bruise on the palm of the left hand?"

"Yes."

"Image five shows a major injury to the back of the head. I think we can detect through Michael Stokes's hair a swelling measuring ten by five centimeters?"

"Yes."

"And in the next photograph, image six, where the hair is shaven, we can see the same swelling, and here it is very bruised with a bluish-purple appearance; the skin isn't broken, and there are no signs of blood?"

"That's right. Yes."

"Image seven is an image of a dissected right testicle with evidence of some bruising." Sonja pauses, and a couple of the male jurors—the lean thirty-year-old and the bearded man, who I imagine's a teacher—visibly wince as they absorb the image. "And I understand you always do this dissection in a postmortem?"

"We do. Yes."

The lawyer steps back from her lectern, as if she as much as anyone else needs some time to absorb this catalogue of injuries. When she speaks, it's as if it pains her even to ask. "Dr. Chatterjee. Can you tell us, out of all these injuries, if there was a single one that caused Michael Stokes's death?"

"Yes." He is emphatic. "Underneath the bruise at the back of the head is a fracture which shows that the head hit the ground with some force. That force would also severely shake the brain in the skull and tear some of the blood vessels linking the brain to the inside of the skull. They would have bled into the space between the skull and the brain, causing a large acute subdural hemorrhage around the front and base of the brain. It's the fracture—and the subsequent hemorrhage—that caused his death."

"And is there anything special about the pattern of injury to the scalp, skull, and brain in this case?"

"Yes, it's what's known as a *contrecoup*—or opposite blow—injury. It occurs when a moving head hits a solid object, in this case the floor. When that happens, the skull stops dead as it hits the surface, and that's where the bruising and fractures are. But the brain isn't fixed inside the skull and so it continues to move and gets ripped away from the opposite side of the skull, stretching the tiny blood vessels. That causes the bleeding which occurs around the front of the brain."

"So, the contact was at the back of the head, but the main brain injury was to the front?"

"Yes."

"And that is typical of a moving head hitting a stationary surface, rather than being hit on the back of the head by an object?"

"Yes. Exactly that."

And I hear the thud of his skull hitting the floor after his roar of surprise.

After what feels like an inordinate time, Sonja continues in her low, serious tone, confirming that the marks on his palms fit with him flying backward down the stairs.

"And the distinct injury on Michael Stokes's cheek?"

"The mark on his cheek, the deep laceration, is fascinating. That is to say it is deeply unusual. It looks as if it is the result of a blunt object such as a key being thrust into his left cheek by a right-handed person in a blow."

"If you look at tab four in your folders, you will see exhibit one," Sonja tells the jury, and there's the inevitable delay as they find it. "It's a photo of a key to the front door of Cleaver Square, belonging to Emma Webster. Analysis of this key after Ms. Webster's arrest revealed a trace of Michael Stokes's blood. And it's not disputed by her that this laceration was caused by this key.

"The next injury, shown in image two, was caused by a ceramic bowl snatched from the console table in the hall. That bowl has never been found, but it is an agreed fact that it was thrown in the recycling bin." She pauses, and I shift in my seat, always unsettled when she mentions the bowl. "And finally, we turn to the bruising to the right testicle." Another beat. "How was this likely to have been caused?"

"By a forceful blow to the scrotum commensurate with him being struck in that area, or, perhaps more likely, with being kneed."

There's another lengthy pause. More rearranging of her papers as the prosecuting counsel prepares to piece together these details.

"Dr. Chatterjee, from these injuries, is it possible for you to arrive at a *likely* scenario which explains how Michael Stokes ended up at the bottom of a flight of stairs with a fatal skull fracture?"

"Well, it's not for me to speculate, but the injuries suggest Michael Stokes was gouged on his left cheek with the keys and struck on his temple with a sharp object. The bruising to the palms of his hands arose as they slammed into the floor, and the head injury, of course, was caused by his head smashing onto the concrete floor just before this. The groin injury was caused by him being struck there by an object such as a knee."

"And the injuries to the cheek, the temple, and the testicle would indicate he was assaulted?"

"Yes, they would." He gives her a look as if to say this is obvious.

"Could the force of this assault have been sufficient to send him down the stairs?"

"My Lady," Tom stands. "My learned friend is leading the witness."

"Quite so," says Judge Costa.

"Let me rephrase this," says Sonja Jackson smoothly. "Are you able to comment further on any likely scenario?"

"No." He gives a self-deprecating smile. "It's impossible to say. I can't say that any one incident might necessarily have caused him to fall. You have to remember he had consumed enough alcohol to make him unsteady. He might simply have tripped over his own feet."

Dr. Chatterjee gives a firm little nod, and I feel a rush of gratitude toward this clever expert witness, who refuses to be corralled into giving an explanation that does not fit within his precise, forensic boundaries, and who refuses to push the facts to fit a narrative the prosecution requests. "He might simply have tripped over his own feet" is a line that will be chewed over just as much as "he was a good man" and "delightfully tipsy," when the jury come to deliberate.

Sonja Jackson looks dissatisfied, but she gives the pathologist a quick nod and asks him to remain where he is.

"Dr. Chatterjee," Tom begins, and his tone is courteous and urbane: two fellow professionals, two *men*, taking the measure of each other. "You have told us that Mike Stokes had drunk a sufficient amount for his alcohol levels to be double the legal drunk-driving limit, and confirmed that this might cause him to be unsteady?"

"Yes, that's right."

"And you've said you cannot specify that any one part of the struggle caused him to fall."

"Agreed."

"Is there any evidence he was pushed?"

Ash Chatterjee gives another little self-deprecating smile, as if he is sharing a favorite joke. "I always say that if I find a handprint in the middle of someone's back or on the center of their chest, I'll know they've been pushed." A murmur ripples through the jury, appreciation at his little jest. "Without that, it is impossible for a pathologist to claim this. There were no such marks, and so, no, there was no pathological evidence to prove that he was pushed."

My throat tightens. It's a critical moment. As Tom sits back down, I watch John Pearson ease back into his seat, and Alice's ramrod shoulders ease.

———

It is ten past four on a Friday afternoon, at the end of the first week of the trial. The judge glances at the clock that has been ticking down the time and suggests that, since there are some administrative matters to attend to, it would be a good time to stop.

"Shall we say Monday morning, 10:30?" she asks the lawyers, as if this is a social agreement.

Both agree.

"Very well." She turns to the jury. "We'll meet on Monday morning at 10:30 a.m."

The jurors shuffle out and the public gallery clears. There is the sound of feet clattering backward; the shuffle of bags and coats; the thud of a door, high above us, banging shut. Then a pause. The judge's eyes flick upward to check that no member of the public lingers. When she's satisfied, she gives a small sigh, the closest she has come to implying satisfaction. "Mr. Tillett," she says.

And Tom confirms that, when the prosecution case concludes on Monday morning, he will be making a submission that there is no case to answer on the basis there's no evidence I did anything other than defend myself when faced with an intruder. In other words, the case should be thrown out.

He had told me he would be doing this, but it is only now that I let myself believe this could possibly happen. That this whole nightmarish situation could be over very soon.

"Do you think we'll be successful?" I ask once we're conferring in a consultation room.

"We can but hope."

It's not the fulsome response I was hoping for. He smiles at me kindly. "Enjoy your weekend with your daughter."

It could be the last of her childhood. It's hard not to feel as if this is a reprieve.

Forty-Two

18–19 JUNE 2022

FLORA

There is so much Flora wants to tell her mum over the weekend, but she ends up feeling as if she's said nothing important. Nothing about how much she misses her, how scared she is, how frightened she is that this will be the last weekend her mum ever spends at home.

She knows her mum's anxious, too. She does that thing where she's trying too hard: filling the days with too many treats—homemade blueberry pancakes for breakfast; smoothies; superfood salads; chocolate and the suggestion of a movie night, the two of them curled up on the sofa in a way they've stopped doing recently, her mum staring at her too long, as if she can't believe she's hers. Then she goes and says something completely embarrassing. "You do know you're beautiful, don't you, Flo? You do know how much I love you?" And Flora mutters something about loving her, too, only she's not sure her mum hears because it's all a *bit* too intense, although that just about sums up life since last summer. Ever since her mum got that acid-threat letter. Since she did that *Guardian* interview and Leah made it quite clear how much she hated Flora. Since Flora sent that photo to Seb—and life changed forever.

Obviously, they don't talk about that. Because it was her doing that that led to this: her mum being on trial for *murder*. She can't tell her mum how horribly guilty she feels. Because, if it wasn't for her, then clearly Mike wouldn't have hassled her and the two of them wouldn't have had a fight. She can't imagine her mum physically fighting. Even when she's angry with her—and she *was* angry about Leah, even if she dressed it up as "disappointment"—she always stays icily, freakishly calm. But no, if it wasn't for Flora, then Mike would be alive, and her mum wouldn't be drifting around the house, failing to hide the fact she's been crying. Her mum wouldn't be facing up to the fact that in a week's time she might be in prison.

But she is, and here, as her dad might say, they are. Having this weird weekend in which they are tiptoeing around each other, neither capable of saying what's bugging them at all. Flora wants to scream at her to just be normal. But nothing is normal these days. Her mum keeps stopping and looking at things or touching things—her Orla Kiely mugs and those awful paintings that Flora drew when she was nine or ten: of Marmite, their dead cat; and of the two them, her mum in an apron, standing by a pile of books, and Flora in pigtails gripping her hand tight. They have big smiles and rosy cheeks, and although Flora has orange hair and her mum's is dark, they are clearly mother and daughter. Her mum sighs as she touches the picture, then goes back to cooking. And on Sunday morning, they go for a ten-mile hike.

It's such a relief to be out: to feel her calves burning as they climb to the top of the most punishing hill and gaze at the sea far into the distance. The people below look like Playmobil figures, and just for a minute Flora pretends that they've escaped reality, that those people belong to a different world.

Then a golden retriever bounds through the gorse, and a hearty family with two teenage children. Flora loves dogs, but she hates families like this: a bit smug—she just knows the children play county-level sports and get straight As—a bit too wholesome in their sturdy boots and wick-away tops.

"Good morning," they chime because that's what hearty families say when they're walking on the Downs on a June day.

Flora sees the flash of fear in her mum's eyes. She's not dressed like usual: her hair's tucked under a baseball hat, and she's barely wearing any makeup; is in jeans and a T-shirt. She doesn't look like Emma Webster, MP. Her mum mutters a hurried "Hello," and looks down, not wanting to be recognized. And as they pass, a flicker of curiosity crosses the woman's face.

"Was that who I think it was?" the husband says as they thud down the track, his voice confident and too loud.

"Yes, I think so. Don't look back," his wife hisses, her words carried on the breeze.

Flora wants to punch her. She really does. And it looks as if her mum feels similarly: her face has gone red and crumpled with deep, deep shame. It's really weird, but at that moment, it feels as if Flora's the parent and her mum's the child. She reaches for her mum's hand and briefly squeezes it. "It's okay, Mum. Just ignore them. It's okay."

But it isn't, and they both know it isn't. That family, with their nosiness, with their judgment, have brought the real world crashing back down around them. *Was that who I think it was? Yes, I think so. Don't look back. Don't risk any interaction! Oh my God: can you imagine what would happen if she spoke to us? What's she doing out and about anyway? An alleged murderer! It's only alleged, Gareth. No smoke without fire, Gwynnie. No smoke without fire. Do you think she did it? Well . . . the police must be pretty certain, mustn't they?*

Flora imagines all this as she watches their retreating backs. *This is my mum you're talking about,* she wants to shout after them, *and she's worth a hundred of you.* But of course, she doesn't. She's a good girl. Well, she's not, but she is trying very hard to be one—and so she tries to distract her mum. To chat about other things just as Emma does when she wants to make Flora feel better. What they should have for lunch; whether to bake a chocolate cake when they get back; how she might get a tan if it keeps being sunny like this. Good job she put on some high-SPF sunscreen: well, she *is* an English Rose. This said in the hope of prompting a smile because they both know Flora hates the way she looks. But then her voice wobbles because her mum might not be around this summer to nag her about suntan cream—or anything else.

Her mum's not responding to any of this, though, and she looks a little bit lost.

"Mum?" Flora can't help feeling frustrated. "You're not listening, are you?"

"Yes, I am."

"What did I say then?" She stands in front of her, suddenly aware she's more powerful. Her mum's so slight she could push her over the edge of the path.

"I— You were talking about dinner?" Her mum hazards a guess.

"Mu-uuuum." And she can't help it. She's so frustrated she turns and starts walking back down, a question fired over her shoulder. "Are you even interested in anything I tell you? I'm not going to talk if you can't even be bothered to listen to me."

She plows down the path, the gorse and branches scratching at her thighs, the air thick and claustrophobic. Her chest is tight with too much pent-up anger and sorrow and *exasperation*. Tight, too, with the pressure of her love.

———

Later, she and her mum go over to see her dad and Caroline, which is usually cringeworthy: everyone trying to pretend they are terribly adult about the situation, despite her mum typically being dismissive of Caroline and Caroline being just the tiniest bit possessive of Dad.

Today, though, things seem a bit easier. Perhaps it's helped, Mum having Caroline at court for a day last week. It certainly helped Flora, having someone to report back, and she knows Caroline is going to suggest she return this week. If not, Dad says he'll go.

The adults get cups of tea, which they take onto the patio, and Dad suggests she give them some time to chat for a few minutes. "Bit of oboe practice?" he suggests, which shows he must be desperate to get rid of her because he's not a fan of the instrument. Still, he's tone-deaf, so what does he know? She makes noncommittal noises and drifts upstairs. No one seem to have thought through the fact her bedroom's directly above them—just as they didn't when she eavesdropped on their conversation about the *Chronicle* stalking her mum, and what Mike might know about her and Leah. But then they always underestimate her. Did they really think she wouldn't want to know what they were talking about?

"Do you know what I really feel like?" her dad asks, now that he thinks she's busy getting her oboe out instead of looking down from her window. "A G&T."

"Good idea." She hears relief in her mum's voice, as if she's recognized something in her dad, some good reminder of their marriage. There's the click of pop tabs being pulled, the clatter of ice cubes, the hiss of tonic being poured. It's still hot outside, and they could be just a few friends catching up over a drink. But Flora catches a glimpse of her mum's face: the way in which the strain of the past few months slips just a little, like a mask she's been holding carefully in place.

"Oh, David," she says. "I'm so sorry. I'm just so sorry." And she puts her two index fingers below her bottom lashes as if to stop herself from crying. "How's she doing?" she asks after a while, and Flora realizes she's talking about her.

"Honestly?" her dad asks. "She's a bit of a mess . . . She's not sleeping. Her schoolwork's pretty nonexistent, though she's spending a lot of time on her laptop. One of last week's searches was the average sentence for murder." He looks down into his melting ice cubes, then drains his drink abruptly, and Flora hears his voice go tight as it does when he's trying to keep his anger in check. "You know she blames herself for what happened?"

"That's ridiculous. *I* was the one who panicked, who got into the fight with him. I was the one who got involved with him in the first place. This would never have happened if I'd just stuck to being a history teacher, as you wanted. If I hadn't tried to become an MP."

"Well, then you wouldn't have been you. And this wouldn't have happened if he hadn't got into your house," her dad corrects her in his dogged way and Flora realizes he must have really loved her mum and wonders why he had an affair in the first place. "You can't blame yourself for this any more than she should."

There is a pause then, and Flora sees that her mum is crying quietly now, as if it's a relief that someone recognizes this. Her dad pats her arm clumsily across the table, and for once, Caroline doesn't do anything to indicate she's pissed off by this show of affection. She doesn't look thrilled, but she's okay.

"We both think it would help Flora enormously if I came up and watched from the public gallery again this week," her stepmother says at last. "My reporting back helped her—and to be honest, it helped David and me, too. Made us realize quite what you're up against. Would that be okay?"

Her mum nods and gives her a look that seems almost grateful, and

Flora is reminded that they used to like each other, even if Mum was never as pally as Caroline wanted. Not for the first time, she thinks how weird her family is.

"And—have you talked to her about the worst-case scenario?"

"You mean prison." Her mum's voice is brittle, now. She doesn't help herself. "No, I haven't. I don't want her to consider that that might happen."

"She's not stupid, Emma," says her dad. "She's already preparing herself for the possibility. If you can't discuss it in detail with her, I think we'll have to. Unless you're absolutely positive you'll win?" There's a pause, during which her mum gives a long, dramatic sigh. Then her dad asks, more gently, "How are you feeling about the case?"

"My lawyer's going to try to get it thrown out."

"That's absolutely brilliant."

"I haven't mentioned it to Flo. I don't want to get her hopes up. I can't let myself believe it, either. He doesn't fill me with confidence that he'll be able to succeed."

And Flora picks up her oboe because she can't listen to this anymore, and begins a study, haunting and mournful. Over and over, she goes, perfecting the phrases until she plays each run confidently. And there's something mesmerizing about the process of practicing, and the study itself: as if the call and response captures the swirl of difficult emotions she's experiencing—frustration, shame, fear—and as if by perfecting it she can briefly block out everything that's happening.

Everything she can't bear to think about, let alone hear.

Forty-Three

20 JUNE 2022

EMMA

Monday morning, I am back in court, and the prosecution case is almost over. All that is left is for them to discuss a voicemail and some texts, and to play some agreed-to clips of interviews to highlight how my story changed.

First up is an edited clip of me stumbling through the story of the fight in my police interview on 11 December after I've been called out for lying by Detective Parkin. It makes for car-crash TV. An interview with a politician who has dug herself into a hole and is now trying to resurface with a little dignity. I want to watch through splayed fingers, to block my ears. If I'm convicted, it's a clip the broadcasters will play in their news packages. The sort of clip to go viral. *OMG, what's she doing! Keep on digging. How completely* stupid *do you have to be to be a politician? Not just stupid but dishonest.* I can just imagine the glee if it's retweeted or WhatsApped: are the jurors similarly disparaging? *Stupid* and *dishonest. Well, what do you expect of a politician? Of course, she's a liar! Goes with the territory.*

And then they are shown a second clip, timed 9:36 p.m., from the interview later that day. I look shifty; Detective Parkin sounds as if he has the bit between his teeth.

"In your first police interview today, you suggested that Agnes Molnár might have broken the ceramic bowl?"

"Yes. That's right."

"The thing is, we've just interviewed her again. She remembers dusting it and putting it back on the console table where it was when she left."

I shrug, not helping him out.

"And when your housemate Julia Cooke returned, she noticed the bowl on the table had gone." I remain silent, looking pinched. "And foot-age taken by Officer Berwick's body cam clearly showed it wasn't there. In addition," he continues, and it sounds as if he is enjoying laying this evidence out like cards from a pack, "a detailed search of the house has shown tiny shards from the ceramic bowl in the gaps between the hall floorboards. Can you tell us how they might have got there?"

"I don't know. If the bowl was broken by Agnes, and she has lied about it, there would be bits in the gaps, wouldn't there?"

My face darkens as I say this: shame flooding my cheeks and voice. Watching, from the dock, I feel that flush again, remember the embarrass-ment of knowing I'd been caught out lying. I hadn't been honest about this final detail because I knew it would reflect so badly on me. Having persisted in lying, how much worse would it look to then confess?

"You see the thing is," Detective Parkin continues, "the postmortem suggests the blow to Mike Stokes's temple could have been caused by a ceramic bowl of this size."

Some response seems required of me, but I still don't help.

"And the funny thing is, the lab has pulled out all the stops and done a preliminary analysis of Mike Stokes's clothing—in particular his overcoat—and guess what? We've found tiny slivers of the bowl in the fiber there."

Beside me, in view on the screen, John Pearson clears his throat. I've ignored his advice about making no comment throughout this interview, to my detriment. But how can I resort to this strategy, now it seems inev-itable I'll have to come clean?

"I used the bowl," I say at last, my voice very quiet.

There is a very lengthy pause, and I feel the need to fill it: to offer up my justification.

"I was terrified. I didn't know if he had a bottle of acid or what he was going to do next. I'd dropped the keys but he came at me and so I just reached out to grab anything. I lashed out and struck him with it and it broke as it landed. Afterward I cleared it away."

Judgment seeps through that interview room, and spills so that I can feel it running through the court. I can't look at the jurors, keep my eyes fixed on the screen.

"And how did you clear it up?"

"With the dustpan and brush. It's kept under the stairs."

Am I imagining a sharp intake of breath from the ample woman with the Chelsea bun face?

"So, let me get this right." The detective's voice is filled with incredulity. "You swept up the pieces with a dustpan and brush from under the stairs before going down to check on Mike Stokes?"

"Yes."

"And what did you do with the pieces?"

"I wrapped them in newspaper and threw them in the recycling bin, which was just outside."

"The recycling bin which you knew would be collected the next morning?" He leans back and raises his eyebrows at the audacity of my behavior.

"I wasn't thinking of that. I just wanted to clear it away." On the screen, I am pitiful, my body hunched over, my fingers twisted in a nest. "Look, I panicked," I go on. "It was Julia's favorite bowl, and I knew she'd be upset."

"You didn't think she'd be more upset by the fatally injured man in her kitchen?"

"I panicked," I repeat, my voice catching and the words coming out in clots, "because I knew everyone would think the worst of me."

I sit with my head bowed as Sonja stops the video, and I imagine every person in the court nodding along with my analysis. My reputation could not be lower at this point. *Well, what are you going to do about it?* I shake my dad's challenge away. There's nothing I can do about it. I am broken by the narrative that's been spun about me.

And there's more. My voice fills the court, but this time it's the voice message I left for Mike on 4 December, the day the *Chronicle* published the "gaunt and anxious" photos. And here my voice isn't tearful or panicked but packed tight with anger. "Mike, you *fucker*. Leave me *fucking* alone."

The hard *f*'s and *k*'s kick out. The abuse sounds jarring in this environment. There's a clear disconnect between the me trying to look demure in the witness box and the raw, visceral me who barked this order, voice shrieking under the strain. Ash Bob recoils as if slapped in the face; Permed Rita purses her mouth. I bet some of these jurors will have erupted like this, have sworn at those who've betrayed them. But I bet none of them would have done so if they knew their abuse would be heard in open court—and, worse, reported in the media. If it was picked over, discussed, scrutinized; if they were reduced to someone who screamed "you fucker" down the phone.

I look down, and when I risk looking back at the jurors, they're busy listening to the man in charge of the case, Detective Nick Cutler, who is reading out text messages between Mike and me in the run-up to and immediate aftermath of our Soho meal. Texts that suggest I was excited about it; that I felt warmly toward him. And for a split second, I am sitting across a candlelit table from Mike. Wine has been drunk; confidences shared; I'm warmed by the knowledge I'm with someone I can trust; the atmosphere's freighted with that delicious, flirtatious anticipation. And then Mike's soft gaze hardens, and I am facing him at the top of the stairs.

There are a few further exhibits for the jurors to note and find in their folders: the receipt from our dinner on 17 November; a credit card bill for the Luxury Inn, where we spent the night together. I have admitted staying there with him—they've seen me do so in the edited clip—so I've no idea why they need to pore over every detail. They are even shown TV footage of my statement on 9 December, outside St. Stephen's Entrance: my voice ringing out more confidently than I thought at the time, speaking of discovering "an intruder who'd fallen to the bottom of the stairs."

Sonja also notes that it's an agreed fact that the lights fused: in their folders, there's evidence from an electrician about this. The filament bulb in the lamp on the hall console table had blown, tripping the electrics: there's a photograph of the bulb, its glass smudged gray as if with smoke. The electrician notes that while the basement kitchen and stairwell had been rewired, the ground floor and upward required this work. There's even an email from Julia to our landlord, dated 7 October 2021, accusing him of having employed "cowboy builders," after complaining about the lights tripping "yet again."

And now Detective Cutler is answering a few questions regarding the bowl. No, officers didn't search for the pieces at the local recycling plant given that I had admitted to its use. No, shards weren't found in Mr. Stokes's head wound, but were found in the cracks between the floorboards in a corner of the hall and traces were found on his overcoat. There are corroborating photographs—and Sonja Jackson directs the jury to the relevant place.

"It is an agreed fact that the ceramic bowl was used, even though the pieces were not retrieved," she notes.

"It is," the detective says as his eyes bore into me, steel blue from a runner's tanned face. Through being in overall charge of the inquiry, he knows the case inside out, and it's clear he doesn't like me.

I am so conscious of this that I almost miss Sonja Jackson's quiet, almost anticlimactic conclusion. "My Lady. That concludes the case for the Crown."

Forty-Four

20 JUNE 2022

EMMA

As soon as Sonja finishes, the jury goes out. This is the midway point, and Tom is going to make a submission that there is no case to answer. Though I've barely let myself believe he will be successful, I feel the tiniest glimmer of hope.

This is a clear householder case, my lawyer tells the judge, in his characteristically calm, rational manner. I was acting in self-defense and used reasonable force against a trespasser: someone who was refusing to leave my home at the time.

"The Crown's case is that the push that propelled Michael Stokes down the stairs was deliberate and grossly disproportionate to the threat imposed. But we know from the pathologist that there is no forensic evidence that there was a push at all, and certainly no evidence such a push was either forceful or reckless. The evidence in this case is inherently tenuous and speculative," he adds.

He goes on to argue that the body cam footage, taken by Officer Berwick revealed I was in "a state of shock," and asks the judge to bear in mind Mike's behavior in waiting in the dark, my shock at discovering him there, the lack of anyone to help me, my desire to protect my home.

This is the way things are done in court: hackneyed terms, dry language, legalese masking the horror of what happened. I think of my heart spiking as I heard the creak of Mike's footsteps, of the chill terror that spread from my bowels and up through my body as I sensed an unknown shape at the back of the hallway: someone broad and male who was lurking in the dark. The fear that a stalker was about to fling acid, or a Twitter troll take a razor to my face. Tom's words bring me back to the present:

"This was a moment of crisis in a domestic case. A moment of extreme terror and distress. It is a most extraordinary case where one can, from a defense point of view, say that a jury is forced down an avenue of concluding that, in these circumstances, the violence was not unreasonable—or unjustified."

Sonja answers various questions, and there is a detailed discussion of a point of law—section 76, subsection 5A of the Criminal Justice and Immigration Act 2008, which Judge Costa consults in her *Blackstone's*—and reference to a Court of Appeal case, which clarifies that, when an intruder enters a house, "the householder is entitled to some latitude as to the degree of force." Tom refers to these authorities slowly and reads the relevant statute with precision. There is nothing rushed or ill-considered about his argument, and he is forensic in his consideration of the law. But the words, the minutiae of what is being discussed, slide over me like running water. I make notes, trying to marshal the argument, but it seems futile and so I stop. Because, despite the dryness with which this is being expressed, this is a very human story, and surely the judge can empathize with it?

Judge Costa makes a couple of notes. Nods sagely, chews on the end of her glasses. She has received briefs from both sides, she tells us, but would like to give the issue a little more thought and time. Despite Tom trying to manage my expectations, I can't help feeling optimistic, my apprehension at having to give evidence easing as I try to interpret the judge's expression. There's another break. I know I should go and speak to Caroline, who has been watching from the public gallery, together with Freya Jones, who has also traipsed all the way from Portsmouth to support me, but I'm too wired and anxious. Tom shepherds me into a consultation room.

"How do you think it went?" I ask. "What do you think?"

He tugs at his left earlobe, gives his frustratingly frequent response: "Hard to read."

An hour later, we have our answer. At length, Judge Costa runs through her detailed thinking. The jury must grapple with two questions: whether the degree of force was grossly disproportionate and, if it wasn't, whether it was unreasonable in the circumstances given the possible mitigating factors such as my shock at coming upon him, the darkness of the house, my vulnerability, and Mike's behavior at the time. Hope flutters in my chest. By listing these factors, of *course* she understands. As a middle-aged woman, she'll have known what it's like to be followed down a dimly lit path, will recognize that whisper of terror, can imagine it multiplied tenfold in her own home.

And it seems I'm right as she stresses the subjectiveness of her thinking: her ruling is peppered with personal pronouns—"in *my* view," "to *my* mind," "*I* really don't see." I let myself believe all will be well when she notes "the evidence of intent to kill is at best tenuous, in my view." But no. However "compelling" Mr. Tillett's submission, Judge Costa "has come to the conclusion that the question of whether the defendant's acts were grossly disproportionate remains a matter for the jury." I sit, teasing out the phrasing before the incontrovertible fact slaps me in the face with the force of a bucket of cold water.

The case has not been thrown out. I will have to carry on.

Forty-Five

20 JUNE 2022

EMMA

I am nervous as I enter the box. No public speaking appearance has come close to this. All the physiological tells are there. My palms prick with sweat; my heart starts to race. I reach for the plastic cup of water placed by the side of me, conscious that everyone can hear me drinking it, aware that I am causing delay.

I replace the cup, tell myself that of *course* I can give a good account of what happened. That if I can discuss Amy Jones's humiliation in the Commons, if I can speak unflinchingly of porn and oral sex, if I can brave every single person I have met since Mike Stokes struck his head on our kitchen floor and, more precisely, since I was charged with his murder, then I can give a good account of what went on.

The stakes couldn't be higher, but like the conscientious politician I am, I have prepared for this: considering how I will respond when questioned about the most problematic aspects of what happened: lying, sweeping the bowl away. Let's face it, around 5 a.m. most nights, I can be found reliving what happened that late afternoon in December. I think of little else, these days.

Tom gives me a smile, head cocked to one side like an inquisitive finch. His eyes are kindly, and I have never been more grateful for his calm certainty. He will walk me through some basic facts; leading on questions that require a "yes" in agreement; establishing a rhythm—question, answer, question, answer—all designed to build the impression I am straightforward and honest. That I am more than eager to help.

And so he begins, asking me my name, address, occupation; providing the broad brushstrokes that give us a general picture of someone, but offer no light and shade, no true insight at all. Still, they succeed in warming me up. Almost imperceptibly, my voice, which has been slightly too high, settles into a lower register; shifts into the friendly but authoritative tone I use when in the Chamber, or when I've been interviewed for TV. I sound like Emma Webster, MP, and I begin to engage with Tom and the courtroom, looking from one juror to the other but never settling on any face for too long. This is my chance to persuade them that my reaction was natural, inevitable even, given the pressures I was under.

This is my chance to persuade them I am not guilty of murder.

Tom quickly establishes that this is not just the first time I have stood on trial, but the first time I have ever been arrested.

"Yes."

"And when you gave your first account, on 8 December, was this your first experience of talking to the police?"

"Well, no," I say. "Unfortunately, I've had to make statements to the police about previous threats that have been made to me—when I was sent a letter threatening an acid attack, for instance, and when I had a flurry of rape threats after I spoke about revenge porn in the House of Commons. But yes, this was the first time I gave a statement to the police about someone being found in my home, and obviously, later, it was first time I have ever been in any trouble with the police."

He tells the jury we'll learn more about the threats I experienced as an MP, but first he talks me through some basic biographical detail. I'm divorced with a teenage daughter; I've been an MP for almost four years and before that was a teacher. Prior to Mike's death, I split my time between the house in Cleaver Square and Portsmouth. I work long hours, too.

"Twelve-hour days?"

"Often fifteen or sixteen if you include responding to emails. And six days a week."

It's all designed to build a version of me to counter the one provided by the prosecution. I'm an extremely hardworking single mother. I might have a job that sounds impressive, but I am really no different from any of them.

I answer politely, as if keen to help. I want to paint an appealing picture as I stand, insistently smiling, like the conscientious public servant

that I am. At the same time, my life sounds small: one daughter, no partner, a workaholic. Do I sound relatable? Not for the first time, I hanker
for a bigger family: two older brothers to protect my girl, a steadfast husband watching from the gallery. Extra support, but a family—all boatlike
shoes clogging up the hall and massive appetites—that would make me
look more normal. Mine is too quiet, too unassuming, and I wonder if
this makes me less trustworthy, more suspicious.

I can't dwell on this, though, because Tom is continuing with his
questions: his voice pleasant and conversational but driving the narrative
forward.

"And this might sound impertinent, but how heavy are you?"

"One hundred twenty-two pounds. I think I was one hundred thirty-
seven when this happened, but I'm one hundred twenty-two now."

"And how tall are you?"

"Five foot nine."

"Are you a sportswoman?"

"No!" I smile at the thought, feel the tension that's tightened around
my temples begin to ease. "I don't have the time. I bought some running
shoes, but then I received the letter threatening the acid attack and I felt
vulnerable running outside. And besides, when I'm not working, I'm
spending time with my daughter."

"You don't work out in a gym?" This said with a wry smile.

I glance down at my slim wrists that look as if they might snap and
wonder why anyone might think that. I'm not wearing the trouser suit
today. It's come to have too many negative connotations, and I'd felt
superstitious shrugging it on this morning: as if I was pretending to be
a stronger woman than I am. Instead I'm wearing a close-fitting jersey
dress: navy, conservative, unadorned. I had thought it would look somber,
but when I looked in the mirror of the court bathroom, I saw that I was
too slight: my clavicles pronounced, my ribs showing through my upper
chest, my breasts flattened like chicken fillets butterflied for a schnitzel.
My ringless fingers are knuckles and bone; my watch strap hangs loose.

"No," I say at last. "I don't work out in the gym."

"And forgive me, but have you ever been in a fight before: a physical
attack?"

"No!" This isn't a question we'd discussed, and I sound suitably affronted.

"So, when you and Mike Stokes became involved in a physical fight, that was your first experience of this?"

"Yes." I swallow. "Nothing like this has *ever* happened to me before."

Tom allows the court to take this in before he talks me through the level of abuse I've experienced. He reads through the text messages I'd received on my personal phone; directs the jurors to a photocopy of the acid-threat letter; notes that I'd received ninety abusive emails and 6,382 abusive tweets in the six months before the day in question, that these intensified after the *Guardian* feature and the start of the Amy's Law campaign.

"'May your death be long and painful,' that's just one of them, I believe?" He directs the jurors to the relevant section of their files, and they riffle through them. "'I'd take a razor to @emmawebsterMP's smug face, only it would blunt it,' that's another." He beams at me, and I remind myself he is repeating these words for a reason: to convey the emotional strain I was under. "What effect did these threats have on you in the run-up to 8 December?"

"They frightened me. I didn't realize it at the time, but I was living in a state of constant vigilance and fear."

He gives me another reassuring smile, and I know this is it. We're about to discuss how well I knew Mike Stokes, all necessary but potentially difficult, and his smile reminds me he'll go gently with me. Sex lurks in the wings. But Tom will cloak this as a deeply regretted aberration; will do everything he can to make the fact we had sex, on just one occasion, sound a mere irrelevance.

"How did you get to know Mike Stokes?"

"Just as a lobby journalist. I worked with him on a few stories."

"What sort of stories?"

"Mainly about violence against women. I'd give him a quote if he wanted a reaction to something. And then, in October last year, we began to collaborate on the Amy's Law campaign."

He asks for more details on this, and as I speak, my pride at what we achieved is palpable. I glance up at the gallery, trying to see Freya, and the fact that she is here, that she has made the journey from Portsmouth, fills me with some much-needed confidence. I feel a flicker of fire in my belly. I am a good MP, a good woman. We did a very good thing, despite our collaboration leading to this: his death and my trial for murder. The thought emboldens me.

"Thanks to our work together, the sentence for such crimes will be increased and victims will be automatically granted anonymity. They'll still have the ordeal of a trial to go through . . ." And here I falter. This feels self-referential and I can't appear to be craving sympathy. "But their reputations, if the offending footage can be removed—admittedly another, difficult matter—can be rehabilitated in the future."

"You must have felt very proud to have brought this about?"

"Yes, absolutely." *Pride goeth before a fall.* "But mostly relieved on behalf of the women who experience this."

"And I think that, on 17 November, you and Mike Stokes went out for a meal to celebrate."

My throat tightens. "Yes."

"As I understand, that's perfectly normal behavior for politicians and journalists?"

"Yes. I would often have lunch, and sometimes dinner, with contacts. It's a good way of building up trust." I pause, aware not just that this sounds rarefied but also that this trust was very much betrayed. "It was the first time I'd had dinner with Mike, but we fixed on the evening because it fitted best with our diaries. He booked the table and was the one who suggested we meet."

"And we have heard that, after the meal, you spent the night together?"

"Yes." I make myself look at the jurors as I say this, seeking eye contact with the women in particular. "It was something I instantly regretted. It was completely uncharacteristic. I have never done anything like that before."

"We are not here to judge." Tom gives me a reassuring smile, though of course that's precisely what the jury will be doing throughout this trial, and it's hard not to believe that some of them will be judging me, as a middle-aged mother, for this one-night stand. "And after you spent the night with Mike Stokes, how did you leave it? What did you say to him?"

"I made it plain that I didn't think it was something that should be repeated."

"And how did he react to that?"

"He wasn't happy about it." My voice dips as I remember the limpid hurt in his eyes.

"And what happened then?"

"I left him, quite abruptly. It was just before six. I wanted to get out of there."

"And a couple of hours later, at 7:57 a.m., you sent him a text message in which you said: 'Last night was lovely. Sorry to rush.' It's in tab ten in your bundle," he directs the jury. "Can you explain why you sent that?"

"I felt I'd been perhaps a little brusque. I didn't want him to think I was rude."

"And I think we can see that Mr. Stokes read that, but didn't reply?"

"I didn't receive a reply, no."

"And then, again in tab ten of your bundle, there's evidence of a phone call you made to Mr. Stokes at 8:46 p.m. that day, lasting two minutes and twenty-eight seconds."

"Yes."

"Can you tell us what you said then?"

"I told him I couldn't contemplate a relationship. That I had enough on with work, and with looking after my daughter."

"And how did he react to that?"

"He was dejected and then quite cold. His attitude had definitely changed."

"And I believe from that point on your relationship was strictly professional and you sought to distance yourself from him?"

"Yes. I didn't want to hurt his feelings further, so I tried not to see him."

"And I think there was no contact between you until he texted you, on Monday, 29 November."

"Yes."

"If you look at your bundle"—he half turns to the jury—"you will see that message, sent at 11:53 a.m. that day: 'Been contacted about a story involving Flora. Be good to hear your side of it. Victoria Tower Gardens in ten?' By which I think he meant ten minutes?"

"Yes." And now my voice cracks because Flora's behavior will now be examined in more detail, and though it can't be reported, every single person in the packed public gallery will hear of my daughter's stupid teenage shame.

"And I believe you met him there, to discuss your daughter?"

"Yes." It is hard to get the word out.

"And that you went straightaway, arriving at about 12:05?"

"Yes," I say, remembering the whip of fear that ran through me, the growing certainty about what he was going to say.

"Now we have heard from Rachel Martin that the two of you appeared to be having an argument. Were you arguing?"

"I wouldn't say so, no. An argument to me suggests raised voices. I would say it was a discussion. Perhaps a heated discussion. Like any parent, I was desperate that he didn't write about my daughter in his paper. I reminded him he couldn't. That he'd be breaking the law, because of her age. But I also knew he could find ways of getting at me. I was frightened, feeling desperate, feeling hugely protective of my daughter—and so I may well have appeared fraught."

"Did you say: 'I will come after you'?"

"No." I shake my head, not wanting this to be the sort of thing I would *ever* say. "And he clearly wasn't threatened by my behavior. In fact, as I spoke to him, he smirked."

Tom smiles. The worst of this is over, but I need to remain resolute. "According to Miss Martin, you 'stormed off'?"

"I wouldn't say I 'stormed off.' I walked away from him. He had suggested that I 'cooperate' on a story: open up about Flora's experience in a feature. I told him he would get nothing from me."

"And how did the conversation end?"

"By my moving away. I didn't feel it was helpful"—I pick my words carefully, aware I sound like a politician—"for us to continue talking."

"And I think you then left the phone message with Mike on Saturday, 4 December, which we've heard already? 'Mike, you fucker. Leave me fucking alone.' "

"Yes," I confirm. "This was five days later, after the *Chronicle* published a picture of me looking disheveled, and a story saying I was 'gaunt and anxious' because of 'family issues.' It was the snide innuendo: the clear inference my anxiety was caused by my teenage daughter and the insidious pressure the paper was putting on me by publishing this.

"It isn't language I'm proud of," I admit. "It's not language I have ever used toward anyone before. I clearly never imagined it would be heard or read by anyone else. But there was something particularly horrible about being spied on in my home. The fact I swore shows how unsettling I found the situation. It sounds naive, but I felt as if he'd betrayed me. I couldn't believe someone who had once appeared sympathetic, and who I'd been intimate with, would be prepared to do this. It wasn't revenge porn—I was dressed in the photo, in a dressing gown—but it still felt invasive, prurient, and like an act of revenge."

Tom waits a little while, and when he speaks, his tone is particularly gentle. "And I think that there were a couple of calls to his mobile after that, later that day, at 2:03 p.m. and later at 4:17 p.m., but you didn't leave a message?"

"I was ringing to apologize. I was deeply ashamed of having spoken to him like that." I think of my fear, too, that this was all rich material for a future character study, and my panic that in phoning twice, I'd only conveyed my anxiety. "I didn't leave a message because I wanted to speak to him in person," I say.

"And did you have any contact with him after that?"

"Not directly, but I did arrange for a lawyer's letter to be sent to the *Chronicle*, on 6 December."

"And just for clarity, you didn't send him a message via Messenger asking him to meet you at your home in Cleaver Square at 4 p.m. on 8 December?"

"No." I am emphatic. "I think I might have used Messenger to contact him once a couple of years ago, long before we worked together on the Amy's Law campaign. But I would always text him. And I *never* invited him to either of my homes."

Tom nods, and says he has no doubt the jury will remember that the IT expert, Mel Reed, could find no proof that the message came from a device belonging to me. Then he gives me another of his trademark reassuring smiles, shuffles some papers, gives everyone time to assimilate what I've told them. Because we are about to embark on the meat of the evidence.

"If we can turn to the day in question, 8 December," he says, and he starts to walk me through the buildup to what happened, spending time establishing my state of mind: the fact I was feeling so on edge I suffered a severe tension headache; that I left work early, cycling fast.

"I believe the journey took you around twelve minutes. You were cycling at quite a pace to cover just over three miles in that time, given that you would have stopped at two traffic lights. Was there a reason for that?"

"I was scared," I say. "I thought I was being followed at the lights. Given that I was being stalked, my reactions were heightened. I felt intensely wired."

"And it's fair to say that when you arrived home, your heart was beating at a rapid pace?"

"Yes. I bent down to lock up my bike, and when I stood back up, I felt quite dizzy." And I'm there, white lights clouding my vision as I stand clutching my bag and helmet, fighting against the light-headedness that makes the sky tilt and spin. Night has fallen as I walk up the steps, but the light above the door goes on automatically as I put my key in the lock and push . . .

"And what happened then?"

I am back there: standing on the step, the door swinging open, the alarm not sounding, the inside light not being on. There must be a simple explanation why the alarm hasn't been set, I tell myself—Agnes forgot to set it, or the lights must have tripped—and simultaneously: I'm going to have to deal with it, aren't I? Because that's what any competent forty-four-year-old woman has to do.

"The alarm didn't sound, and the inside light switch didn't go on, so I found the flashlight on my phone and rearranged my keys so that they were splayed between my fingers—and then I went into the house."

"And what happened then?"

"I started heading to the cupboard under the stairs, to the fuse box because I hoped that was the reason, but I thought I heard a tread, a creak of a floorboard, so I stopped and called out. Said something like: 'Hello.' Then: 'Hello. Is anybody there?' A figure came out of the shadows at the back of the hall, from the door on my right, the one leading to my bedroom . . ." I pause, grateful that the jury have visited Cleaver Square; that they can visualize this. "I didn't recognize him at first; I just thought he was an intruder—perhaps a burglar. Eventually I think I managed to shout at him. I said something like: 'Get out. Get the fuck out of my house.'"

"And what happened then?"

"He said: 'It's okay. It's Mike'—and then he came toward me with his palms raised—I guess it could have been a peace gesture, but it was dark, and I was intensely frightened. I'd paid for the lawyer's letter warning him off—so I couldn't understand what he was *doing* in my house. And then he came right up to me. Put his hands on either side of my upper arms. I dropped my mobile in shock, heard the screen crack. I could see his eyes glinting in the dark, feel the pressure of his hands, smell the wine on his breath. I managed to pull away, and I screamed at him again to get out. But he just stood there. 'You messaged *me*, remember,' he said."

"So, you had asked him twice to leave, and he refused."

"Yes."

"And what happened next?"

"He grabbed me again and sort of gave me a little shake, still with his hands on my upper arms, just above my elbows. And he repeated that thing about *me* wanting to talk to *him*."

I scan the jurors, frustrated at being unable to express how incomprehensible this all felt: him *saying* this and *being* there. It's critical I convey this—and yet how can they understand my panic at his feverish insistence; too much alcohol, combined with self-confidence, convincing him he was right? A minute earlier, I'd been fumbling with my bike lock, wanting to shrug off my wet coat, empty my bladder, make a cup of tea. And now? I was in his grip, his warm breath on my face, his fingers pinching tight.

"And what did you think he meant?"

"I hadn't a clue. I thought someone must be trying to set me up—but I also couldn't work out what he was doing in my bedroom—maybe trying to unearth information on Flora or me?" My thoughts had snagged on him rifling through my drawers, bras spilling as his fingers laced through my things, but it was a fragment of an idea and I barely had time to process it. "I felt terrified by his intrusion. I sort of wrestled to get away from him, but the more I did, the more tightly he gripped."

"And what happened then?"

"I couldn't get free, but I managed to bring my right knee up and into his groin. It was a pure fight-or-flight instinct, though I must have made contact because he bent over and swore, as if he was furious with me."

"And what happened then?"

"He sort of shuffled backward, but just as abruptly stood up—and then he grabbed hold of me again."

"And where were you by this stage?"

"We had moved to the back of the hall and were below the bunch of mistletoe that hung from the second light fitting. I had my back to the front door; he was facing me; the stairs leading downstairs were to his right." I swallow. We all know about the stairs. "He glanced up, and I think he must have seen the mistletoe because he lunged at me, as if he wanted a kiss." I feel him gripping my neck, the force of him yanking me closer. "I said something like 'get *off* me,' but he had put his left hand behind my head."

"Did he manage to give you a kiss?"

"Not quite. His face was right next to mine, but in order to grip my neck, he'd released my right arm. I managed to twist away, brought my right hand up, and smashed my keys against his left cheek."

"Were you in the habit of striking men in the face with a brace of keys?"

"No." The question is so ridiculous I sound appropriately <u>indignant</u>. "I'd never struck anyone before in my life."

"And how did he react to that?"

The memories flow thick and fast then. An <u>unedifying fight</u>: dirty, scrappy, painful; him grabbing and grasping, me flailing and lashing—and at the end, Mike lying at the bottom of the stairs.

"Ms. Webster?"

"I'm so sorry." I take a sip of water, throat tight as I remember the soft menace of his voice.

"How did he react after you hit his face?" Tom repeats, his tone firm and insistent. We are at the heart of the matter, and I can't lose my focus here.

"After I hit him, he let go of me and put his right hand to his cheek. He swore. Said"—and here I remember the shock in his eyes—" 'You fucking bitch.' It was that that frightened me the most. His animal ferocity. His contempt. You think you might know someone, if you trust them enough to sleep with them, but that's so naive." I pause. You can't libel the dead, but you can tarnish their reputation and I'm doing so spectacularly. Josh hasn't been in court since last week, but Cath is: did she know Mike like this? I clutch the wooden top of the box, suddenly blindsided by a memory of someone else from further back, when I was much younger. My breath quickens. The fear of judgment has always been there.

I force myself to count as I exhale, but Tom is indicating I should go on, and the court is transfixed, waiting for me to continue.

"After I struck him, he looked unsteady, swayed a bit. Then he came at me. I was frightened, really frightened. I'd dropped my keys, but there's a console table in the hall with a ceramic bowl on it and I reached out, just to grab something, anything, then sort of flailed at him with it. He staggered back a bit and I heard it smash—but it didn't have much effect because he came at me again, and so I put my hands up to push him off me and they struck his chest. But I wasn't trying to push him down the stairs." I look from one juror to the next, desperate to convey my horror because this is the key moment when I have to convince. "I know it's illogical, but right at that moment, I thought he might have some acid, that he might be connected to the person threatening to attack me with acid. And then it happened. He tilted backward. Sort of swayed as if he'd overbalanced. It started in slow motion and then it happened very quickly. And suddenly . . . well, he was falling down the stairs."

"Can you describe how he fell?"

"I couldn't see it. I just heard this awful thud after his roar of surprise."

"And when he fell, you didn't rush down to his side, to try to help him?"

"No."

A pause. Tom's tone is neutral and nonjudgmental. "Why was that?"

"I was in complete shock. The whole thing just felt utterly surreal."

"You didn't think to ring an ambulance?"

"No—for the same reason. I was frozen and utterly terrified. Frightened that he was dead; and frightened that, as soon as anyone else was involved, they would question why Mike had broken in and why he was interested in Flora or me."

I look at each and every one of the jurors, not just the women but the skinny man and the mountainous student, the elderly Asian man, the bearded fortysomething I suspect is a teacher. I am not lacking in compassion, I try to tell them. These were the actions of a woman pushed to extremes. "I know this wasn't logical, or rational, or kind. I know it isn't possible to justify this decision. But Mike knew what my daughter had done to another girl. He thought it was a story because he thought I was a hypocrite, and he was willing to use her to get at me. I was terrified of what it would do to her—how it would break her—if this came out."

"And yet you must have known *rationally* that his accident in your home couldn't be covered up?"

"I wasn't thinking rationally. From my entering the house to his landing at the bottom of the stairs must have taken less than a minute. The shock of discovering him in my home, the speed at which the whole thing blew up was just incredible. I'd never been in a fight before; I'd never seen someone fall in a dramatic accident, when moments earlier they'd been lunging at me."

"And yet, although you didn't go to his side, you *did* sweep up the smashed ceramic bowl and place it in the recycling bin outside?" He says this with characteristic delicacy, though he is forcing me to address the most problematic bit of the evidence.

"Yes." I am choked with shame.

"Can you tell us why you did that?"

"It was Julia's favorite bowl. I was mortified that I'd broken it. Desperate to hide what I'd done. To tidy it away." I give an odd cackle that makes me sound mad. "I know that sounds insane. There was a man injured at the bottom of the stairs, and I was worried that Julia might be furious about a broken bowl . . ." I tail off, unable to better express my thinking. "And yes, as I swept it up, I realized it was proof we'd fought. That I'd hurt him. And I knew that would lead to questions about the reason we'd done that—and about Flora and me."

We touch briefly on the mistletoe: the accusation I'd moved it straight after the attack to accuse Mike of initiating a sexual assault, and that, in doing so, I'm guilty of further calculating behavior.

"The Crown has suggested that, in the immediate aftermath of this fight, you had the wherewithal to move the mistletoe. Did you do that?"

"No." I am emphatic. "I moved it before I left that morning, but neither of my housemates saw that because I was the last to leave."

"There's also the issue of the blood splatter," Tom goes on. "Why did you wash it from the stairwell that night?"

"Because I didn't want any physical reminder of him. He had frightened me so much that I didn't want any trace of him there."

And then we're onto my behavior with Julia; my initial account with Officer Berwick; and my first interview, on 11 December, with the police. Each time, Tom asks me why I wasn't honest: why the truth that we'd fought only emerged once Officer Parkin began to lay out the full extent of the evidence against me.

"I was terrified that if I told the police what had really happened, they'd discover I'd had sex with him," I explain. "That would be bad enough, but it would be worse if they started wondering why the *Chronicle* had then printed that picture with the inferences about my daughter. Once they looked into that, they'd find what Mike had discovered about Flo. And I know that the police would have evidence of her caution on their system—but I wasn't thinking logically. I was desperate to protect her. I didn't want this to be a story that would haunt her forever."

I don't add that, once I'd uttered that first lie to Julia and to Officer Berwick, it became harder to row back. Because as soon as I admitted the truth, I lost my reputation for honesty, for integrity, for being an uncharacteristically straight-talking politician.

As soon as I admitted the truth, I became seen as a liar.

———

By the end of my telling my story, I feel spent. And yet the adrenaline needs to keep firing. I need to remain alert.

Tom finishes with three questions designed to be those the jury will remember.

"Emma Webster: did you have any intention of killing Mike Stokes?"

"No."

"Did you intend to cause him serious harm?"

"No."

"What do you feel when you remember the events of that night?"

"Regret," I say, and my voice starts to crack, and I can't believe that I'm about to fall apart now, although perhaps it doesn't matter; perhaps it is good to show this contrition. "Shame and regret," I add, because it's not just my genuine regret that he died; it's my knowledge that my reputation will be bound up with his death, with this case, every moment from now on.

"There's not one day when I don't regret what happened."

Forty-Six

21 JUNE 2022

EMMA

If I was nervous about giving evidence when guided by Tom, my fear intensifies the next day when Sonja Jackson rises to cross-examine me.

I smile at her automatically. Am I doing so to appease her? The smile's instinctive, if misguided. I want to persuade Sonja, to win her round.

But it's more than that. Outside the courtroom, she's a woman I would want to get to know. I imagine we'd have much in common: two middle-aged women using their intellect and their sense of right and wrong for the public good; two women managing to succeed in still male-dominated worlds, enduring criticism, even risking their personal safety (because entering a cell to meet a client can't be without jeopardy). And Sonja Jackson, as a Black female lawyer at the very top of her profession, has thrust through more glass ceilings, fought harder, achieved far more than I have.

Perhaps that's partly why I smile now. I want her to like me—of course I do. I want her to empathize with my experience, to go gently on me even. But I'm also trying to acknowledge that the odds have been stacked against her, and that to have attained her success she'll have had to be far more effective than any white man. Embarrassed liberal that I am, I suppose I'm trying to convey that I sense the pressure she is under to catch me out, to score points, to nail me emphatically. And yet I can't help but hope she'll be sisterly.

"Ms. Webster," Sonja begins, "I just want to clarify a few things. I'll try not to keep you for long." She gives me a guileless glance as she looks up from her papers.

And I realize that the idea of empathy based on gender plays no part in a court.

"Now, it's an agreed fact that you have told several lies during the course of this investigation?"

I stand there mutely, immediately in the wrong. "Not several," I manage.

She does a sort of double take as though surprised I might be disquieted by this statement.

"You don't agree that you lied?"

"I—I gave an erroneous account when the accident first happened because I was frightened of the consequences."

"I think most people would call that lying," she says, turning to the jury as if they are all in agreement. "But let's go through the ways in which you gave an 'erroneous account.' First: you lied to your housemate, Julia Cooke, when you told her you arrived home to discover Mike Stokes at the bottom of your stairs?"

"Yes."

"You lied to Officer Berwick, didn't you, when you repeated that account, going into detail about how you found him?"

"Yes."

"You lied to the paramedic, telling him that when you found Mike Stokes, he had fallen—a lie that could have impacted on his treatment?"

"I very much regret having done that—but yes."

"And am I right, you continued to lie to your family and friends?"

"I didn't go out of my way to discuss it with others."

Sonja Jackson frowns, a crease of a V forming between her groomed brows. "Does that mean that you told your daughter and your colleagues the truth?"

"No."

"So, you persisted with your original lie when you spoke to your other housemate, Claire Scott; when you spoke to your daughter; when you were asked about what had happened by your parliamentary team and colleagues; when you gave a statement outside the House of Commons about this?"

"Yes." My voice dips.

"And then, when Mike Stokes died and the postmortem revealed a laceration on his check that couldn't be explained by his falling down the stairs, and a blow to his temple that was also caused before he fell—and we know this because it created a blood spatter up the walls—even then," she says, pausing to emphasize the significance, "even *then* you didn't tell the truth?"

"I changed my account once this happened and I was interviewed by the police."

Sonja Jackson pauses for a moment, gives a little shake of her head.

"You didn't in your initial interview, did you? It wasn't until the second police interview that you did so."

"Yes," I say.

"And we've heard that initially you claimed that perhaps the cleaner had broken the bowl?"

"Yes."

"Even when the police presented you with evidence of shards of a ceramic bowl in the cracks between the floorboards, you persisted in suggesting Agnes could have broken it—despite knowing she'd been reinterviewed and denied it?"

"Yes." I want to shrink away.

"To be clear, you only admitted to what you'd done—the fact that, instead of going to help Mr. Stokes, you'd swept up the shards, using a dustpan and brush from under the stairs, and placed it in the recycling bin—in your second interview, at 9:36 p.m. on Saturday, 11 December, nearly nine hours after you were first arrested and after you had already changed your account?"

Heat creeps up my face as I remember frantically sweeping up the shards, then wrapping them in an old copy of the *Evening Standard*; intent on getting rid of the evidence, ignoring the fact Mike was lying at the bottom of the stairs.

"I told the truth about our fighting near the start of my first police interview on December 11. I wasn't honest about the ceramic bowl until the second interview, later that day. I deeply regret that," I say.

"It wasn't until your police interview, on the evening of 11 December, that you told what you *now say* is the whole truth." She looks at me intently, emphasizing my mendacity as vibrantly as if she had applied a neon highlighter.

She is really milking this, but "Yes," I say.

"You see, the problem is, Ms. Webster"—and here Sonja Jackson's gaze sweeps from me to the jury so that she encompasses them in her observation—"that it is hard to know if you're telling the truth now, in this courtroom. How are we to know if the version of events you now offer is what really occurred?"

"My Lady." Tom gets to his feet.

"Miss Jackson," says the judge. "Please confine yourself to questions rather than comment."

"My Lady." Sonja gives a deferential nod. "Perhaps I can phrase it another way. Ms. Webster, you persisted with a tissue of lies for *over three days*, right up until the point, during your second interview on Saturday, 11 December, when it became not just unconscionable but impossible for you not to tell the truth. Given your tenacity, your persistence, in lying, I am going to suggest to you that there is no reason the jury should believe a word you say.

"Your Ladyship." Tom bobs up again, his usually urbane tone tinged with irritation.

The judge dismisses him, with a shake of her head.

"Ms. Webster?" Sonja Jackson says.

"I have taken an oath," I say, looking at each juror in turn and galvanized by a sudden, intense anger. "And I am telling the truth in this court."

The prosecuting lawyer pauses a while: long enough for the pause to feel sardonic. Perhaps I am paranoid, but as she glances down at her notes, she seems to be hiding a smirk.

"If we can turn to your relationship with Mike Stokes, we have heard that you had worked together on the Amy's Law campaign, and I think there are some two hundred and fifty text messages between you that month alone?"

"Yes."

"You met for coffees to discuss the story, there are eight phone calls listed regarding it, and, of course, you went for a meal to celebrate what you'd achieved together?"

"Yes."

"In fact, you trusted him so much you were willing to have sex with him?"

I curb the instinct to glower at her; look in appeal, instead, to Tom.

"Ms. Webster?"

"I have said that was a major error of judgment. It never happened again."

"But it's fair to say that whatever your feelings about him in the immediate run-up to his death, he was far from a stranger?"

"Yes," I concede.

"In fact, two hours after you left him on the morning of 18 November, you sent him a text message: 'Last night was lovely. Sorry to rush.'"

"Yes, I did."

"That suggests you felt quite amicably toward him?"

"I did at that point, although I was quite clear I didn't want the relationship to continue in a phone call later that day."

"And after you rejected him, in that phone call, his behavior altered. 'It was clear he didn't want anything to do with her,' Rachel Martin told us. He had an animus against you. And he was going to get at you through the story about your daughter?"

"My Lady." Tom stands. "The defendant cannot possibly know Mr. Stokes's motivation or his state of mind."

"Quite so," Judge Costa says.

"My Lady." She gives a nod of feigned contrition and moves on. "It's fair to say that whatever Mike Stokes's motives in pursuing this story, you were angry with him when you met on 29 November in Victoria Tower Gardens to discuss your daughter?"

"I wouldn't say I was *angry* when I met him."

"You were seen jabbing your finger at him and 'storming off.' I'd say that indicated you were angry with him, weren't you?"

"I suppose I was angry when I found out he wanted to run the story. I didn't want him to run the story about Flora, no."

Sonja tilts her head gently, her tone softer, more conversational.

"Flora's the most important person in your world, isn't she?"

"Yes, she is." My heart squeezes tight.

"And the idea that he would expose her made you furious."

"I felt protective, as I think any parent would."

"She was a fourteen-year-old girl. And you were furious he thought she was fair game: that he didn't think she should be protected?"

"I thought he was behaving in a way that was immoral and illegal—and I told him that. I also instructed a lawyer to remind his newspaper of this."

"And when the *Chronicle* printed a photo of you on 4 December, and the story suggested you were 'gaunt and anxious,' that fury spilled over?"

"No."

"No? We've heard the voicemail you left for him. 'Mike, you fucker. Leave me fucking alone'?"

"I was angry with him when I left the message." My voice rises in frustration. "But that doesn't mean I felt any sustained anger toward him."

There is a pause as Sonja lets my show of emotion reverberate around the courtroom, and I look at the female jurors. Ash Bob, Permed Rita, the Chelsea-bun-faced woman, the one my own age in a too-tight jacket who looks permanently tired—all of these, I suspect, are mothers—and I want to ask how they would behave if their child was threatened like this.

But Sonja is changing tack, coming at me from another angle, and I'm unsettled by her dexterity, her nimbleness at keeping one step ahead.

"If we can turn to the day in question, 8 December," she continues, giving me a smile that says there's no need for me to lose my temper. "You have told us that you opened the door and felt acute anxiety because the alarm hadn't gone off?"

"Yes," I say.

"We have seen extensive evidence of you being trolled on social media?"

"Yes."

"We have seen that you were sent abusive text messages?"

"Yes."

"That a letter was delivered to your office threatening an acid attack?"

"Yes."

"In fact, you were so frightened in that instance that you called the local police."

"Yes," I repeat.

"And yet, when you arrived home and discovered your house in darkness, without the alarm being set, you didn't call the police?"

"No."

"You didn't call PLaIT, the Parliamentary Liaison and Investigation Team, the police team for MPs concerned about their security?"

"No."

"You didn't knock on a neighbor's door to ask for help—even though we now know Alex Marber was at home?"

"No. I didn't know he was there."

"You didn't even step back into the street and phone one of your housemates, or your cleaner, to check if they'd forgotten to set the alarm—or indeed, if they were still in the house?"

"No."

"Or unlock your bicycle and cycle off?"

"No." Frustration rags my voice.

"Despite this catalogue of abuse, despite already feeling 'intensely wired,' as you put it, you didn't back away in the street but instead chose to enter the house, with your keys clutched in your right hand like a weapon?"

"Not like a weapon. I mean, I didn't intend to use them as such."

"I'm sorry." Sonja Jackson gives an apologetic little glance down at her notes. "I thought you said: 'I rearranged my keys so that they were splayed between my fingers'?"

"Yes."

"That sounds as if you deliberately created an impromptu weapon?"

"It's something I always do when I'm walking alone in the dark and sometimes when entering the house. It's something lots of women do," I appeal to her, because *surely* she's done this herself or heard of others doing it?

"And this protection was something you were prepared to use, wasn't it?"

"I just did it instinctively—I suppose I thought it might act as a deterrent." My voice is rising in exasperation.

"A deterrent you armed yourself with and were willing to use; that, in fact, you did use?"

"Well, yes," I concede.

"I suppose what I'm struggling to understand is this," the lawyer says. "If you really felt so anxious that you thought you needed some sort of protection, and you improvised with metal keys to provide this—why on earth did you enter the house?"

"I don't know," I say. "Every day, I regret that decision. Perhaps I just felt that, as a forty-four-year-old woman, I needed to override this anxiety. Perhaps I was tired of feeling scared."

From the public gallery there comes an odd, triumphant shout, hastily shushed, and a ripple of recognition. I wonder if this comes from Caroline, or if she is part of this. I risk looking at the jurors and think I spy a collective shift in sympathy. The woman my age looks pensive; Ash Bob seems strained. I have struck a chord. They, too, know how it feels to fear the sound of footsteps behind them as they walk down a quiet street in the dark.

But Sonja Jackson gives no indication that I may have a point.

"After entering the house, you step into the hall and are quickly aware that someone is there," she sails on. "But Mr. Stokes immediately identifies himself and he raises his hands in a sort of 'peace gesture.' In other words, he tries to defuse the situation by being conciliatory, isn't that right?"

"It didn't feel like that. I was frightened. I didn't understand why he was in my house—or why he was refusing to leave."

"He puts his hands on your upper arms. That's a sort of placatory gesture, isn't it? He had put his palms up, in a peace gesture, and now he, a man you had worked with closely and who indeed you had had sex with, was trying to calm you down?"

"In the context of his having inveigled his way into my home and then refusing to leave, it didn't feel the least bit placatory," I say, because I am furious that she is depicting him like this. It's as if she believes in a different reality.

And yet she seems impervious.

"Just to be clear, although you entered the house with an impromptu weapon—the keys you would go on to smash into his face—Mike Stokes didn't have a weapon, did he?"

"No—but he'd put his hands on me."

"But you were the one who attacked him. Who kneed him in the groin?"

"I was frightened." Her expression is serene while I am assailed by the memory of his eyes, the grip of his fingers, the utter conviction that he was going to hurt me. My breath is light, panic mounting at the memory of what happened and how she is twisting it.

"Did you attack Mike Stokes by kneeing him in the groin while he had his hands lightly on your upper arms?"

"Yes—but I was trying to get him away from me!" Why can't she understand this?

A cool, appraising look. She takes her time. "Well, in actual fact that worked. He bent over and 'shuffled backward.' But you went 'down the hall,' so farther *into* the house. Why pursue him when what you wanted was to get away from him?"

"I think I didn't want him going back into my bedroom."

"But you were chasing him in precisely that direction?"

I feel hopeless; unsure of what to say.

"He had doubled over and was shuffling away from you, but you didn't take advantage of this fact and use the opportunity to run out of the house?"

"No."

"Instead you pursued him deeper?"

"*He* was the intruder. *He* was the one who should have been leaving!" The injustice of this is overwhelming.

"And according to your account, after you'd gone after him into the house, he then *lunged* at you and put his hand behind your head as if for a kiss?"

"Yes."

"So, after you knee him in the groin so painfully that he swears and doubles over, he tries to kiss you?" She turns to the jury as if to indicate she is incredulous and is rewarded with smiles of agreement from a couple of the men. "He swore, in pain, no doubt, and then he *came in for a kiss*? Now I'm going to suggest that your memory of the order is wrong. Isn't it more likely that, feeling a little merry and believing that you had invited him to your home, perhaps hoping for a reconciliation, he tried to kiss you—and that you kneed him then, to force him away?"

"No. That's not what happened," I say.

"That order would make much more sense."

"It's not how it happened," I repeat, sensing that some of the jurors are unconvinced.

"And then we come to the mistletoe."

I go cold.

"You say that after you had kneed him in the groin, he lunged toward you for a kiss."

"Yes."

"And you assumed he was inspired by the mistletoe."

"Yes."

"Where exactly was the mistletoe at that point?"

"It was hanging from the second light fitting near the back of the hall and next to the entrance to the top of the stairs."

"How dark was it at the back of the hall?"

"Fairly dark, but I could see Mike's face from the light that was shining down outside the door."

"So, Mike Stokes was in pain, and he was standing at the back of the hall in the dark—and yet, in this state, he somehow notices the mistletoe hanging above him, and decides it would be a good idea to give you a kiss?"

"I can't tell you what his thought processes were, but that's what happened, yes."

"You see, I'm going to suggest to you that he didn't notice the mistletoe because it wasn't hanging there."

"Yes. It was."

"I'm going to suggest that he tried to kiss you at the front of the hall, before you kneed him in the groin, because that's where the mistletoe was hanging, wasn't it?"

"No. It wasn't," I say.

"And it would be perfectly possible for him to see those berries, glowing in the light of the lamp outside the door?"

"No. That wasn't where it was," I insist. Her certainty is astounding, and I can't see how I can fight against it in any way.

"Ms. Cooke has told us that when she'd left for work, the mistletoe was hanging from the first light fitting close to the door entrance, and she was surprised that it had been moved when she came home?"

"I moved it before I left for work that morning."

She raises her left eyebrow. "Can you explain why you did that?" she says.

And I go through it all again. Our pathetic argument about its positioning and how I'd subsequently realized I was in the wrong.

"It just wasn't worth antagonizing her, especially since I'd be leaving. So, just before I left, I took it down from the front light fitting and reattached it to the second."

There's a long, excruciating moment in which she manages to convey her utmost skepticism by saying nothing. *Do you believe this catalogue of lies?* her most pregnant of pauses says. And I'm bemused that what I'd thought was an act of kindness, an admission I'd been in the wrong, has backfired so spectacularly.

"You see, I'm going to suggest you didn't move it before leaving the house that morning but *after* you pushed Mike Stokes down the stairs."

"No," I insist.

"That by moving the mistletoe, you gave yourself an excuse for pushing him. You could allege that he'd tried to kiss you—to assault you even; that you pushed him off; and that, by an unfortunate coincidence, it just happened to be at the top of the stairs?"

"That's not what happened." I say. "Besides," I add, and I know it's a risk to challenge her, but I can't help myself: I'm so incensed by her plowing on with her narrative, "if I'd been so calculating as to move the mistletoe, why wouldn't I stick to that story with Officer Berwick—instead of claiming I'd found him at the bottom of the stairs?"

Another long, cool look of appraisal. *That backfired*, I imagine her thinking. *You've not only flagged up that lie but irritated the jurors by appearing too clever by half.* And I am suddenly tired of this merry-go-round of questions, but I need to concentrate because, like a boxer in a ring, she is off the ropes and coming at me again.

"So he tried to kiss you—and you smashed the keys into his face."

"Yes."

"And then you thought he was going to retaliate? You said: 'He came at me.'"

"Yes."

"In fact, he came at you full of 'animal ferocity'—so in a threatening manner."

"Yes," I say.

"And as he moved toward you, you then picked up another weapon—the bowl—which you smashed against his left temple?"

"Yes—but it didn't seem to deter him."

"And then you pushed him in the chest."

"Yes—but only to get him away from me."

"So, were you merely putting your hands up in appeal, or did you apply some force?"

And this is the key moment of the trial, isn't it? The point when I need to convince the jury. I pushed him away—of course I did; I couldn't not, could I?—but, in these circumstances, how much of a push is too much?

"I suppose there was some force. I did push back, but only a little." My voice strains upward in my desperation not to be disbelieved. "And I didn't push him deliberately in the direction of the stairs."

"So, although you've already kneed him in the groin and smashed your keys into his face, then hit him across the head with a bowl, you didn't use any substantial force when you pushed him away from you?" Sonja signals her disbelief to the jury, swiveling around to them and then back to me. "I am going to suggest to you that, in this heightened state—where you had already kneed him in the groin and smashed your keys into his face—you shoved him fully knowing that you were doing so right at the top of the stairs."

"No."

"You deliberately shoved him at the top of the stairs."

"No."

"And you then failed to run to his side or to call an ambulance—and instead you spent the time sweeping up the bowl with the dustpan and brush and throwing it in the recycling bin, which would be collected the next day. You then rushed around, moving the mistletoe from the first light fitting, and securing it to the second, all so that you could claim he tried to assault you—and that this was your justification for pushing him down the stairs?"

"No. That's not what happened!" I say.

"I'm going to put it to you, Ms. Webster, that you were very angry with Mike Stokes for threatening you and Flora with exposure—and hinting at this through the publication of this unpleasant story, and intrusive photograph, in his paper."

"No."

"That you were angry because he was effectively stalking you."

"No. His paper was stalking me, yes, but not specifically him."

"He, through his paper, was stalking you because you'd rejected him, and he was using Flora, the most important person in your life, to get at you because of that rejection."

"No. That's not what happened," I say.

"You'd been angry with him before, by the river."

"Well, yes. I think that was only natural given what he was proposing! But that doesn't mean I wished him any *harm*."

A pause while Sonja lets this statement land. Then she continues: "Only this time you didn't walk away, did you?"

"No."

"You were so angry, you sent him a message luring him to your house in Cleaver Square."

"I didn't!" I'm so exasperated my voice spirals and is shrill. How is she allowed to persist with this, and why is she no longer looking at me, but staring ahead at the judge, impassive? "As I've repeatedly said, I *didn't* send that message. It didn't come from me!"

"And once you were there, you assaulted him with two weapons: the keys to the cheek and the bowl to his temple. But that wasn't enough, was it?"

"No."

"And so you deliberately pushed him down the stairs."

"No. That's not what happened," I say.

"You pushed him down the stairs meaning to kill him or cause him serious harm."

"I didn't."

"Because he was threatening you and your daughter."

"No."

"He was getting at you through your daughter because you'd rejected him."

"No!"

"He was threatening to ruin both your reputations."

"No!" I look directly across at the jurors, imploring them to believe me.

"And then you swept up the broken bowl and moved the mistletoe to cover your tracks—all very calculating behavior for someone apparently in shock. All very strange behavior for someone who'd acted in self-defense."

"No."

"And you didn't call an ambulance, you left him unconscious at the bottom of the stairs for *eight* minutes, because you had wanted to kill him outright, and now you wanted him to die."

"No!" My reaction is too loud. Not a shout, but a statement of outrage, because she won't look at me, won't acknowledge an alternative viewpoint as she bombards me with this. And I'm incensed that my reputation—as a good woman and a decent person—has been trounced so effectively.

A curt, tight smile. Sonja looks directly at the judge, shoulders back, posture relaxed, her body language conveying she is calm and in control while I have clearly lost my temper.

"No further questions," she says.

Forty-Seven

21 JUNE 2022

EMMA

I feel emptied after my pummeling from Sonja: as if I've had a severe bout of food poisoning and my insides have been drained away.

I make myself face the jury, trying to read skepticism, suspicion, or disbelief. Have I convinced them? I didn't send the message and I didn't move the mistletoe, but I *did* sweep up the ceramic bowl, and that smacks of ruthlessness. Of calculation. It's hard to explain as the result of momentary panic.

And I don't think I succeeded. Christ. I know I haven't succeeded. I look to Tom for reassurance, but his expression, as he rises, is opaque. He'd warned me he might reexamine me briefly, to clarify any lasting impression created by Sonja, but it feels like a weakness him having to do so. An admission that we didn't convince.

He is quick and to the point, asking three questions to clarify my intent and convey that my behavior wasn't disproportionate.

"Ms. Webster, when you pushed against Mr. Stokes at the top of the stairs, did you believe it was necessary to use some force to defend yourself?"

"Yes."

"If you used a scale of one to ten—ten being the most terrified you have ever been in your life, one being moderately frightened—how would you rate how you were feeling?"

"Ten—or rather, off the scale."

"When you pushed, did you consider that the force was grossly excessive?"

"No. I didn't have time to think. I acted out of instinct. I pushed him away but only because I was so incredibly frightened." And here my voice breaks, and I see Mike coming at me, his voice savage, his breath hot on my face. "I can't overstate how terrifying it was, particularly as someone who'd been stalked, trolled, threatened, to come across him like this."

He gives me an almost imperceptible nod. I've done well, the look says.

And then it is over, and I am engulfed by a sense of anticlimax. This was it: my last chance to give an account of my actions that was so persuasive the jury couldn't fail to acquit me.

And I am not so sure I have managed it.

———

There's a short break while we wait for Jazz, the next defense witness, to be summoned. I meet Caroline and Freya, who tell me Sonja came across as a bully.

"How is she allowed to do that?" Freya questions. "She wasn't listening to you. She kept ignoring what you were saying. The jury didn't like it at all."

"What about the bowl?" I fret. "How did they look then?"

"Well . . ." Caroline's eyes flit to Freya: they've been discussing it, and it's clear she's trying to be tactful. "Obviously that's not so great, but it's just one point."

I don't think any of us are convinced.

Back in the dock, I fiddle with my cuticles, pressing the dead skin down with my thumbnail, taking a certain grim satisfaction in exposing the crescent half-moons and forming ridges of hard skin. My brain feels sluggish: incapable of fully processing how I've done but registering that the only part of the trial over which I had any control is over. I tug at a shard of skin on my ring finger. It's tender. A sphere of scarlet balls and smears.

———

My despondency lifts, a little, when Jazz enters the box. Tom had reassured me that the witnesses detailing the pressures I experienced as an MP would help counter the impression given by Sonja. And with Jazz's entrance, it's as if a window's been opened and we're suddenly breathing cool, refreshing air. It's partly her posture; partly, perhaps, her clothes. With her jewel green dress, resin hoops, and blunt red nails, she looks vibrant and young. I think of her as being mature beyond her years, but seeing her dressed to please herself and no one else, I'm reminded that she is only twenty-six. The jury visibly perks up: interested in what this charismatic young woman has to say.

Tom talks her through the details of her job, and I wonder if the jurors are recalibrating their opinions of this young millennial with her distinct South London accent. Parliament is still viewed as stuffy and elitist—a world of middle-aged white men who bray at one another; an Old Etonian prime minister who has no concept of poverty—and yet this bright, assured young woman also works there.

She speaks with authority about dealing with trolling and social media, and I'm reminded of quite how effectively she protects me.

"I took over her Twitter early on. Emma used to try to reply to tweets, but it became impossible for her to keep up with comments, and they soon became aggressive. Really quite full-on. At first the attacks happened when she spoke about violence against women, and they'd last for a good forty-eight hours. But pretty soon they'd happen if she spoke about something uncontroversial like food banks. Literally hundreds of tweets just having a go. Some were really twisted. We took off her notifications, but she still knew they were happening. I used to tell her: ignore them; people are stupid. But really, there are just some very twisted individuals."

"I think we have some examples of some of the threats she experienced printed out here," Tom tells the jury. "If you turn to tab ten, you will see them. If I can hand you this document, Miss MacKinley . . ." He gestures to the usher, who hands it to Jazz. "There are some of the tweets that you forwarded to PLaIT: the Parliamentary Liaison and Investigation Team, at the Metropolitan Police?"

"Yes."

"And would these be fairly typical?"

"These are typical of the tweets I'd forward, or the emails, yes."

"If you turn to tab eleven," he tells the jury, "you can see several examples of those, too. And I think we can see they are peppered with threats. 'Hope you die of cancer,' for instance, or 'Cunts like you should be aborted.'" He enunciates carefully. "I think if you scan through them, you will see various terms of abuse: 'whore,' 'cunt' again, 'bitch'; references to parts of Ms. Webster's anatomy, and to sexual acts they would like to subject her to."

He then reads several of the threats at length, required for them to be recorded as evidence. I press my knuckles to my eyes. I thought I'd become inured to these terms, but there is something shocking about hearing them relayed by a tall, well-spoken man in this courtroom. A man who mouths them as if they are distasteful gobbets to be treated with the utmost contempt.

"I think we have some ninety abusive emails here and some 6,382 tweets," he tells the court. "These are generally abusive but not specific—that is to say they might say Ms. Webster is not worth killing, or not worth raping, or they might be peppered with insults, but they do not constitute actual rape or death threats. As I understand it, you would forward specific threats to PLaIT but not general abusive comments?"

"Yes. That's right. Threats are forwarded, phone calls logged. In the Commons, the mail room scans all envelopes and checks inside them—for blades or toxic substances. So, you'll have corners of envelopes chopped off because the contents have been searched. But in the local office, you don't get that protection: that's how she received the letter about the acid attack, in Portsmouth. If you get a letter like that, you just put it in an evidence bag."

The jurors look surprised by this, even shocked. *Yes*, I think. *This is what life's like if you're in the public eye—perhaps particularly if you're a woman. You need to take these precautions every day.*

"And of course, you'll get the odd constituent who's aggressive," Jazz goes on, and I think of Simon Baxter. "We haven't sought restraining orders, but that was only because Emma didn't want to antagonize. I think we should have done."

They discuss my mood on the day of Mike's death, and Jazz describes me as "jangled, wired, very freaked."

"'Very freaked?'" Tom checks.

"On edge. She burst into tears when she smashed a mug. Her daughter's her life, apart from the job, and her worry about her was what was tearing her apart."

"But in the three years you have worked for her, have you ever known her to be aggressive?"

"No."

"Even when 'very freaked' or 'jangled'?"

"No." Jazz is adamant. "That isn't her style."

And then Tom reads a statement from Sue, detailing the measures taken to protect me before any local meeting: health and safety precautions that seemed necessary but, filtered through Tom's reading, now feel utterly bizarre. The desk and chair positioned so that the chair could be kicked in the way if a constituent lunged at me; the need for a strong mobile signal in the building in case the police had to be called quickly; the clear escape route that no assailant could access, carefully mapped out in advance; the bag searches for knives; and the couple of half-gallon bottles of water always placed on the desk in front of me. Not in case I was thirsty, but in case anyone flung acid.

The court is silent as Sue's words are read out, and the simplicity of her statement, and the quiet detailing of the care she and Patrick have taken over my safety, is so humbling I have to look down.

I think of their loyalty in working for me despite regularly having contempt hurled down the phone at them; of their steadfastness despite knowing that every time they open a parcel, they risk being exposed to something toxic at worst, unpleasant at best. I think of the Simon Baxters we've known. Men who fizz with anger, their aggression only just reined in, the potential for them to erupt, for a situation that appears civil to escalate in a flash, always present.

I accepted that danger was part of the job, but when did I internalize this belief? When did I accept these precautions as normal? And why did I believe my staff should accept this, too?

Gayle Parsons is not a woman you would think would be my natural ally. The Conservative MP for Eddisbury looks as if she models herself on Margaret Thatcher: a teased web of dark hair; royal blue jackets with shoulder pads that unironically reference the '80s; a cupid's bow of plum lipstick, always immaculately applied. In her late forties, she is on the right of the party: a Brexiteer, a libertarian vehemently opposed to the "nanny state." When I had my first sustained experience of the trolls, she surprised me by whispering in the committee room corridor, "Hang in there." Soon after I was arrested, she sent a message, asking if she could offer support.

And so here she is. Appearing as a defense witness to discuss the level of abuse that has become par for the course in our jobs, hers a far more extreme experience than mine: four separate ongoing cases involving death threats, a stalker against whom she has had to take out an injunction after he ambushed her one night and claimed he had a vial of Novichok in his pocket, and a letter sent to her teenage son, detailing precisely how his mother would be tortured before suffering a "painful demise."

The former transport minister is matter-of-fact as she describes this, her tone almost brittle, as if these are familiar anecdotes she has perfected over the years. But the more sardonic her tone, the more evident her anger, a broiling current that threatens to bubble over. And my God, it's powerful.

"Is it any wonder women are leaving Parliament in droves?" she asks, looking from jury to judge to lawyers, demanding that they consider the question. "We do this job in part to have our voices heard, yes, and there are plenty of MPs motivated by their egos, but women like Emma and me do it for the greater good. And it *wears you down*. It makes you a hardened, calloused version of yourself. You stop trusting people. You become cynical. Relationships become impossible; your marriage, the first casualty." At this point, the reporters are scribbling frantically to capture this visceral account. "And if you're not careful, you can start to doubt yourself, to question your sanity. You become deeply afraid."

She pauses. She's a former actress, and she knows how to hold a room: when to allow her voice to dip, when to slow things down, when to use rhetorical tells like repetition. She's not so different from Caroline playing a Mozart sonata, knowing when to lean into a phrase. And as with Caroline, it's instinctive. She takes a breath, and it's as if she has decided to tell it as it really is, even if, in doing so, she detonates her career.

"You tell yourself to fight it, but the fear filters into every aspect of your life. I went away for the weekend to Paris." Her tone is briefly sardonic. "It was hardly the romantic weekend my husband had planned. There were fireworks, and I assumed it was a terrorist attack: another *Charlie Hebdo* or Bataclan scenario. I fell to the floor of our hotel room, crawled under the bed, and hid."

She pauses as the press scribble on, as the jury watch rapt, as the judge looks thoughtful. Even Sonja sits, apparently mesmerized.

"Emma Webster and I are on opposite sides of the political divide, but I know her to be principled, honest, hardworking. Not as ruthless, you might think, as your average MP. I have been a politician for nearly twenty years—and the job has only got more tough. It's the impact of social media and twenty-four-hour news. Story cycles are faster; people react far more aggressively and impetuously. I am surprised, frankly, given the pressures female MPs are under, that this is the first instance of someone acting like this in self-defense."

The court is somber after Gayle leaves: the atmosphere as dank as a late November afternoon when the light has leached away and dusk has fallen. Several of the journalists rush out like theatergoers racing for the bar at an interval. *MP Tells of Fears for Sanity* is a great headline, and her account will be online before the end of the day.

I am so preoccupied by what Gayle has told us that it takes me a moment to appreciate what Tom, also subdued, is telling the courtroom:

"That concludes the case for the defense."

———

Caroline drives me home, and we barely talk. It's a specific type of emotional exhaustion. I have been on high alert, and it is only in the sanctity of David's pristine Volvo that I can finally let go. I shrink into the gray upholstery as the rush hour traffic crawls past, imagining fellow passengers clocking me, noting my behavior. But I am almost beyond caring. In this metal box, I am briefly protected from it all.

"You okay?" Caroline asks at one point, and I nod. At some point, I'll need to tell her I'm sorry for remaining so judgmental, for allowing my bitterness to persist like poison. I still can't imagine behaving as she did, but none of us is infallible. *Thou shalt not kill. Thou shalt not commit adultery.*

I think we all know which one is worse.

She hurt me almost as much as David, but it's been far easier to blame her. To see her as the instigator, him as the hapless man enticed by a siren. I rub my eyes, too tired to consider this now.

I appreciate her support this week. Have stopped seeking ulterior motives: a desire to keep me at arm's length from David, a need to be overinvolved, even a delight in seeing my reputation ripped to shreds. I haven't had the capacity to think in this small-minded way. Instead have chosen to believe what she's told me: that she just wants to make things easier for Flora, that she'll do anything to help our troubled girl.

"I'm sorry," I say, looking out of the window, not making it clear quite what I'm apologizing for. Four years of sustained judgment, or the fact she's having to spend this week in the Old Bailey?

"I'm sorry, too," she says, again not specifying, and it feels as if we've reached some kind of truce.

The traffic is thinning out now, and the car picks up speed as London slips from us. The silence is comfortable: the bigger picture of whether I'll be convicted meaning there's no need to discuss anything else. We continue like this for several miles. I think of Flora. I'll see her tonight, and the relief makes my eyes smart because this is something I can't possibly take for granted. This might be the last night I get to hold her.

"I thought you might have done it on purpose, you know." Caroline keeps her eyes on the road as she says this, her expression bland and non-judgmental. I stare at her profile, jolted from my thoughts, incapable of knowing what to say.

"I thought you might have talked to him about Flora, then pushed him because you became furious. I know how desperate you were to protect her. I saw how infuriating, how cruel, he could be." She sniffs, then says quite deliberately: "I wouldn't have blamed you if you did.

"It's okay. I don't think you did it now." She gives me a quick smile before looking back at the road while I sit stunned. "It was your reaction to Sonja's cross-examination that convinced me. You were so genuinely incredulous about her mistletoe argument, and you're not such a good actor you could fake that." She throws me another quick, appraising glance.

"There's no need to say anything," she continues. "I'm glad you didn't do it, but I wanted you to know I'd understand if you had."

I am silent and shift, restless. Wishing I could slam the door on this conversation, which perturbs me more than she can know.

"Well, let's just hope the jurors don't think I did," I say eventually.

Because tomorrow will be taken up with closing speeches. And then the jury will be sent out.

Forty-Eight

22–23 JUNE 2022

CAROLINE

The lawyers' closing speeches and the judge's summing-up take forever. A day and a half, to be accurate. Watching them, Caroline realizes that all parties are preoccupied with covering their own backs.

No one wants to omit a critical detail. To be the one whose lack of intellectual rigor leaves the door open to an appeal and ensures the higher court will hear it. These lawyers are preoccupied with shoring up the very thing at the heart of this trial. These lawyers are concerned about their reputation.

She barely pays attention to the judge's summing-up. Not that there's anything to distract her: the oddball man hasn't turned up, which is a relief after his unsettling comments during Emma's evidence. (She hopes the security guard had a word, as she'd asked.) But Judge Costa seems determined to document every twist and turn of the evidence, in which Caroline is well versed. She listens carefully to the lawyers, though, because each tells a story: both persuasive; both black and white, with no nuance, no gray. They diverge dramatically, these narratives, from the point at which Emma steps over the threshold of her home into the dark hallway. And rather like the story of the disintegration of David and Emma's marriage—caused or only hastened by Caroline—it's all a question of who you believe.

First, Sonja: unflinching in her depiction of Emma as someone utterly ruthless in killing a man in sheer rage at him intimidating her and threatening to expose her daughter.

"We say that Emma Webster lured Mike Stokes to her house and deliberately pushed him down the stairs with the intention of killing him.

He had threatened the most important person in her world—her only child, Flora—and he'd threatened *her* reputation, both as a mother and an MP.

"You have heard evidence of the aggression she felt toward him, in the immediate run-up to their fight, just nine and five days beforehand. Her threat to 'come after him,' and that extraordinary voicemail: 'Mike, you *fucker*. Leave me *fucking* alone.' Now, whether or not you consider those words a threat, at the *very least* they demonstrate an extreme hostility and anger toward Mike Stokes. A hostility and anger, the Crown says, which she then acted on.

"We say this was no accident. Not just because of the sustained nature of the fight—striking him with not one but two impromptu weapons before kneeing him in the groin and administering the push—but because of her cool and calculated behavior afterward. Because Emma Webster didn't run for help or call an ambulance as any decent person might. Instead she swept up the pieces of the ceramic bowl she had struck him with and put them in the recycling bin to cover up what she did. She then moved the mistletoe in a cynical attempt to depict Michael Stokes not just as an intruder, but as someone who sexually assaulted her. To paint a false picture of herself as the victim, not the instigator of a fight in which she intended to kill him—or at the very least cause him serious harm. She even tried to cover up her traces, later that night, by scrubbing at the blood spatter in the stairwell with bleach and scalding water.

"Ms. Webster denies moving the mistletoe. Or rather, she claims, rather coincidentally, that she moved it before she left for work that morning. What she can't deny is that she repeatedly lied to everyone about what happened that day. She changed her story: at first claiming she found him at the bottom of the stairs, then denying a sexual relationship. She was still persisting with her lie that she found him unconscious when she was arrested on suspicion of murder three days later—and it was only when the wealth of evidence was laid before her that she admitted that Michael Stokes was alive and well when she entered that house.

"She continued to lie about the ceramic bowl, only admitting to using it and tidying it away *nine hours* after arriving at the police station, when the evidence was incontrovertible. And in court, she persisted with her lies, the Crown says, when describing their fight. Because she claims that, when doubled over in pain after being kneed in the groin, and at the back of a dark hallway, Michael Stokes happened to see some mistletoe and was inspired at that point to try to kiss her! And it's because of this that she pushed him.

"Members of the jury, Emma Webster has proved time and again that she is a convincing and quick-thinking liar. So why should you believe a single word that she has said?"

And then it's time for Tom, whose speech conjures up a very different version of Emma: a woman, already burdened with the knowledge she was reviled, who panicked in a moment of intense terror and distress. And Caroline, who understands the fury Emma felt—because she is furious on her behalf, and because she knows she, too, would do almost anything for Flora—wants to cry out that Tom's is the version that should be believed. That this is the account that fits with her understanding of Emma—a moral woman who made a mistake—but it's also the one that gives the benefit of the doubt to any woman confronted at a moment of crisis with the reality of how she might be perceived.

"The body cam footage shows Emma Webster was in a state of extreme shock," says Tom in his reasonable, gentle tone. "Is it any wonder? She had come home and discovered that a man whose colleagues had been stalking her, and who appeared intent on pursuing a story about her daughter, had got into her home, and was waiting for her, in the dark.

"Emma Webster was already extremely anxious. She had experienced death threats, abusive texts, abusive tweets, and she had come home to find her house in darkness and, emerging from her bedroom, a journalist who was hounding her and trying to destroy her and her only child. A journalist who she had spurned sexually, who had already humiliated her in his national newspaper, and who was now behaving in this terrifying, anarchic way.

"She panicked, and for the first time in her life, she became involved in a scuffle. Of course she hit him. She hit him because she was absolutely *terrified*. She wanted to get him away from her, and yes, she hit him out of anger because this man, who was trying to destroy her, had grabbed her, and was threatening her in the one place she should feel safe.

"But just because she fought with him, it does not mean she deliberately intended to kill him. And just because she pushed him, it does not mean she intended to push him down the stairs.

"My learned friend suggests that Emma Webster 'threatened' Mike Stokes nine days before their fight. Ms. Webster denies this. In any event, does 'I will come after you' really constitute a threat to kill? And as for the voicemail? Well, have any of you sworn at someone in the last week? The last month? The last year?" A pause, while he takes his time looking from one juror to another. "And are all of you murderers?"

A slight ripple of amusement runs through the courtroom. *Good*, thinks Caroline. *That struck home.*

"The Crown has to prove their case on evidence. And the evidence is infinitesimally slim. There is absolutely no evidence that Emma Webster sent Mike Stokes that message. Nor, as Dr. Chatterjee the pathologist was keen to stress, is there any evidence that she pushed him down the stairs. Mike Stokes had drunk over double the legal drunk-driving limit and it is perfectly possible that he lost his footing in a split second precisely because he was unsteady on his feet.

"Emma Webster responded in a very human way when she entered her home. She panicked in a moment of crisis, and when he fell, she panicked again. She did not do anything as calculated as move the mistletoe—and it is mischievous of my learned friend to suggest this. Indeed, there is a flaw in that argument because, if Emma Webster had been sufficiently calculating to do this, why would she fail to use this story when questioned by Ms. Cooke or PC Berwick, and instead opt for a panicked lie?

"It is true that she cleared up the ceramic bowl, desperate to hide the evidence of the fight, and Mike Stokes's connection to her and her daughter. And again, to protect Flora and prevent their lives becoming a misery in the press and social media, she lied to Ms. Cooke about what happened, when she came in, minutes later. Having lied, she was then trapped: not knowing how to come clean.

"Emma Webster already knew what it was like to experience sustained abuse for daring to put her head above the parapet. She'd experienced it when she was just trying to work on behalf of her constituents. How much worse would this be if she was suspected of killing a man? And not just any man but a journalist on a leading newspaper who she had had sex with, and who had information he wanted to divulge about her daughter?

"Emma Webster lied because she knew what happens to women who are seen to have done anything transgressive—and she could only imagine what might happen to a woman accused of murder who was already in the public eye."

The lawyer pauses. Every member of the jury watches, and Caroline crosses her fingers as she wills them to believe this eminently reasonable man. Tom waits just a little longer, ensuring the magnitude of what he says next strikes them.

"But just because she panicked and lied about what happened does not mean she is guilty of murder."

Forty-Nine

24 JUNE 2022

EMMA

"All parties in the case of Webster to Court Seven. All parties in the case of Webster to Court Seven."

I am sitting in the canteen of the Old Bailey when the adenoidal loudspeaker sounds abruptly. My hand jolts against the foam cup of my too-weak coffee, knocking it over, and I dab frantically with a crumpled napkin.

"Leave it," says Caroline as the brown liquid streaks across the table, bleeding into my cuff. "It's okay," she adds, mopping away at the pool of liquid, which threatens to spill over. "It will be okay."

It might not be okay. Officially, it's been four hours and twenty-seven minutes since the jury was sent out just after 2 p.m. yesterday. But that time has been stretched over almost a day. Twenty-three long hours, including a night where I lay wide-awake, fearing it would be the last I'd spend in my home instead of a prison. Sometime after 4 a.m., I grabbed two hours' feverish, unsettled sleep.

The worst part was leaving Flora. Is it possible to overwhelm your child with love? I suspect I came close to doing so as I hugged her this morning: conscious this might be the last time I held her for years.

"It's going to be okay," I whispered into her hair, repeating the mantra we've all being telling ourselves. "It's all going to be okay."

Did she believe me? She's young enough to pretend to, old enough to know no one can offer such certainties. She gave me a small, sad smile, and my chest ached at her stoicism and necessary maturity.

"Whatever happens," she said, looking at me so intently I wanted to burst into nervous laughter, "I do believe you." And I started because

I had taken it on faith that she would. Then she'd traipsed back to her room, and I'd climbed into the car to go to London.

Time has dragged since we arrived here, too, which explains our ending up in the canteen with its stench of egg and chips and its coffee like muddy water. "It's a waiting game," Tom explained, half an hour into the jury being sent out this morning. "Nothing we can do."

It's now 12:27 p.m. "What do you think?" I ask Caroline. "Is this it?"

She looks pale but determined. "Might be nothing, but we'd better hurry up and find out."

Now, walking down the vast marble staircase to the courtroom, I repeat the mantra I've been telling myself in the middle of the night, created from carefully curated statistics. Urban juries are less likely to convict; female jurors are less likely to convict; only 63 percent of murder indictments result in a conviction, but only *38 percent of women* indicted for murder are found guilty. *Sixty-two percent of women go free.*

My heel catches on the penultimate step, and I grab at the handrail, stumbling down the last step, my ankle turning, pain juddering up my spine.

"It's okay." Caroline's hand is firm beneath my elbow, catching me, guiding me toward the court, before she leaves to sit in the public gallery. How has it come to this? That I have lost all sense of self-belief and need to be righted by a woman who, until recently, I would have avoided seeing? The question unsettles me, though I've no time for this. *Fake it till you make it*, as Jazz might say. I have to act as convincingly as Sonja. I have to appear stronger than this.

My chest is tight, my breathing shallow as I open the door to the courtroom.

"This might just be a question," says Alice as we file in.

"I know," I say. But I am torn between wanting to stave off the verdict a little longer—and needing the uncertainty to end.

———

The atmosphere, as the jury enters, is dense with expectation. The usher whispers to the clerk and the question—*Have they reached a verdict?*—rustles through the court. I scrutinize the jurors, and the girl in the hijab suddenly glances my way, then suppresses a smile like a small child who knows it's inappropriate to do so. I give her a tentative smile.

She looks down as Alice turns to me with a nod. A verdict. We have a verdict. I feel it in the base of my spine: a chill shiver that seeps into my core. Cath is seated in the well of the court, hands neatly folded in her lap, head bowed. She'll be here for Josh, who hasn't been back since I saw him in the lobby, and I'm selfishly grateful I won't have his eyes on me today.

The court quiets as the judge takes her seat, her gown of red and violet settling around her. She looks at the ranks of silent lawyers and press, clocks the air of heightened apprehension, then gives her clerk a nod.

"Could the jury foreman please stand."

And the woman around my age rises. This woman who has worn a different jacket every day—some tired, some outdated, many straining at the shoulders, all hinting at a different life led before. A woman who initially viewed me harshly—that unflinching assessment on the day the jury were sworn in—but whose expression has sometimes softened as if she understands something of what I've said.

The clerk is speaking now: asking if the jury has reached a unanimous verdict.

"Yes," the woman says.

The air stills, motes of dust listing in a lazy cascade. I want to freeze this moment. To remain in this liminal state. But the clerk is asking another question. The one whose answer we have been building up to for the past two weeks.

"Do you find the defendant Emma Webster guilty or not guilty on the charge of murder?"

And I can't breathe, and I can't hear. It's not just that my chest is bound asthmatically tight; it's that there's a disconnect: my brain can't engage with the words coming out of the foreman's mouth.

It lasts for perhaps as little as half a second—because suddenly they ring out, preternaturally clear.

"Not guilty," the woman tells the clerk. And suddenly other women on the jury—Ash Bob Margaret, Permed Rita, the thirtysomething with cornrows who I have never seen take a note but who has listened with a sharp intelligence—are looking in my direction, as is Alice, who turns, her face wreathed in a beam. From high up in the public gallery there's a "Yes" that sounds as if it comes from Caroline, or perhaps Jazz or Claire, because they said they'd try to make it, and I can't get out of here quick enough because I need to tell my daughter that it's all over. That I'm coming home.

The end of the trial is relatively brief.

The judge thanks the jurors for their time and consideration, and there's a brief discussion about costs. I have remortgaged my house to fund the £160,000 this has cost me, and not all of it will be reimbursed. And then I must face them: the journalists who have sat on the press benches for the past two weeks; the broadcasters, with their furry gray booms thrust in my face. And beyond them: not just the Twitter critics— who will no doubt already be pointing out that a not guilty verdict isn't the same as saying I didn't do it—but also every single person who believes there is no smoke without fire, that a woman charged with murder can hardly be innocent.

Before I step outside the Old Bailey to say a few words, John hands me his mobile.

My daughter answers on the second ring.

"It's Mum."

A sharp intake of breath at the other end of the line.

"I'm not guilty, Flora! They said I didn't do it." My throat rasps with the threat of tears.

"Oh, Mummy." She is crying. Ugly sobs that make her incomprehensible, and tell of months of suffering under the most intense stress.

In the background, I hear David's yelps of delight. "Of course you're not guilty, Emma." Against the background of our daughter's cries, his relief is palpable. "That's utterly brilliant. As if there was any doubt!"

But there was, wasn't there? And as I step onto the street, I feel myself morph into a politician who needs to quell that doubt once and for all, but to do so while speaking with humility, and while recognizing that a sixteen-year-old boy has been left knowing that no one has been held accountable for his father's death.

Shoulders back, head up, voice low, I stand my ground. Breathe in, breathe out. Ignore the shafts of the cameras thrusting at me, the cries of the snappers—"Over here, Emma! Over here!" And as I speak, I realize that I also have a choice: I can be penitent, grateful, suggest that I will retreat from public life having learned the lesson of what happens to women who are outspoken; or I can be, if not defiant, then *steadfast*: using my experience to improve other women's lives.

"Thank you," I begin as I stand flanked by John, and with Caroline and Claire a little to the side, out of view of the cameras. "I'd like to thank my legal team; my colleagues in the Labour party and the staff in my office; and my constituents, who have all been unflinching in their support. Most of all I'd like to thank my extended family and, in particular, my daughter. If the last seven months have been a living hell for me, then I can only imagine how they have been for her.

"This is not a time for celebration. Mike Stokes died because of what happened on 8 December last year, and no one could feel jubilant about what amounts to a tragedy. But perhaps it is a time to reflect on the way in which women's lives can be seen as public property—particularly those in the public eye.

"No woman should have to feel as terrified as I did in the lead-up to this. And if I hadn't experienced a perfect storm of abuse, online and via texts, as well as through letters sent to my office, and if I hadn't been stalked by Michael Stokes's paper—then perhaps his death would not have occurred.

"It is time we look at how we encroach on women's space, both physically and virtually, and to assess why we believe it is acceptable for women to live in such fear. I will be spending some time now with my daughter, but I will not be retreating from public life. I will be not cowed. I will not be frightened, and when I return to Westminster, I will be campaigning on anti-stalking legislation, and on measures to curb social media trolling. In other words, I will be doing everything I can to draw some good from this."

I look up, and on the other side of the road, standing beneath the canopy of a sandwich shop, I see Simon Baxter watching. I go cold. *I'll be watching you. I'll be tracking your every move.* And despite my strong speech and the security guards nearby, my legs start trembling. Because this is what I was talking about and I am frightened, and there seems to be no end.

And suddenly he's walking briskly across the street, and is coming straight toward me.

"I will encroach on your space," he shouts, his face red, the vein on his forehead throbbing as he jabs his finger in my face, "until you do your job properly. I asked you for help, but you ignored me. And then my boy lay down on a train track. He killed himself and you couldn't be bothered to listen."

"I'm very sorry," I begin because I'm not sure what he's talking about. He didn't mention his son when he came to see me, and was so threatening, I refused to engage with his emails. I'm perturbed he felt I ignored him, but I can't see that I'm culpable in any way.

"Emma—cab!" Alice has hailed one beyond the media scrum and ushers me toward it, keen to get me to safety as the reporters turn to Simon. But as I go to the door, my path is blocked by a tall figure.

"Do you have any words of comfort for Mike Stokes's son?" asks Guy Black.

And there is nothing adequate I can say beyond what I said in court: that I deeply regret what happened, that it will continue to haunt me. But I'm not going to continue to apologize for it. Not because I'm a politician but because the jury found me not guilty. I ignore the question, ignore the commotion of Simon Baxter being manhandled by the Old Bailey's security guards, and get into the cab.

Fifty

24–26 JUNE 2022

EMMA

I feel burned out after the verdict. That night, I sleep more deeply than I have since entering Parliament, and when I wake, I feel as if I'm wading through water: sluggish rather than refreshed.

We spend the weekend quietly. I cook food I eat too quickly, after picking at meals for a fortnight; empty the linen basket and watch the sheets billowing on the line. I stuff my court clothes into a black trash bag and hide them in the shed: I can't bear to look at, let alone wear them. I avoid social media. I avoid the papers, though Jazz calls and fills me in on the headlines.

"And what about the *Chronicle*?"

"A line about your 'stony silence.' An interview with Cath and Josh: I can send it, if you like, but you don't need to read it."

"No," I say. Then, with more conviction: "No. Really, I don't."

But Josh preoccupies me, and so I clean the oven, as if by scouring away four years' worth of encrusted charcoal I can purge myself of what happened.

"Mum?" Flora kneels next to me. "Mum . . . can you stop being busy? Can you stop what you're doing?"

I put the scourer down, pull my head out of the oven, and look at her lovely face.

"Mum, can you just *stop* it," she repeats, and I see she is crying. "You don't need to do this."

Later we delete the Twitter app from my phone and computer, do the same with Facebook and Instagram. Jazz will deal with all my social media; I'll interact via formal press releases few people will really want to read.

"Does that feel better?" Flora asks as the app wobbles, then disappears.

"Actually, it does. What about you?"

"It didn't make me happy," she says, gesturing to her laptop, where she has deleted her accounts. "Knowing what people were saying about us. Most of the time, I reckon I'm better off without it."

———

On Sunday morning, there's a knock on the door. It takes me a while to recognize the woman standing there, not just because I haven't seen her properly for four years but because she looks so apprehensive.

"Stef?" I eventually manage.

"I owe you an apology," Leah's mother says.

"No, you don't, not at all." I remember her understandable fury at Flora's behavior the last time we spoke. "Look—do you want to come in?"

"I won't, thanks. You might kick me out." An odd laugh. "At least you might when I tell you why I'm here."

"Go on," I say.

"I heard what they said in court. About the texts. The abusive texts to your personal mobile, not your work one." She stares fixedly at the door-bell as red spreads up her neck. "At first, it was because of that interview. It wound me up something rotten. The fancy clothes you were wearing and all that stuff about not being interested in local people when Flora had already been so snotty with Leah. I'm sorry, but I just had to vent. Then I was angry—" And here she looks at me, and I see not just embarrassment but defiance and hurt. "I was so bloody *angry* about what Flora did and the fact you didn't get it: didn't acknowledge what it was like for Leah. Knowing that that boy and his parents thought she was that sort of girl, knowing that the police had seen that clip—her doing a striptease, all strutting, all sneery—when she was a fourteen-year-old girl mucking around."

She draws breath, but there's more. "Look, I know some of the things she did to Flora weren't exactly *kind*. I'm not proud of her behavior. But you'd have thought she'd sent that boy nudes from the reaction she's had. Boys slut-shaming her; girls, too. What does it do to you, do you think, to have that happen to you when you're fourteen? What does it do to your reputation?"

And I want to say that Leah shouldn't feel ashamed. That everyone knew she hadn't sent this. That she was the victim, and Flora is the girl whose reputation, as a loyal friend and exemplary student, has been ruined. Flora is the one now homeschooling, who has lost all her friends, who has suffered enough because of what she's done. But then I imagine our roles reversed, and I'm sure I'd feel a similar visceral anger, though I'd never resort to abuse. *You think you're so fucking special.* The fact texts like this appeared on my personal mobile, before I changed the number, made them all the more pernicious. What sort of woman sends texts like that to another woman?

Maybe one whose daughter's been shamed by the other's daughter.

I stand there, incapable of articulating any of this, incapable of even saying something as bland as *It's okay.* What does it do to your reputation? It knocks it. It threatens to send it flying like a plate dropped by a waiter through a lapse in concentration, a nudge, or perhaps a glancing blow. Reputation—Leah's, Flora's, mine, Caroline's, even Sonja's and Judge Costa's—is the most precarious thing, built over time, sometimes lost in seconds.

But I don't say any of this, merely manage an odd grimace.

"Thank you for letting me know."

———

On Sunday afternoon, David takes Flora on a long bike ride so she has some release; some escape, I can't help feeling, from my intensity. Caroline joins me in my garden. I offer tea, end up opening a bottle of wine.

At first, we sit in silence, but it's no longer uncomfortable. It reminds me of our friendship at the start. End-of-term drinks; impromptu suppers, Caroline staying for dinner, me delighted by my new, younger friend.

"I can't return to Westminster this week," I say eventually. "I don't feel strong enough, despite what I said outside the court."

"No one would blame you if you concentrated on your constituents for a bit—but it's like coming back after a bad recital. You'll need to face it sooner or later, or you'll lose your nerve."

"There's a debate I want to speak in, a week on Monday."

"Well, there you go."

"Yeah." I sip my cold wine, reveling in the heat of the sun touching the back of my neck like a lover's caress, but still not able to fully relax. There are still too many loose ends.

"The thing I keep obsessing over," I say after a while, "is who sent that message."

"What?" The crease between her brows deepens.

"Who messaged Mike and told him to meet me at Cleaver Square? I assumed he sent it himself—to justify being let in—but what if there's a simpler explanation? No one could engineer it that I'd turn up, and maybe I wasn't meant to. What if someone just wanted *him* to be there?"

A thought that's been nudging away at me crystallizes as I say this.

"It wasn't you, was it?"

"And why on earth would I do that?" she says, and there's exasperation and frustration in her response. Surprise, too, which suggests she's being genuine. "I'd already tried to dissuade him on the Monday—yes, I know you asked me not to, but I don't always do what you want, do I? For God's sake. Of *course* it wasn't me."

"I'm sorry." The thought that had seemed hard and bright a moment earlier turns to dust. I feel diminished for even thinking it. "I'm really sorry."

"It's okay. Just leave it," she says.

I stare at my pot of lavender. It's a meager garden: a neat patch of a lawn, a honeysuckle I've trained over the fence, and this lavender, which is rampant. A bee buzzes, woozy on nectar, intent on draining each sweet drop.

Keen to defuse the tension, I tell her about my relief at deleting my apps and my conversation with Flora. "I'm so glad she's no longer into social media, that she doesn't have a smartphone."

"I agree."

"Less annoying, too, when she loses them."

"To be fair, she's only lost, or broken, two."

"Two in eight months is enough. I could have done without sorting one out for her just before the trial." I pause and realize that I've only done this the once, and I'm sure David didn't help previously. "Did you replace the first one?"

"I think so. Yes."

And there's something in her voice that tugs at me. She's being breezy. Dismissive. Perhaps the subject is tedious?

"When was that again?"

"December. I think she put it in the washing machine by mistake."

"December?" I roll the word around my mouth. "So, she broke it less than a month after she had to give up her iPhone because of Leah. Did she do it deliberately, do you think?"

She shakes her head. "Think she was just being absentminded. And I forgot to check her pockets, don't you remember?"

"No . . ." That doesn't sound the least like meticulous Caroline. A stream of questions I bet neither of us will ever articulate swim to the surface of my mind.

When exactly was this in December? Was there a particular reason Flora wanted her basic Nokia phone broken? Had she made a call from it she didn't want traced?

I stare at Caroline, one thought breaking through my clouded mind like a shaft of light.

Was Flora's phone put in the washing machine on 8 December? Hours after it was used to make calls from London? Hours after my daughter lured the man who was trying to ruin her to Cleaver Square?

"You were so busy." Caroline stares back, and her expression defies me to voice the thought that has burst through with sparkling clarity. *Bury that idea*, her gaze tells me. *Leave it well alone.*

"She left it in the pocket of her hoodie," she continues, "and neither of us checked before I put on the wash. It was completely waterlogged. It was around the time everything happened, so it was much simpler if I just got her a new one. Don't worry. I dealt with it all."

And I can't believe what I'm hearing except that it makes perfect sense.

"And David?" I say. *Does he know of our daughter's involvement?*

"He agreed it was best I dealt with it."

So, that's a yes.

"Thank you," I manage, though I'm consumed by an uneasy mix of gratitude and a possessive anger that she shared this secret with my daughter. "But no more secrets now."

PART FOUR

Fifty-One

8 DECEMBER 2021

FLORA

"We apologize for the delay, caused by an earlier incident on the line," the train conductor announced. A frisson of irritation ran through Flora's carriage on the 12:47 Portsmouth-to-Waterloo service. The train sagged a little lower onto the tracks, gave a hiss of a sigh.

"He must mean a body," said the woman sitting next to Flora. "A suicide," she added, as if she hadn't been abundantly clear. She sniffed, then returned to her thriller. The cover was black with a photo of a dimly lit station platform; the words along the top mentioned death and lies.

Flora shifted in her seat by the window, trying to work out how this would impact her plans, how much it might delay her. She was already pretty stressed, and this really didn't help. She should have known this wouldn't work. Things started going wrong at the station when the fast train she had hoped to catch was canceled, and the one after that. "There are delays on all services," the man at the information desk told another customer. "Best to get on the next train. You'll get there fastest." But she had never been on this slow route before, and she hadn't realized there were *quite* so many stops: Botley, Hedge End, Eastleigh—she got more anxious as the train dawdled at each. Now, between Shawford and Winchester, it had ground to a halt.

"Much more frequent these days, aren't they? Bodies on the line," the woman said philosophically. "Wonder if it's another soldier? There was one who did it last year." She opened a bag of prawn cocktail crisps and munched noisily, crumbs peppering the corner of her mouth.

The smell made Flora want to heave. She checked her phone: 2:27. The train was due to arrive at Waterloo in fifteen minutes, which clearly wasn't going to happen. Perhaps she should just go home? Get off at this stop and wait on the opposite platform for the returning train? Only she couldn't do that. If she went home now, she had no hope of fixing this. Her mum hadn't managed it, her dad couldn't face it, and Caroline had put up her hands and said *"Okay!"* when warned not to do so. It was Flora's mess. She was the one whose life would be over if she didn't manage this. At fourteen, it was up to her to sort her life out.

And she had thought she might *just* be able do it. Perhaps she still could. After all, it had been surprisingly easy to do the first bit: to get hold of Mike Stokes.

She'd gambled on him being so old, he didn't understand Facebook properly and so didn't check for mutual friends when a new message popped up from "Emma Webster" with her usual profile picture; had gambled, too, on Facebook not suspecting it came from a false account and sending it to his spam. Had this not worked, she'd planned to get a message to him via his news desk. But she hated using the phone. It was one thing to leave a message on the school answering machine, claiming to be off sick; another to speak to a real live person while impersonating her mum.

Luckily, the message—*Meet me at mine. 4pm. Have something you'll want to hear*—went through, and he didn't seem to suspect a thing. He'd responded within two minutes.

Great. See you then. 👍

Bit needy. Not to mention stupid. Perhaps he had all his settings open so that readers could send him stories; maybe he was in a rush—but she really thought he'd be smarter.

Still. Maybe he'd fallen for it because she sounded so like her mum. (After all, she'd been listening to her for fourteen years.) The tone was a touch imperious (her new favorite word), a touch intriguing. Enough to make sure he came along. Correct punctuation, too. Always the teacher, her mum *couldn't abide* abbreviations in texts, though she had to put up with them from Flora.

She'd waited a moment, just to check he'd really fallen for this, then deleted the account.

And so, it had all been set. When she sent the message, a couple of hours before leaving, she'd already checked the train times: calculated that if she took the 12:47, she would have just over an hour to walk from Waterloo to Kennington. (Obviously she couldn't take a cab or use public transport: even if she could afford it, she didn't want to be spotted on CCTV.) She thought she knew the way, but she had a printout from Google Maps neatly folded in her pocket. (She'd deleted the history on her laptop.) No iPhone these days. "We think it's best you no longer have a camera on your phone," her dad had said after the Leah thing, and it was the closest he'd ever come to expressing his disappointment. She'd wanted to ask him for a hug but hadn't known how. And so, they'd both stood there, hands hanging ineffectually by their sides, until she'd taken the Nokia and stomped from the room.

The train gave a lurch, and Flora felt a jolt of apprehension.

"Oh. Off again!" the woman said. Then, eyes narrowing: "Why aren't you in school, then. Not ill?"

"Teachers' training day," said Flora, wishing the woman would shut up.

"Is that why you're not in uniform?"

"Yes." No need to mention she had called in, claiming to have period pains. With Caroline and her dad out at work, and her stepmother having rehearsals on Wednesday evenings, neither would know, or miss her. It had all been so carefully planned.

By the time the train pulled into Waterloo, it was 3:47 p.m., and she had thirteen minutes to get to Cleaver Square to meet him. Google Maps said it was 1.3 miles and should take twenty-nine minutes, but she wasn't entirely sure of the way. Still, she walked briskly, and she could run. At least she looked anonymous: hoodie, black puffa, jeans, and Nikes. She pulled her hood up and kept her head down while jogging across the concourse, then realized this might provoke interest and slowed her pace.

She didn't mean to do anything wrong. Later, when what happens at the house comes out, she will remind herself of this constantly. It wasn't her fault she got there too late, that there was a body on the line. But of course, at 3:49 p.m., as the sky shifted from gray to a bleached navy blue, all she was thinking was of how to get to Cleaver Square quickly. She just needed to talk to, or to *beg*, Mike Stokes.

She upped her pace, jogging down streets slick with rain and the mulch of leaves and sodden litter. There were more people than in Portsmouth, and they walked with focus, racing for their trains. She darted around them, turned a corner, realized she wasn't where she wanted to be. She was on a busy road leading to a massive roundabout and perhaps the river, when the map—which she wasn't used to using—said she should have hung a left. She paused, trying to shield the paper from the fat drops of rain, now falling heavily. A car sped through a puddle, the water soaking her sneakers. Head down, feet squelching, she powered on.

Three fifty-six p.m. Would he wait for her? Would he listen? Would he agree if she begged him? She had tried to look persuasive. Had put on makeup, not as thick as Charley Morris but enough to make her look far more confident than she felt. It was partly a disguise. A way of pretending she was someone she wasn't because if she stopped to think about what she was doing, then she got completely panicky.

And now she'd look stupid, she knew she would. A sweaty mess. Incoherent, embarrassed. A silly little girl who everyone mocked, who everyone hated, who everyone would laugh at even more—and worse, *despise*—if she didn't manage to talk Mike Stokes round. Because he clearly didn't understand that if he printed this story, the story Mum and Dad and Caroline had been talking about while assuming she couldn't hear, then her life would be over. The shame would be so intense, she couldn't see how she could carry on. And now she was crying such noisy sobs that a man in a suit was looking at her with real concern, and she had to stop this, stop being such a drama queen, except that fear engulfed her. If he printed the story about her sending that image of Leah, she would be like that body on the line, and like her mum's constituent, Amy Jones.

She would have to kill herself.

Four ten now. She was lost. She was bloody lost. She didn't know where she was or where she was going. Kennington Road? Did this look familiar? A wide London street with elegant terraces and apartment buildings and buses that churned up water as they hurtled past. Her thighs were burning, and her chest was starting to hurt, but her feet were pounding the pavement and she couldn't stop—4:16, 4:17. Come on, come *on*. She could get there, except was this right? The Imperial War

Museum? She backtracked, retracing her steps; realized she *was* going in the right direction. Wanted to scream at herself for wasting more precious time.

It was 4:35 by the time she finally reached Cleaver Square. Too late. She was too bloody late. Soaked from the rain, sweat licking her back, tear marks tracking down her cheeks. Should she just go up to the door? It was 4:36. Would he have hung around? Or would he have phoned her mum? What would have happened then? Would he have been furious? Her breath came out in great juddering gasps. She knew so little about this man.

But she couldn't not try. Not after coming all this way. Not after risking being found out. (And her phone had been buzzing. She'd sent Caroline a text saying she was going into town after school, but she must have been checking up on her.) Perhaps Mike was waiting beyond those cars, sheltering from the rain? She had a key—cut by her mum as a Christmas present, for the very few occasions when she stayed in London—and he might be grateful to be out of the cold? She could make him a cup of tea. Okay, so it would be a bit weird to be alone with a middle-aged man—she's been worrying about that—but she could explain herself better inside. And if he wasn't there, she would ring her mum. Admit she was here, that she was scared of what was going to happen and just needed to see her. She wiped her nose on her sleeve. It would be a relief because she's been so desperate to talk to her about it, to admit how much she's been stressing. (She needn't mention sending the message to Mike. Her mum has secrets, too, and there are some things she doesn't need to hear.)

But as she stepped out from the trees to cross the square, an ambulance siren erupted around her. A wail of a chromatic scale that rose and fell, underscored by a two-tone riff. Manic blue lights, a blur of red and fluorescent yellow, a police car and an ambulance that skirted the corner before hurtling to an emergency stop.

A paramedic ran to knock on her mum's door. She stayed hiding in the shadows as Julia opened it and he followed her inside. Stayed, too, while his colleague went in, then returned for a stretcher; stayed as two policemen entered and the stretcher with what looked like a male figure on it was carried out. She waited until she saw her mum standing at the top of the steps, until she knew that she was okay, and then—though all she wanted to do was to race up and hold her—she turned and ran as fast as she could, sprinting through the shadows, by the park, under the railway bridge, all the way to the station. And all the while her mind was screaming: *Shit, shit, shit: what happened? How am I going to explain why I'm here?*

Her phone buzzed again, and it was only then, in the dark beneath the bridge, in front of the gaggle of men selling artisan donuts and roasted chestnuts at the station, that she saw Caroline's three missed calls.

She pressed her number.

"Flora?"

And before she could help herself, her words were running away from her. "I'm in London. I wanted to see Mum. Something's happened. It's really bad."

"Something bad?"

"Not to Mum but to that journalist. The one who wanted to write about me. He's at her house . . . I made him come. It's all my fault, and now I think he's in an ambulance."

A long silence at the end of the line.

"Caroline?"

"I'm here. I'm thinking." Her stepmother was calm, as if she was telling her to repeat a bar of music she'd scuffed up. "Don't say anything else until you see me. Are you near a station?"

"I'm at Waterloo. I want to come home."

"Get on the first train, switch off your phone, we'll sort this. I'll pick you up."

It was such a relief for someone else to take over that she wanted to cry.

"What will you tell Dad?"

"He's out at the gym. He won't notice. We'll sort this, I promise." A pause, and then she said the thing Flora had been desperate to hear, though she couldn't believe it. "Whatever's happened, this is *not* your fault."

And so she did as she was told. She took the train home, powering her phone off, as Caroline advised, and hunkering down, hood pulled around her. At the station parking lot, she climbed into their Volvo, Caroline having parked away from the CCTV. She told Caroline what she had done and what she saw, trying to persuade herself that it needn't have been a man's body on the stretcher, or that if it was, his injury was unrelated to whatever happened. A fall caused by the slick wet of the pavement, a heart attack or perhaps a stroke. She couldn't find the words to tell her about the police.

"I don't think there's any need for you to mention any of this to your mum or dad, is there?" said Caroline once they were back in their kitchen, where everything was just as it was that morning. "I can't see that it helps in any way to have you connected to him, given the Leah thing."

The Leah thing. The thing that risked defining her forever, the very thing she had been trying to sort out. She started crying as if she were a little girl.

"Oh, sweetheart." Caroline put her arms around her. "It's okay. You're going to get through this. You are *not*—" And here she looked properly angry in a way Flora hadn't seen before. "You are *not* going to shamed for this, you are *not* going to be caught up in whatever's happened, and you are *not* going to have *anyone* making a connection between what happened with Leah and Mike Stokes."

Flora nodded, then had a shower and curled up in bed. In that room of childhood memories, she tried to imagine a time when her mum living in London and associating with journalists was something that would never occur.

Sometime after 10:30 p.m., the landline rang, and soon after, there was a tentative knock on the door. Caroline hovered in the darkness, then came closer. "She's okay; your mum's okay," her stepmother whispered, because of course she knew she would have been worrying.

And Flora willed herself to believe what she said.

The next morning, Caroline woke her up. Six forty-five. A bit earlier than usual. Her mum would FaceTime her at 7 a.m., her stepmother said, to fill her in on what had happened, and she repeated her reassurance that everything was going to be okay.

"I need my phone. She might have texted." Flora raced downstairs to retrieve it from the kitchen where she'd left it charging.

"Ah—slight problem. You left it in your hoodie pocket, and I forgot to check before putting a wash on. I'm afraid it's gone through the washing machine."

"But I didn't leave it in my pocket." She frowned. They were in the kitchen, and she was hunting for it, frantic.

"Don't argue with Caroline," her dad said absentmindedly. As he moved to fill the toaster, he slipped an arm around his wife's waist.

She stared at her stepmother, trying to work out what was going on. Caroline gave her a look that said: *Shut the fuck up.* The hairs on the back of Flora's neck stood on end and she remembered Caroline's clarity last night: *Get on the first train, switch off your phone, we'll sort this.* Remembered, too, the relief of letting an adult take charge.

"Okay, sorry," she said, her tone meek, though she kept trying to catch Caroline's eye when her dad wasn't looking. Her stepmother was having none of it. She fetched her iPad, her movements as precise as ever, her expression as serene and in control.

"Don't worry." Caroline's voice was calm as she came up beside her at the island and placed her palm in the small of her back to reassure, or perhaps to warn her. "Accidents happen. Good job it was a cheap handset. I tried leaving it in rice, but it was beyond saving, so I'm afraid I just chucked it. Better to be on the safe side."

Fifty-Two

6 DECEMBER 2021

MIKE

He knew it was him as soon as he saw him come out of the tunnel from Westminster Tube and start walking along the Embankment. He had his father's saturnine good looks but seemed saddled with a sense of unease.

Luke Jamieson had been keen to meet as soon as possible, and Mike had dealt with enough contacts to know that you snapped up the goodies as soon as they were offered. No point risking them having crises of conscience, realizing that perhaps they weren't being entirely fair in divulging this information. Especially when it was as explosive as this.

"Luke?" he asked as he sat on the other end of the bench from the boy. Boy? He was twenty. Old enough to know what he was doing; young enough to feel the purest, most righteous rage.

Of course, at twenty, Mike had already been working on the *Yorkshire Post* for two years; felt little enmity toward his old man; was too busy concentrating on impressing the bosses so he could eventually move to London, and on trying, and failing, to pull attractive girls. But kids like Luke—rich kids of open-minded parents who got to take gap years and study arts subjects—grew up more slowly these days; had time to indulge their adolescent angst, to expand their minds and obsess about their parents' unconscious bias. Or, to be fair to Luke, their parents' blatant, unapologetic prejudices.

Because Luke's dad was Professor Marcus Jamieson, whose recent columns in the *Record* had managed to offend both the trans lobby— virtually in his job description—*and* second-wave feminists. ("Could it be that their ire is directed at transwomen because, for these dried-up harpies, sex is no longer on the cards?") But it was his dismissal of Black

Lives Matter as a "trite slogan"—a move that had seen him suspended from his professorial post last month—that had made Luke contact the *Chronicle*. As he'd told Mike, in the call Mike had been so eager to take after leaving Caroline Webster: "He's gone beyond being an embarrassment. I actually hate him. I've got to do something to shock him before he gets even worse."

That something was the reason Luke was now sitting on one end of a bench overlooking the Thames, and Mike at the other. The kid—Mike couldn't think of him as a man; maybe "youth" or "kidult" was more appropriate—had clearly been watching too much *Killing Eve*. Even the way he was dressed—the collar of his jacket turned up; his well-cut jaw half hidden, as if by shielding his mouth he could minimize his betrayal—flagged up his awareness he was doing something underhanded. And yet here he was. And in his bag was a slim packet of photos that would give Mike the most incendiary story of his career.

"It's not that I'm a shit son," Luke was saying.

"Not at all."

"I think he just wanted to shock me. Perhaps subliminally to 'cure' me because he can't not know, deep down."

Of course. This wasn't just about his father's transphobia and racism. Luke Jamieson was gay.

"He was drunk when he showed me. Said *he'd* known how to have a good time—and here was some evidence. I think he thought the drug element would shock me—a real party man snorting coke from a young girl's body. But it's the sex and the bullying that will strike you. It's him to a tee. The lording it over the girl. I mean, I know it won't be great for her . . ."

"No." That was an understatement.

"I know she'll be embarrassed, but it reflects worse on him, doesn't it? It'll be his reputation at stake."

God, the young were so simplistic. According to Luke, the package of photographs showed a clearly uncomfortable nineteen-year-old Emma Reynolds as she was then, Emma Webster as she was now, "performing a sex act," as the *Chronicle* would put it, on Marcus Jamieson; having coke snorted off her back; indulging herself, and then being coerced into a bit of girl-on-girl action, both young women apparently drunk and embarrassed at doing this.

Luke had been shown the photos by his father one whiskey-fueled night as Amy's Law was gaining momentum, and Marcus, apparently, had been unable to resist putting her down a peg.

"He hated her becoming more high-profile. Was surprised, not that she'd managed to become an MP, but that she was getting so much airtime. 'Second-class mind,' he said. Perhaps he just wanted to put her in her place by showing me this: asserting he still had the upper hand. That she was literally begging for it . . ."

"I get the picture." Mike felt a wave of self-loathing. If he didn't take the photos now, he'd probably reject them. Would that be such a bad idea? However dejected Emma had made him feel, she didn't deserve this. But it would be a way of getting the desk to drop the Flora story, which he felt increasingly uncomfortable about running. (He kept imagining how he'd feel if Josh was caught stupidly sending a dick pic.) And Marcus deserved it. He was an adult: thirty when this happened. This might be the final blow: the element, on top of his professorial suspension, that cemented his fall from grace.

"I thought him having sex with a student would look pretty damning, and the lesbian action might expose him as a real hypocrite . . . You know how homophobic he can be . . ." Few straight men would be repulsed by a little girl-on-girl action, thought Mike, but there was no point highlighting Luke's naivete, especially as he looked as if he was having second thoughts about what he was doing. "I just . . ."

"You're doing completely the right thing." It was as easy as taking sweets from a baby.

"And you *will* focus on him, not her . . . ?"

"Absolutely." And he could. Marcus was a household name. Perhaps it was more powerful, post–#metoo, to run a story about the depraved commentator, the abusive coke-snorting professor hitting on his girl students, including a now famous figure, than to nose it on an MP and her kinky past. Not that his editor would necessarily see it that way. Still, the important thing was to get hold of that envelope of photographs.

He riffled through them as soon as he had a moment alone in the office, and he felt a troubling pity for her. No wonder she was so brittle, bringing her guard back up as soon as she'd lowered it down. Her affinity with Amy Jones made perfect sense, too. Her campaigning wasn't just part of some broader feminist agenda: the personal *was* the political. Looking through the photos, he recognized the parallels with Amy's case: the fragile curves of a young girl; the sense of coercion; and above all the look of raw embarrassment, of apology and appeasement, in her wide, trusting eyes.

Such a shame she hadn't felt able to open up about this when talking in Parliament, or better still on the *Chronicle*'s pages (where they could have had this as an exclusive). Because think how much more potent her message would have been? Come to think of it, perhaps she could be persuaded to talk now? To turn the screws on Marcus, who embodied everything she despised. He would talk to her before approaching the desk. Suggest dropping the Flora story for her collaboration. He could see her going for that. Obviously, he could pull a fast one if she didn't. (*Feminist MP takes class A drugs and enjoys threesomes* easily passed the *Would you chat about it down at the pub?* test for publication.) But he'd prefer not to do that. In the meantime, he wouldn't share these with anyone. Would be old-school. Just squirrel them away.

The office was probably the best place to hide them. That way he could get his hands on them quickly if needed but no one else would find them. The chaos of his corner was legendary: even Guy at his sharpest-elbowed wouldn't rummage here. On the bookshelves above his desk was a row of files, leaning precariously into the political biographies, while piled on the floor were his cuttings books: oversize relics with yellowing pages and well-thumbed corners; past intrigues, speeches, scandals all packed inside. Beneath his desk, in a clear breach of health and safety rules, were electrical wires, boxes of paper for the printer, a gym bag—brought in a couple of weeks ago and still not used—and, where his feet scuffed against the wall, an air vent. He bent to examine this now. It was set in a panel of the wall that had come loose, and if he removed it, he could shove in the photos and hide them to the side of the pipes.

He took the slim envelope with the twelve pictures that would detonate Marcus Jamieson's reputation, at least in the eyes of the readers of his column, and smear Emma Webster's, and hid it inside a padded envelope; sealed this and placed it inside the vent.

Whatever happened, he was fully in control of the situation.

He had the evidence to obliterate Marcus's career—and Emma's if she didn't agree to cooperate. But until he chose to use it, her secret would be perfectly protected here.

Fifty-Three

18 NOVEMBER 2022

Portsmouth Post (online edition)

An Iraq War veteran who "terrorized" Portsmouth South MP Emma Webster has been given a five-year restraining order and warned that if he breaches it, he faces jail.

Simon Baxter, 53, of Victory Way, Southsea, threatened Ms. Webster outside the Old Bailey minutes after she was found not guilty of murdering a political editor, in June this year.

His threat to continue to "encroach on her space" followed a campaign of messages on social media and via email, which "just managed to avoid being illegal while creating a sustained air of menace," James Jacobs, prosecuting, said.

Saira Singh, defending, told the hearing at Westminster Magistrates' Court that the ex-marine had been consumed with anxiety about the mental health of his son, Will, 28, another veteran, and had believed Ms. Webster was uninterested in helping him. Will Baxter died by suicide on 8 December 2021, and Mr. Baxter held Ms. Webster partially responsible for this.

Mr. Baxter, a security guard who fought in Iraq in 2003, was issued with an order preventing him from coming within 100 yards of Ms. Webster's office, or her homes in London or Portsmouth.

Fifty-Four

19 DECEMBER 2022

EMMA

The mistletoe takes me by surprise. I am choosing a Christmas tree in a farm shop, just outside Portsmouth, when I spy the bunches thrust into plastic buckets. It's been a particularly good year for mistletoe, the shop assistant says. A cold winter equals fat berries, and these are creamy and waxy like opalescent pearls. The leaves are elegant, too, olive green and tapered. "The Romans believed mistletoe symbolized peace, love, and hope, and would protect a home from evil," says the girl, pointing to the brown label tied with red gingham ribbon on which this is written. It's that kind of farm shop. It's a bit more complex than that, I want to say. In Norse mythology, a mistletoe spear brought death. The Victorians believed bad luck would befall any woman refusing a kiss beneath it.

I shiver. Silly to be so superstitious, but it's just over a year since Mike's death, and this was always going to be difficult. Don't get me wrong: in many ways, I've managed to move on. A week after my acquittal, I returned to Westminster, where I've campaigned on anti-stalking legislation and tightening social media regulations. I live with Claire, in a modern apartment with extra locks; have a core of colleagues who remain supportive. But I'm not stupid: I know that many still view me with suspicion.

So, it's been difficult, and I've spent the past week thinking of the immediate aftermath of that late afternoon in December. Still, the mistletoe brings me up short so that my breath is caught in my chest, and I have to move away from the overpriced foliage, the boughs of fir and sprigs of holly, and abandon my basket with its artisan mince pies. I walk briskly, conscious that I'm drawing attention to myself but not wanting to be seen because my breathing is shallow now, fluttering away, making me dizzy, and I only just manage to keep it together before getting outside and stepping behind a timber-clad barn.

And I'm there, that late afternoon last December, the wind skittering against my back, the rain trickling down my neck, as I push the door open, my mind catastrophizing, my body semaphoring my fear.

The tread of a hard sole on a floorboard, the creak of leather.

"Hello?" I wait for a moment, heart in mouth, telling myself it's my imagination. Then, trying to sound more assertive: "Hello? Is anyone there?"

And a man steps out from the door leading to my bedroom. A broad-shouldered, shadowy presence. My throat thickens. "Get out. Get the fuck out of my house!" I hear myself shriek.

"It's okay. It's me, Mike," the figure replies.

He strides forward and puts his hands on either side of my upper arms. He's too close to me: I can smell the red wine on his breath. His eyes shine: manic. "You messaged me, remember? You wanted me to come here?"

None of this makes any sense, and nor does his smile: warm, almost nostalgic, but coupled with an unpredictable excitement that lights up his eyes and flits across his face. I've pulled away, but he grabs my arms again and gives me a shake. And my reaction's instinctive: I bring my right knee up into his groin and try to force him the fuck away.

"Fuck!" he says, staggering back. "Fuuu-uuuuuk." He breathes heavily, doubled over, then stands back up and seems to compose himself. "You didn't need to do that! Fuck's sake. I thought you *wanted* me to come here?"

"Get out. Get *out*!" I scream, but I can't get him to turn around in the direction of the door, so illogically I drive him deeper down the hallway, still shouting, and batting him with my hands to get him away.

"Hey!" He catches my wrists, holds his ground. His fingers tighten, digging into me like pincers. "I just want to talk," he says.

He releases my wrists, holds his hands up in a peace gesture, though he's as fired up as much as I am: there's that glint in his eyes, an edge to his voice. "I've no idea why you're behaving like this when you wanted me here, but I've an idea to run past you." He pauses, and I'm so shocked I seem incapable of moving. "This isn't about Flora," he adds, and his voice is soft and intimate as if he's sharing a secret or, because there's a bubble of laughter in it, a joke and he's leading up to the punch line. "I know all about Marcus, you see . . ."

"Marcus . . ." My tone's too light, too high. He couldn't know about us, could he? Marcus couldn't have shown him the photos that I know he's kept?

I shift away, hoping I can escape not just from him, but from the nightmare of what he's saying. Because if I'm panicked by his being here, then the shock of what he's told me—that he and Marcus have been conspiring to expose me—feels like a second blow.

"God knows why you'd reject me when you went for the likes of him. Why you let him humiliate you as well. The girl-on-girl action for his pleasure, you down on your knees."

"I don't know what you're talking about." My throat feels strangled.

"Oh, come on, Emma. I've got the photos. Him snorting coke off your back. You and that other girl. And the more explicit stuff. He must have developed them himself. It's all there plain to see . . ."

And I think of the pained phone call I made to my ex-tutor before deciding to stand as an MP when I'd begged him to hand the photos over. He said he'd destroyed them, but the tone of his voice told me he was lying. Besides, it wasn't in his nature to relinquish such power over me.

And now Mike has the photos. And I can't compute quite why they would conspire to do this to me, but I know one thing: I am *not* going to let him publish them.

He's talking fast because he knows he has the upper hand, and he knows that I will listen. "Don't worry about it," he's saying, and in his enthusiasm, he comes even closer, until we're both beneath the mistletoe, hanging, as I said, from the second lampshade. I glance upward, see the berries glowing in the meager light from the streetlight, sense a tangle of twigs. He follows my gaze and gives a smirk: does he think he can kiss me? His breath is hot on my face. "Forget the story about Flora. This is far more relevant to Amy's Law. And we can do this in such a sympathetic way."

And suddenly he is putting his hand behind my neck, as if to pull me toward him. And I'm frightened at him doing this and enraged at him trotting out this line. Because I know that, whatever he says about dressing it up, he will reduce me to that nineteen-year-old who went along with an older man's wishes because she was worried he would think her unadventurous, frigid, naive. And I'm consumed with such an intense fury—for Marcus, for him, for every man who's made judgments about me—that for the first time in my life I lash out at someone and smash my keys into his face.

"Fuck—what the fuck?"

And then it gets nasty. A scuffle, the court will be told, but that minimizes it: this is raw and terrifying, my instincts heightened by fear and rage. I grab at the console table, trying to lay my hands on anything that might help; pick up the bowl; clumsily thrust it at his head. He staggers away as the sound of the bowl breaking on the floor stops us both for a moment.

"Jesus Christ! I am going to fucking ruin you," he rages, coming at me.

It gets blurry after that. Or at least I later told myself it did: that I didn't mean to do it. That I put my hands up to defend myself and merely shoved him away. But the truth is, I *was* furious. In the heat of the moment, it wasn't just that I didn't care what happened to him but that I *hoped* to really hurt him, to scare him, to make sure he never humiliated me again. That he never cut me down to size, erasing all the good I have ever done; ensuring I would never be taken seriously; would have my reputation smeared so effectively I would always be that girl who gave Marcus Jamieson oral sex and let him photograph her doing it, head tilted back afterward, a look of faked pleasure on her face. Type "Emma Webster" into Google and this would pop up. It would be what I was known for. This would be the thing people thought of when they mentioned my name.

I pushed, and then I watched with a growing sense of horror, fascination, and, for perhaps a millisecond, vindication as Mike lost his balance and swayed and tipped.

There was a roar of surprise and then a thud. I didn't go to him at first. Powered by adrenaline and terror, I swept up the pieces of the ceramic bowl, wrapped them in the day's *Evening Standard*, and shoved the pieces in the recycling bin, which, I dimly realized, would be emptied early the next day.

Then I stood at the top of the stairs, looking down, not feeling any need to rush and help, for one long, shameful moment, before grief and guilt and a sense of common decency kicked in. I stood, catatonic with shock and the most intense, searing anger that he had threatened me and my daughter, that he was willing to smear us in this way.

I made myself go down the stairs, of course; perhaps only dallied for a couple of seconds, my fear of what I would find—of how he was—growing more acute with every step. Later I would fret and extrapolate. Had Marcus shared the photos elsewhere? What about Mike? Would the *Chronicle* still run them? Immediately after the verdict, I was certain they would. A fierce one-two: a *fuck you, you think you've got away with it, but we know what you're really like, and we'll publish and be damned, anyway.*

But then I could think of nothing other than the fact there was an unconscious man lying at the bottom of my stairs. A man I'd worked with. A man I'd slept with. A man investigating my daughter and me.

And I worked out very quickly what I might do and say to try to salvage the very thing he had sought to tarnish.

My reputation.

Fifty-Five

29 DECEMBER 2022

RACHEL

It's a thankless task: clearing out a desk. Still more when its previous occupant is unable to help you.

Rachel has put off finishing this job for far too long. The police had pored over the contents after Mike's death, and yet there is so much *stuff* still to throw out: a mountain of old notepads, expense sheets, and business cards; yellowing Post-its with telephone numbers and cryptic squiggles of shorthand; and—the most useless relic of a journalist's past since the contents can now be accessed by a simple search of the tabloid's archive system online—Mike's old cuttings books.

She drags the four large books from beneath his old desk. They'll have to be recycled or go to the dump. That feels quite brutal, but it's time for brutality after no one tackling this for a year. She had woken on Christmas Day and known she had to clear it all out. New Year, new broom. No use being sentimental. No one needs Mike's old words. They were all online—and these belonged in the recycling, didn't they?

Christ, but it's dusty down here. She sneezes, tendrils of dust tumbleweed-ing, getting up her nose, settling in her hair. His gym bag went with the police, but there are boxes of crap that they handed back: notes and letters she'd vowed to go through properly. She heaves, pulling one box out so that it topples and knocks against a panel in the wall behind his desk that appears to hold the air vent. *This place is a pit, isn't it? Vacuuming should spruce it up*, she thinks, sitting back on her heels.

If she is honest, there is a large part of her that's ambivalent, not just about clearing out the remainder of Mike's desk but about continuing in his shoes. Yes, the promotion's great. The pay raise is more than welcome, and becoming political editor of the second highest-selling national paper at the age of thirty-three, impressive, particularly because she's a woman about whom the paper's execs, though knowing they shouldn't, might fret about future maternity leave. But she's lost her love of the job. It's not just that her colleagues have changed: Guy becoming a foreign correspondent, currently in Istanbul, with Rome, Paris, and New York no doubt lined up; and Sam, another bit of posh, joining them. It's not that she doubts it's relevant (because it's never been more important to hold this rotten government to account). But when she gave evidence against Emma Webster, it left an unpleasant taste.

Yes, she'd killed Mike, robbing Josh of a father, robbing *her* of a dear friend. But when Tom Tillett asked if Rachel had ever been put under surveillance, photographed in her dressing gown, or told that secrets humiliating to someone close to her would be printed, she'd felt almost ashamed. *If you're a public figure, then you're fair game . . . And if you're a politician . . . you're open to greater scrutiny.* She still believes that, but she also knows the media are more prurient about women than men. And she admires Emma for her persistence. It's hard succeeding in a career in which casual misogyny is rife. Rachel, spying her own glass ceiling, feels some solidarity.

She feels for her, too, with Amy's Law being rebranded not just as Mike's legacy but his brain wave. (It's been difficult writing stories without mentioning Emma, but this first draft of history has her firmly edged out.) Rachel wishes her well. Really, she does. She could claw some way back up the slippery pole if she only stopped campaigning against sexual violence and opted for something worthy but dull. But this will always hang over her, and her obit will describe her as "the MP tried for murder." Because, while disgraced male MPs have been able to rehabilitate themselves, there is something particularly pernicious about a stain on a woman's reputation.

Emma needs a break. She needs to be cut some slack. Not by the *Chronicle*—the desk is brutally unforgiving—but by the rest of the media. Time for them all to move on. Perhaps Rachel will be able to do so once she has tidied away this desk, as if by removing every vestige of Mike she can clear her guilt at the way in which Emma was treated—and her nagging anxiety that, had the paper not hounded her, Mike's death wouldn't have occurred.

Time to deal with this shit. She bends under the desk using the vacuum cleaner's nozzle to get at the corners, conscious that Mike would never have done this; nor Guy; nor Ben, her deputy; nor this new chap, Sam. Perhaps it's this realization that makes her ram the vacuum against the wall a little too hard. The paintwork's scuffed already: no one will notice, but she'd forgotten about the dislodged paneling, which now clatters off. Bugger. The House of Commons might be dilapidated, but she ought not to make it worse. Gingerly, because you're never less than six feet from a rat in London, she fumbles inside the hole to find some way of securing the paneling or slotting it back on. But her fingers brush against some sort of package, shoved to one side. Clumsily she grips it, pulls it out.

And it's a brown padded envelope, sealed but unmarked, and inside there's a smaller envelope containing photos. She rifles through them, feeling pretty dirty because they're X-rated, some of the snaps that spill out. With a burst of recognition, she sees, too, who the main players are, and she knows, in her gut, that these will be more corrosive, more explosive, more permanently damaging to Emma Webster's career than any previous story about any female public figure. Understands, too, that these would have been far more damaging than any story about Flora and revenge porn.

And though Rachel will always be a newshound at heart, she also knows that in 2022 the sexual behavior of women will still always count against them. And she decides that this is something the world doesn't need to see.

Later, when she burns Mike's old notebooks (after filleting them for useful numbers, and finally checking there are no golden nuggets buried inside), she will cut each photograph into thirty-two tiny pieces and shove this shiny confetti into the bottom of her trash. Do the negatives still exist? Are there copies? Will Marcus ensure they resurface? For a split second, she'll prevaricate, wondering if any of these could be true—but no. She is doing the right thing.

And later still, when she opens a bottle of red and toasts her old colleague, she'll remind herself of this; note, too, that Emma now owes her—and that there'll come a point when Rachel will call on her to pay her dues.

But for now, thanks to her, Emma Webster's reputation is safe.

Acknowledgments

Reputation required more research than any of my previous novels. Some contacts can't be publicly acknowledged. Those who can include Eloise Marshall, KC, without whom this really couldn't have been written; Graham Bartlett, former chief superintendent and police procedural adviser and author; and Dr. Richard Shepherd, forensic pathologist, and author. Any errors are entirely mine.

My heartfelt thanks, too, to Heidi Allen, Luciana Berger, and Jess Phillips; to Kevin Maguire, Helen Morris, Sam Raincock, Jim Rayment, and Tom Watson; and to Ayla Boz, India and Freya Grigson, and Anna Tennant. All were unfailingly helpful and kind.

My US publishers, Simon & Schuster, have shown immense enthusiasm and patience in waiting for this novel. My grateful thanks to my editor Emily Bestler, of Emily Bestler Books, Lara Jones, and Gabrielle Sevillano; and to Libby McGuire and Dana Trocker; Ariele Fredman, Maudee Genao, James Iacobelli, Paige Lytle, and Sonja Singleton as well as the entire sales team.

Over the pond, at S&S UK, huge thanks to Clare Hey, Hayley McMullan, and Jess Barratt; and to Suzanne Baboneau, Ian Chapman, Sara-Jade Virtue, Polly Osborn, Gill Richardson, Dom Brendon, Rich Vliestra, Joe Roche, Louise Davies, Saxon Bullock, and Tamsin Shelton. I feel immensely grateful for such excellent publishing teams.

As ever I am indebted to my agent, Lizzy Kremer, at David Higham Associates; to Maddalena Cavaciuti and Kay Begum; the DHA rights team; and my TV agents, Penni Killick, and Sylvie Rabineau at WME.

The court scenes were written as I gave notes on Netflix's *Anatomy of a Scandal*. Thank you to Bruna Papandrea, Liza Chasin, David E Kelley, Melissa James Gibson, and SJ Clarkson for making me an executive producer and involving me in the process. I feel as if I learned a great deal and *Reputation* benefitted enormously.

Many thanks to John Harris who kindly provided the name of Jago Harris via an auction at the Bath Literary Festival, and to the bloggers, booksellers, and authors who have pushed me up their TBR piles and championed me.

Finally, all love to my ever-supportive family. The third lockdown meant many weekends working: to my husband, son, and daughter— thank you. I'm so glad it was worth it.

This novel is dedicated to my daughter and niece. Neither are Floras or Leahs. Both are bright, kind, thoughtful young women of whom I could not be more proud and who I would have loved to have known at fourteen.

Author's Note

On October 15, 2021, Sir David Amess, a veteran Conservative MP, was stabbed to death as he held a walk-in clinic in his Essex constituency. Following the murder of Labour MP Jo Cox, in June 2016, it was the second killing of a serving MP by a member of the public in just over five years.

The murder, for which an ISIS fanatic was given a whole-life sentence, led to discussions in Parliament about how to improve MPs' security, with politicians revealing how inconsistent and inadequate security had been.

The stabbing took place after I had finished writing and editing *Reputation*. As of writing, in April 2023, MPs still meet with constituents in person at regular "surgeries" with no automatic protection from the police. Each politician is now given a security assessment, and receives a standard package such as alarm systems, CCTV, and personal alarms for staff. But, while some practical measures can be taken to guard against physical threat, it remains to be seen whether anything sufficient will be done to quell the extreme hatred public figures, and in particular female politicians, currently experience online.

REPUTATION

SARAH VAUGHAN

*This reading group guide for **REPUTATION** includes an introduction, discussion questions, ideas for enhancing your book club, and a Q&A with author **Sarah Vaughan**. The suggested questions are intended to help your reading group find new and interesting angles and topics for your discussion. We hope that these ideas will enrich your conversation and increase your enjoyment of the book.*

Introduction

The bestselling author of *Anatomy of a Scandal*—now a Netflix series—returns with a new psychological thriller about a politician whose less-than-perfect personal life is thrust into the spotlight when a body is discovered in her home.

As a politician, Emma has sacrificed a great deal for her career—including her marriage and her relationship with her daughter, Flora.

A former teacher, the glare of the spotlight is unnerving for Emma, particularly when it leads to countless insults, threats, and trolling as she tries to work in the public eye. As a woman, she knows her reputation is worth its weight in gold, but as a politician she discovers it only takes one slip-up to destroy it completely.

Fourteen-year-old Flora is learning the same hard lessons at school as she encounters heartless bullying. When another teenager takes her own life, Emma lobbies for a new law to protect women and girls from the effects of online abuse. Now, Emma and Flora find their personal lives uncomfortably intersected—but then, the unthinkable happens.

A man is found dead in Emma's home. A man she had every reason to be afraid of and to want gone. Fighting to protect her reputation, and determined to protect her family at all costs, Emma is pushed to her limits as the worst happens and her life is torn apart.

Another breathless and twisty novel from an absolute "master of suspense" (*CrimeReads*), *Reputation* brilliantly illustrates that it isn't who you are that matters . . . it's who people think you are.

Topics & Questions for Discussion

1. Why do you think Sarah Vaughan chose to open with the scene of Mike's murder? How is it effective in setting the novel's tone and introducing us to Emma? What do you learn about Emma before you even know her name?

2. There are many pieces of ironic foreshadowing in the early chapters of the novel, including Emma's t-shirt that reads "Well Behaved Women Seldom Make History." Find other examples of foreshadowing and consider how they help set the mood of the novel.

3. There is much commentary in the novel on how women are judged by society and the gendered rules they must follow to maintain their good reputations. Emma comments that in her photoshoot, she thought she looked serious, but "I just looked as if I took myself seriously (a cardinal sin for a woman)" (p. 11). In what ways is taking oneself seriously as a woman shown to be a tricky thing to do in our world?

4. Compare and contrast the three main women in the novel, Emma, Flora, and Caroline. How are their motivations similar? How do they differ? Was there a character with whom you empathized more?

5. Before the murder, Emma has a good reputation, both in her public and private lives. Find examples of where and how her good repu-

tation protects her. How do characters describe Emma? Would you describe her in the same way?

6. Emma's motivation for going into politics was her father, who used to ask her "What are you going to do about it?" when faced with injustice. She explains, "[It] was the rallying cry that had inspired me to study politics and history, the first in my family to go to university" (29). How does knowing this detail about Emma influence your understanding of her subsequent choices? Do you think this rallying cry motivates other characters in the novel?

7. What details does Sarah Vaughan include to create the tense, claustrophobic atmosphere of Emma's life in the days leading up to Mike's murder? In what ways are they paralleled in the subsequent trial?

8. Although Flora more obviously deals with mean-girl bullying, adult women in the novel experience or make bullying remarks as well. How does the adult bullying resemble the teenage kind, and how does it differ? Do you think the stakes are any higher or lower?

9. Emma makes the decision to answer the detectives' questions in her initial interview, despite her lawyer telling her not to comment. Emma explains her need to cooperate is "that old desire to be a good girl, to always answer questions" (158). Where else do you see Emma trying to please in a similar manner? Do Flora and Caroline do the same?

10. Vaughan uses epigraphs from *The Duchess of Malfi* and *Othello*. Read or watch these plays and explore the ways in which they examine reputation. Why is Malfi particularly pertinent?

11. How responsible do you think Flora is for what happens at Emma's home on December 8th? Flora blames herself, thinking, "If it wasn't for Flora, then Mike would be alive, and her mum wouldn't be . . . facing up to the fact that in a week's time she might be in prison" (232). How did you feel about this assessment before the twist, and did you reconsider Flora's feelings of guilt afterward?

12. After the verdict is reached, Emma answers a few questions from the press. When asked what she feels when she thinks about the night of December 8th, Emma responds that she feels "Shame and regret . . . There's not one day when I don't regret what happened" (259). Do you think Emma regrets what she *did* or regrets getting *caught* and having her reputation tarnished?

13. Were you shocked by the revelation that the whole family was somehow involved in the acts of December 8th and its cover-up? What elements surprised you the most? Would you have gone to the lengths Emma, Caroline, and David did to protect Flora?

14. Once you learn the second twist at the end—what part of Emma's past she is so desperate to keep secret—go back and read a few of the key scenes. How do you understand them differently with your knowledge of the last few chapters of the novel? What techniques does Sarah Vaughan employ in order to give double meaning to many of Emma, Flora, and Caroline's thoughts and statements?

A Conversation with Sarah Vaughan

Q: Sarah, you were a political journalist for many years. How did you draw upon your past job experiences to write *REPUTATION*?

A: I used the skills I learned as a political journalist: observing MPs, interviewing them, and researching key issues—such as revenge porn—and I drew on what I'd call "the texture of Westminster": my knowledge of the protocols, the architecture, and certain scenarios, such as the MP giving a statement outside a certain entrance. (Though there is some dramatic license, i.e. I know Emma would be told her question in chapter five was too long.) Equally, I used my experience having covered court cases to write the court scenes, although I also shadowed a criminal barrister in a two-week murder trial to make sure these scenes were accurate. When I was a political correspondent, Twitter didn't exist, but it didn't require much research to gain an idea of the extent of the misogynistic abuse experienced by women in public life.

Q: A character in the novel mentions that it's surprising, considering the amount of online threats and trolling happening, that a politician hasn't committed a murder or assault before. Was that a point of entry for you when you began writing this novel? Was there a first moment of inspiration that led to writing *REPUTATION*?

A: The starting point was an interview with a female MP in which she described having nine locks on her front door and a panic alarm by the side of her bed. I wondered what it would be like to live under this level of threat. At the same time, in the spring of 2019, several other women MPs—including my own—were experiencing extreme abuse online, in person, and via anonymous letters. I'd just written about a mother's judgement being warped by postnatal anxiety in *Little Disasters*. Now I wondered how a public figure might act if she was exposed to threats from numerous different sources. If I put her in sufficient jeopardy, how might she react if she was filled with fear?

Q: Why did you choose to write Emma in the first-person point of view and all other characters in third person? What effect were you going for?
A: Writing her from the first person and the other characters from the third was a deliberate decision to privilege her viewpoint. It was an efficient way of getting inside her head and, I hoped, to try to engender sympathy.

Q: What were your favorite scenes to write? Were there any that were especially difficult to write?
A: I found myself most moved when writing the Flora scenes: I was bullied at school and there is a lot of me in Flora, Emma's 14-year-old daughter. The most "fun" parts were probably those in the POV of the least attractive characters: Simon Baxter, a constituent who's furious with Emma, and Marcus Jamieson, an academic turned extreme right-wing commentator. In fact, the easiest bits to write were Marcus's shock jock tabloid columns. It felt like such a joy to write a bit of opinionated journalism. Perhaps I've missed my calling!

Q: What research did you need to do in order to bring this story to life?
A: I interviewed several MPs about their experience of abuse and the safety measures they've been forced to take; I shadowed a criminal barrister in a two-week murder trial and discussed points of law with them. I read Law Commission documents on potentially changing the law on revenge porn and news stories detailing victims' experiences. I interviewed friends of my teenage daughter, and their parents, about online bullying; I talked to a forensic pathologist, who kindly talked me

through injuries that would be sustained if someone fell down the stairs. I checked details with an IT expert who gives evidence in court cases, and an electrician to ensure a plot detail made sense; and I ran my police interviews past the retired detective turned police procedural adviser I work with, who also advised me on blood spatter. The bulk of it was written once the pandemic had started, so I had to rely on Google Maps a little since we weren't allowed more than five miles from our home, but I chose to write about areas of London I already knew.

Q: Many of your novels depict the moral challenges faced by women balancing high-pressure jobs and high-pressure family issues. What intrigues you about intense situations and the questions that arise from them?

A: Great question. I suppose people react in dramatic and sometimes unexpected ways when they're put in intense situations, and that hopefully leads to a compelling, exciting read. Although I try to write beautifully, I'm writing books which are marketed as thrillers, even if they are also psychological dramas, and so having a great hook and strong plot is crucial. When I was researching this book, a detective told me no one could swear they would never commit murder. His argument was that if one of my children was being physically threatened, or worse, I might react in a murderous way. I'm interested in putting women in high-pressure situations and seeing what happens then.

Q: Was there a character whose point of view you especially liked writing from? Who did you find most challenging to write?

A: Having said I loved writing the Marcus columns, I also enjoyed writing from Mike's viewpoint. I was a journalist for fifteen years, and so there was a certain nostalgia in conjuring up his world. I probably found Caroline the most challenging to write. We don't necessarily view her sympathetically, and I wanted to play with the wicked stepmother trope but still ensure people were sufficiently invested in and intrigued by her to want to read.

Q: At what stage did you decide that Flora wasn't the only thing Emma was protecting? How did you go about writing scenes where you could only hint at what was really at stake and what Emma's true motivations were?

A: As soon as I knew Marcus was going to be a character (and we have our first reference to him in Chapter Nine. It wasn't something I seeded in later drafts.) At the risk of creating a spoiler, I do think her desire to protect Flora is paramount: she would have reacted in the way in which she does even without the added motivation we learn of at the very end.

Q: Why did you decide you wanted to explore what one's reputation means—and what it means to tarnish it, or be protected by it? What intrigued you about the issues surrounding the idea of a good reputation?

A: *Reputation* is the third of my novels to explore the judgment women are exposed to. In *Anatomy of a Scandal*, I'm asking the reader—and jury—to judge Olivia in a rape trial (and to judge Sophie's behavior in remaining loyal to her husband and Kate's in prosecuting him). In *Little Disasters*, it's mothering that's scrutinized: Liz makes a professional judgment about whether Jess is a good-enough mother, and the mums at the school gate all chime in. With *Reputation*, I'm looking at how high-profile women are judged as they navigate public life, and how teenage girls are bullied by their peers. I didn't set out to explore the theme of reputation but I knew early on that the Duchess of Malfi was an influence, and then as soon as I remembered the Othello quote I use as an epigraph it all slotted into place. In all three books, I'm conscious that a woman's reputation is more precarious than a man's—by which I mean we still judge women more harshly than their male counterparts and are less forgiving.

Q: What are you working on next?

A: I don't want to give away any details but another thriller/psychological drama about power and judgment, again inspired by news stories.

Enhance Your Book Club

1. Find a recorded or live production of *Othello* or *The Duchess of Malfi* and watch it as a group. Discuss why Sarah Vaughan chose to use quotes from both plays for *REPUTATION*'s epigraph. How do they relate to her novel? Are there other lines you would have chosen to use?

2. Find a recent article about a female politician. See how the woman is described by the journalist and compare it with the ways Emma is described in the novel's fictional media reports. What have you learned about the depiction of women in the media by reading Sarah Vaughan's novel? Are there elements you'll be more wary of when you read or watch the news or scroll through social media now?

3. Check out more of Sarah Vaughan's books, such as *ANATOMY OF A SCANDAL* and *LITTLE DISASTERS*. To find out more about Sarah, visit sarahvaughanauthor.com, or follow her on Twitter @SVaughanauthor.

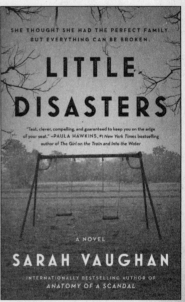